Shooting at the Stars

Shooting at the Stars

Linda Taylor

WILLIAM HEINEMANN: LONDON

Published by William Heinemann in 2002

1 3 5 7 9 10 8 6 4 2

First published in the United Kingdom in 2002 by William Heinemann

The Random House Group Limited
20 Vauxhall Bridge Road, London, SW1V 2SA

Random House Australia (Pty) Limited
20 Alfred Street, Milsons Point, Sydney,
New South Wales 2061, Australia

Random House New Zealand Limited
18 Poland Road, Glenfield
Auckland 10, New Zealand

Random House (Pty) Limited
Endulini, 5a Jubilee Road, Parktown 2193, South Africa

The Random House Group Limited Reg. No. 954009

www.randomhouse.co.uk

A CIP catalogue record for this book is available from the British Library

Papers used by Random House are natural, recyclable products made
from wood grown in sustainable forests. The manufacturing processes
conform to the environmental regulations of the country of origin

Printed and bound in the United Kingdom by
Mackays of Chatham Ltd, Chatham, Kent

ISBN 0 434 00997 0

To Margaret May Green 1908–1978

*'We are all in the gutter, but some of us are looking
at the stars'*

Oscar Wilde

Acknowledgements

My thanks to Jacquie Robinson at Amelia's of Sevenoaks for telling me her inspirational story; to Kenny Green for Emile; to Fiona Burgess for cheerful help with background research; to Ian and Shahpur for miraculous technical and moral support and Alex for additional enthusiastic help; as ever, my love and thanks to my family especially to Sue, Julie, Jackie and Rachel, for fun, friendship, practical help and keeping me going. To Elizabeth Wright for her unbending support and all at the Darley Anderson Agency. Thanks to Kate Parkin and all at Random House. Thanks to my great friends Margaret, Gale and the amazing Rebecca for being there in every eventuality.

My gratitude, always, to my grandmother, Margaret May Green, for teaching me to keep my eyes on the heavens and my feet on the ground.

Chapter One

The smile Greg gave Caroline was so sudden she knew he hadn't intended it to be as meaningful as it appeared. But smiles delivered by athletically handsome chemistry teachers were not to be sniffed at, and Caroline couldn't help offering him a grin in return.

He had stumbled across her in the Space Gallery, gazing at the Apollo 10 command module in awe. She had been daydreaming in the peaceful silence that had descended on the vaulted caverns of the Science Museum. The students had vanished to various corners of the vast building and in the last precious moments before the museum closed the Space Gallery was hushed, cosy and spotlit, cosseting her.

'Now, how did I know I'd find you in here?' he teased her. 'You do know it's ten to six don't you? They'll lock you in if you're not careful.'

'I'd like that.'

'I'll bet.' He chuckled.

They both pondered the command module for a while. It was difficult to tear herself away from it. To think where it had been, what it had done, awed her. Then Caroline suddenly panicked. 'Where are my students?'

'Safely accounted for. Antonia's being very efficient. She's grouped everyone outside the main entrance.'

'Ah yes, Antonia. She's amazing, isn't she?'

'Yep. Just as well we brought an English teacher along to organise us.'

Caroline smiled at him. He shared her love of science and although his area was chemistry, hers physics, they had much in common. Having the opportunity to teach, to pass that enthusiasm on, was a bonus. They'd talked a lot about their shared passion in the year and a bit that they'd worked together at the girls' school.

Looking at him now, flush-faced, his eyes bright behind his glasses, with tight-knit dark brown hair, olive skin and a quirky sense of humour, Caroline wondered why she didn't fancy him. She knew quite a few of the female members of staff thought he was sexy. He was an enthusiastic teacher, with as much energy as she had herself, and he had applied his passion for sport practically, running an after-school football club for those girls who were keen. To Caroline, though, he was an ally and a friend.

'Looks like you'll have to come again another day and spend several hours just looking at this thing here.' He nodded at the capsule as a voice over the tannoy urged any stragglers to leave.

'I'll be back next year,' Caroline assured him. 'I've loved it here since my granddad first brought me when I was a little girl. I was running so fast along the pavement that I fell flat on my face and got huge grazes up my arms and legs. He picked me up and dried off my tears, then said, "Trying to get there faster than the speed of light, Caro." I'll always remember that.'

'That's such a sweet story.' Greg sniffed and pretended to dab at the corner of his eye while Caroline playfully slapped his arm.

'Every word of it's true. I started young, you know.'

'When I was a little boy,' Greg said, 'I blew up my mum's salad bowl.'

'I can just picture you doing that.'

'My friend Robert and I collected a load of fireworks, emptied the powder into the biggest bowl we could find, threw in a lighted match, and ran. The rest, as the cat could have testified, is history. My mum was livid.'

'Livid? Why? Was it an expensive salad bowl, then?' Caroline asked.

Greg laughed. 'You see? That's why I like you, Caroline. Anyone else would have instantly sided with my mum. She tells that story to my girlfriends now. She actually thinks it's funny.'

'My grandfather helped me to build a rocket,' Caroline breathed, gazing back at the command module and wishing that she was allowed to climb in it, just for a minute, to see what it felt like. 'It was only a small rocket, but it took off, and it went up in the air, then came down and broke the glass in the greenhouse. It was amazing.'

'He was the mad inventor, wasn't he?'

'Mad?' Caroline thought about it. 'No, he wasn't mad. But everyone was poor on account of him. Nobody minded.'

They both disappeared into their private thoughts until the tannoy jolted them again.

'It really is time to go,' Greg said. 'Come on.'

'See you next year,' Caroline whispered to the command module.

It was already dark outside, the illuminations of the museums and the dazzle of the streetlamps making the cluster of buildings look orange and very grand.

Antonia was glancing at her watch impatiently. The coach had pulled up a few yards along the pavement from the exit, and Caroline had been chatting animatedly to Greg as they emerged from the building and trotted through the freezing January air towards the promise of soft seats, heating and a cosy journey back to Kent, although judging from the traffic seething through South Kensington they were going to catch the London rush hour.

Seeing Antonia's lips tighten as they approached her, Caroline felt chastened for losing track of time. All the girls were already on board. Although Antonia was the eldest of the three of them, somewhere in her early forties while Caroline was thirty-five and Greg thirty-one, it was too slight an age difference to account for the sudden feeling of being a naughty child that Caroline experienced. Perhaps it was because Antonia was a mother and well practised in the art of killing looks. Caroline had often seen her cousin Lizzy produce exactly such an expression when her two young boys were playing up. For Caroline, single and as likely to enter into motherhood as Antonia was to shake down her hair and take up a career in lap dancing, it was a case of watching and learning.

'Sorry, Antonia,' Greg pulled a rueful face. 'I found Caroline elbowing all the kids out of the way so that she could design her own rocket.'

'Did that last time I came,' Caroline quipped then bit her lip at Antonia. 'Sorry, it was the—'

'Space Gallery. I guessed as much. I think we all know about your passion for astronomy by now.' Antonia smoothed her hands over her blonde hair, finding the clip at the back of her head and patting it as if to reassure herself that she was all in one piece.

'Sorry,' Caroline muttered again, blushing.

Caroline never quite knew where she stood with Antonia. She was often acerbic, but a spark of humour seemed to lurk in her eyes. Antonia had stepped in for this trip at the last minute when one of the maths teachers had dropped out with a savage cold, and Caroline felt a pang of sympathy for her. She was always a keen volunteer and Caroline knew she ran the drama club very successfully. Caroline had been to a performance of a play Antonia had written herself and it had been extremely funny. But she was a more apt mentor for trips to the Barbican or Stratford-upon-Avon. At times during the day she'd looked a bit out of her depth, probably much how Caroline had felt when she'd been taken once to a lengthy reading from *The Waste Land*. After initial curiosity and effort came a strong desire to run out of the room screaming.

Antonia was an extremely attractive woman. She had silver-blonde hair, shoulder length and always caught back in a stylish clip, a fair skin, wide blue eyes and symmetrical features. She dressed elegantly, and sometimes with a hint of femme fatale. Some days a suit would be moulded around her perfect figure, and the heels of her shoes (and her skirts) would creep up an inch or two. She wore finely crafted necklaces and rings, and often added bold, striking earrings to her repertoire. She wafted expensive scent along the spartan school corridors, so you could always tell if she'd been that way five minutes before you.

Caroline, on the other hand, dressed fairly simply and was usually too busy thinking about something else to remember to wear perfume or jewellery. Her hair was

5

short and dark brown, her eyes brown, her features unremarkable, as far as she could tell. She had a normal share of womanly undulations, but she'd never worried about her looks. She was a happy person with a busy mind.

The girls took quickly to Caroline. At the Further Education college where she'd taught previously, the students had just turned up to classes (or more frequently, hadn't) and Caroline had had much less of a holistic influence on their lives. It was one of the reasons she'd sought a school teaching post.

Caroline admired Antonia, even if she felt held at arm's length by her. She'd learned that Antonia was divorced, with a teenaged daughter who she was bringing up on her own. She realised that her life was difficult and that she covered any private worries with a sheen of slick professionalism. Caroline had little to worry about beyond her job, other than the mortgage and light pollution. Antonia had a great deal more responsibility in her life, and she also had to teach English, which Caroline couldn't do if she tried until she exploded. So elusive, so hard to pin down, so . . . well, emotional. Not Caroline's bag at all. Antonia had quite enough on her plate, Caroline had decided, and tried always to be as friendly as possible towards her.

Now she gave Antonia a warmly encouraging smile, as she looked cold and fed up. 'Did you enjoy yourself today? Your group seemed to find it quite exciting.'

Antonia gave Caroline an ironic look. 'This is next year's GCSE bunch. They get excited by things in baggy trousers holding microphones.'

'Landing on a meteorite was brilliant,' Greg enthused. 'Very *Star Trek*.'

6

'My group landed on the meteorite,' Antonia said flatly. 'And one of them threw up.' Caroline wondered if she saw a twitch of the lips behind the facade of composure.

'They didn't throw up during your *King Lear* performance last term, even during the eye-gouging scene,' Greg returned with a wink. 'Selective, aren't they?'

'I just wondered where you two got to this afternoon,' Antonia said with a raised eyebrow. 'I thought two scientists might have been better prepared. Your lot seemed to be scattered all over the place. Did you think of drawing up a plan of some kind to make sure we all covered the important galleries?'

Greg scratched his head. Caroline chewed her cheek.

'Well, no, we just wanted to do as much as possible,' she defended, realising uncomfortably that Antonia had a point. 'The idea was for it to be a bit –'

'Free range,' Greg finished for her. 'So that they could sense the fun, and the energy of it.'

'Why,' Caroline asked Antonia a little coyly. 'What did you do?'

'Systematically worked upwards, ending with Medical Instruments on the top floor.' Antonia's blue eyes warmed with a flash of humour, but then were peaceful again so that Caroline wasn't sure if she'd imagined it.

'Oh. I forgot about Medical Instruments.'

'My point exactly.' Antonia turned to mount the steps to the coach. She glanced over her shoulder, looking, at that moment, in a squirrel-grey overcoat with a snowy collar and an arch expression, very Hollywood. 'You guys may have rationalised the world but it's just as bloody well you've got people like me to organise it.'

7

'I thought you decorated it, Antonia,' Greg laughed.

'I do that too,' she said in an aside. 'It's called multi-tasking.'

In the coach, Caroline took a seat at the front. Antonia sat on the other side of the aisle. Subdued conversation and occasional giggles came from the seats behind. Caroline slipped off her coat and settled back. Outside, the late January air was clear and cold, the South Kensington museums glowing like Gothic mansions under their spotlighting. She cupped her hands to the window to block out her reflection and tried to peer up towards the sky. There were no clouds tonight, which was no doubt why it was so cold. It would be a good night for viewing. If it didn't cloud over later, she could go out into her shed, set things up and have a look. A thread of anticipation slivered through her veins and she smiled to herself. All in all, a busy and fun Saturday.

Antonia shifted along in her seat to allow a space for Greg to sit next to her, which he dutifully did. Caroline thought she heard a well-timed giggle from the back. Very little went unnoticed by this horde, and what they didn't notice they generally made up anyway.

A plaintive voice from the back begged for the driver to put music on the radio, which was denied. Caroline's mind wandered as the engine rumbled beneath them and the coach drifted off into the London traffic. The voice at the back became more insistent.

'Please can we have the radio on? Mrs Clarke, isn't music the food of life?'

'The food of *love*.' Antonia turned round in her seat to view the perpetrator, but a fateful smile on her face was followed by one from Greg, and Caroline herself, which

8

ensured that the radio went on. 'Damn it,' Antonia said as she settled next to Greg again. 'I thought I had my facial muscles drilled like new recruits. You never know when they're going to let you down.'

When Antonia got home she scooped up the mail from the doormat, frowning. Sonia was thirteen, and trying to house-train her was like trying to teach a cat to jet-ski. She sifted through the mail quickly. A couple of official-looking envelopes, something for Daniel, the lodger she had taken in to help make ends meet, and a letter in her mother's handwriting. She could smell burnt toast wafting from the kitchen. *Blind Date* was on in the living room, and Sonia was chuckling.

She nudged open the living-room door and peered inside. Sonia was in the lotus position on the rug, apparently practising a new exercise while she gazed at the television.

'Hello love,' Antonia said, her frown disappearing and her heart warming to see her daughter's lanky form, her flyaway pale hair, her overly long flared jeans and clumsy trainers. Sonia turned dark brown eyes towards her mother, which instantly lit up. Her soft mouth split into a wide grin. The eyes and the grin she had inherited from her father.

'Hey, Mum! Look at this one, isn't he disgusting? I bet she picks him. If only she could see him.'

Forgetting her annoyance at finding the mail strewn across the hall carpet where it had landed, Antonia took off her coat, dropped her handbag on the sofa, and sank down next to her daughter, ruffling her hair.

'Good day?'

'Don't,' Sonia pleaded, moving just out of reach. 'I've

got stay-in conditioner on it. You'll get your hands slimy.'

'Okay. Get your history project finished?'

'Hmmn.' Sonia nodded, eyes turned back to the screen. 'How was the spod museum?'

'Spoddy. But surprisingly good fun. Daniel's out, is he?'

'Gone to London. Staying over with some friend. I reckon he's got a girlfriend up there.'

'I wouldn't be surprised if he has got a girlfriend,' Antonia mused, glancing at the screen and cringing in unison with her daughter as the disgusting one was picked for the blind date. 'Which is good, as we get more weekends to ourselves.'

'I suppose. I quite like him though. I mean, he's hardly ever here, which is what you wanted, but I like it when he is here.'

'Yes, he's a bright thing. I quite like having him about.'

'Do you fancy him?' Sonia asked bluntly.

'Of course not.' Antonia was surprised. She thought about it for a moment. Daniel was a good-looking and affable young man, but he *was* young, and he was busy with his friends in London most of the time. It had been hard to get to know him – which Antonia had considered ideal in a lodger. He paid her money, slept in his bed most weeknights, then vanished. A perfect arrangement.

Antonia's cottage was in a mid-terrace row, on the borders of a town close to the girls' school where she worked. She had chosen not to live in the same place as the school, knowing from experience just how overwhelming physical proximity could be in a job that

10

already demanded your heart, soul and liver on a plate. The town was near enough, and it was small and pretty. Sonia, lively and bright, but not studious, hadn't managed to get a place at the grammar school where Antonia taught, and was educated locally instead. It was a good school. Antonia approved of it, Sonia loved it, and Antonia had never wanted Sonia to suffer the teasing which would have resulted from her mother teaching in the same establishment. They were both happy with the way things had turned out.

Daniel had replied to the advertisement for a lodger she'd placed in the local paper. He'd just received a transfer down to the nearby Ministry of Defence establishment. He drove between the cottage and Fort Halstead during the week, then most weekends, and some weeknights too, took advantage of the proximity of the town to London by getting the train up to see his old crowd. University friends, Antonia imagined, always feeling slightly sorry for Daniel that he'd landed a job, albeit a high-flying one, down here in the sticks.

'You really don't fancy him, do you?' Sonia said, looking relieved and disappointed in equal measure. 'Why's that?'

'Well, he's too young for me for a start, I know very little about him, and I would imagine we wouldn't have much in common. But he's friendly, and pleasant, and he's neat which at least means *one* of my charges cleans up after themselves.' She punched her daughter's arm playfully. Sonia giggled.

'I guess he is a bit young for you,' Sonia agreed. Then, looking more thoughtful, she added bluntly, 'It's not because he's black, is it?'

'For heaven's sake, Sonia, you know me well enough

to know that's a stupid thing to say. Daniel's just Daniel.'

'Who do you fancy, then?' Sonia persisted.

'Nobody. I have some good male friends, and that's quite enough for me. And in any case, I'm not looking for people to fancy,' Antonia advised her daughter. 'Unlike you, madam, with your rotating head.'

Sonia blushed. 'It's my age. It's not my fault.'

'Yes, that's what your father said when he ran off with Tasha.' Antonia pulled herself up. Her legs were aching after the day's prowling around the galleries, and she was starting to feel tired. 'What I need is a glass of wine and some food. I take it you're still hungry, or did a loaf of toast fill you up?'

'I'm starved,' Sonia said, her eyes widening. 'Can we have your special lasagne?'

Antonia was really too weary to start fiddling with cheese sauces, but she nodded. 'Yes, all right then. You're sure you've done your history?'

Sonia nodded vehemently. Antonia went into the kitchen, poured herself a glass of red, and pulled out one of the pine chairs around the table. She sank into it thankfully, ignoring for the moment the toast crumbs and the unwashed plates and mugs in the sink. The wine brought sensation back to her limbs, and, taking a breath, she thumbed her way through her mail.

After she'd skimmed through a bill, the newsletter from the local drama society, and her mother's letter, she opened the last envelope.

It was from her doctors' surgery, and she had to look at it twice. It wasn't what she was expecting. Apparently her recent cervical smear had shown abnormalities in the cells, and she was being recalled for further investigation. With the letter was a leaflet describing a variety of investigative processes. Antonia read it all, and again, and again, then sank back in her chair, taking a larger sip of her wine, and stared at the wall. The angles, spikes and blades of the medical instruments she had seen earlier in the day played across her mind. Rusted saws, curved knives, swabs and leather cases filled with tools of pain.

'Oh sod,' she said.

Chapter Two

Lizzy wasn't sure what she was doing, standing in the freezing air at nine o'clock on a Saturday night, above her only a mustard-coloured glimmer from a streetlamp and the musky light of a full moon, in front of her a complete stranger's door. The air smelt of cold. An odd mixture of chimney smoke and metal. She wriggled her fingers in her gloves, pulled her furry hat over her ears, braced herself, and rang the bell. She stepped back and waited.

It was a solid door. There was a chink of light showing through a gap in the thick curtains of a front window, so she knew that 'The Spinning Fate' (modest rates, discount for students, unemployed and OAPs) must be in. She had spoken to him briefly on the phone to make the appointment, and he sounded pleasant enough. In fact, she'd thought at the time that he'd sounded enormously surprised to get her call. Now she tried to picture him. Probably with a scarf, hooped earrings, a fake tan, and a heinous cackle. Or perhaps beaded trousers and an embroidered waistcoat, with long flowing hair reeking of herbal oils, and sandals made out of compressed lentils. The thought made her nervous. David knew where she was and she had her mobile at the ready, so she had covered herself in case the fortune-teller turned out to be a seducer in the guise of a spinning fate. She'd have liked David to have come

14

with her but she knew he'd have ruined it by guffawing and, above all, he had to stay and babysit for the boys. So here she was, on her own, on a whim after seeing the fortune-teller's small advert in the local paper, and she had a strong urge to turn and run back to her car.

The consolation was that Caroline's house was in the street parallel to this. In fact, The Spinning Fate's house must have a garden that backed onto hers. Caroline, Lizzy's cousin, lived at the bottom of the long hill that led down from the town centre, the opposite end of town from Lizzy and David's house. But Lizzy was often down here (more often than not, David teased her) dropping in on Caroline, talking and catching up on family news. If the fortune-teller turned out to be a weirdo, Lizzy could always make a quick excuse to leave and pop into Caroline's for an hour or so. She'd noticed her cousin's lights on as she'd driven past, so Caroline was in, possibly in the garden with her telescope pondering the night sky.

Lizzy gazed upwards while she waited for him to come to the door. It was a beautiful night. She couldn't assess the sky in the same way that Caroline did. It seemed highly unromantic to consider the twinkling lights as elements, chemicals and molecules. Lizzy's mother – Caroline's mother's sister – had been the odd-ball in a chaotically inventive family. Where the others took great pleasure in dissecting, dismantling, rebuilding, analysing and testing things, Lizzy's mother was a poet at heart. When Lizzy was a little girl, her mother had told her that the sky was acres and acres of knitting, and the stars were dropped stitches where the light beyond shone through the holes. Somehow Lizzy had never been able to get that idea out of her head.

The door opened a crack, and Lizzy heard a man's voice.

'Back, Shirley! Come on, out of the way, Birdbrain.' A deep sigh. 'All right, if you want to go and play with the traffic, don't let me stop you, but don't expect me to come and scrape you off the tarmac. That's it, away from the door. Thank you *so* much for not killing yourselves.'

The door opened further, and Lizzy peered ahead curiously. Part of a face appeared around the side of the door.

'I'm sorry, can you squeeze in? This lot will run out into the road if I open the door too wide, and cars come racing down this road at a rate of knots. I don't want them flattened.'

Lizzy felt heartened. He didn't sound like a weirdo, although she'd only seen the top of a reddish-blond head very briefly, and in shadow with the hall light behind him. He hadn't got a headscarf on. He was probably fine. Even so, Lizzy took her mobile out of her bag and decided to keep it in her hand for now.

'Please, do come in,' he said again. Lizzy stepped over the threshold, and slid into his hall. He closed the door behind her, breathing a sigh of relief, and smiling at her. 'Thanks. I know it seems a bit odd, but if you've ever had cats, you'll know what I mean. They see an open door. Zip, they're through it. Just like that.'

Lizzy gazed around the hall. Three cats were slinking away from her. One sat perched on the bottom stair. A rotund black beast with yellow eyes. It winked at her. The other two slithered away like pompoms on strings. One side of the hall wall was lined with shelves crammed with books. It made the hall very narrow, which was why she'd had to slide in sideways. A musty,

16

old library smell came from the books. It wasn't unpleasant. Standing just in front of her, looking a little nervous, was The Spinning Fate.

He was younger than she'd expected, probably somewhere in his mid-thirties. He was tall, with dishevelled dark blond hair which had a hint of red about it. The ends of his hair lay on his shoulders. His skin had a sheen of healthiness, like a suntan except that it was natural. He had a patrician nose, curved, sensual lips, and clear eyes, a greenish colour edged with dark lashes, that she was now trying very hard not to stare at. In short, he was utterly stunning.

Lizzy swallowed, fingering her mobile phone.

'What do we do now?' she said, when she could speak again.

'Do? Oh, I see. Tea, I think,' he said.

'Is that what you normally do?' Lizzy asked, as she followed him through the hall and into his front room.

'Normally?' He seemed puzzled as he hooked a stray bit of hair awkwardly behind his ear.

'It's just, I've never had this done before.' Lizzy blushed, wondering if she should apologise. 'I don't really know what the form is. But I do promise not to laugh.'

'Oh, I see.' He raised his eyebrows. 'You know, I really don't mind if you laugh. I think that's allowed. Have a seat somewhere. I've put chairs at the table in case you want the tarot, but just sit where you like. How do you take your tea?'

'Er, milk, one sugar. Thanks.'

He disappeared, leaving Lizzy to peruse his front room. It was a mess, but Lizzy couldn't help thinking it was a friendly mess. She began to relax. There was a sofa with a throw over it, adorned with a grey cat curled up into a sleepy ball. It had so much fur, Lizzy couldn't tell which way up it was supposed to go. Bookcases lined the walls, the books stacked unevenly, some half-hanging from the shelves, some upright, some in piles. A carved rocking chair took up one corner, with an askew cushion that had a cat-shaped dent and a film of ginger hair on it. There was a portable TV in the corner, with a teetering pile of magazines on it. Apparently it served as a coffee table. There were globes everywhere. Very small ones, lined up on one shelf, and several more, shiny, detailed and football-sized, placed around the room somewhat haphazardly. A large yellow ochre and brown globe with a heavy brass fitting sat on the floor.

Lizzy turned around. There was a large tropical fish tank along another wall. It was brightly lit, the water clear, a silver stretch of sand along the bottom. Within, fascinating arrows of vivid colour darted in and out of swaying ferns. Lizzy dropped to her haunches and put her face close to it in wonder. She'd never found fish interesting, but these little creatures were quite beauti-ful. The boys would have loved it. She settled herself comfortably on her knees, noting that the rug beneath her, which was decorated in black and maroon with haunting Eastern geometric patterns, had probably been hoovered recently. It was no wonder the room felt so homely. The light from the tank and two honey-coloured standard lamps gave it a comforting glow, and a soft sound of bubbling came from the water. And, Lizzy noted, it was full of life. She was starting to feel confident that The Spinning Fate, while not at all what she expected, was not weird.

'Here's the tea,' he said, and Lizzy stood up to take it.

'Thank you.' It was a Garfield mug. She took a sip. And nice tea too. She found herself wondering if he was married, and if so, where he might have found room to fit his wife into his small house. 'How many cats have you got, then?'

'Just the six now. Lucy died. But don't feel sad, she was really old. I know, it seems like more, but that's because they run about, and you see them twice without realising it. I mean, visitors do. I recognise them, of course.'

'You like globes? You've got a lot of them.'

'Oh, yes. I don't collect them. Well, not deliberately. But they fascinate me.'

'Do you travel a lot, then?'

'Sometimes. But with the globes it's more about perspective. Looking at the world from the outside. As if you were far away, looking down on yourself. It's like those ten-foot-long school photographs. You can gaze at them for hours, trying to pick out your own face in a sea of pink blobs, and it's always tricky. I could never tell which one was me. The globes are the same sort of thing.' He cleared his throat self-consciously. 'If you see what I mean.'

Lizzy didn't really. She said instead, 'The fish are wonderful. I didn't think I liked fish, but I could look at your tank for hours.'

'That's what everyone says.' He smiled, seating himself at the round table, and indicating that Lizzy should take the chair opposite him. Lizzy noticed that on the scuffed surface of the table (which also had a few coffee-mug rings on it) was a small cardboard box with curious images on it, and a crystal ball. It sent a frisson over her.

'They're not that much trouble to look after either, surprisingly,' he went on. 'It's only buying crates of distilled water that's a job, everything else is easy. Lovely, aren't they?'

'Do your fish have names?' Lizzy asked, trying not to think about the crystal ball for the moment.

'Yes.' He looked a little embarrassed. 'But anyway, Mrs Carter, I don't want to waste your evening for you, what would you like me to do?'

'Oh, call me Lizzy,' she said, sipping her tea again. 'Well, what do spinning fates normally do? I'm not really sure what I want. Just for you to read me my fortune, I suppose.'

'Spinning fates?' He looked baffled for a moment, then gave a short laugh. 'Oh God. The name in the ad. Of course. You can just call me Tom if you like, it's a bit less of a mouthful. Well, normally I – er.' He stopped to scratch his ear. 'Well, I make tea, then we sit here, and then we decide what to do, then we do it, then – then you go home.'

Lizzy nodded uncertainly. He didn't seem very sure. She wondered for a moment if he was a charlatan. Not that she'd know the difference between a real spinning fate and a fake one, but she'd come presuming that he would know at least a little about what he was doing. She hadn't much experience to go on, but she'd certainly never seen a spinning fate in a rugby shirt and jeans before. Perhaps she would have felt she was getting more value for money if Tom had been draped in scarves and wearing fragrant sandals. But he hadn't asked her for any money yet. In fact, he hadn't seemed sure of what his standard rate was when she'd asked him on the phone.

20

'Well, I'll tell you what. We'll leave the crystal out of it for now. My grandmother was excellent at that, but in truth I'm not so good. It's really there because it's pretty. I've never seen anything in it.'

'So you're not psychic then?' Lizzy asked, starting to feel let down. 'I mean, how do you do this?'

'My grandmother was,' he said earnestly. 'It was a gift she had. She could do anything. Tea leaves, palms, crystal ball, tarot. She always told me I'd inherited some of it.'

'So – you see visions then? Or – what's it like?'

'Nothing like that. I think we'll do the tarot, shall we? Then I can look at your palm, if you like.' He removed the lid from the box, unwrapped a pack of elongated cards that looked quite old from a dark blue silk cloth, and began to shuffle them. Lizzy noticed his hands. Quite rough, the knuckles reddened. 'It's more of a gut feeling,' he went on as he shuffled. 'I can't really explain it. I'm not even sure myself if it's what being psychic's all about. Perhaps it's just intuition. I do know that people find the readings helpful.'

'So you have done this before, then,' Lizzy said, very relieved.

'Oh, yes, of course. I'm sorry, you must have been wondering.'

'It's just, you know, the table, the jeans.' Lizzy blushed, feeling shallow. 'The lack of beads. And there's not a joss stick in sight.'

He smiled gently, and Lizzy felt her stomach somersault. She was deeply in love with her husband, she was sure of that, but it didn't stop her being a woman.

'All that's just gloss, Lizzy. It doesn't mean anything. My grandmother used to do readings over a glass of

21

stout and a Woodbine, sitting at her kitchen table with her curlers in.' He shrugged. 'I'm afraid that's me. I'm not very big on gloss. But perhaps you're right. Perhaps a paying public expects a bit more of a show. I'll think about that. It should probably look a bit more professional. Yes, I'll give it some thought. Thanks.'

'I'm not sure what "professional" is for a spinning fate. But it's fine, really,' Lizzy assured him. She breathed quietly to herself. One of the reasons she'd wanted to come out and do this, on her own, without David and without the boys tonight, was because she felt she was losing sight of herself. Only with Caroline did she truly feel like an individual again, and even then she often felt that Caroline was better defined than she was herself. It was if her cousin was a three-dimensional, solid being, but she herself was an elusive shape, at times almost transparent. It wasn't that Lizzy was unhappy, just a little unsure of who she was these days.

'So, now you shuffle, and I'll shut up for a bit, and just think about yourself.'

Lizzy took the cards, her skin tingling as she felt them in her fingers, and hesitantly began to shuffle. 'Like this?'

'You can be more robust. They won't break.' He smiled. 'I'll just go and feed the cats while you do that. Back in a bit.'

Lizzy shuffled like fury while Tom was out of the room. He left her alone for a few minutes, in which time she felt a sense of peace descend on her. There was something about this house that made her want to curl up on his sofa, like one of his cats, and snooze the evening away. It was very restful.

He returned, and sat down again.

22

'Okay, now place the cards on the table and cut them with your left hand, into three piles.'

'Does it have to be my left hand?'

'Yes. Don't ask me why, though. Now put them back together in any order that suits you. Fine, here we go then. I'll do you what's called the Celtic Cross, gives you a better overview that way.'

Lizzy watched with fascination, her pulse speeding up a little, as Tom laid out the cards on the table. She tried to imagine what the symbols and pictures might mean, and gave an audible sigh of relief that the infamous reaper hadn't appeared.

'No death then,' she laughed.

'That's a myth. The death card is actually very positive. Change, cutting out dead wood, moving on.'

'Really?'

'Yep, but it's not there anyway. Right, let's have a look.' He cleared his throat. 'Your distant past is so happy. Good childhood, plenty of sun there. Healthy and strong, not just you, but your wider family. You're lucky. You've had a good foundation in life.' He gave a quiet laugh. 'Yes, that's very clear to me. You're a happy person. You have a lot of friends, people love being around you – and your family's like that. I can't see any problems there. You had a wonderful time.'

Lizzy pressed her lips together. She was determined not to be too impressed by him. Besides, if he'd had to make a stark choice between a happy and a disastrous childhood, he had a fifty per cent chance of being right. So far it could be luck. As it was, he was spot on. But he wasn't looking at her for confirmation. He was gazing down at the cards, a frown crossing his brow.

'Can you take another card, from the top of the pack, and put it over this one here?'

Lizzy did as she was told. The images meant nothing to her. She could see a lot of swords, but that could mean anything. They both fell silent. Tom put his elbows on the table and considered the cards carefully. He shook his head, lost in thought.

'Would you mind very much giving me your hand, just for a second?'

Lizzy obeyed. She didn't even think about arguing with him. She put out her hand, and, momentarily, he held it. Then he let it go again. She watched his face for clues. His mouth curled and straightened, and when he finally looked at her again, his green eyes were troubled.

'What is it?' Lizzy whispered.

'Not long ago, it's like a black cloud covered the sun. Not just for you, but for everyone around you. But it was worse for you. It threatened to take the bloom from your happy nature, if anything could.'

Lizzy's throat tightened. 'Go on.'

'Probably six or seven years ago. A tragedy in your family, but it was very personal to you. Something that filled you with pain. Oh dear, I'm sorry to bring it up again when you've been managing so well.'

Lizzy swallowed down the hard lump that had risen in her throat. 'I thought you were meant to predict my future.'

'I don't really predict. Things change. Depending on decisions you make, your reading can be different in a matter of days. But this is telling me something very sad about your past,' he said softly. 'I'm so sorry, I should have explained. It's a full picture, you see, to place you, to visualise your soul and what's made it what it is.'

24

She managed in a choked voice, 'It's all right. You've brought it up because it has to be brought up again. I can't keep pretending I've got over it.'

'I – I think I see. It's something buried deep within you, but it's still hurting. Like a sword, stuck in your body.'

Lizzy tried to take a breath.

'My – first child. Six years ago. A little girl. She was premature.' She gasped. 'Her name was Elizabeth. She lived for two days. Forty-three and a half hours to be precise. There's not a day that passes when I don't think about it.'

Tom put his hand across the table, and Lizzy found herself taking it. A tear dribbled down to the end of her nose and hung there. He squeezed her fingers.

'I'll go and get a box of tissues,' he said.

Caroline was surprised to hear the doorbell ring at nearly eleven o'clock. She'd just come in from the garden, finding herself too cold, even in three sweaters, a windcheater and woolly hat, to stand out there any longer.

She'd been marvelling at the unclouded sky. A rare event, as this January had been mostly overcast and grim. Tonight it was clear, and very cold. The full moon had transfixed her and she'd been in her flip-top shed, or, as she preferred to call it, her amateur observatory. It was in essence a garden shed, but designed specifically with a stable concrete floor and permanently fixed pier to take her beloved Meade telescope, with a roof that slid off on a metallic bracketed arm on one side to allow her to observe. Her parents had helped her to set it all up when she'd moved in, and it had been an exhilarating exercise. This evening she'd been scanning her regular sites in the sky and logging details for as long as she could before she froze. Finally her fingers were too numb on the pencil when she moved away from the telescope and sat at the computer desk attempting to make notes. She downloaded as much information as she could into the laptop and decided to take it inside for further analysis. Just too cold. Winter. Her nemesis.

A sheen of ice was already forming over the path and the grass was spiked with frost as she secured the detachable slope of the roof back to the shed and locked the door. She'd stood silently in her compact garden, her head back, gazing up into infinite space, lingering over Perseus, one of the first constellations her grandfather had shown her, before settling on Vega, her favourite star, which was low and dazzling. It was an irksome fact of life that the astronomy club had to book viewing sessions at bigger observatories in advance. Her shed was too small to take more than one or two visitors comfortably. You could never really tell, weather forecasts being what they were, when you were going to be blessed with ideal observing conditions, especially in the Northern Hemisphere in the middle of winter. One or two of the members had small telescopes set up at home, as she did herself, but they were limited and not all the members benefited. It would have been a fabulous night to gather at an observatory. They'd have to plan the next viewing night better. But nonetheless she knew she wouldn't be the only one out tonight dressed up like an egg cosy. Even if you were only armed with powerful binoculars it was a night to make the most of.

Squinting at Vega, Caroline hadn't realised how cold

she was getting until an insistent scuffling at the high wooden fence at the bottom of the narrow garden distracted her. There were bushes down there that in the summer held promise of gooseberries and redcurrants. In the winter they were sharp brown stalks that rustled in every gust of wind. Her house was one in a row of Victorian terraced town houses and the gardens were back to back with those of the houses in the street beyond. Whoever owned the house that backed onto hers had some sort of big dog, she'd gathered. It clawed at her fence a lot. It wasn't a very sturdy fence, but if the animal was doing any damage it seemed to be on the other side. And it didn't bark, thankfully. As she was walking up her garden path to the back door, she'd heard a man's voice speaking to the animal.

'How did you get out? You'll freeze to death. Come inside now.'

Caroline let herself back into her bright, warm kitchen and pulled the blind down over the window in the kitchen door. Her intention was to make a hot coffee and spend an hour or two on the Internet before bed. She tried to catch up with developments via the Web whenever she could. She took off her woolly hat, wind-cheater, and two of her jumpers, and just as she was making her coffee, the doorbell trilled.

At the door Caroline called a quick 'Who is it?' and heard, 'It's me, Lizzy, open up,' in response. She pulled the door open, ready with bright eyes and a warm smile.

Lizzy erupted into Caroline's impeccably neat hall-way and threw her arms around her cousin, planting a kiss on her cheek.

'Everything all right?' Caroline asked, laughing as Lizzy maintained a strong grip on her arms. She had to bend a little to kiss her cousin's cheek, given that Lizzy was a few inches shorter than she was. She disentangled herself and looked at her properly.

Lizzy's fair cheeks were flushed, her furry hat was on back to front, and her curly blonde hair was sticking out and ruffled. She was not the sort of woman who'd be blown away by a puff of wind, but tonight she looked fragile. More worryingly, she had smears of mascara under her eyes, and she looked as if she'd been crying. Caroline was instantly suffused with worry.

'God Lizzy, what's happened? Is it the boys? David?'

Lizzy shook her head. 'No. They're fine. It's me.'

'What is it?' Caroline breathed, fear touching her. Lizzy meant the world to her. She was family, and also her best friend.

Lizzy laughed. 'I don't know. That's the thing. I don't even know what happened. But it was the most amazing thing I've ever experienced. I feel – I feel absolutely fantastic.'

'You do?' Caroline's eyes widened. She knew Lizzy was more emotional than she herself would ever be. But Lizzy was also practical, a great organiser, and anything akin to an artistic temperament only emerged on very rare occasions. Bewildered, Caroline took her coat and hat, hung them neatly up on the coat hooks in the hall, and led her through to the kitchen.

'Oh, and I've brought back the trousers you lent me. Don't fit, I'm afraid. I'm too porky round the waist at the moment, but I've got this red blouse I bought and hate. You can have it if you like it.'

'Great. Thanks,' Caroline took the plastic bag and set it to one side, concerned about Lizzy's strange frame of mind.

'It seems quiet in here.' Lizzy danced through the house. 'I must have had the cold in my ears outside. Or maybe it's my thoughts making me think it was noisy before.'

'Sometimes it is too quiet in here.' Caroline gave Lizzy a curious look. 'I'd better make you a coffee.'

'Make it something stronger and if I take a liking to it David can pick me up. He's got Brendan with him, so he can babysit while David comes to get me. They're watching some sort of fighter plane documentary that David taped. You know what they're like with the plane things.'

'Brendan?' Caroline tutted as she found a bottle of white wine in the fridge and poured Lizzy a glass, picturing David's laconic Australian friend. 'In which case, they'll be on the Fosters. You'd better get a taxi.'

'Okay.' Lizzy sank into one of Caroline's clean white kitchen chairs, and watched Caroline place her glass of wine on a coaster and slide it over the equally spotless white table towards her. 'Aren't you going to have one with me?'

Caroline guessed now that her Internet session would have to be put off until the next day, but she couldn't think of a nicer distraction than a glass of wine with Lizzy.

'Okay, I'll join you. But you'd better tell me what this is all about. If I didn't know you better, I'd swear you'd just had wonderful sex with David for the first time, but I know that can't be true.'

'Just as well I didn't go straight home then.' Lizzy flopped her elbows onto the table, gazing over at Caroline, who took a seat opposite her, with subdued excitement.

'Or, I'd say you were in love. But as you're always in love with your husband, there's nothing new in that. Sickening pair that you are,' Caroline teased.

Lizzy took a sip of wine. 'There's this man. I met him this evening.'

'A man?' Caroline froze. For a horrible moment, she wondered if Lizzy had fallen in love with somebody who wasn't David. Lizzy must have seen the horror on her face, and waved her hands quickly.

'No, no, no. Not like that. I met a man this evening, because I went to his house to have my fortune told,' Lizzy said. She paused. 'Exactly. That's why I didn't tell you before.'

'What did I say?' Caroline defended.

'Nothing. You didn't have to. It was the expression on your face, as if you were chewing pickled onions. So do you want to hear about it, or are you going to go square on me and start lecturing me about scientific probabilities?'

'I want to hear about it, of course.' Caroline curled her fingers around her wine glass. 'And I'll try not to make you feel silly, all right?'

'He was amazing,' Lizzy said. 'The things he knew. The things he just couldn't possibly have known that he told me about, and then we talked about them. And, oh God, Caro, some of it was really painful, but it was stuff I hadn't been talking about, not to David, or Mum, or you, or anyone. Things I'd had hidden inside. It all came out.'

'I'm not sure I like the sound of this,' Caroline said quietly.

'He wasn't spooky, or funky, or any of those things you think fortune-tellers are.'

'Deluded is the word I'd use.'

'He wasn't that either. He was factual, and honest, and spiritual. Just the way he saw the world, and the universe.'

'It's a universe, whichever way you look at it.'

'You know those old school photographs, the ones that have the whole school included?'

'The ones where you can never find yourself?' Caroline laughed.

'That's just it. I hadn't thought about it in that way at all. There was just something about him. I can't put it over. It's as if he had a light on inside him.'

Caroline couldn't bring herself to answer. Her cousin, lovely as she was, was rambling. When Lizzy glanced at her appealingly, she gave a short nod instead. She didn't want to bring Lizzy down, she hated to do that, but she had thought she was slightly more sane than this.

'So we went through the past, and the present, and talked a bit about the future.'

'Tall, dark stranger?' Caroline quipped, deciding humour was probably the best way to avoid any awkwardness.

'No, not at all. In fact, that was the incredible thing. He talked about choices, and opportunities, but he said he believed each individual was in control of his or her own destiny, even though destiny threw surprising things into your lap. So we talked about everything, right back to me meeting David at the nightclub years ago.'

'Lizzy,' Caroline said kindly, 'that was chance.'

'And he made me feel so fulfilled,' Lizzy went on. 'I felt important. He has a way of seeing the world, as if we're all souls, singing individual songs, joined together in a kind of – choir.' Caroline raised her eyebrows expressively and Lizzy giggled. 'He put it better than me.'

'I do hope so,' Caroline said. 'And what did he charge you for all this?'

Lizzy looked at her blankly, then clapped her hand over her mouth. 'Oh my God, I forgot to pay. Or he forgot to ask me. Oh hell, that's really awful. It just slipped my mind. I was so full of inspiration when I left, and he seemed happy it had gone well, so he waved me off, and that was it. It was free.'

'So what does he call himself, this guru of yours?'

'The Spinning Fate,' Lizzy said.

Caroline nearly sprayed her mouthful of wine across the table. She wiped her mouth. 'Please tell me you're joking.'

'But that,' Lizzy waved a finger in admonishment, 'is only because he thought he should have a name like that to attract customers. It's like a stage name. I think he'd even forgotten what he'd called himself in his ad. His real name's Tom. He explained it. Apparently there were three Fates in mythology. One gave out fates to people, one was the fate you can't avoid, and one was spinning.'

Caroline got up and topped up Lizzy's glass for her as Lizzy began to hum happily under her breath. She sat down again and looked at her cousin more seriously. She felt protective of her suddenly. Lizzy had such a warm and trusting heart. She didn't want anybody messing with it.

'Lizzy,' she said. 'When people claim to be able to tell you what will happen in the future it can have a funny way of making decisions for you. I don't think it's healthy. These people rely on statistical probabilities and self-fulfilling prophecies. The rest of it is guesswork based on your eagerness for it to be true. That's about all there is to it.'

'That's it, you see. He just inspired me. I can't explain it. He didn't actually predict anything.'

'Not much of a fortune-teller really, then,' Caroline said with a twinkle in her eye. 'No wonder he didn't charge you.'

'I'll send him a cheque,' Lizzy said earnestly. 'I tell you, Caro, it beat yoga, or toe-plaiting for young mothers. It was the most therapeutic two hours I've ever spent in my life.'

Caroline let this thought sink in. Lizzy certainly looked good on it, if a little unearthly. Perhaps there had been no harm in it. It was ludicrous, but perhaps not an entirely wasted evening from Lizzy's point of view. She tried another angle.

'Did you tell David where you were going?'

'Of course.' Lizzy looked surprised. 'He always knows what I'm doing. He thought it was a bit of a joke, but said it'd be good for me to have an evening off doing something for myself. In fact,' she added mischievously, 'David suggested I should take you with me.'

'You've got to be out of your mind.'

'That's what I said. Mind you, Caro, he's gorgeous.'

'I know David's gorgeous. I have eyes.'

'No, the fortune-teller, Tom, I mean, is gorgeous.'

Caroline didn't answer. Lizzy's eyes took on an added sparkle as she said the word 'gorgeous' and Caroline prayed silently just once more for good measure that Lizzy hadn't formed a crush on this fortune-telling freak. They were both silent for a moment, lost in their own musings. Then Lizzy said suddenly, 'You used to have a globe, didn't you?'

'Yes,' Caroline said vaguely. 'And I've got a newer one I bought at Greenwich Observatory by the computer in the front room. Why?'

'There was a big one by your bed for years when we were kids. One of the lighting-up ones. It was even there when you did your A levels.'

'That's right.' Caroline smiled at the memory. 'I used to turn all the lights out, lie in bed and look at it, lit up in the dark, like an orb floating out there in the blackness. It used to make me feel as if I was in space.'

'It's a shame you lost it along the way.'

'I didn't. It's up in the spare room. Why?'

Lizzy sipped her wine. 'I think you should go and see Tom.'

'Over my dead body,' Caroline said.

Chapter Three

Caroline lay in bed for a few more moments, rubbing her eyes and wishing she hadn't had that last glass of wine with Lizzy before the taxi had arrived to take her cousin home. She had a busy Sunday ahead. Internet research, typing up the minutes of the last astronomy club meeting, Sunday lunch with her family, a pile of marking and preparations for the week's lessons. It was a chilly morning, and the central heating had only just kicked in. She reached tentatively for *Astronomy Now*, whipped it from the bedside table and snuggled back under her *Star Trek* duvet.

At ten o'clock her neighbours put the radio on and *Steve Wright's Sunday Love Songs* throbbed through the wall. Caroline got out of bed and darted to the shower while Whitney Houston trilled at her. After her shower she found her neatly ironed and folded tracksuit in the bottom drawer, and put it on. She blasted her hair with the hairdryer, ruffling it with her fingers until it was a short, dark brown mass of warm strands. She pulled on clean sports socks, her trainers, and trotted downstairs. A strong coffee and a glass of cold water to refresh herself, then she headed out of the door for her Sunday morning run.

The sky was white with opaque cloud from horizon to horizon. Caroline frowned up at it and picked her way carefully down her short garden path, through the gate and onto the sloped pavement which ran alongside the main road. Frost formed a thin glassy layer on the tarmac. She turned up the hill and tentatively broke into a slow jog.

Today she ran up the hill towards the town then turned back before the High Street, down the sleepy lanes where the houses were huge and set back beyond leafy boundaries. Evergreens swayed on either side, giving off a crisp, lemon-tinted scent of pine. Birds arrowed between the trees. Caroline longed for the soft sun on the buds, the primroses in the bank, the first whoop of the wood pigeons.

Further down the lane were smartly renovated terraces. At the foot of the circuit was a busy road, one of the three main roads that formed a triangle around the town. From there, it was pleasant to jog away from the traffic – not that there was much in a small country town on a cold Sunday morning – and back up Randolph Road which was lined with Victorian terraces and ran parallel to the road Caroline lived in. The path was thickly coated with frost, the glimmer of sun attempting to break through the cloud far too weak to have any effect. It was a steep incline, and Caroline plodded on, her calves aching. She stopped to gather her breath outside the newsagents, her attention caught by a rack of newspapers on the outside wall.

Edwin Hartley greeted her inside the shop.

'You're a hardy one, aren't you? Not much of a day for running. Them pavements are deathly out there.'

'That's true.' She stooped over the row of papers laid out along the bottom shelf and scanned the headlines. 'You have to take it slowly. How are you today?'

'Can't complain. I'd rather be in here than out there.'

The bell tinkled at the door as another customer came in. Caroline squatted to examine the papers more closely, torn between an *Observer* article on secondary school education and a *Sunday Times* feature on NASA. Someone hovered close to her and she glanced up.

She vaguely recognised the man. He looked at her with a glimmer of recognition too. Where had she seen him before? Perhaps here, or in the local Co-op, or one of the small cafes at this end of the town. He was tall, with blondish-reddish hair in a state of disarray which looked as if it might be permanent. He was dressed for the weather in a thick leather flying jacket, jeans, and boots. After looking him up and down, she met his eyes again and realised he was studying her too. She glanced away quickly.

'Hi there,' he said.

'Hello,' she said casually under her breath, and went back to scanning the papers.

'Daisy's not outside, is she?' Mr Hartley called over with something like despair in his voice.

'She's tethered. She's quite safe,' the stranger replied. Then added, 'I'll be quick.'

'Could you please?'

'Excuse me.' He bent over Caroline, scooped up a pile of newspapers, hoisted them under his arm and took them to the counter. Caroline peered at the window curiously, but small ads and a couple of posters blocked an outside view. Daisy had to be a fearsome dog if Mr Hartley was so insistent on her being tied up. The blond man didn't look like someone who'd have a pit bull, but you never knew with people. Mr Hartley poked at the till with lightning speed, the stranger paid, and turned

37

for the door. He glanced at Caroline once more, then left the shop.

'Oh Daisy!' The exclamation came from outside. Caroline continued to watch in fascination as he strode back in with a handful of chewed-up *Sunday Sports*, thumped them on Mr Hartley's counter, and emptied his pockets of change. Mr Hartley took the money and offered a purposeful look of disapproval. 'I'm sorry,' the stranger said. 'It won't happen again.'

He left, giving Caroline a rueful smile on the way out.

She stood up, having opted for the NASA article. She regretted that she couldn't just sweep up an armful of papers, buy them, and see what was inside them later, as the blond man had done. She was one to filter everything for content first. But she didn't have time to read ten Sunday papers. He obviously had nothing better to do.

'Daisy must be quite an animal,' she probed as she paid Mr Hartley.

'Tell me about it. Penned up, that's where she should be, not out there, eating my livelihood.'

Caroline agreed sympathetically, and, deciding that the strange man's attractive green eyes didn't make up for the fact that he was obviously an anti-social lout with a dangerous dog that went around terrorising newsagents, she left.

'Hello love. How's my favourite niece?' Doe asked as she opened the door with a glass of wine in one hand.

'Hello Doe.' Caroline greeted Lizzy's mother with a kiss. 'Have David and Lizzy made it yet? David had Brendan round last night. I bet they were poleaxed by bedtime.'

'Ah, Brendan. Such a dish. So grabbable. If someone doesn't grab him soon, I think I might have to.' Doe tossed her silk scarf around her neck and raised her eyebrows suggestively. 'And he's got a lovely bum.'

'Just a shame he talks out of it,' Caroline quipped.

'Brendan's in the other room.' David appeared in the hall and gave Caroline a kiss. He was always cheerful, his eyes deep blue within a slim, ruddy face. 'So keep your voice down. He fancies you, and you don't want to blow it, do you?'

'You, shut up.' Caroline thumped his arm. 'Where's Mum?'

'In the kitchen.' Doe disappeared through the arch into the front room. 'Building something.'

'What's she building?' Caroline asked David, who shrugged.

'God knows. Lizzy's doing dinner. I think your mum forgot to put something in the oven. Your dad's in the garden with the boys. They're checking out the hedgehog kennel.'

'Ah. Okay. See you later then.'

David followed Doe through the archway into the front room, and Caroline could hear Brendan laughing (how he managed to laugh with an Australian accent, she wasn't sure).

She wandered through the large dining room. The table was draped with a cloth. The cutlery was still in a heap at one end of the table, and there were a handful of plates dotted around haphazardly. Through the patio doors, at the end of the wide, disorganised garden, she could see her father on his knees on the grass with Lizzy's two boys, all peering intently into a wooden box. He wouldn't care whether his knees were getting wet

39

through his trousers or not. He wouldn't even notice. The heavy brass standard lamps around the room bathed it in a golden glow, and a tantalising aroma of roasting chicken threaded its way through the warm air. It was home, and Caroline felt a swell of emotion. From the kitchen, she could hear Lizzy chatting brightly, and the distinct sound of sawing.

'Hi!' Caroline announced herself in the doorway. Lizzy was basting the chicken, which would account for the wonderful smell, and Caroline's mother, Stephanie, was on her hands and knees on the lino, sawing the legs off a small table. Stephanie glanced over her shoulder, a strand of grey hair slipping from her chignon and falling over her eyes, and smiled.

'Hello Caro. Can you just grab the other end?'

'Sure.'

Such things were normal to Caroline. In her parents' house, anyway. She'd been brought up this way. In creative chaos, her mother had always joked, so she thought nothing of it. Perhaps her own home was so neat purely because she'd been brought up in a mess? She hadn't given it much thought. Caroline slipped off her coat, hung it over one of the chairs around the kitchen table, and obliged. 'What do you want me to hold onto – these legs?'

'Please dear. I've got one off, but it's tougher than it looks. We were just talking about Phil.'

Caroline's interest perked up. She was very fond of Phil, her younger brother. He had married a German woman, Luzie, whom he'd met when he was travelling in Germany. For a while, they'd been living in Hamburg together. Caroline was vowing to get out there to see them both again soon.

Phil hadn't inherited much of his family's scientific curiosity, but he'd always had a fascination for foreign travel seething in his veins, and it had made him more restless than any of them. He was twenty-seven now, eight years younger than Caroline. He'd always been her baby brother. Phil had been a source of worry for all of them as he grew up. He couldn't settle into university, so he left. He couldn't stick at any of his jobs, so he left those too. Every so often he'd disappear, leaving a note saying something like, 'Gone to Europe. Be in touch.' Once Stephanie had rung Caroline in a panic when she'd received a letter from Swaziland (she was sure he'd said he was going to Switzerland). Once it had been a phone call. 'There's some sort of coup going on so I've had to postpone coming home for a bit.' On another occasion it was a call on a satellite phone from Nepal. 'It's fucking freezing!' he'd told Stephanie, who'd bawled 'Language!' at him as they were cut off.

'How is Phil?' Caroline quizzed. 'Did he ring?'

'Just a quick call this morning.' Stephanie paused in her sawing. 'He said he and Luzie had had some sort of row but that they were making it up. I do hope he's settling down.'

'They're bound to row, Stephanie,' Lizzy said wisely. 'They're married.'

'Well, I suppose so.'

'Did he sound happy?' Caroline asked with big-sisterly concern.

'Oh, well yes. I have to say he did. But then, he's always happy. He was a happy baby. Even when you tried to suffocate him with talcum powder, Caro. He just giggled.'

'There you are then,' Lizzy said. 'It's a blip, nothing

more. David and I have rows, they don't mean anything. Sometimes I want to push his face into the Magimix, but that feeling passes in a few seconds.'

'I did once consider pushing Howard off a hotel balcony when we were on holiday in Crete,' Stephanie smiled. 'But that was because he was admiring a woman in a bikini sunbathing below us, and I realised pushing him on top of her would hardly be a punishment. That was a long time ago.'

'And how are you today, Lizzy?' Caroline flicked Lizzy a glance. Lizzy groaned.

'David had a bottle of wine in the fridge waiting for me. He said he thought I'd need it after my outing. We stayed up later than we meant to, so Brendan slept over, and the boys were up at six, as usual.'

'Lizzy's being wonderful,' Caroline's mother said. 'The potatoes were done and nothing else was, but she's got it all in hand now. Right then.' She turned the table onto its back.

'What's this for, Mum?' Caroline clung onto the upturned legs of the table while her mother sawed.

'For the boys, but the damned legs are too long. I bought it to go with those chairs we had in the shed.' She nodded over at two diminutive plastic chairs which had been sprayed with silver paint. Some of the paint had missed and hit the boiler, giving it a streaky effect.

'Ah, I see. Have you measured the legs now?'

'Yes. Just hang on, nearly there.'

'I rang Tom,' Lizzy called over as she popped the chicken back in the oven and turned her attention to topping and tailing sprouts.

'Tom?' Caroline shifted position, her knees starting to hurt from the pressure of the lino.

42

'Tom!' Lizzy widened her blue eyes expressively. 'You know. Of the spinning fate fame.'

'Oh God Lizzy, not him again.' Caroline winced as a splinter of wood flew past her face.

'Sorry,' her mother said.

'That's okay. Lizzy, why did you ring him?'

'Because I owed him money. And do you know what he said?' Lizzy flipped a sprout over the draining board and into the saucepan with expert precision. 'He said forget it. He said, as long as I got something out of it, he felt very content. Then he laughed and muttered something to himself like, some entrepreneur I am, but I don't think I was supposed to hear that. But he's so unusual, Caro. I can't really explain it. It didn't surprise me that he didn't mind about the money. There's something very giving about him. It made me feel really good about the world.'

'I'd feel really good not to have to pay for the benefit of a load of bollocks myself.'

'Caroline!' Her mother sat up, wiped her forehead, and frowned severely. 'There are parents present. Watch your language.'

'Sorry Mum. Here, let me do the last two legs. They're closer to me.' She was handed the hacksaw and tape measure, pencilled in a line on the leg, and began to saw while her mother held onto the table.

'I feel I should give him something, though,' Lizzy mused, lobbing another spout towards the saucepan.

'How about a crash course in reality,' Caroline said under her breath.

'My favourite sheila!' Brendan's twang reverberated around the kitchen. Caroline averted her eyes and sawed on. She was well aware that Brendan amplified his Australian characteristics in her presence because he knew she thought him the worst kind of macho Australian male, so played up to the image devilishly. 'Blow me, all my favourite sheilas in one room.'

'Hello Brendan,' Caroline said, head down.

'And Caro too. Sorry, I didn't spot you down there.' Caroline gave him an evil look. He grinned at her.

Brendan and David both worked at Fort Halstead, the nearby Ministry of Defence base. They'd known each other for seven years. It seemed to Caroline that Brendan had been around for ever. He had dark hair which he always wore in a ponytail, thick eyebrows, and lively black eyes. There was something unashamedly male about him that made the hair on the back of Caroline's neck prickle at times. Sometimes she even wondered . . . but she stopped herself there. He was a family friend, and she wasn't on the lookout for lovers, especially of the 'treat 'em mean to keep 'em keen' variety.

Caroline wasn't sure what Brendan actually did at work but knew he had a master's in electronic engineering from Melbourne, whereas David's role was more angled towards administration. When he and David had first met, Brendan had been married. Lizzy had always said it was what brought them all together as friends. They were young married couples, in the same boat. A couple of months later Brendan wasn't married any more, and had relished his single lifestyle ever since. He was godfather to both of the boys, and a regular visitor to David and Lizzy's. It seemed to Caroline that when Brendan was fed up, or lonely, or between girlfriends, he headed for Lizzy and David's house and refused to leave until he felt better.

44

Caroline's father arrived through the back door that led from the kitchen into the garden with the two boys in tow. Jacob was five, Michael four. They were all talking at once, and Howard had huge wet patches on the knees of his trousers which nobody noticed.

'Stephanie!' Her father addressed her mother loudly over Caroline's head. Jacob took the opportunity to skid across the lino on the sawdust and Michael followed.

'What is it, Howard? Did you scare the hedgehog away?'

In reply, Caroline's father held out a set of wind chimes, long cylinders of bamboo that Caroline knew her mother had made to hang from the hazel in the garden. His expression showed that he was deeply offended. 'That Glenda Hope-Potter next door has complained about the noise. We have to take them down.'

'Oh no.' Caroline's mother looked despondent. 'And the boys loved them.'

'Well, if we have to, we have to. God forbid that we should offend the Hope-Potters.' He put his foot on the pedal bin, and ceremoniously dropped the wind chimes inside. He let the lid fall with a snap. He put up a finger to Caroline, and wagged it. 'But I tell you, Caro, if they dare to complain once more about us talking at night on the bedroom balcony, I swear I'm going to – I'm going to really say something.'

'They complained?' Caroline set herself on the last leg of the table. Jacob grabbed one sawn-off leg and used it as a light-sabre. Michael took up another, and they had a mock fight on the floor until Brendan knelt down and prised the legs from the boys, whispering, 'Splinters, they hurt,' to them, with a wink.

45

'I'd taken your granddad's old telescope out there,' Caroline's mother explained to her. 'And you know how quiet we always are up on the balcony. We're very respectful. But it was such a clear night, and I could see so much, I called Howard out of bed, and he joined me. And, apparently, it upset the Hope-Potters.'

'Not as much as the wind chimes,' Caroline's father said before leaving the room, not storming out – he was too gentle and thoughtful a man to storm anywhere – but swiftly, for him. He was obviously deeply upset.

'Go to him,' Caroline's mother urged her quietly. 'I'll get the last leg off.'

'Okay. You might try using a bigger saw, Mum. This one's almost blunt.'

'I'll take the wind chimes, if you don't want them,' Lizzy suggested.

'By all means.' Stephanie nodded towards the bin. 'Help yourself. I'm sure you'll find somewhere to put them, and you don't have any Hope-Potters next door to you. Damned people they are.'

By the time they were all seated around the dining-room table, Howard was mollified, and things were back to normal. He had forgotten to take his magnifying glasses off since showing the boys an electrical circuit he was putting together where coloured lights flashed in time to the theme tune from *Bob the Builder*, so when Lizzy put a plate of food under his nose which must have seemed huge, he jumped and clasped his chest in shock. Stephanie called, 'Glasses!' He looked up, his brown eyes enormous behind the lenses, said, 'Eh?' then remembered, and took them off. Brendan, sitting next to

46

him, and opposite Caroline, put them on instead and tried to make her laugh.

The boys had decided to sit in the kitchen to have a meal by themselves and shrieks of laughter came through the hatch. They'd been seated around the sawn-down table when Caroline had gone back to the kitchen to get the salt and pepper, which everyone else had forgotten. She'd noticed that the table sloped, despite careful measurements. The boys were having great fun watching their plates slide around.

'You did say forty centimetres for each leg, didn't you Mum?' Caroline queried along the table, to her mother who was at the opposite end from her father.

'Forty? Yes, dear.'

'Strange.'

'That table,' Howard said, as if he was on another train of thought altogether, 'needed the legs sanding. Would have left splinters all over the place. I took it into the shed and smoothed off the ends. Should be right as rain now.'

'Ah,' Caroline said discreetly, and helped herself to some carrots.

'Your mum,' Howard said, smiling, 'is a bit bonkers. She gets it from your grandfather.'

'What's your excuse then, Dad?' Caroline dipped into the cauliflower cheese and groaned with delight. 'Lizzy, that's superb.'

'My excuse is that I married her,' Howard beamed. 'Let's drink to that.' He held up the gravy boat, peered at it, put it down again and picked up his glass instead.

'Not even a glass of wine today, Caro?' Brendan asked across the table as the others entered into a spirited conversation which revolved around memories of

Caroline's grandfather. She glanced at Brendan in vague annoyance, wanting to listen.

Her grandfather had been very special to her. He had inspired them all, but Caroline knew that she and her grandfather had shared a particularly close relationship. He had been unique, the kind of man whom she would never meet again in her lifetime. He was creative and scientific in equal measure, and always off pursuing a new project. He lived life without stopping to worry about what others thought. He defied convention without even meaning to. He had died ten years ago, and now she tried to remind herself that she shouldn't feel pain at the thought of losing him, but foster loving memories instead. It was hard. Sometimes she still wanted to sob her heart out at the mention of his name. Brendan, even though he'd practically been adopted by them all by virtue of the fact that his own family were in Australia and everyone in Caroline's family loved him, had never met her grandfather. It made it irritating that he wanted to talk while she wanted to delve into delicious memories of the things her grandfather used to do. She answered Brendan absently.

'No. Got work to do.' Caroline's attention was dragged away from the discussion. 'Take the magnifying glasses off, Brendan. You're putting me off my sprouts.'

Brendan removed the glasses and put them on the table. 'You don't allow much time for fun, do you?'

'I have lots of fun.'

'Sure. Secretary to the local astronomy club. Out-of-school activities, marking exercise books, research.' Brendan quirked a dark eyebrow teasingly. 'It's pure rock and roll, isn't it, pumpkin?'

'You chase women, I chase meteors,' Caroline bantered.

Brendan smiled. Since he'd asked Caroline out for 'some fun' on the day his divorce had become final some years ago and she had rejected him as a Lothario, he was used to her put-downs, and seemed to enjoy them. Being horrible to each other had become a sort of habit.

'Okay,' he shrugged. 'I'll try to understand. But tell me this, when was the last time you really got passionate about someone?'

Caroline passed the gravy boat down the table. 'I get passionate about things all the time.'

'No, not things, someone. A person. You know. A fella.'

He was flirting. Caroline felt the colour rise in her cheeks. 'Ask me another.'

'We should drink to something,' Lizzy was saying. 'It's not that long till Stephanie and Howard's anniversary. How about that?'

'How about drinking to true love?' David winked at Lizzy.

'You have fantasies,' Brendan said to Caroline in a hoarse whisper as conversation hummed around them, his eyes sparkling. 'I've seen your *Star Trek Voyager* duvet on the washing line.'

'You're rambling.' Caroline widened her eyes warningly at him.

'But I know what you want.' He nodded confidently. 'You want to express yourself passionately to another warm human being.'

'And that would be you, would it?' she shot at him. There was a meaningful pause and she felt her skin burn. She recovered herself quickly. 'You're just talking about meaningless sex.'

Brendan laughed. 'What would you know about meaningless sex?'

'Thankfully,' Caroline said, raising her voice, 'very little.'

'Do you know,' Brendan said earnestly, 'I really believe you.'

Howard was on his feet, holding out his glass. He glanced down at Caroline, distracted. 'What do you know very little about?'

Caroline thumped her knife and fork down on her plate. 'Meaningless sex!'

'To – meaningless sex!' Howard announced, holding out his glass and finding a silent table facing him.

'I'm sorry.' Caroline pushed back her chair, red-faced. 'I'll be back in a minute.'

'Caro?' Caroline turned to hear her mother's voice. She'd gone to find solitude in the cold fresh air on the upstairs balcony that led off from her parents' bedroom. She'd been fingering her grandfather's brass telescope on its stand that her mother now cherished, gazing over the ramshackle garden, listening to the conversation rising and falling as it drifted through the ceiling from downstairs, lost in her own thoughts. She'd been annoyed at herself for letting Brendan get under her skin. It wasn't personal, but she'd suddenly taken his comments about sex personally.

'Mum.' Caroline put out her arms, and they hugged.

'This old thing.' Stephanie ran her fingertips over the telescope. 'It means so much to us. All of us. Your granddad left us so much that isn't solid. Ideas, a way of

50

thinking.' She sighed loudly. 'But this, when I touch this, I feel as if he's right here, standing at my shoulder like he used to, telling me how to focus, where to point, what to see. You know he never really left us, don't you?'

Caroline nodded. 'Yes.'

'But you, Caro. You were his special girl. And of all of us, you're the most like him. I can see him sometimes, in your eyes, the way you move, even the things you do with your hands when you're explaining something. There's more of him in you than in me, or Doe, or Phil – certainly than in Lizzy.'

'Thanks, Mum. That helps. It's just sometimes, I miss him so much.'

Stephanie was a solid woman, as tall as her daughter, and with a womanly shape. When she put her arm around her shoulder, Caroline felt protected and comforted.

'He's a tough act to follow.' Stephanie laughed under her breath. 'When I was a girl, I used to think there wasn't a man in the world to compare to my wonderful dad. But I was lucky. Howard came along, and that was it. I was hit by a thunderbolt. He wasn't like Dad at all. He was Howard, with all his Howardly ways, but my God, I loved him.'

'Yes,' Caroline breathed.

'We're lucky, you know. We lost Granddad, and poor Lizzy lost the baby girl. And Phil's been a worry at times, but he's always come through. We're blessed, I always feel. There's so much love in this house. So much in all of us. And you, Caro. It shines from you. You don't know it, but you're quite beautiful. All the more so, because you just don't realise it. You have a . . . how can I put it . . . a glow. It comes from the inside.'

51

Caroline was stirred, and held her mother tightly. 'Thanks, Mum.'

'So what's troubling you?' Stephanie whispered into Caroline's ear. She stood away from her and looked at her quizzically. 'I'm your mum. Tell me.'

'It's so silly. I don't even know. I just – I went out jogging this morning, and the world was in limbo. The buds on the trees are snapped shut, the sky was just a thick mass of cloud, even the sun was being kept on hold. None of the shoots are coming up yet, it's far too early. And this thick frost, lying everywhere, on the earth, on the pavement. It's like a lid on a box, keeping everything inside. I just feel as if everyone's asleep. The world's asleep. I'm asleep too. I'm trying not to be, but – you see? I can't explain it.'

Stephanie squeezed Caroline's arm.

'You always hated this time of year. Even as a little girl. It kept you from being outside. I remember you in the summer, disappearing all the time. I'd lose you for hours, and I'd look upstairs, but your bed would be empty, and Howard would just glance up and say, "Don't panic, Steph, she'll be in the deckchair." And there you'd be, in the garden, curled up in the deck-chair, breathing in the summer night air, staring up at the sky.'

Caroline felt a nostalgic tear probe her lashes. The memory was so clear to her.

'I think I just want that. A little bit of home in my home. You know I like the house, and it suits me, but it does seem a bit empty sometimes.' Caroline laughed. 'Perhaps I should get a deckchair.'

'What about this amazing telescope you're saving up for? I know you wouldn't want Granddad's. The one you've got is far, far better. You can't plug this thing into a computer.'

'Oh, it's fine. The one I've got is great, it's just that the more I save, the better the telescope models are that come out, and trying to keep up is quite hard on my salary. I guess that's part of it too. I just feel today that nothing's moving forward. Then bloody Brendan started on about sex.' Caroline tutted, feeling more cheerful as her mother laughed under her breath.

'You know, I'm very fond of Brendan,' Stephanie said. 'Even if he can be a twit at times.'

'Yes, me too. It's like having a surrogate irritating little brother when Phil's not here.'

Stephanie raised her eyebrows. 'Not such a little brother. Brendan's practically the same age as you. And he is rather handsome, with those big brown eyes. Nice shoulders. I've even got used to his ponytail.'

'Mum!' Caroline eyed her mother curiously. 'You're not trying to pitch him to me, are you?'

Stephanie smiled. 'I know you too well to do that. I'm just saying that he's a nice man. One of the family. You know, he was talking about going back to Australia.'

Caroline frowned. For some reason she felt disappointed. 'Back home?'

'He's just mulling the idea over.' Stephanie kissed Caroline's cheek. 'I don't think you're the only one who's frustrated with life not moving on at the moment. Come on, let's go back in. It's freezing out here, and Lizzy brought a crumble for pudding.'

Brendan caught Caroline in the hall as she was pulling on her coat ready to leave for home.

'Caro?' He looked unusually sombre. 'I'm sorry for teasing you earlier. I took things a bit too far.'

Caroline was mollified. 'Forget about it. It's not you, it's me.'

Brendan threw back his head and laughed into the air. 'Christ, why do women always say that to me?'

'Well, the others are probably lying to you. But I'm being truthful. I'm having a bad hair day, so don't give it a second thought.'

'Thanks, doll.' Brendan held Caroline's shoulders and dropped a kiss onto her cheek. It was a warm kiss, and he planted it firmly. Caroline stood still, slightly disturbed, as he strode away to find the rest of the family in the front room. She touched her cheek with her fingertips. It was a long time since Brendan had kissed her. He seemed to have avoided doing so in recent years, perhaps because he thought it would annoy her, perhaps because he didn't want to, or perhaps because he sensed it might awaken a response in her. It had felt rather nice. Lizzy arrived in the hall as Caroline was heading for the front door.

'Glad I caught you. Listen, don't worry about Brendan today. He's in a funny mood.'

Caroline pulled her gloves on and gave Lizzy a quick hug. 'I'll take your word for it. I have to fly. You take care. Oh – and I wondered if you could make one of your wonderful cards. Something lovely and romantic.'

Lizzy's blonde eyebrows shot up in what looked like hope. 'You want to send someone a romantic card? Who? Not . . . not Brendan?'

Caroline laughed. 'I mean for Mum and Dad for their anniversary. You do those funny little figures so well. Plenty of time but I wondered if you'd think about it.'

'All right, I'll do you one. Oh, and one more thing.' Lizzy stopped Caroline as she was opening the door. 'I want to ask you again. Will you go and see The Spinning Fate? Tom, I mean. Just for a laugh, even?'

'No,' Caroline said firmly.

Chapter Four

Nina McArthur was twenty-six. She had frizzy blonde hair, and was often asked if it was permed, but it wasn't. She lived in a two-bedroomed Wimpey home just outside Reading with Graham, who was a pharmacist.

Nina's life had started to become interesting when she was twenty-one. It was then that she'd taken a job as a sales rep for a pharmaceutical company, selling products to independent chemists. Before that she was working as a sales assistant in Boots, living with Paul who was a mechanic, and didn't look much beyond her job, their bedsit above a bicycle shop on the Bath Road, Friday and Saturday at the pub, and avoiding her parents. She'd moved out of home and into the bedsit with Paul when she was sixteen, a move that was met with comprehensive indifference from her mother, who was watching television at the time. As Nina had left the house for the last time, her mother hadn't so much as raised her vodka bottle in her daughter's direction. Her father had been away on an overseas driving trip, so there hadn't been any cause for a farewell on that count, and Nina wondered how long it would take him to notice that she'd moved out when he came back. As he never made contact despite her having left a note with her new address and phone number on it, she never found out.

Her relationship with Paul had been an easy-going

one. Sometimes she'd wondered if he minded one way or the other whether she lived with him or not. He smoked a lot of pot, which made him very uncomplicated but not exactly stimulating company. In the beginning she partook too, but after a while she got bored with sitting around gazing contentedly at walls, and left him to smoke with his friends while she found herself something to read, or went out with her own friends instead. But she and Paul jogged along well, and most of the time they got on comfortably with the other people who they lived with, which was as well as they all had to share one big kitchen. Nina did her best to turn their bedsitting room, on the top floor, into a kind of home. She made curtains for it, and placed plants and dried flowers around to cheer it up. At Christmas she always put a tree up and draped it in decorations. Paul worked in a garage, which meant that he had the aroma of diesel clinging to him when he got home from work, but he was active in bed, which Nina liked. After a while, it started to seem as if their only real communication was in bed.

When she first took the job as a rep, Nina's life expanded. She met new, interesting people. Then, one day, when she was twenty-two and a half, she walked into a pharmacy in Reading to discuss sales with the manager of the shop, and for the first time in her life became the passionate object of someone's desires.

Graham was a qualified pharmacist, as well as the manager of the store. He was thirty-five, smart, and smelt of aftershave. Although not what one might call manly, Graham was attractive in his own way. He was slim, a little taller than her, with clear eyes behind steel-rimmed glasses. She liked his eyes. They were a cool blue, and he blinked a lot when he saw her. She'd been wearing a new skirt that day, one that hugged her hips and had a discreet split up one leg. Graham spent a lot of time looking at her legs while they were talking. Nina was flattered, and it sent a tickle of excitement up her spine. This man – this intelligent, educated, professional, mature man – obviously fancied her.

He asked her out to lunch to discuss business further. While she was bluffing like mad his eyes were all over her. She found herself slipping her jacket over the back of her chair to show her figure off better. She had a good figure, Paul's friends always said so, and the way Graham's blue eyes brightened suggested that he thought so too.

For two months Nina went out with Graham without telling Paul about it. Paul was usually either getting stoned at home, or getting stoned at someone else's house, so he didn't really notice that anything had changed. Then one night when she and Graham been out for a Chinese meal, Nina went home with him afterwards. He lived on a geometrically neat estate of new homes. His was a small, clean house, with a square of lawn for a back garden, and beech hedges rising up at the foot of the garden where the estate met a field. From his bathroom window (which Nina opened to get a look outside) she could see over the field, to the lights of the suburbs of Reading. A bat zipped over the garden and darted off into the night. She took a deep breath, and could smell cut grass. It was so different from the smell of engine oil on Paul's clothes. The garden consisted only of a sparse lawn, with no shrubs, no plants, no features, but this was a new house, and Graham was obviously a busy man. And he was a man, after all, and a chemist, and they weren't famous for being creative. Perhaps the place needed a woman's touch?

Downstairs, Graham offered her a brandy. The sitting room was small and square with a three-piece suite in dark blue which matched the lampshades and curtains. The carpet was cream and smooth. Graham put a Belinda Carlisle CD on. Nina could remember some of the songs from when she was a girl. She sank onto the sofa with a glass of brandy, knowing that she had now drunk too much to drive home, but no longer intending to drive home. Graham took off his jacket, readjusted his glasses, and sat next to her, putting an arm along the back of the sofa.

He talked for a long time, about music, his job, friends he'd met at university. She noticed he often said, 'you'd like her', or, 'I think they'd like you' and she felt warmed and flattered that he treated her like a mature woman. She listened, pretending to be polite, laughing a lot and sitting at an angle which she thought was seductive, wondering what Graham would be like in bed. He seemed very nervous. She wondered why when he was all of thirty-five, twelve years older than herself and a man of the world. Surely *she* should be the one who was nervous?

She was a little bit nervous. Not about making love with him. She was too experienced from her relationship with Paul to worry about the physical side of things. But nervous about what it might mean for the future. She'd already pictured a Christmas tree in the corner of the room, a smattering of warm, loud, laughing children rolling over the carpet. It needed some life, and some character. A big hairy dog perhaps, with floppy ears and appealing eyes, to put hairs on the white cushions on the sofa, or that very clean cream carpet. Nina was already trying to build a home.

Graham had reached out and stroked her soft frizzy hair with fingers that seemed very hot as they rested on her scalp.

'I get very lonely,' he said. 'All my friends are married, or in couples. I feel like an oddball.'

'No, no you're not at all!' She sat up straight and touched his knee. 'I don't think you're odd. I think you're lovely.'

They had kissed. A tender, hesitant kiss. Then Graham had stood up and put out his hands.

'Please come upstairs with me.'

So it wasn't like being clubbed over the head by a caveman and dragged off by the ankles to his cave, but it was gentle and pleasant, and Nina was led upstairs by Graham to his bedroom, which was also very clean and very neat. He closed the curtains, put on a bedside lamp, sat on the edge of the bed, and removed his clothes. Nina did the same, realising there was more than one way to make love. They lay on the bed together and Graham ran his hands over her body.

'You are so beautiful.'

'Take your glasses off,' she'd instructed him. 'I want to see you properly.'

He did, and she felt a thrill when she saw that his eyes were lovely without his glasses. Very blue, and very clear. And the way he blinked at her, as if he was deeply unsure of himself, touched a chord inside her. Whether it was love, or compassion, or an answering gentleness that was latent in herself, she wasn't sure. They lay for some time, while he felt her skin, her breasts, her thighs. She waited, wondering if he was going to leap on her, as

Paul usually did, but he didn't. So she gently moved over him instead, and they made love.

'Come and live with me,' Graham said, after he had recovered his breath, and Nina was lying over his chest.

'Yes, I will,' she said.

So, at nearly twenty-three, Nina had summoned up her courage and packed up her car ready to move in with Graham. She drove to his house. The lights were on, and he was waiting.

'I made you some dinner,' he said, as she came into the house. 'I wasn't sure if you'd have eaten. Shepherd's pie and peas. Is that okay?'

'Yes!' Nina said, dragging her holdall inside and bursting into tears. 'This is all so new. I hope I'll make you happy.'

Graham patted her shoulders a little awkwardly as she threw her arms around him. 'You'll be fine, Nina. You just need some guidance.'

Why they'd never got married, Nina wasn't entirely sure. She had met his friends, and they had all encouraged it. They were delighted to see that he had a girlfriend, and so clearly a serious one – after all, they were living together within two months. That had to be an intense love affair. But it wasn't intense. It was comfortable, and easy, and Graham was besotted with Nina, that much was clear to her. At least, he was besotted with her physically. And his life, his friends, his commitments, were so different from the world she'd known. Nobody ever seemed to get very drunk, or laugh much. They were serious, intelligent people, and very earnest. The wholesomeness that had been lacking in her life was here in abundance. It was refreshing, but it was also daunting.

'I hope you can do dinner parties,' one of his friends, Joanna, had said early on in their acquaintance. She was an attractive red-haired woman with a pert figure, married to Jonathon. They had all been university friends, Nina had discovered.

'But the house is so small. There isn't a dining room. Just a kitchenette and a living room downstairs.'

'No, *do* them, I mean,' Joanna had said, piling fresh mayonnaise on top of a delicious-looking potato, walnut and chives salad and stirring it around the bowl. They were at Joanna and Jonathon's house for a Sunday afternoon barbecue, and Nina was pretending to help Joanna in the kitchen. In reality, it meant watching her. 'Graham's an ambitious man, for a quiet little mouse. He needs an impressive wife to help him get on. What can you talk about?'

'I'm not his wife,' Nina had defended, very intimidated by the thirty-something Joanna, and the thirty-something friends who were strewn around the long, sunny garden in chairs, chatting amiably. She wasn't sure she was too keen on the knowledge that his friends thought of her boyfriend as a mouse, either. 'I'm his partner.'

'Same thing. You see we find your anecdotes about house-sharing and package holiday mishaps quite amusing, but head office won't.' Joanna whipped some marinated lamb from her fridge, and placed it on a plate. 'At these tedious social functions, the men in suits like nothing better than an entertaining woman who can talk about something,' she produced a carving knife and started slicing the lamb into chunks, 'other than sun-burn and ouzo, or housemates who don't wash up. It's too studenty.'

'Studenty? I've never been to university. How can it be studenty?'

'It's too young, then,' Joanna clipped back. 'Maybe if you had been to university, you'd know what I mean.'

'I read a lot,' Nina defended, her face reddening as she watched Joanna's deft fingers at work on the food. 'I could talk about a lot of things. I just didn't think anyone would be interested.'

'It's a start. Now be a love and take that out to Jonathon.'

On the way home, in the new car which Graham had bought, and which still smelt suffocatingly of plastic, Graham stopped Nina from opening the window.

'I'll put the air conditioning on,' he said.

'I just want to feel the fresh air on my face,' she protested.

'The air conditioning won't work if you open the window,' he said, and put it on. 'That potato and walnut salad Joanna made was lovely. Did she give you the recipe?'

'No,' Nina admitted.

'You might like to ask her for it when you send her a thank-you note. And ask her how she marinated the lamb too.' He rubbed his stomach through his shirt contentedly. 'Jonathon's a lucky man.'

'Yes,' Nina couldn't help agreeing, withdrawing her fingers from the button which controlled her window.

She felt so inadequate. So gauche, young and stupid. Of course she didn't know how to marinate lamb, or throw together a fantastic salad, or buy the right sort of wine for an afternoon barbecue as Joanna had apparently done without thinking about it. She didn't know how to say the right things to the men Graham

63

needed to impress to get on well in his job. She was only herself, with her anecdotes of the life she'd known, and the life she knew now. But, she realised, that wasn't going to be good enough. She would have to learn from Graham, learn from Joanna, and from all his friends. It was a challenge. But faced with a challenge, Nina wasn't one to be daunted.

On their first Valentine's Day together, Nina bought flowers and placed them all around the house while Graham was still at work. She bought a bottle of champagne, she marinated lamb in the way that Joanna had told her, and put together a potato and walnut salad. She'd bought Graham a Parker pen, a beautiful one with a golden nib that rolled over the page. She wrapped it up carefully in paper covered in silver stars, and stuck a big bow on the top. On the card she wrote 'Thank you, for everything'. She watched out of the living-room window to see his car pull into the drive next to hers. It was all a surprise. He would be pleased. He was Graham, a kind, sensitive, intelligent man. He'd realise she'd done all this to please him.

As he stilled his car engine she dashed to the kitchen, feverish in her desire to do everything perfectly, and put the lamb under the grill. She wanted to recreate the sumptuous smell that had wafted over Jonathon and Joanna's garden on that hot afternoon. That would bring back happy memories for Graham. He came into the hall and looked Nina up and down.

'Surprise!' she said, producing the chilled bottle of champagne from behind her back.

'That's nice,' Graham said, giving her a smile. 'But let's drink it when we get back. I'll have to drive, so I have to watch my intake.'

'We're going out?' Her spirits fell. But then they rose again. Was Graham more romantic at heart than he'd led her to believe? Yes, he could well be the sort of man who would whisk her off to a candlelit restaurant. He could afford it. The lamb wasn't important.

'I'm sure I told you ages ago? It's Joanna and Jonathon's anniversary. We're all having dinner together in town. In an hour, in fact, you'd better get ready quickly.'

As Nina was dashing around the bedroom trying to find something suitable to wear, she heard a shriek from downstairs. Her hair wet, her face half made-up, she flew from the bedroom and pounded down the stairs.

'What is it?'

'There's a bloody fire in the bloody kitchen,' Graham said, his face pink. 'I've put it out now, but God knows what damage it's done to the oven. How could you forget that you were cooking?'

'Oh my God! I'm so sorry!' Nina flapped pointlessly around the kitchen. She couldn't see any damage at all, but her lamb was in the washing-up bowl, being pounded by a stream of cold water from the tap.

'And those flowers in the living room have left orange pollen on the carpet. I've moved them. That's the sort of thing that will stain permanently, and devalue the house once I come to sell it.' Graham must have seen Nina's face fall. He added more sympathetically, 'They're pretty, but just not practical in a small house like this. Perhaps one day when I've got a bigger house, with carpets that don't matter . . .'

'It's all right, I understand.' She kissed him quickly to prevent any bad feeling. 'And it's your house after all. I should have asked.'

'Well, maybe. But it's a nice thought. Look, why don't you get ready, and let's be out of here in ten minutes? Okay? I don't want to let them down. They're my best friends.'

Much later, when they were in bed after their meal, Graham reached out and touched Nina to show his interest. He waited. As usual, she moved over him and kissed him into passion.

'You are a lovely girl,' he whispered to her. 'I'm sorry Joanna gave you a bad time tonight.'

'It's all right,' she whispered back. 'I didn't mind you telling her about the lamb. It was really stupid of me. It's no wonder she thinks I'm too young for you.'

'You're only as old as the woman you feel,' Graham quipped, stirring inside her, and they made love. 'We can take the champagne to Christopher and Jill's house-warming,' he said afterwards. 'They'll appreciate that.'

'I thought *we* could drink it. Just you and me,' Nina said, rolling away from Graham.

'Lovely girl, you mustn't try so hard,' he said, gazing at her thoughtfully. 'You do go over the top sometimes. Joanna's right on that count. Try to calm down a bit. That way, they'll all like you.'

'It's so hard to get it right,' Nina said to herself, as she gazed up at the ceiling.

Now, at twenty-six – a full four years since she'd met Graham and moved in with him – Nina had got it right. She knew how to marinate a lamb, how to throw together a potato, walnut and chives salad, and even how to make a good, fresh mayonnaise. She'd gone with Graham to the garden centre a few times, and had let him choose a selection of shrubs in big pots to brighten up the tiny garden. She'd never impulsively spread flowers all over the house again. In fact, she'd never bought anything for the house since that occasion without asking Graham's advice first. After all, it was *his* house. He never talked of 'when we sell the house,' only of 'when I sell the house'. He would never have realized that the emphasis was like a little, sharp dart hitting her skin.

But Nina had a comfortable, neat home and a live-in partner who neither drank himself into oblivion like her mother, or smoked himself into a coma like her ex-boyfriend. As long as she didn't impose her personality too forcefully on either the house or the partner, life was peaceful, and at times she really felt quite happy. They made love frequently enough for it to be what might be considered normal, and, sometimes, Nina was fulfilled by it. At other times, she wished Graham would just come home from work, fling off his glasses, throw her over his shoulder and take her out into the field beyond the garden and ravish her there, with the oak leaves rustling overhead and the twigs digging into her back. But Graham was not that sort of man. Graham liked to gently demonstrate his willingness to be passionate, then Nina would be passionate enough for both of them. He'd even told her once, in a rare moment of rashness after a couple of drinks, that she was a very exciting lover. The realisation that she pleased him had made her happy.

There wasn't going to be a chance to create the Christmas she'd never had in Graham's house, and that was a disappointment. But Nina buried it inside herself, inured to years of anticlimax. After the orange pollen on the carpet incident, she was fairly sure that Graham wouldn't take kindly to pine needles sprayed around his living room, which had turned out to be the case. When she'd suggested decorating the house for their first Christmas together, Graham had frowned.

'I don't see the point in messing the place up. We'll be spending Christmas at my parents anyway, and I've always found saggy tinsel and flashing lights to be very tacky. We could put a string above the gas fire and hang some of the more tasteful cards on it, if you'd like to do that?'

Christmas with Graham's parents was a must. Nina's mother and father knew where she was, but relations between them had not changed since she'd lived at home. She'd tried ringing them once or twice, just to see whether anything had progressed. But it was as if she'd never existed for them, except to cause them aggravation.

'No, we don't want a bloody duty visit,' her father had raged at her down the phone, prior to her first Christmas with Graham. 'You're living your own life now. You always were a loner. You just get on with it.'

So Christmases, in the time that Nina had been with Graham, consisted of visits to his quiet, precise, subdued parents, who seemed to approve of Nina in a non-committal kind of way. Meanwhile the home that she lived in remained untouched by the colours and moods of the changing seasons. The Christmas that had just passed had been no different. But now Christmas was behind them, it was late January, and Nina was driving home from work.

It was cold and overcast. Nina parked her car in the driveway, climbed out, and retrieved her briefcase and appointments book from the back. She'd stopped off in Reading on her way home from her round of meetings and had bought a couple of novels. She grabbed the thin plastic bag which contained them.

The sky was pewter grey, and it looked as if it might snow. That would make the field at the back look pretty. While she found her key in her handbag, she glanced at the small patch of grass that was the front garden. Graham said that he wanted it to be gravelled over, with a shrub placed on either side of the front door. Nina was diplomatically arguing the case with him. It seemed crass to churn up the living, thriving grass and earth, and suppress it with lumps of stone. She really wished Graham didn't want to do that. But he said it was practical, and that it would increase the value of the house. 'Low maintenance,' he said. She put down her bags on the doormat, and crept over to the edge of the front lawn, rubbing a few strands of grass between her fingertips. Her fingers smelt bitter afterwards.

With a deep sigh, she took herself indoors. The stench of carpet cleaner hit her immediately. Graham insisted on using a powdered carpet freshener every time the carpet was hoovered. He did as much hoovering himself as Nina did. In fact, she did as much as she thought was necessary, and he doubled up on her efforts, making this surely the cleanest home in Berkshire. But he was over-doing it a bit. The smell was stronger than when she'd left the house this morning for an early appointment in Bracknell. He must have hoovered again after she'd left.

Nina dumped her bags on the bottom stairs. When Graham came home he would complain about them blocking up the hallway, but he wasn't due until ten that evening, as he was on the late-night chemist roster. She went through to the sharp white surfaces of the kitchenette to make herself a cup of tea.

Four years was a long time to live in the same house as somebody. Now Graham was talking about putting the house on the market and moving 'up' to something detached. Nina was doing well in her job and earning good money. While Graham still paid the mortgage, she paid half the utility bills, and they cut food bills down the middle. But he hadn't talked about Nina putting her salary towards a mortgage in another, bigger house. Nina hadn't pressed the point, not really knowing what she felt about it. It would seem a very permanent step, and Graham was very careful about his steps. She was also so used to him saying, 'When I sell the house . . .' that it was hard to know at which point he was actively going to do something about it.

She kicked off her shoes, left them lying in the hall, and took her tea through to the living room. Tomorrow night they were due at Joanna and Jonathon's again. Some sort of do, for some sort of reason, Nina didn't want to think about it. Joanna had turned out not to be such a bitch as she'd first thought, and in a way Nina quite liked her. But she was so bloody smug, and a woman could only take so much smugness from another woman without undergoing a very powerful, if silent, revolt. If only Nina had her own friends to counter Graham's, but it hadn't really been possible to keep her old friends. They had all trundled off in such different directions, it would be too strange to contact them again. They'd all known her as the rebel she was, dropping out of school, getting drunk at the weekend, playing pool up at the Rising Sun, living in the bedsit with Paul. That was a past life. It couldn't be part of her present life. Nina had friends she'd made through work, but somehow they all linked back to Graham, and somehow they were all the same as Graham, Joanna, Jonathon, Christopher and Jill.

Nina pulled a face and slumped on the sofa. She put her stockinged feet up on the arm and closed her eyes. She lay there for half an hour, just breathing and thinking, her tea turning cold on the glass-topped coffee table which was placed with, mathematical precision, parallel to the sofa.

What she needed was a video to transport herself away from starter homes, cream carpets and the smell of Shake 'n' Vac. She had time to watch a film before Graham came home. She put *Dances with Wolves* into the machine. When she had these strange moments of suffocation, she found that *Dances with Wolves* provided the most effective therapy. It was like a craving, when the body was telling you that you needed a certain kind of nourishment. She would watch Kevin Costner roughing it in his shack, alone with the wilderness and his wolf, and feel as if she'd taken a handful of vitamins with a glass of milk.

She put it on, curled up on the sofa, and watched.

Much later, as Wind In His Hair was rendering his dramatic parting cry over a mountain ridge, the front door flew open, and Graham burst into the living room and stood before Nina looking very intense. She pulled herself up in astonishment.

'I'll move my bags. I just wanted to unwind, I had such an early start this morning.'

'I didn't notice your bags,' he said, and put down his briefcase. 'I've had amazing news. Wonderful, amazing news. I'm so happy.'

'God, what is it?' Nina was puzzled by Graham's expression. It certainly looked like joy. 'A promotion? They're moving you to Head Office?'

'Joanna's pregnant,' Graham announced, his voice breaking with emotion. 'That's why we're all invited over tomorrow for a big do. They were going to announce it then, but Jonathon was so excited he rang me at work this evening to tell me first. I mean, he told me first, after their parents. I'm so happy, and honoured, and flattered. And it's so perfect for them. Joanna will be the most wonderful mother.'

'Oh!' Nina stood up, not quite knowing what to do. 'That's lovely. I know it's what they've wanted for some time.'

'No, it's not at all planned, it's a total surprise.' Graham frowned at Nina. She bit her lip. Graham was very proud of his closeness to his friends. It would probably be a really bad time to tell him that Joanna had confessed to her, over the washing-up about a year ago, that they were trying for a baby but nothing was happening.

'I'm sure it's a big surprise, even if they half wanted it,' Nina said. 'Well, let's break open a bottle or something.'

'Nina.' Graham clasped her to him, and planted a big kiss on her lips. 'It's made me think about everything. The continuity of my name, your happiness, the thought of a life out there, becoming a little Joanna and Jonathon. It's very profound.'

'Yes,' Nina said uncertainly. A little Joanna and Jonathon. A child that would be trained at an early age in the arts of salad-making, lamb-marinating, and dinner party conversation. No such child could ever possibly feel as awkward, stupid and naïve as Nina had been made to feel. That child was more likely to have mastered such arts by the age of two.

'I'm thirty-nine, Nina,' Graham said earnestly. 'It's what my parents want. I'm about to buy a bigger house. There'd be room.'

'Room?'

'Room for . . .' Graham paused, his eyes twinkling. In the background, Nina could hear the closing music to *Dances with Wolves*. She'd wanted to see Wind In His Hair galloping away, and Kevin Costner trekking off into the snowy wastes, the future an adventure to him. But Graham was holding her upper arms. 'There'd be room for a baby, Nina. That's what I'm saying.'

It was funny, because four years ago Nina had sat on that very sofa, in that very living room, which hadn't changed since she'd lived there, and formed a mental picture of children crawling around and messing it up. It had seemed a happy thought. But perhaps then she'd thought she would have more of a voice in the way things were done in Graham's house. Now, hearing him say the word 'baby', her reaction surprised her. She felt alarmed.

'Graham, I'm only twenty-six.'

'Don't you see how good it could be? If we have a baby now, it would be almost the same age as Joanna's baby, and they'd be friends as children. We'd have even more in common with them than we do already.'

'This is a bit sudden.' Nina pulled herself away and looked at Graham kindly. 'You've sort of sprung it on me.'

'Nina,' Graham said, putting his hands on her shoulders. 'You're young, you're healthy, I can't see any reasons for complications. And you're beautiful too. I think it would be perfect.'

'Hang on,' she half-laughed. 'You sound like a farmer sizing up a heifer for good breeding stock.'

'I'm completely serious,' Graham said, his blue eyes shining from behind his glasses. 'Nina, shall we have a baby?'

Chapter Five

The astronomy club meeting was going to be a quiet one. It was a chill evening, the wind nipping icily, and on such evenings, enthusiasts as the club members generally were, the gatherings tended to be a little thin.

They met at the All Saints' Methodist Hall, in a back street of the town. It was close enough to bus stops and the railway station for the one or two members who didn't have cars to get there, and there was parking space around the back for those that did. They rented the hall for fortnightly meetings and it was ideal in many ways. It was big enough, had plenty of chairs for fuller gatherings, had a small platform that they could put visiting speakers on, and room to set up the club projector. It also had central heating, but on winter evenings by the time it kicked in it was time to leave. So, on nights like tonight, members turned up muffled in scarves, hats and thick coats, and kept them on until it was time to go home.

Caroline had joined various astronomy clubs in the past, when she'd had time and could find one close enough. Compared to others, this was an unusually small group, with a tendency to be disorganised. Caroline had found it as soon as she'd got her feet under the table in her new job. She knew there were bigger clubs in neighbouring towns, and some really quite professionally run much further afield, but somehow she'd become fond of this local group, odd as it was at times. On her first evening the members had been curious about her, possibly because at that time she was the only woman present. The way some of them had looked at her, she'd wondered if they'd ever seen a woman before. But by the end of the evening they'd been so impressed with her enthusiasm and background knowledge, they'd asked her to be the club secretary.

Since then she'd worked on setting them up with a web page, encouraged them to think more clearly about the aims of the group, and tried to suggest events that would bring new members in. She was sure that the club could do more than just provide a venue for discussing their own thoughts. It could help to promote more public interest in astronomy locally. She was getting resistance from some of the more established members, who wanted it to stay cosy and small, but she soldiered on.

Tonight she parked her car around the back, trotted over the gravel with her scarf up to her nose and opened up. There was a small, musty-smelling entrance hall where she felt her way to the lights and switched them on. In the kitchenette off to the side she found the heating controls and turned the heating on. The radiators in the hall clunked loudly but wouldn't do much else other than make tantalising noises for a couple of hours. Still, their rent covered a nominal heating charge so Caroline was determined to use it.

She was the first, arriving as always a quarter of an hour before the others to open up. The chairs were stacked against the walls from a previous event, so she set about dragging them out into a row at the front, her fingers still enveloped in her thick gloves, her nose not venturing from the cocoon of her woolly scarf.

The front door swung and banged shut as somebody came in. She continued to arrange the chairs, deciding optimistically to add another row. She called out towards the entrance hall.

'Put the kettle on!'

Ten chairs in each row? That was ludicrously optimistic. Caroline put her hands on her hips, assessed the chairs, and straightened them. Then she dragged a table across the wooden floor so that it sat at the front facing the rows and down the hall, and put three chairs behind it. One for herself, Dylan, the chairman of the club, and Roderick, whom they called president of the club. Roderick had been the president of the club since he'd founded it in 1971. He was now eighty-nine, and turned up to every meeting despite not being able to hear the contributions clearly or add to them much. He seemed to enjoy himself immensely, but as an active committee member was as much use as a chocolate teapot. Hence Caroline had suggested delicately when she'd become club secretary that Dylan, a member for ten years, an avid observer, and an articulate man, might take the role of chairman, leaving Roderick with his stately title intact.

There was a fair amount of shuffling in the kitchen. Caroline frowned, images of Roderick wrestling with the Calor gas stove in response to her barked order alarming her. She sped up the hall towards the kitchen.

'Roderick? I can make coffee. Don't you worry.' She stuck her head around the kitchen door. A strange man had his back to her and was bending over the sink. Her nerves fluttered. She never usually thought about strangers walking in during the few moments while she waited for the others to arrive, because they never did. The reality was a little unnerving. He turned round.

'Oh, hello,' he said.

She blinked at him. It was the same man with the green eyes and ruffled reddish-blond hair whom she'd seen in Mr Hartley's newsagents. He was in solid climbing boots and jeans with a thick black overcoat over the top.

'Hello,' she said.

'Are there any matches?'

'What are you doing?'

'You told me to put the kettle on.'

'I wasn't . . . I didn't really mean it,' she blustered.

'You meant it figuratively?' He raised an eyebrow. 'Was it a metaphor?'

'I mean, I thought you were someone else.' She might have smiled at the absurdity of her own comment, but she was still trying to reconcile the image of this man in the newsagents, and from wherever she might have seen him before, with his presence at her astronomy club. It was a small town, but it wasn't *that* small. For a start, most people commuted. They left home before the sun came up and got back after it had gone down. Then they had a whisky and fell asleep before the cycle started again. They weren't people she saw around much, either in the town or at her club. Even in a small town, familiarity on someone else's terms was jarring.

'What are you doing here?' It came out a little bluntly, a result of her jolted nerves.

He scratched his ear. 'There was something on your web page about meetings.'

'My web page?'

'The astronomy club's page. I was searching for, well, various things on the Internet, and up popped a link, to clubs. And this one was there.'

'Oh.' Caroline continued to stare at him. It wasn't that she meant to be rude. It was just odd that he'd turned up again, and this time at her astronomy club. It needed explaining, then she'd be nice to him.

'It said that beginners were welcome,' he said, looking very unsure of that fact.

'Oh, you're a beginner? Well, I see now. Yes, of course beginners are welcome. I'm very keen to have beginners along. We've all got to start somewhere. I'm hoping to have some beginners' evenings arranged before too long, where we can go through some basic things, and get people started.'

'Shall I put this on then?' He indicated the full kettle.

'Yes, do. Matches are in the top drawer.' Caroline watched as he lit the stove, turned it down to a safe heat, and placed the kettle there. He extinguished the match between his finger and thumb, and put it on the draining board.

'But, er,' she continued, 'I'm not sure if you'll find tonight's meeting much help to you. For the beginners' meetings I'm hoping to hand around some planispheres to demonstrate how they work, and do overheads and handouts. Charts of basic constellations. How to find your way around the night sky, that sort of introduction. I think you'll find tonight's discussion a bit involved. One of our members wants to talk about binary systems; Dylan – he's our chairman – has been taking some photographs of moon craters that he's going to show round, and I was going to discuss speakers for future events. That's if we get time for all that, with general feedback too. Otherwise the overall topic's really about the winter sky, and what to look out for at this time of year.' Caroline started to feel a little mean. She was supposed to be encouraging beginners, not putting them off. It was just that she hadn't expected this enigmatic man to be her very first beginner. She wasn't quite sure what to do with him. She should have practised on someone else first. 'You might find something to relate to in the winter sky discussions,' she finished, a little more warmly.

'Oh, I'm not here for the detail,' he said, as if he was enjoying a private thought. 'It's more the abstract. I'm curious, so here I am.'

She hadn't managed to put him off. Caroline wasn't sure if she was relieved or disconcerted by that thought. There was a laconic air about him. It was a slight drawl in the way he spoke, a way of lingering over his words, as he seemed to linger over his thoughts. She wasn't sure what it was about his manner that was so striking. It was as if he wasn't in a hurry. Perhaps it hit her because she always was.

'I'm – I'm Caroline,' she said. 'I'm sorry, I should have introduced myself. I'm the club secretary.'

He put out his hand. 'I'm Tom,' he said. She shook his hand. He flexed his fingers after they'd shaken hands, as if they were very stiff, and put his hand into his coat pocket. 'Interesting,' he said.

A brief silence followed. 'Interesting?' Caroline said, as he didn't explain the remark.

'It's nothing. Just that . . . Well, I've seen you before. In a couple of places.'

'Yes, I've seen you too.'

80

He nodded, and they looked at each other for a second or two. Caroline's eyes fell first.

'Nice town,' he said absently. 'Small. Quiet.'

'It's – it's all right. Bit close to Biggin Hill,' she said.

'Why's that a problem?'

'The VOR beacon. It means the planes circle overhead here.' As he looked unenlightened she added, 'It affects viewing. The lights. On the planes. That circle overhead. On their way to Biggin Hill.'

'Ah yes, I see.'

'And Gatwick.'

'Ah yes, Gatwick too.'

They both stood for a while, waiting for the kettle to boil.

'So, have you been doing this long?' Tom asked.

Caroline willed someone else to arrive. She'd already organised the chairs, and she didn't feel she could leave Tom to make coffee all by himself in the kitchen. But it was very small in there. Cold as the tiny kitchenette was, she was starting to feel warm inside her layers of clothes. She suspected he was playing with her.

'Er, yes, all my life. What did you mean by abstract?' she said.

'Abstract?'

'You just said you were here for the abstract. What did you mean?'

'Oh.' He smiled. 'Yes, I did say that.'

The door banged, and Caroline heard Dylan's voice. 'Hello the hall. You here, Caro?'

'That's Dylan,' Caroline explained, and made her exit quickly. She met Dylan with a bright smile. He looked surprised. Well, perhaps she was usually too pre-occupied at the beginning of a meeting to smile at

81

everyone, but she was pleased to see him. She had started to wonder what she might do if nobody else turned up. Apart from Roderick. He always turned up. She couldn't quite imagine herself, deaf Roderick, and blond Tom with his strange comments, holding a very comfortable meeting between themselves.

Dylan was a tall, portly man, in his late forties. He was genial, with a very pleasant wife whom Caroline had met, and four boisterous children. He commuted up to London and held down a job that he hated. Something to do with insurance, Caroline had never probed into it much. He was one of the members who had been keen to elect her as secretary of the club from day one, and he was usually in tune with her thoughts. Tonight he was wearing a large furry hat with ear-protectors.

'Are you going on an Arctic expedition?' Caroline asked him.

'Bloody earache.' He pulled a face, and removed his hat. 'It's been getting worse. I hate this time of year. The nights are so miserably cold for observing.'

'We're making coffee,' Caroline said, realising the 'we' was euphemistic, seeing as she'd left Tom in the kitchen. 'And we've got a beginner,' she whispered to Dylan.

'A real beginner?' Dylan raised his bushy eyebrows. 'That's great.' He made his way down the hall towards the table where he usually sat, and looked around vaguely. 'Where's the beginner?'

The kettle whistled sharply from the kitchen. 'Making coffee,' Caroline admitted.

'You sent the beginner into the kitchen to make the coffee?'

'But now that you're here, I'll send him out to you and make the coffee myself.'

82

Caroline retrieved Tom from the kitchen. He'd found the mugs in the top cupboard, had put eight out on the draining board, and set the coffee, sugar and Coffee-mate beside them. 'I didn't know if you'd brought fresh milk along,' he said. 'The stuff in the fridge is off.'

'Go and talk to Dylan,' she instructed, ushering him out of the door towards the hall. 'He'll tell you about the club.'

As nobody else arrived in the next ten minutes, Caroline took the coffee out to Tom and Dylan. She perched on the edge of the table and listened to their conversation, finding it hard to work out exactly what they'd been discussing. They seemed to have gone off at a wild tangent. Caroline pretended to be fascinated by a lump of Coffee-mate in her drink.

'I'm curious about your fish analogy,' Dylan was saying. 'It's an interesting way of looking at it.'

'Fish?' Caroline questioned.

'If you consider fish in a pond,' Tom said, cradling his mug in his hand and looking directly at Caroline. 'All they know is that pond. The shimmering surface of it is the limit of their universe. A fish could never know that there is a whole world beyond the pond.'

'And?'

'Imagine if you could speak to a fish. You tell that fish about a world of air, and wind and mountains. Of eagles and forests, deserts and pyramids, arid steppes, verdant fields full of animals grazing in the sun. Of giraffes, anteaters, humans. Of skyscrapers and underground train systems.'

She pursed her lips, determined not to be moved by the fertile imagery he so easily produced for her. 'And?'

'And beyond the mountains, wind and eagles was a

huge universe full of other worlds of fiery liquids and amorphous gases, and moons and stars. And that was only just what we could see.'

'Your point is?'

'The fish would say, "What have you been smoking?"'

She managed to straighten her face and suppress a laugh, and decided to stand up rather than lean on the table. It made her feel taller. There was something about the way Tom's clear eyes were holding hers that seemed to indicate a challenge. 'And?' she said.

Tom shrugged pleasantly enough. 'We've got no reason to assume that we are any different from the fish. If somebody came to us with a story of something we couldn't relate to, we'd assume they were insane too. The assumptions we make can only be based on what we know. Our experience is limited to similes, analogies, comparisons. Figurative speech, if you like.' He offered a slight smile.

'Like a metaphor?'

'That kind of thing.'

'Penetrating,' she said drily.

'But you can only compare like with like,' Tom went on. 'I'm not convinced that there's any such thing as fact. There's only empirical evidence. By which I mean, evidence based on an individual's experiences, or past impressions. It has to be subjective.'

'I know what empirical evidence is,' Caroline informed him.

'I thought you would.'

'There is nothing that can't be expressed in the language of science,' she said. 'Even metaphors and similes can be scientific.'

84

'I take it you don't read poetry then.' Another smile appeared briefly.

'We're an astronomy club,' Caroline said, hoping her tone might take the wind out of his sails a little. Dylan was rubbing his chin thoughtfully and looking temporarily lost for words. 'We examine what's in the sky.'

'What you can see.'

'And what we can deduce, based on what we know at any given time. Science moves on all the time, it's evolving. You can't accuse it of not being flexible.'

'But it is arrogant,' Tom said gently. 'It claims to be the only avenue of exploration left to the sane individual. That doesn't make it any closer to discovering the truth.'

'Truth?' Caroline suddenly had a gruesome thought. Tom was one of these evangelical born-again Christians who was on a mission to ridicule any scientific progress. 'You're not from the Flat Earth Society by any chance?'

Tom laughed, and pushed a hand through his hair. She noticed his red knuckles again. Perhaps he'd worn them out by knocking on innocent people's doors and instructing them that science was rubbish. 'No, I'm not from the Flat Earth Society.'

The front door slammed, and Dylan, who'd been watching the exchange between Caroline and Tom wordlessly, seemed relieved. He moved up the hall.

'Roderick. See anyone else as you came in? Anyone in the car park?' Roderick always walked to the hall from his house, which was only ten minutes away. He lived on the exclusive, quiet lane edged with evergreens at the top of the hill that Caroline sometimes jogged down during her Sunday run. The houses were old, craggy and gorgeous there, and the spot commanded magnificent views of the Weald of Kent. Roderick was a life-long bachelor. He seemed very proud of that fact, having proclaimed to them all many times that his life was just what he would make it if he could start it all over again. Caroline was secretly impressed by his genuine contentment. He insisted on walking to the club, whatever the weather, as he loved the night air. Otherwise Caroline would certainly have offered him a lift. Each time she did, he dismissed her suggestion roughly.

'Eh?' Roderick, a long black scarf wound partly around his neck, the rest around his arm and tailing away to the ground, made his way slowly up the hall, his expression brightening as soon as he spotted Caroline. 'Caroline, my dear!'

'Hello there, Roderick,' Caroline greeted him. 'I hope there are more coming. I know it's freezing out there, I'm not very optimistic.'

'Snow forecast,' Dylan said, helping Roderick reorganise his scarf before he stood on one end and choked himself. 'And some of these guys come in from the villages. I wouldn't be surprised if they've been put off by the weather.'

'Carl,' Roderick said, pointing a shaky finger at a wall, indicating the direction of the car park. 'And William.'

'Ah, that's good. Anyone else? I hope so.' Caroline slipped away from Tom to fiddle with the chairs again.

Why she was experiencing such a prickly reaction to Tom, she really wasn't sure. The shock of being on her own in the lonely old hall with a complete stranger could in itself account for a prickly reaction. She'd been very surprised to see him again, as she *had* noticed him in the newsagents, and in honesty taken quite a good look. She might have stared at him then, but that was only out of curiosity. So it had given Caroline a pang of unease to find him at her astronomy club meeting, almost as if he'd sensed her curiosity and acted on it by turning up to allow her to assess him at closer quarters. But she knew that was utterly impossible. He couldn't have known who she was, and certainly not that she'd be at the astronomy club.

But there was something else that was getting under her skin. It was as if he was toying with her, and perhaps even with the club. People didn't normally turn up and launch into philosophical reasoning before they'd even got through their first cup of coffee. It wasn't what Caroline had been expecting. Tom was obviously intelligent, articulate, and frankly not like other people. But what was his angle, and why was he there at all? And did it actually matter? Why on earth was it bothering her so much?

Carl and William walked in together a few minutes later. Carl was in his late twenties, with fine, shoulder-length fair hair and a red face, a leather jacket, and faded jeans. He strode in with his motorbike helmet over his arm. William had obviously arrived in his car. He looked pristine, still in a suit as if he hadn't changed since work, probably close to fifty, with swept-back hair, a cleft chin and round glasses. A second later Patrick arrived in a mac, rubbing a dusting of snow from his bald pate.

'Snowing,' he said, taking a coffee from the tray on the table where Caroline had set a few mugs out. 'Only light, very wet, and not settling.'

'So much for winter sky observations then.' Carl winked at Caroline. 'You're a cherub. Here, come rain, sun, wind or snow.'

87

'I never did cherubic very well,' Caroline answered. 'It's nearly half past eight. Should we wait for anyone else?'

Lesley arrived. A pretty but skinny, pale woman in her mid-twenties with a nervous manner, more a bean string than a beanpole. Caroline had been delighted a few months ago when Lesley had turned up for the first time. She was an assistant librarian in the local library with a good background knowledge that had only gradually emerged. She never contributed much, but Caroline, ever keen for a woman to show an interest in her subject, was pleased to see her.

'Sorry I'm late,' Lesley whispered.

'Lesley! You brave thing. Grab a coffee.'

'Meetings are usually fuller than this,' Dylan advised Tom jovially. 'You've caught us on a quiet night.'

'Who's this?' Roderick demanded, shuffling towards Tom and pointing his finger. He squinted at Tom closely. Caroline kept her mouth shut.

'This is Tom,' Dylan told Roderick. 'Tom, this is Roderick, our president.'

'I'd curtsey, but I've got a dodgy knee,' Tom said. 'I'm very pleased to meet you.'

'Hmmn? You from the *Courier*?' Roderick turned to Dylan and said in a loud whisper that everybody could hear, 'He looks like a journalist. I've met a few in my time. Better look sharp. Need a good press.'

'Shall we get on then?' Caroline decided to take control. As she, Dylan and Roderick settled in their chairs behind the table, and the others gathered in the front row, she pondered on whether Tom might actually be a journalist. Well, if he was, so what? There wasn't much of a scoop to be had at the local astronomy club.

She could see the headline now. 'Local club claims to have found truth, but dismisses fish analogy.' How the town would riot against that one. There'd be tear gas in Waitrose. She waited for Dylan to open the meeting.

'Welcome again, all, and a particularly warm welcome to Tom here, who's turned up to have a look at us. As you all know, Caroline and I are very keen to encourage beginners to attend, so Tom, you are most welcome, and I hope you enjoy the evening. Caroline's going to run through the minutes of the last meeting, and after that we'll try to get through as much as we can tonight . . .'

Caroline glanced at her watch again as it was nearing ten o'clock. Dylan had handed around his moon crater photographs, to much praise; Carl had led a lively debate about binary systems which had somehow veered off towards a general free-for-all on the latest Hubble space telescope photographs, and all the time she'd been darting her eyes towards Tom. She'd wondered if he'd leave, or fall asleep, or leap up and say something startling. So far, he hadn't done any of those things. There was a slight lull in conversation. They'd all had another coffee, between craters and binary systems, and Caroline felt wide awake still, but she was aware others had further to travel home than she had.

'Caroline?' Dylan turned to her, pulling his coat around his body as the radiators were still clunking teasingly but refusing to deliver any heat. 'Do you want to finish up?'

'Does anyone want to check the state of the snow?' she asked, looking at Carl. 'You're only on two wheels. If you want to leave now, you should.'

89

'Hey, I'm cool.' Carl laid a relaxed arm over the back of the empty chair next to him. 'I've been biking all my life. I know how to ride the snow.'

'I'll have a quick look.' William went outside to check, and came back with a report. 'Still snowing, still wet, not settling, but cloud cover is total.'

'Bollocks,' Carl said.

'But they said it'd clear up soon,' Lesley said quietly, going red. 'It should be a better sky for observing by next week.'

'Okay, well I'll keep this brief.' Caroline concentrated on her notes. 'I've updated the web site. Have another look at it, and you'll see members' observations is a new page on there. If anyone's got any photographs they want me to add, bring them along or get them to me as attachments. I'm going to set up an observing evening at a rural site where we can go as a group. I'll have more on that next time. And I have a list of suggested speakers. I've done printouts so that you can go away and think about it. I've also done some pointers for winter sky observation as we talked about earlier, if we get the chance in this weather. I'll hand them around.'

'What about the slides you promised?' Carl asked. 'You keep saying you're going to give us a blow-by-blow description of how you set up your observatory shed complete with piccies. I mean, we all want to hear your story properly. You did say you'd do a presentation on it.'

'I did tell you about my shed, in the pub last time but one. And I showed you all my shed not long ago.'

'But you still haven't given us a proper talk on it.'

'Good point.' Dylan raised bushy eyebrows enthusiastically. 'We're all keen to hear your account of what you did, Caroline.'

'All right, I'll schedule it in to a meeting.' Caroline blushed slightly with the attention, and passed her printed sheets to Tom, who was at the end of the row. He took one for himself, and obligingly handed them on to the others.

'Most of this you know already, although some of you might not be so clued up,' Caroline said, putting on her impassive teaching air to include Tom. 'Just to remind you there's a meteor shower forecast for the early spring and we just might get a clear view of it from the Northern Hemisphere. We'll talk more about that next time. Meanwhile, don't forget that at this time of year and especially this month Mars is visible in the morning if you're an early riser, and Venus is a beauty in the evening sky.' She couldn't help letting out a deep sigh. 'If only we had the chance to appreciate it more. God, I hate winter.'

'Hear, hear,' Carl groaned, leafing through the handouts. 'Can we have all of these speakers please?'

'Budget, Carl, some of them might want fees. I'll have to check. And we're small. We can't exactly fly anyone in from SETI on a promise of ten eager members. Or five even, based on tonight.'

'SETI?' Tom spoke for the first time in an hour and a half. The others turned to look at him. 'You're talking about Berkeley's SETI project? The Search for Extra-terrestrial Intelligence?'

Caroline felt ruffled, which was silly. It was she herself who a while ago had bullied everybody at the club to download the SETI screensaver for their computers. She eyed Tom, trying to make him out. Was he about to crack a funny about little green men? 'Yes,' she said.

'Okay, that's great.' Tom pulled himself up in his chair. 'Are you taking questions now?'

'Well,' Dylan interjected hesitantly, 'given the time and the snow, it may be time to think about home, or pub.'

'Pub!' Carl inserted, waving a hand in the air as his vote while assessing his handouts.

'What? Is it over now?' Roderick called to Dylan, handing back one of the enlarged black and white photographs of the moon surface.

Dylan looked at Caroline. 'Did you have anything else on the agenda? We could always take questions in the pub.' He sounded hopeful.

'Well, the only other thing was to think about the summer star party,' Caroline said. 'But as we're so depleted this week, we could discuss it when there are more of us here.'

'Yeah, star party,' Carl waved his hand again. 'I'm up for that.'

'What's a star party?' Tom asked, looking at Caroline. She bit her lip.

'Carl? Would you like to enlighten Tom?'

Carl grinned. 'Star parties are the best. You go and sit on a great big hill somewhere, and you take all your stuff with you. Telescope if you've got one, binos, charts, torches, coolboxes full of grog. It's an all-nighter, summer thing. Very sociable. It's usually a great big gang, regional event. You get to meet other clubs that way too. And you just lie back, and think of the universe. Very cosmic. I love 'em. Best night of the year.'

'That sounds interesting,' Tom said down the row of chairs to Carl. 'Really does.'

'Yeah well, I could tell you more about it in the pub. Can we go there now, Caroline?'

Caroline felt prudish. She didn't particularly want to be faced with Tom in a pub. She wasn't really sure how to handle him. His comments had been odd when he'd first arrived. 'I'm not here for the detail, it's more the abstract.' Who on earth, who was the slightest bit interested in astronomy, couldn't be interested in detail? It was all about detail. Tom was sweeping detail under the carpet in preference for unanswerable questions.

'Tom, did you have a question you wanted to ask now?'

'Pub, man,' Carl said in a hushed voice, putting on his leather gloves and picking his crash helmet up from the floor.

'Well that would depend,' Tom said. He again addressed Caroline, as if she were the only person there. 'Will you be at the pub? I'd like to hear your thoughts.'

'On what?' Caroline put her papers back into her folder.

'On where it all began. I read a theory about black holes. It suggested a different way of looking at nothingness. I mean, to accept a Big Bang, one has to accept that before it there was nothing. I wondered what your definition of nothing was.' Tom caught Caroline's eye as she tried to look busy. 'All right, I understand, it's late. It's too big a question to ask this time of night. Forgive me.'

'What does he want?' Roderick called to Dylan, who was all of one foot away from him. 'A photograph for the article?'

'No,' Dylan called back. 'He wants to know about the Big Bang.'

Roderick squinted at Dylan. 'What? At a quarter past ten?'

'Apparently so,' Dylan replied loudly, giving Tom a friendly smile.

'You can't do that!' Roderick declared, trying to stand up. 'Not at a quarter past ten. There's not enough time. It's insane. Where is he?' Dylan waved a hand in Tom's direction, and Roderick leaned over the table to focus. 'It's an engrossing topic, don't get me wrong. But you can't do that at a quarter past ten. We could be here all night.'

'It's all right,' Tom said, tucking his handouts into his coat pockets without any apparent offence. 'I realise that. Apologies.'

'It's why we're all here, man,' Carl said. 'I mean, don't apologise. Come and have a beer. We all go to the pub by ten usually. We're not the nerdy no-fun bunch you've probably imagined. Astronomy's a peach. You meet people, stimulate your brain, ponder a universe beyond Ikea and *Brookside*, and, would you believe it, we like to get pissed too, just like everybody else.' Carl laughed as he stood up, all six foot four of him, and swung his crash helmet, gazing ironically along the row of seats at Tom. 'What did you expect? Norman Nomates? If you did, you're going to be educated.'

'Who's Norman?' Roderick quizzed Dylan. 'Is he coming to take the photographs?'

Caroline rubbed her forehead. The icicles had just about defrosted on the chairs, but she was suddenly feeling warm again. 'Tom,' she said, without looking up, 'are you a reporter? It might be as well to say so, if you are.'

'No, I'm not a reporter.' Tom put his hands out in appeal. 'Honestly, I'm not.'

'Right,' she said decisively. 'In which case, as there's not really enough time to come to a conclusion on the meaning of life before we get enveloped by snow, and as Carl's itching to go down the pub, and as Carl's probably voicing what everyone's secretly thinking, let's close it down now. Anyone who wants to talk further, reconvene in the Chequers, up in the High Street. Thank you very much for turning up tonight in the foul weather, thanks to all of you for photographs and contributions, and,' she added sweetly, 'I'm so pleased that we had Tom here tonight. Perhaps you'll join us another time, Tom?'

Tom nodded. 'You can count on it.'

Caroline kept a straight face. 'Dylan? Any final thoughts?'

'Pub,' Dylan said. 'As soon as we've locked up. See you all there.'

'Is that it then?' Roderick stood up, regarding his watch. 'When are the photographers coming?'

Most of the others scrambled for the door and headed for the pub. Caroline was relieved to see that Carl was with Tom, and was chatting to him animatedly as they moved out of the hall, and although Tom glanced back once over his shoulder, he was led out of the door by Carl. 'There won't be any photographers tonight. No photographers. No reporters,' she told Roderick.

'I agree. Keep the bastards at a distance.' Roderick arranged his folder under his arm.

'Come on Roderick.' Caroline tucked the end of his scarf into his coat. 'I'll stroll home with you.'

'Home?' Roderick stared at her. 'Walk me home? I'm

not a child, Caroline. Thank you very much, but I'll walk home on my own, and I'll enjoy it immensely, as I always do.'

'He may not enjoy it that much in thick snow,' Dylan muttered, collecting the last coffee mugs from the table and taking them back to the kitchen to wash them up.

'Are you sure?' Caroline asked Roderick, wanting to offer help, but not wanting to offend him.

'Sure? My dear, much as I respect you, which without doubt I do, I am not in the habit of repeating myself. I am a lone creature. No marriage, no children, no family. I'm very content with the way things have worked out for me.'

'No family at all?' Caroline couldn't imagine such a thing.

'They're all ill-tempered peasants and I'm glad to be rid of them. My life is delightful and I wouldn't have it any other way. When I die I shall leave all I have to the pursuit of knowledge, which is a very worthy cause. Now please remove your foot from the end of my scarf, then I shall be able to move.'

'If you're sure.'

'I am.'

'All right then.' Caroline stepped off Roderick's scarf, and he wafted away. Once the door had banged shut behind him, she was alone with Dylan in the hall. He seemed to have done all the clearing up. They were both still in their coats. She touched a radiator to see if it had come on as she walked down the hall. 'Oh, hang on, I feel warmth.'

'It'll be warmer in the Chequers. Are you coming?' Dylan said.

'I'm not sure. I've got a busy day tomorrow.'

'You're not put off by Tom, are you?' Dylan regarded her kindly. She almost thought of him as a benevolent uncle sometimes, and he was looking at her in that way now. 'He's an intelligent man, with interesting questions. You seem to have taken against him, though.'

Caroline laughed as she wrapped her scarf around her neck, ready to face the cold outside. 'Of course I'm not put off by him. And I haven't taken against him, Dylan.'

'Well, he mentioned SETI in a quite knowledgeable way, and he wanted to talk about the origin of things. I thought those were two of your favourite subjects.'

Caroline and Dylan reached the small entrance hall together. He checked the kitchen and turned the heating off. She put her fingers over the panel of light switches as he opened the front door.

'Normally, they are,' she said.

'Just not sure of where he was coming from?'

'Or where he was going to,' she said. 'All done?'

Dylan paused on the doorstep. Beyond the open door, Caroline could see wet snow drooping towards the ground in soggy flakes, and disappearing once it touched. 'No pub for you tonight, then?' Dylan asked again.

'No pub for me tonight,' Caroline confirmed, and turned off the lights, leaving the hall in darkness.

Chapter Six

'What in God's name is she doing?' Antonia murmured under her breath. Standing in the staffroom next to the window, nursing her mug of coffee, she peered out over the empty tennis courts towards the hockey pitches on the dome of the vast playing field. The recent snow hadn't settled, but the air remained chill, the clouds threatening, and it looked as if it would snow again. Out in the abandoned wintry scene a host of little stick figures in their full winter uniforms were leaping about like Lowry characters, clutching fruit. Leading this bizarre spectacle, yelling instructions through a loudhailer, was Caroline.

'It's her solar system thing.' Greg stopped and grinned at the sight. 'Amazing, isn't she? Must fly, got to set up an experiment for the next lot.'

Antonia looked round, irritated, as Greg disappeared from the staffroom. Why did lobbing fruit around on a frozen hockey pitch in the middle of winter qualify as 'amazing'? Was she really losing her sense of humour? The only other person around at that moment was Gerry Bream, the long-serving biology teacher with the wire-wool beard and a sensitivity to match. They all avoided him if they possibly could. She swung back to stare moodily out of the window again and sipped more of her coffee. Her skin bristled as Gerry came and stood next to her. A faint smell of stale pipe smoke reached her.

'It's all very well being trendy,' Gerry whined as he squinted at Caroline and her class cavorting over the horizon with a water melon held aloft. 'But it's traditional methods that get examinations passed.'

'I'm not sure Heather would agree with you.' Antonia always wanted to disagree with Gerry, whatever he said, but it was easy on this count. 'She's not exactly reactionary, is she? Been a breath of fresh air to this place. Everybody thinks so.'

'Oh I'll grant you that at first Heather was a little different from the previous headmistresses. We weren't used to high heels and tight skirts in our Head, but I don't think any of us complained on that count.' Gerry sucked on his teeth and Antonia cringed. 'But she values experience and loyalty as much as the next Head. I think we'll all see that when it comes to replacing Hilary as Head of Science, experience will triumph over novelty.' She could feel, rather than see, him nodding in agreement with his own statement. 'I trust you know what I mean, Antonia. After all, us old hands need to stick together.'

'I'm not exactly an old hand. Either in the years I've been alive or the years I've been here.'

'Well, no. No, of course,' he simpered charmingly and her stomach lurched.

'What, then, do you mean?' She was being dis-ingenuous, knowing exactly what he meant. The current Head of Science was retiring and a replacement would have to be found. Gerry was obviously asking her to endorse him as the best candidate for the post whenever the topic came up in the staffroom.

'Oh you know. Gregory. Caroline. The new blood in our department. Oh they're terribly popular with the girls, we all know that. They're young, ebullient, energetic. Of course they're popular. But let's see about their reliability. A Head of Department needs sticking power. I think you and I have proved that we have that in abundance, Antonia.'

'Perhaps. I don't see Caroline going anywhere, though. She seems very happy here.' She avoided mention of Greg. There was something about his manner, the things he talked about socially, the way he envied some of his friends who weren't in teaching, that did make her wonder if he might not stay around for much longer. Having said that, he'd already put in a few good years' service with the school. Caroline had been with them for over a year now. As much as Antonia had been edgy about her at first, she couldn't help admiring the way Caroline conducted herself in her job. She was damned good at it, and she wasn't going to have the mediocre likes of Gerry slagging off a gifted professional. She pursed her lips and concentrated on the exhilarated girls running about with their items of fruit. They were having a wonderful time.

'I expect they can hear that megaphone in the huts. I hope Heather approves,' Gerry tutted. 'Such a ludicrous waste of lesson time. She could have put the fruit on the desk, or passed it around the class. I mean, how is she going to demonstrate distances of kilometres?'

'What do you mean?' Antonia asked, then as Gerry rocked back on his heels and took a breath, instantly wished that she hadn't.

'I mean, even if you start off with the distances of your first few planets from the sun, Mercury, Venus, et cetera, measured in metres, from Jupiter onwards you're talking about kilometres.'

'I presume that's why she's chosen to do it outside then. Over there, at the edge of the school field, she can show them just exactly how far it is to the next one.' Antonia nodded. She probably wouldn't have said any of this to Caroline's face, but she was genuinely intrigued nonetheless. 'It's a great idea. Very visual and I bet the girls will remember it. I wish I'd had a science teacher like Caroline. Might have changed my life.'

'She won't make Head of the department, though,' Gerry said edgily. 'She's only been here a year.'

'Yes, shame isn't it?' Antonia said, and walked away.

'What are you doing?' Graham walked into the bedroom and stood by the bed, staring, as Nina emptied her wardrobe and laid her clothes on the duvet. It was a good question. The philosophical answer was that Nina had realised that before she could ever have a child of her own, she needed to know who she was. She had to place herself in time and space, to discover her true identity and to become happy, and she had realised that she could do none of those things under Graham's roof. But she was fairly sure Graham wouldn't understand that, so she chose to answer him literally.

'I'm packing.'

He stood in silence, watching her. It had been a while since he'd got home from work. First she'd heard him go into the kitchen and make himself a sandwich. Sometimes he did that when he thought she wouldn't notice, as if there wasn't enough food to go round and he had to sneak some for himself. When she made a snack, she always asked him if he wanted something and then always made what he chose. It was one of the differences between them, she supposed. But she'd liked looking after him. Perhaps it was because nobody had looked after her so she knew how it felt to be ignored. She hadn't wanted him to experience what she'd grown up with. But now she was starting to think that he'd been looked after rather too well over the years, by his mother and now her. He seemed to expect it rather than to enjoy it. She'd heard him make his sandwich, and then he'd hoovered the downstairs of the house. She'd been able to smell the lemony bite of the carpet freshener as she'd found her capacious holdall in the back of the wardrobe. She wondered whether she'd feel nostalgic every time she smelt carpet freshener in the future. It was far too early to tell.

'Where are you going?' He pushed his glasses up to the bridge of his nose, looking sweaty. Hoovering often did make him sweaty. She thought that was because he was so thorough.

'I'm going off to find myself.'

He blinked erratically at her from behind the steel rims. She imagined that if they were holding this conversation without the evidence of the suitcase and holdall in front of them, he might have been dismissing what she was saying by now.

'You're what?'

'Well,' she began, as she folded her trousers and slid them into the opened suitcase on the bed, 'if I explain it at great length, after you've listened you'll snort and say, "You mean you're going off to find yourself!" so as I know that's what I really mean I just thought I'd save time and say it.'

'Oh, I see.' Graham began to give sharp, knowing nods. 'I get it now. Those sales conferences, nights away. There's someone else, isn't there?'

'Nights away?' She tried to remember the last time she'd stayed away overnight. Graham didn't like her staying away. He liked to know where she was. Between his sheets, in other words. 'Oh, you mean the two days last year in Chelmsford?'

'Yar, yar, whatever. I should have known. You did it to the last bloke, of course you'd do it to me. Once a slapper, and all that. I should have listened to Joanna.'

Nina stood up straight and looked at her boyfriend with dislike. He was referring to the fact that he had taken her out before she left Paul. She hadn't been happy about that herself. It was her lack of a home, she now realised, that had made her so scared of losing what she had, where she lived, who she lived with. That was why there had been an overlap. How silly she'd been. 'No, you shouldn't have listened to Joanna, you should have married Joanna, shouldn't you? Except she wouldn't have you.'

'What do you mean?' He paled.

'She told me once. I think it was meant to prove to me that she could have had you if she'd wanted you but had better taste than me, or something like that.'

'Nina! I can't believe you'd talk about Joanna like that. After everything she's done for you.'

'Yes and I'll be sure to send her a thank-you note.' She stuffed her underwear into her holdall in handfuls. 'I'll ignore your insults. They don't matter now.'

'All right, all right.' Graham crossed the room, took a handful of Nina's underwear from her bag and put it back in the drawer. 'I'm sorry I called you a slapper. You're not. Okay? I'm just a little bit shocked to find my fiancée moving out without even warning me.'

'Your what?'

103

'Well what did you think I meant when I told you it was time for us to have a baby? I wouldn't have one outside marriage, would I? My parents would never speak to me again. So come on, put all this back, let's go downstairs, I'll make us a weak gin and tonic so that we can calm down, and let's stop all this nonsense about finding yourself. You've found yourself here. You're happy. You've just panicked because I've mentioned a baby, but you'll get used to the idea. It's what you want in your heart.'

'No, it isn't,' she told him factually, scrunching up her underwear and putting it back in the bag again. 'And by the way, you don't *tell* somebody when it's time to have a baby.'

'What's the difference? Oh for Christ's sake, that's just semantics.'

'It's because you don't know the difference that I'm going.'

'Well you could hardly have one without me, could you?' He sniggered, and in that second Nina realised just how unappealing he was and how little she loved him. The thought made her stronger.

'Excuse me please, I need to get to my shoes.'

He stood aside, swallowing loudly. 'So where do you think you're going then?' He sounded nervous now. Perhaps he really was starting to believe her.

Nina put her hand on her hip and took a deep breath. She was definitely going, she knew that. Issuing smart comments at him wouldn't make it any easier. And, for all the numbness in her heart, she didn't want to hurt him. She found it difficult to hurt anything. 'Do you really want to know?'

'There's nowhere for you to go. You haven't got

anybody else, that's the truth of it. You're nobody without me.'

She shook her head at him sadly. 'It's not much to be proud of, is it Graham? Sole ownership of a house, car and girlfriend.'

'It's more than you've got. Even your car belongs to the company. What have you got to show for your life, eh? Where's your house? Your car? Your . . .' he paused elaborately, '*family*?'

She shot a startled look at him, the tears pricking her eyes. He knew where to hurt her. She roughly pulled the zip across her holdall and snapped down the lid of her suitcase. She'd already cleared her things out of the bathroom. Anything else that she'd forgotten would just have to go to hell. She sniffed and wiped her nose.

'I'm going now. Please don't make a scene.'

'Oh yes? Where? Come on, tell me. I'm dead curious.'

Nina heaved her holdall onto her shoulder and struggled to pick up her case with the other hand. 'Please stand aside.'

'You're not going home, are you? To your delightful mum and dad? The alcoholic and the lout who spends all his time laying prostitutes on his European long-haul drives? The one who didn't notice that you'd left home?'

'Get out the way Graham.' The tears shot down her warm face in streams.

'Oh, I know,' his eyes brightened unnaturally. 'It's back to boyfriend number one. Paul the druggie. He'll take you back, that's if he's still alive.'

'Shut up.' She plodded across the impeccable cream bedroom carpet. The house still smelt as new as it did the first evening she saw it. The memory of that time was sharper than ever before. And she'd only realised when she was packing just how little of its contents were hers. Certainly no ornaments or decorations, no furnishings, nothing from the walls. It was like leaving a hotel. It would make going to stay in one all the less painful by contrast. She loped down the stairs, the suitcase banging on the ground. Graham followed a few steps behind, taunting her in a strangled voice.

'I tell you Nina, if you take one step out that door I'm never welcoming you back here again.'

She opened the front door and heaved her bags outside. Once they were dumped on the doormat, she collected her coats from the hall cupboard and heaped them all over her arm. Graham wrestled one with a black fluffy collar away from her.

'I bought you that. I'll have it back, thank you.'

She laid the rest of her coats over her bags and went back inside, her breath coming in painful gasps. Graham shadowed her into the living room, to the TV and video. She picked up *Dances with Wolves*.

'Oh no you don't.' He took it out of her hand and put it back. 'That's mine.'

'It's not,' she managed, her voice tight. 'I bought it. We were together at the time, in Reading Smith's, but I paid for it. It's mine.' She could feel her voice getting smaller as he grabbed it and hid it behind his back, shaking his head.

'I thought you'd do this if you ever left. Suddenly things that are mine become ours, don't they?'

'It's not even ours, it's mine,' she whispered. 'Please give me *Dances with Wolves*. You don't know how special it is to me.'

'You can't have it,' he said, and she was shocked by the meanness in his face.

She blundered out of the house without her video. 'Goodbye Graham.'

'You little fool.' He narrowed his eyes at her as she edged away towards her car on the drive, lugging her bags with her. 'This is all you've got. How can you walk away from it?'

Nina smeared a tissue across her face and slammed the boot once her bags were safely stored inside. Graham ran out to her in his socks as she opened the driver's door and looked back at him.

'No, don't go!' he rasped at her. 'I'm sorry for everything I said.'

'Goodbye.' She got into the car and shut the door. Graham's face appeared at her window, screwed up with anguish. He banged on the glass with the corner of *Dances with Wolves*.

'Open the window! I want to talk to you.'

'Can I have my video, please?' she attempted. The video was symbolic. She watched it to remind herself of who she really was.

'What? No, of course not.' He put it behind his back. 'It's mine, I told you. I just want to talk sense into you.'

She started the engine, her breath coming in sobs, and quickly put the car into reverse. She shot out of the drive so fast that he was caught off balance. Her last view was of him on his bottom on the tarmac, gesticulating at her wildly.

'This is your home!' she heard being yelled into the night as she steamed around the neat avenues of the estate and out towards the main road, where she put her foot down on the accelerator and let the engine roar.

*

'What are you lot gossiping about?' Antonia asked, expertly juggling several plates of pizza as she nudged open Sonia's bedroom door later that night. Two of Sonia's best friends had come round for a pyjama party as it was Friday, and the one night of the week Antonia always allowed Sonia some leeway. Her daughter was swamped with homework most of the time and especially at the weekends. Antonia understood all too well that if she didn't have occasional nights off to let off steam and forget about assignments, Sonia would become overwhelmed. There was nothing wrong with a bit of frivolity. Besides, Antonia had been sitting quietly downstairs with a pile of marking on her lap and one eye on *Frasier*, her mind neither on the television nor the work, but completely overtaken with dread at the thought of her forthcoming medical investigation, and she'd found the explosions of laughter coming through the ceiling comforting.

Antonia was trying hard not to panic. She had read all the leaflets, and stared hard at the date of her new appointment. She now had to undergo something called Colposcopy. This meant that somebody would do an internal examination and take small biopsies to check the extent of the problem. So far so vague. No doom-laden certainties yet, but neither could she assure herself that everything was all right. Of course, Antonia hadn't mentioned a word of it to Sonia.

What would she say? She wouldn't have dreamt of worrying her daughter, who was now reclining face down on her bed, with her feet on the pillows, her toenails varnished a gothic shade of dark purple, a Mills and Boon romance in one hand, which, judging by the rapt attention of her two friends, she had been reading aloud from. Sonia was relaxed, happy, secure, something Antonia had striven to achieve for her ever since her divorce. There was no way she was going to mess that up with frightening uncertainties.

Antonia couldn't talk to her own mother about her health problems either. Widowed and alone now, her mother had become more used to complaining than listening in recent years. Antonia reasoned that it was understandable, but it was still difficult to be around. A seed of negativity had entered her mother's soul, and with the passing weeks and months its roots gained a firmer hold. No doubt she would nag Antonia about her previous smoking habit. Antonia had finally managed to quit when she was thirty-nine and struggling financially to keep herself, Sonia and the house together. Her mother would say, 'I always knew the fags would get you, just as they got your dad,' and Antonia would be in a corner about it again.

She might have talked to Greg – he was turning out to be a good friend. But gossip had a way of boomeranging. Antonia never failed to show up for work and she knew that if she had to take significant time away from school to deal with this, it would invite comment. It would be appalling if word of the big C got around the school, and people started treating her with sympathy, or suspicion, or, worse, avoided her because they didn't know what to say. Who knew how a rumour of ill health might affect her standing, and her job security. It was better not to risk it. Especially as it was all likely to blow over.

So Antonia kept her thoughts, her fears, and her quiet distress to herself, smiled brightly at the three flushed-faced girls lazing over their novels and magazines, and for all anyone could have guessed, she was at that moment as content as a woman could be.

'Thanks Mum.' Sonia struggled up, took the pizzas, and handed them round. 'Mum, why does this say "manhood"? Why can't it just say "dick"? I mean, we all know it's a dick.'

The girls snorted. Imogen went bright red. Antonia knew that not every teenager was her mum's friend as well as her little girl.

'Because "dick" is ugly slang,' Antonia responded reasonably. 'And it would ruin the tone of the romance.'

'Not much romance in this one. It's pure sex from beginning to end. It's not even funny either. The other Mills and Boons we've got are much better.'

'If you want romantic and funny, why don't you grab one of my Jane Austens from downstairs?' Antonia said. She loved to relax with a good Mills and Boon romance herself once in a while, but the teacher inside her was difficult to repress.

'Can we stay up and watch *Pride and Prejudice* tonight?' Sonia brightened. 'The whole five hours?'

Antonia glanced at her watch. 'If you were going to do that, you should have started . . . ooh, about five hours ago. I promised your parents you'd all be clear-headed tomorrow. You've got a violin lesson at nine tomorrow morning, haven't you Imogen?'

'Yes,' Imogen admitted bleakly.

'Well then.'

'Mrs Clarke? Can I ask you something?' Katie, strewn across a bean bag and waving her painted fingernails asked, blushing. As both Sonia and Imogen burst into further giggles and rolled over, Antonia guessed this was something they'd been planning.

110

'She'll say no,' Sonia said with good humour, cramming half a pizza into her mouth in one go.

'Nothing more about sex please,' Antonia appealed. 'I'm far too old to remember any of the details.'

'It's – well –' Katie looked at Sonia for support. 'It's just that we saw an advert in the paper. For a fortune-teller. And we'd like to go. For Sonia's birthday treat.'

Antonia leant against the door frame and considered the girls' faces. All eyes, alert and eager, were turned on her in hope.

'Why would you want to do that?' she hedged.

'Emma saw a fortune-teller at a fair, she said it was brilliant fun,' Sonia said. 'This old woman told her all sorts of things she couldn't possibly have known. She said she'd spend most of her life in Africa and she said she'd meet her husband when she was twenty-seven, he'd be blond and play the piano, and they'd have four children.'

Antonia listened.

'So we just thought it'd be brilliant if we could see one. It'd be such fun.' Sonia rolled over and pretended to be a dog begging. 'You know you want to say yes. You do, you do.' She stuck out a finger and attempted to hypnotise Antonia by rotating it in her direction. 'Mother say yes, Mother will say yes, when I snap my fingers the word you will say is yes. Oh go on, Mum. It'd be really different.'

Antonia considered the suppressed excitement of the three girls. Romances, stories, possibilities, wasn't that what everyone imagined might happen, whatever their age? What else made you get up every morning, day after day? Not the knowledge that such things were the stuff of dreams, certainly. And although she and Rick had tried to make sure that Sonia was never caught up in any of their conflict, Antonia could sense that Sonia must have memories, of the upsets, and the coldness, and the very lack of romance in her own two parents' lives. And now, with a mother who refused to entertain the idea of boyfriends on the grounds that she didn't want to disturb her daughter's life, and also due to the very plain fact that she'd felt unable to withstand the turbulence of any further romantic involvement since her divorce, wasn't it natural that Sonia would dream of something she'd never seen? Did Antonia have any right to taint those heartening dreams with her own cynicism?

'Well . . .'

'Oh go on,' Katie urged in a hushed voice, and went puce. 'Sorry.'

Antonia smiled. 'The thing is this, girls. If you were at a fair and popped into a fortune-teller's tent it would be a laugh. I did it myself with some friends when I was a lot younger. I can't remember much about it. But I don't like the idea of you visiting somebody's house. It all sounds too serious.'

'It's not serious.' Sonia sat bolt upright, sensing that progress was being made. 'Not at all. This one calls himself The Spinning Fate. I mean, come off it. How can that be serious? And he's the only one that's local. Otherwise we'd have to go to Tunbridge Wells.'

'He?' Antonia frowned. 'How do you know it's a man?'

The girls looked at Sonia, who blushed.

'I rang him up. I wanted to ask you first, but I knew you'd say no unless I'd found out a bit more about it first, and could persuade you.' She added in a whisper with upturned eyes, 'And it is for *my* birthday treat.'

'Oh Sonia,' Antonia tutted at her. 'I'm disappointed in you. You shouldn't have pursued this without asking me. And what's more, Katie and Imogen will have to ask their parents too. Not everyone thinks these things are just a bit of fun.'

'My mum said it's okay,' Katie said. Antonia held her gaze. Katie was far too gentle to lie, and Antonia knew all Sonia's friends were slightly in awe of her, aware that she was a teacher.

'I haven't asked mine yet,' Imogen admitted. 'But that's because Sonia only told me about it tonight. I can ask her tomorrow.'

'I only rang him to see if he'd do a discount for a group booking.' Sonia looked at Antonia sheepishly. 'And he said yes, he would. I just thought it'd be a great party thing. We've never done anything like this before. It beats watching videos or going out to dinner. And I *know* you always do great theme parties and I *know* they're brilliant, but this would be magic.'

'I was thinking of another theme party,' Antonia said at the same time. They gave each other knowing looks.

'And he said he'd do a home visit if we liked,' Sonia pressed. 'You know, like a guest appearance.'

'Well.' Antonia scratched her head. 'If he's local, it *would* have to be a home visit. I'd want to monitor what was going on. But I don't know where we'd put him. I'm really not sure about this, Sonia. It sounds far too adult. And you're only thirteen.'

'Going to be fourteen,' Sonia asserted.

'It's still only fourteen, love.'

'Right. Only fourteen. As if girls didn't get married at that age all down through history. If I was medieval I'd have twenty-four children by now,' Sonia protested.

'Thank your lucky stars that I'm not fixing you up with some corpulent sixty-year-old noble from Bologna just because it'd be a good family alliance. Believe me Sonia, you've got it good. Being married young was no fun.'

'All right, don't have a cow. The point being we can have him round here. We could do it round the kitchen table or something. Or in the living room?'

Antonia thought hard, the pros and cons of the idea swaying her. She could see the girls' point. It was an unusual thing to do for a birthday party. But were they too young, too impressionable? As long as the fortune-teller didn't take himself too seriously, she guessed it might be safe. She'd have to be sure it was all in fun.

'Oh please, Mum. We want this so much. I promise if you say yes I'll never ask you for anything again. Ever.'

'I'll have to talk to the other girls' parents about it. I'd like to know what they think.'

'Yessssssss! Re-sult!' Sonia rolled over and kicked her legs in the air.

'No, not result. Not yet, but I'll think about it. Now put some proper clothes on.' Antonia eyed the skimpy nightclothes the girls had adorned themselves in. It wasn't so much a pyjama party as a lingerie contest. 'If Daniel comes in later, he'll have heart failure.' Antonia left the room, but hesitated, and stuck her head around the door again. 'And no Graham Norton on the portable.'

'Thanks for the pizza.' Katie almost choked on a mouthful, and seeing the sparkle that had entered all three girls' eyes Antonia took herself downstairs again, contemplating the fact that the last thing she wanted to know was what might happen in the future. There was comfort in ignorance. Nobody needed to remind her at that moment that fate was spinning.

Daniel did come in, an hour later. Antonia had been gazing at the television, her marking set to one side, a glass of wine in one hand which she'd hardly touched. She heard the front door close quietly. She blessed Daniel for being such a thoughtful man, and also realised that there was some kind of soft porn on the screen. She grabbed the remote and quickly flicked over to a Hammer Horror film on BBC1.

Daniel put his head cautiously around the door.

'Ah, you're still up. I saw the light on but I guessed Sonia might be in bed.'

A resounding thump from the ceiling followed by shrieks of laughter caused Daniel to turn his eyes upwards. He sucked in his cheek to disguise a laugh. Antonia had noticed the way he did that. It was quite endearing. But she was too dazed, had been locked into her own thoughts for too long that evening, even to raise a smile. Her face felt numb. Daniel regarded her sympathetically.

'You look wasted, if I may say so. Are you all right?'

Antonia sat up straighter on the sofa, smoothed a hand over her hair, found her clip was still neatly in place, and considered Daniel with a slight frown.

'Of course. I'm fine. How did your evening go?'

'Work do. Not bad, but they're not really my kind of people. A couple of guys were there who I'm good friends with, but other than that, it was a bit dull. I'll leave you alone then.'

How she'd been blessed with the lodger from heaven Antonia wasn't quite sure. She hadn't really done

115

anything to deserve it, and she'd heard such horror stories from others when she'd first come up with the idea.

'There's a bottle of white open in the fridge. Help yourself to a glass if you like,' she said.

'Ah, thanks. Yes, perhaps a small one before bed. I'm not much of a drinker.'

'You're welcome to sit in here, Daniel. I know I was a little firm with house rules when you first moved in, but I had to be careful, not knowing you. It's fine . . . you know . . .' Antonia's voice tailed away as her gaze drifted back to the screen. What was she going to do if the news was bad? What would happen to Sonia? If she ended up losing her job, spending half her life in hospital, too ill to be able to be a proper mother, would Sonia go and live with Rick? How would her daughter cope with that?

'I'll get a glass,' Daniel said.

Antonia hardly heard him. Then she shook herself up and tried to concentrate again. The slamming of the bedroom door, followed by the bathroom door, followed by the bedroom door from upstairs revived her. She went out into the hall.

'Girls! Quieten down!'

She settled herself back on the sofa, and took a sip of wine. It soothed her. When Daniel returned, he tapped on the door first.

'You sure you don't mind me joining you? Just for five minutes or so?'

'Sure. Go ahead. I'll be going to bed soon anyway. Stay up and watch TV for a bit if you like. I don't think you're likely to disturb the girls – it's more likely to be the other way round.'

Antonia watched Daniel perch politely in the arm-chair. He looked very smart, in a dark suit, white shirt and maroon tie, which he'd loosened a little. The crisp white of his shirt complemented his dark skin tone. She wondered idly if he had many female fans at work. He was a good-looking man, bright, and young. Still unattached as far as she knew.

'Did I tell you I've got a teenage niece who lives with my mum in London? I was living there too before I came down here,' Daniel ventured.

Antonia shook her head. 'No, I don't think you did. You mentioned brothers and sisters in London, but no details.'

'She's my older brother's kid,' he smiled. 'She's thirteen too.'

'Ah.' Antonia relaxed back into the cushions and a smile tugged at the corners of her tense mouth. 'That would explain why you haven't strangled my daughter yet.'

'I lived at home for a few years until I got this posting down here. So I'm pretty used to it.'

'You should have put that in your letter when you responded to my ad,' Antonia mused. 'I probably wouldn't have bothered to interview anyone else. What's her name?'

'Natalie.' He sat back more comfortably in his chair. 'She's my little angel. And of course, she thinks I can do no wrong. I like that.'

Antonia gave a small laugh. 'Yes, men do like to be worshipped. I know all about that.'

'Well, we all need at least one adoring fan.'

'I'm sure you've got more than one,' Antonia teased. Daniel took a sip of his wine before grinning, and she realised that her comment had sounded too flippant, possibly even a little flirty. That wasn't what she'd meant. It was only an observation. She stood up quickly. 'I'm going to go to bed now. Do make yourself at home down here, and I'll try to make the girls shut up and go to sleep now.'

Daniel stood up. 'Actually I'll just take this glass up with me and do some reading in my room. I'm bushed too. Goodnight. Thank you for the wine.'

He left the room before Antonia could. She marvelled at his diplomacy while she turned off the television and the lights. She found herself feeling very glad that Daniel had decided to come home that night rather than take off to London to see his friends. He'd pulled her from mawkish speculation, and she felt a little better. She heard Sonia encounter Daniel on the landing. He cracked a joke about making an appointment to get into the bathroom in a house full of women, before his door closed firmly. There was subdued giggling from Sonia's room, and by the time Antonia had cleared up in the kitchen, had locked up and was making her way upstairs, the house was draped in peaceful silence.

Lizzy took herself into the diminutive spare bedroom, and closed the door. It was nearly midnight. David had fallen asleep in front of a video they'd both been watching, and the boys were tucked up in bed. She could have woken David and encouraged him to come up to bed now, but she'd chosen not to. The boys were usually up and thundering about by around six in the morning. But if she'd woken David they would have got into a sleepy conversation and he would have been expecting her to come to bed too. Then if she'd explained that she wanted to stay up for a bit, he would have queried her choice, saying, 'The boys'll be yelling in our ears in a few hours.' So instead she'd crept away to have a few precious moments by herself, where she could think.

She'd stopped on the landing to listen to the sound of the boys' breathing. She loved to do that before she went to bed. The house was a small modern unit on an estate that had been new in the Eighties. It had three compact bedrooms, and the boys shared a room with single beds either side of a painted wooden storage unit that Stephanie and Howard had made for them. Lizzy had hovered outside their door, absorbing the stereo sounds of breathing. The soft breath of the boys was punctuated by throaty snores drifting up from David downstairs. Her family, breathing. She adored them all.

She'd met David when they were both very young. They'd grown in the same direction since. They were good friends, and they still got a thrill out of seeing each other in the bath.

Before she had become pregnant, Lizzy had held down a demanding job. She'd worked for a local newspaper, selling advertising space, and in a short time had been promoted to a managerial position, aware that they thought very highly of her there. She'd loved the bustle of the office, the deadlines, the frenetic scramble to sell the space, and the contact she had with lively people. She didn't want to go back to that job. But she was pining, secretly, for a sense of fulfilment beyond the emotional bond that tied her to her family. She felt guilty even privately admitting it.

She and David had always wanted a family. Issues of not being ready, or one partner wanting children while the other hung back, or postponing the idea for some future epoch, had never even occurred to them. She had worked throughout her first pregnancy.

Then the little girl had arrived early, and they had lost her after two days. Lizzy could still see her tiny hands and feet every time she closed her eyes. She could remember the smell of the special unit, the sharp angles of the incubator, the very moment that they realised that Elizabeth had slipped away from them. Both Lizzy and David had been stricken with grief. The family had supported them fantastically. So much so that eventually Lizzy had felt it would be self-indulgent and morbid to dwell on it any further. And once she was pregnant again, and the pregnancy carried full-term, and the adorable Jacob bounced into their lives, she and David were so overcome with joy that it seemed indecent to take them both back to the despair they'd felt at losing the baby girl.

The fact that she still mourned at some point every single day but locked her feelings inside had left Lizzy feeling hollow. Tom, the fortune-teller, whose advert had seemed so shallow but whose personality had been so deep, had let her talk about it. Just to be allowed to be honest about how she felt had thinned the fog that had been lingering around her heart. It was as if a tiny shaft of sunlight had made its way through that dense cloud.

With that release had come something else too. She had gone on to talk to Tom about what she wanted to do with her life beyond David and the children. She'd been able to spill her thoughts out haphazardly in a way she would have found impossible with anyone else. She was proud of being a mother and the time she spent with the boys was, she knew, precious. In a few years they would lose interest in spending time with her. She and David both made the most of that, and relished it. But Lizzy's problem was that she was losing sight of who she'd once been. A young woman with a flair that people recognised. A flair for what? That was what she didn't know any more. Her dreams and ambitions seemed less defined than they ever were.

Tom had said something, out of the blue. He'd remarked that she might enjoy exploring her creativity further. Lizzy did one 'thing', something that everyone around her knew her to be good at.

She made cards.

It had started for practical reasons. When she and David were first married, she'd never been able to find a card she liked enough to send anyone on the right occasion, and David had said casually, 'You're artistic enough. Why don't you make your own?' So she had.

Not wanting to take the artistry too seriously, and putting her sense of humour into it, she'd collected buttons, cut up tiny pieces of fabric, used everyday bits and pieces – anything from paper clips to shreds of wool or sequins – to create little figures on cards, paint features on them, and turn them into caricatures of people she knew. From the very first one she'd sent, a birthday card for David's brother, her efforts had been rewarded. She could pinpoint a personality with a few tiny details. From then on she'd always made her own cards, and now close friends or family often asked her to make one for a special occasion. Her most recent commission was Caroline asking her to make an anniversary card for Howard and Stephanie.

Lizzy invested in good quality card which she bought

from an art shop in the town. She took great care in sticking on her miniature creations, and had worked on a professional style of calligraphy to place a personal-ised message on the front. She was often asked where she'd bought the finished products, which was the nicest compliment she could ever be paid. It made the few snatched hours she spent making her cards some of the most fulfilling of her life.

Lizzy sat down at the narrow dressing table she'd squashed into the little room, pulling up the plastic folding chair which was the only one they had spare. The folders and envelopes in which she stored ephemeral bits and pieces to use for her cards were spread out over the single bed. Once she had started to sketch an idea on a piece of paper with a soft HB pencil, she might have been in an open field, or in the studio of her dreams. The room dissolved, and the images in her head possessed her.

She found a flat piece of balsa wood, about a foot square, copied the shapes she'd sketched in pencil, and picked up a scalpel ready to cut them out. Her fingers paused over the wood before she cut it. She held it up instead, turned it around in her fingers. An idea came to her. Wouldn't it be more interesting to mount the figures on a piece of wood? She'd seen something similar once. It was a three-dimensional picture, with intricate wooden features. Couldn't she do the same, but taking her own style and the caricatures she enjoyed doing so much, and create a solid picture, something that could be hung up on the wall, rather than a card?

Her ideas racing, Lizzy emptied her folders and envelopes onto the dressing table, swirled her fingers through the assortment of bric-a-brac in front of her, turned the balsa wood over, and began to create something new.

Chapter Seven

'God, I need a drink,' Greg announced as he swept into the staffroom. 'Has everyone buggered off home already? The last bell only went half an hour ago.' He stopped, his shoulders hunched, and gazed at Caroline bleakly. 'You don't fancy a drink, do you?'

Caroline, who had been cornered by Gerry Bream, biology teacher and possibly the most irritating man in the world, was delighted to see Greg.

'And that's why,' Gerry had been saying, stroking his wiry dark grey beard, 'we should all be using the trains to set an example to each other.'

'Greg, how are you?' Caroline slid away from Gerry, poking folders into her bag, and heading purposefully towards the door.

'Ah, Gregory.' Gerry spun round on spindly legs. 'Here's a man who understands all about ozone. Why, tell me, do you insist on still driving to work when there's a perfectly good railway station ten minutes' walk away?'

The problem with Gerry wasn't so much what he said, but the fact that he said it at all. Caroline had run across teachers before who were unable to stop lecturing beyond the boundaries of the classroom. They brought out the gum-chewing rebel in everyone. It had got to her, and now she could see that it was getting to Greg. A defiant look had swept across his face.

'Er, don't know Gerry. Ask me another.' Greg widened his eyes at Caroline. 'Speaking of cars, let me walk you to yours, Caroline, seeing as we're both leaving now.'

'Yes, I'm leaving right now,' she emphasised.

'And me too.' Greg gathered his things like a whirlwind.

'Did somebody say pub? I may have misheard, but I don't think so.' Gerry ho-hoed.

'I was thinking of dropping into the Chequers on my way home,' Greg said. The Chequers, as he and Caroline both knew, was an appealing pub in the town where Caroline lived and that Greg had to drive through anyway on his way home. Gerry, who lived in Paddock Wood and relied on trains, would be taken right out of his way.

'Chequers, Chequers . . . is that walking distance?'

''Fraid not.' Greg told Gerry where it was. Gerry scratched his chin through his beard. Small flakes of skin drifted into the air, and Caroline and Greg shuddered in unison.

'I think I know the one you mean. The station's not five minutes from there. If one of you can give me a lift, I can get a train back easily.'

'A lift? Are you quite sure you want to be party to ozone depletion?' Greg said.

'Very thoughtful of you, Greg, but as my beloved lady is at her upholstery evening class tonight, and as the one little pleasure I permit myself is my pipe and I'm not allowed to smoke it in the house, upholstery evening class or no, I would very much like to join you for a swift one. And when I say swift one, I mean, of course, a drink.' Gerry guffawed and Greg's face fell in tandem

125

with Caroline's. 'What nobody else seems to realise is that car-sharing is a way forward in these self-serving times. Now, in the States—'

'Actually Greg,' Caroline said apologetically, 'I'm pretty done in. I probably should get straight home and prepare things for tomorrow.'

Greg gave Caroline a startled look.

'Just us men together then, Gregory.' Gerry rubbed his hands together. 'A pint, a pipe and some man talk. Now that would be pleasant.'

Greg edged up to Caroline and pretended to read a notice on the board. 'Caroline, if you leave me alone with Gerry, I will personally ensure that you never breathe again.'

'Well, I . . .' Caroline hesitated. A quick trip to the pub with Greg to relax would have been welcome. But to combine relaxation with Gerry Bream was like trying to combine a stag night with teetotalism. On the other hand, she felt that she was becoming very repetitive these days. She seemed constantly to be saying 'no', 'another time' and 'just not tonight'. Was she all work and no play? Was she becoming really dull?

Antonia swept into the staffroom at that moment, her high heels clacking on the tiles, a waft of delicious scent enveloping them all. She glanced round at them, made a vague noise of greeting, and headed straight for her table in the corner.

'Antonia, my dear lady,' Gerry Bream began.

'I'm not your dear anything,' Antonia rallied as she gathered her belongings.

'You see, I get terribly confused by these politically correct times. A poor man doesn't know what he's allowed to say these days. Ladies don't like to be called

126

girls any longer, and yet I use the term "girl" by way of a compliment, as I do "lady"' What nobody seems to realise is—'

'My name is Antonia,' she said, picking up her bag. 'And if you've got something to say, stop all this prevaricating and just come out with it.'

Looking slightly confused, Gerry stuck out his chin, rolled on his heels and proclaimed, 'We are going to the pub, Antonia, and I am inviting you to join us.'

'Oh Christ.' Antonia let out an audible sigh.

Caroline suppressed a laugh. For some reason Antonia always got away with expressing what everyone secretly thought when it came to the one or two grating members of the male staff. Caroline thought it was probably because they were in love with her.

'I'm not particularly in the mood for pubs.' Antonia glanced at Greg, who mouthed, 'Please?' Caroline could guess that Greg had visions of her abandoning him to Gerry, pipe, flaky skin, lectures and all. 'Where are you going?' Antonia seemed to waver, but she was unsmiling as she pulled on her coat.

'Chequers,' Caroline said quickly so that Antonia would know that she wanted her to be there too. It had been a while since she and Antonia had relaxed together. It would be nice to get to know her a little better.

'Well it's on my way home, and Sonia's got gym straight after school tonight, so I'll join you briefly,' Antonia said. 'But on one condition. Nobody talks about work.'

'Agreed,' Gerry said, reaching for his mackintosh and umbrella. 'And perhaps you would be so kind as to let me travel with you in your car, Antonia. I'll be getting a

127

train home of course, so I would only be imposing on you for a brief, but hopefully pleasant, interlude.'

Antonia raised her eyes to the ceiling and led the way out of the staffroom.

As Caroline and Greg strolled through the car park, huddled into their coats to shun the wind, Greg murmured, 'Thanks, Caroline. I couldn't have stood being alone with Gerry Bream in a pub. Not after the day I've had. I know he's not evil, but he gives me the creeps, and he spouts such utter balls sometimes. I just keep having this horrible feeling that he's gay.'

'And I keep having a horrible feeling that he's straight.' Caroline reached her car. 'Poor Antonia.'

They looked over at Gerry attempting to open Antonia's door for her, which was causing something of a struggle since she had the keys. She shooed him away, and they heard the whoop of the central locking and Antonia barking, 'Just get in will you?'

'Looks like I'm not the only one who needs a drink,' Greg said.

There was a fire blazing in the stone hearth, and the public bar was warm. The Chequers was an atmospheric pub, maintaining much of its sixteenth-century flavour. The ceiling was low, yellowed and threaded with dark oak beams. The floor was hatched with stone flagging and soft lighting flickered from the unevenly plastered walls. Caroline sometimes came here with Lizzy, and it was the astronomy club's favourite pub to tumble into after meetings as it was genuinely rustic, friendly, and free of loud music. Two barmen seemed to alternate shifts, both easy-mannered with goatee beards and ponytails. Caroline found it hard to tell them apart.

Greg was already at the bar as Caroline arrived. There was no sign of Antonia and Gerry.

'What are you having?' Greg asked, sipping the froth off a bitter shandy that he'd ordered for himself.

'Better be something soft.'

'You only live down the other end of the main road, don't you? Have something weak.'

'Yes, I could have just one, I suppose, but . . .' Caroline spotted the crackling fire, and a table that looked wonderfully inviting near to it. The thought of nestling there for a bit before heading home was quite appealing.

'Yes, I know. Marking, lesson-planning, form-filling, got to keep a clear head, bla di bla, bollocks bollocks,' Greg said, rolling his eyes. 'One drink, Caroline. Now that Gerry's managed to muscle his way in, you'll need it.'

'A white wine and soda then. That should last me.'

'It's a bummer,' Greg said after he'd ordered Caroline's drink. 'I really wanted to talk to you alone.'

'Is everything all right?' They picked up their drinks and headed towards the fire. There was still a threat of snow in the air and the night was closing in sharply outside. They seated themselves either side of the table, which had four comfortable chairs placed around it. Caroline hoped that Gerry wouldn't sit next to her when he arrived and cover her in his beard scratchings.

'Well, yes.' Greg took another sip of his drink. 'Well, no, not really. I just fancied a chat, with a good friend.'

Caroline felt a flicker of affection for him. 'What a nice thing to say. I'm glad you think of me that way.'

'But you were the only person around.' Greg gave Caroline a broad wink. 'No really, I do think of you as a friend. I've got mates, of course, outside school, but they don't really get the whole picture. None of my friends understand why I do this for a living. They seem to have a lot more freedom than I do.'

'And more money,' Caroline said, thinking longingly for a second about the telescope of her dreams.

'Well that's partly it.' Greg looked a little uncomfortable. 'That's why I've been thinking about moving on to greener pastures.'

Caroline was taken aback. She knew Greg loved teaching, liked the school, and was doing well there. He'd probably be in line for a promotion if he hung around. When Hilary, the current Head of Science, retired, Caroline thought that Greg stood the best chance of being asked to fill her shoes.

'Moving on?' she queried with concern. 'What do you mean?'

'I've been offered a job. At a school in the north.'

'A better job than this?'

'It's, erm . . .' Greg shifted in his chair and took another peck of his shandy. 'The thing is, it's a private school. All boys, quite a small place, but very good academically.'

Caroline allowed this bombshell to sink in. Greg had been a state-school boy himself, and she'd heard him say before how much he wanted to be a part of the state system. She hadn't ever expected to hear anything like this from him.

'A private school?'

'They've got a lot of extra-curricular activities. And they're big on sport as well as academic subjects. I used to love the combination of all that. I was captain of the rugby team at university. Played football too. I guess it's always been great to get out of the lab and work all that

130

energy off running about in the mud. It would fulfil both sides of me, you see. The classes would be smaller, the labs better equipped, and I could do some sports coaching as well. There'd be less paperwork, and more time to do interesting things.'

'I see,' Caroline said quietly.

'It's not just the money, which of course is much better. But it is a factor. I mean, I'm young. There are things I want to do, to have the money to do.'

'Well so do I, Greg.' She couldn't help sounding disapproving.

Greg leaned back in his chair, assessing Caroline with a worried frown. 'But you'd never consider going private.'

'Me? No, I wouldn't. But I'm not you.'

He let out a harrowed sigh. 'I knew you'd react like this.'

Caroline fiddled with a beer mat. 'I'm not really reacting. That wouldn't be fair. It's got to be your choice.'

'I know what you think, though. It's plastered all over your face. And you know that deep down inside, I agree with you.'

'Greg, I'm not you. This is your personal decision. Whatever's plastered over my face is my problem.'

'Room for a small one?' Gerry Bream's voice boomed over their heads. He sidled around the table and sat himself down next to Caroline. As he rubbed his hands together and scratched his beard, she was left to ponder in bafflement Greg's series of announcements. For some reason it suddenly brought Brendan into her mind. If Greg were to go off to his school in the north, and Brendan were to go back to Australia, that meant two very good male friends would go out of her life. But was her worry about Brendan purely on account of losing his friendship, as it was with Greg? Or had those teasing black eyes of his finally worked their magic and seduced her into thinking about him as a lover?

Greg stood up to allow Antonia to settle at the chair next to him as she arrived at the table with drinks for herself and Gerry. Caroline wondered whose decision it had been that Antonia should buy the round. Gerry was infamous for refusing to put his hand in his pocket. It was usually stuck in his beard.

'Nobody minds if I smoke, do they?' Gerry had already whipped his pipe out and was stuffing tobacco into the bowl.

'What about the ozone layer?' Antonia sipped a gin and tonic.

'Ozone? No, no. You explain it to her, Gregory, you're the chemist. I'm sure you can do this on automatic pilot by now.'

'She doesn't need it explaining to her, thank you,' Antonia retorted. 'I was pointing out a certain level of hypocrisy, not asking for a lecture.'

'I don't really think any of us are in the mood to discuss fuel emissions just now,' Greg advised Gerry.

'I thought you were dead against pollution of all kinds, Gerry?' Caroline quizzed him, annoyed that he'd burst into their conversation just when she'd wanted to find out more of Greg's thoughts. 'Doesn't that include air pollution?'

'Give a poor chap a break, Caroline,' Gerry grinned, revealing crooked, off-white teeth. Caroline instinctively leaned away from him. 'Life holds so few truly self-indulgent pleasures. A man has to be allowed one or two sins that give him satisfaction. Of course, I don't mean sins of the female variety. That would never do, working as I do in an environment bursting with healthy young girls.'

Caroline felt vaguely sick, and she heard Antonia give an impatient sigh.

'Smoke your pipe. I don't care. I'm a reformed smoker anyway, and it's too late to care about damage to my bloody health now.'

'Of course, it helps being an obscenely happily married man,' Gerry croaked on, lighting his pipe and puffing plumes of blue smoke into the air. 'There are very few things I have asked of my God in life, and I've been blessed with them. Good health and a happy marriage. Without those two integral elements, I don't think life would have been worth living—'

'Oh Gerry . . .' Antonia took a breath. 'Just fuck off.'

There was a stunned silence.

Gerry was slack-jawed as he gaped at Antonia. Greg and Caroline stared at her too. Antonia was sharp, often, and drily humorous at times, and they all threw expletives about when they knew the students weren't listening. But this was a personal insult, not just in the vocabulary, but in the tone that it had been issued. Antonia's cheeks were flushed as she downed her gin and tonic in one and stood up.

'Antonia!' Gerry protested.

'My apologies, Caroline, Greg,' she nodded at them. 'I should never have joined you. I have things to do. See you at work tomorrow.'

She left. They all stared at her empty chair after she had swept out of the pub, leaving the door to bang shut behind her. Nobody seemed to know quite what to say.

'I don't think it's a crime to have a happy marriage.' Gerry stuck out his chest, putting his chin defiantly in the air. 'There is no need for that language. It may not be fashionable to stay with one's spouse these days, but I'm not going to apologise for the very stable and loving environment which I am very proud to call my home.'

'Yes, but Gerry, perhaps it's not wise to gloat about it in the presence of three unmarried people, one of whom had a particularly upsetting divorce, and is bravely getting on with life on her own without all the luck you've had.' Greg sounded remarkably restrained, Caroline thought. Personally, she felt like punching Gerry in the face. Antonia had looked seriously upset. She could tell, not just from her outburst, but from the strained look around her eyes and mouth. Caroline stood up quickly.

'I'll be right back.'

She sped out of the pub, faced the wind, and ran round to the gravel car park. Antonia had just made it to her car and was about to get in.

'Antonia! Hang on a sec.'

Antonia waited, her hand resting on the opened car door, until Caroline reached her. Her face was very pale. She looked as if she wanted to either cry or break something. Caroline knew that feeling.

Caroline gathered her breath. 'Please don't rush off. Gerry's an arse. Greg's sorting him out. Look, why don't you stay with us for a bit?'

'Not now, Caroline,' Antonia said tensely. Her eyes were glittering, whether from anger, unshed tears, or the cold, Caroline couldn't tell. She knew, though, that she had never seen Antonia let slip her professional veneer in this manner before. She was always poised, even out of school.

'Are you all right?' Caroline quizzed, shivering as a blast of icy wind caught her hair.

'Yes, I'm all right. I'm going to go now. I'll see you tomorrow.'

'Look, if you want to talk, or anything, just – well, just say.'

Antonia's cheeks tightened. 'See you tomorrow, Caroline.'

'Yes, see you tomorrow.'

Caroline watched Antonia drive away in a screech of tyres and join the main road. Then she made her way slowly back to the pub. Her mind far away, she pushed open the door, and walked into the back of two men in heavy overcoats who seemed to have just arrived.

'Sorry,' she muttered.

One of them turned around and looked at her. It was the man with the green eyes again. Tom.

'Hello,' he said. He looked surprised. She was too troubled by Antonia's exit, though, to really register seeing him again.

'Hello,' she said vaguely. He was standing in her way. She couldn't get past him until he moved. On the other hand she couldn't think of anything to say to him.

'I enjoyed the club meeting the other night,' he said. 'I was hoping you might come to the pub afterwards. We had a lively chat.'

'I'm sure. It's usually lively.' Beyond Tom, she could see Greg and Gerry stuck into conversation. It looked as if they might be having an argument, but she was too far away to hear, and now the pub was filling up there was a background buzz of voices.

135

'It was a shame you didn't come,' Tom said. He seemed to be watching her for a reaction.

'I don't always do the pub afterwards. Depends on my mood.'

'And I don't seem to have put you in a very good mood that evening. I probably should have rung or e-mailed someone first, to say I was coming.'

'Sorry?' Caroline pulled her attention back to Tom again.

She hoped that Antonia wasn't going to get caught for speeding on the way home. She concentrated on Tom's face for a second. Now she was closer, she could see that he had an unusual mouth. It was very male, but at the same time sensitive, with a wide teddy-bear shape very apparent if you looked at the corners. Was he laughing? If so, was it with her, or near her? The reddish tinge of the bulbs in the wall lamps brought out an auburn hue in his hair. He was older than she'd thought. She'd put him initially in his early thirties. Perhaps the shoulder-length dishevelled hair made him look younger. But he was probably in his late thirties, give or take a year or two. What did it matter?

She still couldn't think of anything to say. She was wondering how long it would be before Greg killed Gerry.

'You – um. You seemed a bit put out when I turned up at the club,' Tom said again, looking unsure.

'Oh, no I wasn't.'

'No. Well, maybe we could discuss things another time. It would be interesting. Perhaps you'd like to . . .' He tailed away, watching Caroline's face. She frowned, as Gerry seemed to be thumping his fist on the table. Tom followed her line of vision, and glanced over his shoulder. 'Oh, I'm sorry, you're with friends.'

'Yes. I don't usually come here on my own.' Caroline edged past Tom. He moved closer to his friend at the bar to allow her to pass. 'Thank you. See you around then.'

'Yes. Yes, I'll see you around,' Tom said.

When she reached the table, Caroline was relieved to find that the two men weren't having a fully fledged row after all. It seemed that Greg was being very reasonable, and Gerry was overdoing the mannerisms. Caroline gave Greg a sympathetic look as she slipped back into her chair, taking the opportunity to edge it a good few inches further away from Gerry's.

'Gregory is telling me that marriage isn't an essential component of one's happiness in life,' Gerry announced to Caroline, as if she'd be aching to know what she'd missed. 'And I am asserting that it is. A man needs solidity. A warm home, an understanding woman. The family is the rock on which our society is built.'

Caroline took a big swig of her drink. If it hadn't been for Greg, she'd have liked to have screeched out of the car park herself in order to avoid any further Gerry-isms. But what was Tom doing here? Now that she was seated, she could see him at the bar, getting drinks with his friend. Both men were tall, solid figures. His friend had short, spiky, very black hair. Both were handsome, quite dashing additions to the little country pub. As Tom was paying for his drinks, he looked over at Caroline. She felt a rush of blood to her face. She'd been discovered staring at him.

She looked away quickly, and turned her full attention back to her own table. She would just ignore the fact that Tom was there.

'What nobody seems to realise is,' Gerry went on,

137

'that without marriage, the fabric of society falls apart.'

Caroline tutted. 'Gerry, why are you telling me this? You know I'm a single woman and I'm quite happy that way. You're welcome to your opinions but I don't share them.'

'I bet you,' Gerry pointed a finger that had a yellowy stain on it, 'that I can deduce a great deal about you from your single state. I bet that you haven't had the advantage of observing a good marriage at close quarters. And with divorces so rife, it's no wonder that marriage is an uncool thing to do now. Nobody grows up knowing anything other than broken homes and single parents. I'll put money on your background.' Gerry put his hand in his pocket, pulled out a pound coin, and slapped it on the table. Caroline noted mentally that it was the first time she'd ever see him produce any money in public. 'There. Tell me I'm wrong.'

Caroline squinted at Gerry in irritation. 'My parents are very happy, thank you. As are the rest of my family, including my happily married aunt, brother, and cousin. And there's no reason on earth why having divorced parents would make you want to be divorced yourself. I'd imagine the reverse is probably true. If you got married, you'd want it to work. However, I don't want to get married, euphorically married relatives or not.'

Gerry sucked on his pipe, and lit the tobacco again. 'You say you're happy, but you're not,' he declared, ignoring Caroline's information about the satisfactory state of her family's marriages. She noticed that he slipped his hand on the table and took back his pound coin quickly. 'No woman can be single, and happy. It isn't the natural order of things. Look at Antonia.'

'Gerry, I think that's enough,' Greg said in a low, firm voice.

'Well, if a poor old chap isn't even allowed to voice an opinion these days without the PC brigade jumping down his throat,' Gerry huffed.

Trying to ignore him, Caroline shot another sneaky glance at Tom. She watched curiously as he and his friend took a table at the other end of the bar. They both sat down, slipped off their coats, and crossed long, denim-clad legs. An eye-catching pair of men, it had to be admitted. They said men hunted in pairs. Perhaps they were out on the cop? They certainly had the attention of two young women who seemed to have come for a drink from work and were offering subtle glances in their direction.

'I said, tell me that you're really happy, and I'll tell you you're deluding yourself,' Gerry insisted, swivelling in his chair to face Caroline. She turned to him in annoyance. He was far too idiotic, she always thought, to be taken seriously, but she wasn't in the mood for this.

'You could try minding your own business.'

'I said it was enough, Gerry,' Greg repeated. 'We've come here to relax, not to be interrogated. Let it drop.'

'Oh, I'm terribly sorry to be the one to ask uncomfortable questions.' Gerry's cheeks flushed with indignation. 'But it's our job to have enquiring minds. At least, that is my understanding of—'

'Oh for God's sake,' Greg said, running a hand over his thick brown hair and looking more exhausted than angry. 'Please shut up now. You've made your point.'

'If Caroline can convince me she's happy to be on the shelf and nearly forty, then I'm a Dutchman. That's all

I'm saying. At least Hilary was married.' Gerry had raised his voice.

'*What*?' Caroline had just taken a sip of her drink, and nearly spurted it across the table.

'Hilary. She can hold down her job because she's got stability behind her. That's important.'

'Hang on, Gerry.' Caroline tried to reason. 'You're not saying that—'

'I'm saying that the Head of Science job can't go to somebody insubstantial like Caroline.'

'Right, that's it.' Greg stood up. 'You apologise for that comment, right now.'

'I most certainly will not.' Gerry puffed wildly on his pipe, his eyes bulging. 'I am saying what I think.'

'You are such a dickhead.' Greg leaned over the table.

'And using language from the gutter in an attempt to intimidate me into not having a point of view is the behaviour of a lout,' Gerry said in a shrill voice.

'Forget it.' Caroline stood up. 'I honestly don't care what Gerry thinks about me. I'm just going to go home.'

'To your empty house. That is the only point I am making. A spinster of a certain age reaches a point where she knows she's missed the boat. And that is why you could never head the department. You just aren't well-rounded enough.'

Caroline picked up her glass, which was half-full, and threw what was left of her drink into Gerry's face.

The moment she had, she was shocked at her own behaviour. She put a hand up to her mouth. Their part of the pub had fallen silent. Gerry's face was dripping, a few bubbles from the soda fizzing in the wiry strands of his beard.

140

'Oh,' Caroline breathed. 'Sorry about that, but you deserved it.'

Gerry blinked back at her.

'You don't know when to bloody stop,' Greg stated. 'Come on Caro, I'll walk you to your car.'

Greg strode out of the pub with Caroline. As she reached the door, her eyes met Tom's. It was impossible to tell what he might be thinking. She wound her arm through Greg's and they stepped out into the cold evening air.

'Oh God!' Caroline burst out laughing as they jogged around the pub to the car park. 'Let's get out of here before he follows us with another lecture.'

'That slimy little know-all,' Greg fumed. 'He's had that coming for a while, but I've never heard him this bad before. I'm sorry you got the rough end of it.'

'I'm not worried about what he said,' Caroline told him, finding her car keys in her bag. 'I think I was more annoyed with him for upsetting Antonia. But God knows why I threw my drink at him. I've never done that before.'

'I nearly decked him.' Greg stopped walking as they reached Caroline's car. 'And don't worry, men are notoriously hopeless at guessing women's ages. He probably needs his eyes seeing to as well as his nuts.'

Caroline laughed. 'Well, so much for chilling out. You look like you're going to go home and thump the sofa for a good couple of hours before you calm down.'

Greg tutted, but a smile tugged at his mouth. 'Bloody Gerry. I hope his trains home are all cancelled, and he has to sleep under a newspaper on the platform.'

'I feel sorry for his wife. No wonder she goes out every night, flower weaving, or whatever it is she does.'

'Yeah.' The wind whipped them both into a shudder. 'Look, about the job at the other school. I know you wouldn't dream of mentioning it to anyone else, but don't dwell on it too much yourself either. I'm really not sure what I think yet. It's all a bit of a new idea. Don't judge me too harshly for it.'

'Course I won't,' Caroline soothed. 'How can I blame you for looking at your options? If it makes you feel any better, I've sometimes wondered if I should have followed the research path and gone into a job that was more to do with pure science. I could be working on the Mars mission now. Imagine that.'

'I remember. You've said that before.'

'But I love what I do and I'd never do anything else. That's just me, though. We all need to wonder how things might have been different. The fact is, you're thinking of acting on it.'

'You wouldn't make a decision based on money though, would you?' he probed her.

'No,' she said after considering the question. 'But the fact that money's a factor for you doesn't make you immoral.' Greg laughed and Caroline felt a little easier. 'Look, I'm going to head off now. You know how it is. Friday tomorrow. End-of-the-week panic.'

'Yep, you're right. Let's get going before bloody Gerry reappears.'

They parted company, and Caroline drove home, her thoughts turning back to Antonia. If she'd had her phone number, she might have rung her. But would Antonia find that intrusive? They really didn't know each other that well. And she might think Caroline was prying. She hadn't looked as if she wanted to discuss anything with her. No, it was probably best left alone, and not mentioned again. Everyone had bad days. When they did, they usually liked to be allowed to get over them privately.

And as she pictured Gerry's shocked face, covered in her white wine and soda, she shook her head. Where had that idea come from? It had been a reflex. She very much regretted doing it, even if he did deserve it. She was normally a happy, good-natured person, and not prone to flashes of anger. Well, it just went to show what any woman was capable of in the presence of Gerry Bream. Antonia had told him to fuck off, and Caroline had drenched him in white wine. She wondered how often his wife threw his boil-in-the-bag cod in parsley sauce in his face, and left him covered in it while she ran out to her evening classes.

And Tom, the blond, green-eyed man with the odd line in questions, had seen what had happened. Well, that ensured one thing, at least. He wouldn't turn up to the astronomy club again. He'd be convinced now that Caroline was a dangerous virago who was best avoided. But she'd had the opportunity to observe that he was very good-looking, which she hadn't really registered properly before. Perhaps it was a shame he wouldn't come to the club again. But it probably wasn't a shame. He was fairly strange.

The room in the cheap motel was spartan. It was in an annexe, away from the main reception, reminding Nina of a Butlin's chalet they'd been to many years ago when she was a child. It was the only holiday they'd ever had together as a family, and as her mother had spent the entirety of it paralytic and her father had disappeared for most of it, either gambling in the arcades in the town, getting drunk as far away from her mother as possible, or seeing other women, it hadn't been much of a holiday. Nina had spent her time with the Redcoats, who she now realised must have felt sorry for her. Little orphan Nina. One of them had lent her a book on a day when the weather was particularly wet. It was a James Bond thriller and she'd devoured it from cover to cover. He'd been surprised when she'd given it back to him the next day and asked if he had any more. She'd been eight at the time.

She heaved a sigh, arranging her toiletries in the bathroom to try to make it look like home. She hung her clothes up in the wardrobe, set out her shoes and squirted some perfume into the air to get rid of the smell of damp walls and mouldy carpet. Two of the bulbs had gone in her room, one in a wall light and one in the lamp next to the bed. The gloomy lighting, the dowdy furnishings and orange and black swirls on the thin carpet gave the place a decidedly tired air. She'd already had supper, having bought a Cornish pasty and some salad earlier in the day. She'd eaten it a little while ago, with her fingers, at the tatty writing desk in the corner of the motel room.

She hadn't told anybody she worked with what she'd done. As her job was mobile, she could base herself anywhere and they wouldn't know. She made appointments over the phone and she visited people. She so rarely had to go into the head office at Bracknell that she'd sometimes wondered why she lived so close. Most of her work was in the south, but not that much of it in Berkshire. The region she covered was more south-east than south-central. But at least her colleagues' indifference gave her time to gather herself. Nobody would think to ask her whether she'd set off from the two-bedroomed house she shared with Graham that morning, or a shabby motel room. In fact, the colleagues she was friendly with were decidedly underwhelmed by Graham, something she was well aware of but didn't broach with them, and they never asked her anything about him.

She opened a can of Coke, plumped the lumpy pillows behind her and leant back on them. The television that optimistically faced her from a bracket on the wall refused to come on when she pressed the remote control. After a further fifteen minutes of fiddling with various combinations of pressed or unpressed buttons, Nina gave up. She'd have to mention it to them at reception in the morning, though from the feedback she'd received from the staff in the motel so far, she wasn't too optimistic about anything being done about it in a hurry. She was too weary now. She just wanted something to take her mind away from what was going on. She found a novel she'd been looking forward to reading and opened that instead.

As she read, her eyes flickered away from the book. She gazed over the dull room, the suitcase and holdall stacked in the corner, the row of shoes. She wondered what Graham would be doing now. Oh, of course she knew the answer to that, and an ironic smile lifted her full lips. At Joanna's, getting filter coffee and sympathy. She'd reassure him that he was too good for Nina, which he knew already. She probably had a friend lined up to meet him already, one of her forty-something London cronies, desperate to sleep with anything to get pregnant. But that was a cruel thought, and Nina only ever felt guilty when she'd been cruel. If only she could watch her video of *Dances with Wolves* now and nourish her spirit. If only her heart and soul could be taken away from the stench of dampness and decay, from musty bed linen and spinach-coloured wallpaper, and lifted right up into the sunshine. She turned over, thumped the pillow, and tried to get back to her book.

She was putting it off because she didn't feel strong enough, but she knew what she had to do. Slapping the book down, Nina sat up, sipped her Coke and stared at the wall. The motel was only a temporary solution. Once she'd realised that she couldn't live with Graham any more she'd had to go straight away. She was too honest to stay with him once the relationship was dead and buried in her heart. She could manage financially at the motel while she got herself sorted, but then she needed to find somewhere to live that was more permanent, a room or a very small flat. But before she could do that, she had to make a decision on where she wanted to live, and given that she had no ties to anybody any more, she might as well have closed her eyes and stuck a pin in a map of England to see where it took her. And that brought her back to the thing that she was putting off.

Heaving a deep breath and closing her eyes for sustenance, Nina took the phone from beside the bed and moved it to her lap. Time passed, her heart beating so hard that she could see her shirt rising and falling. She licked her lips, gathered her courage, picked up the handset and dialled.

She kept her eyes tightly shut whilst the phone rang. She prayed that it wouldn't be answered. That would be one way of getting this absurd notion out of her head. But eventually, just as she was about to hang up and put the phone back on the bedside table, her mother's voice came down the line.

'Hello?' A sharp sound, too loud. Nina glanced at her watch. She would be drunk by now. Then she panicked and nearly hung up anyway. 'Who's there?'

'It's me,' Nina swallowed her words and tried again a little louder. 'It's me, Mum. Nina.'

'Nina. Well Jesus Christ, Sheila, it's royalty. I suppose you want me to drop everything and talk to you just because you're in the mood, but you'll have to make it quick because I'm busy. Sheila's here.' Sheila was one of her mother's collusive drinking friends, so was often at the house. Nina could hear their neighbour's voice in the background, saying something along the lines of telling the little bitch to go to hell. 'Yes, Sheila says you always were a selfish cow with ideas above yourself.' Nina heard Sheila say something about bloody books. 'She says you were always a snob with your books, using long words just to impress people. What is it then? I've got no money so don't ask me.'

Nina bit back a reply. She'd known it would be hard to come into contact with her mother again, but she had a reason and she couldn't back down. 'I want you to tell me about anybody I'm related to.'

There was a stunned silence on the other end of the phone, then her mother's voice was muffled, she assumed that she'd put her hand over the receiver, then Sheila screamed with laughter. 'You bloody what?'

Nina hardened her voice, filled with resolve. 'I said, tell me about any relative you know about who is still alive. I want to contact my family.'

'Oh get frigging lost. There is no family.' The slur was prominent in the voice.

147

'If you don't tell me, I'll shop Sheila for moonlighting.' Nina would never have done that in her wildest dreams, but she had to use any tactic she could. She couldn't be sure that Sheila was still moonlighting, but it seemed like a safe bet.

'You bloody little bitch.'

'My family. It's all I want. Tell me who they are.' Nina put her head back against the wall and allowed the tears to roll down her cheeks. She had to keep her voice firm and steady. She heard more muffled voices as a frenetic debate took place, then she heard Sheila say, 'For God's sake tell her then get her out of your hair for good.'

'Mum?' Nina stifled a sniff. 'Tell me. I have to know.'

'There is no bloody family,' her mother was saying, but Sheila was arguing and Nina could hear the neighbour's brittle voice getting louder. She listened to the dialogue going on in her mother's sitting room, able to picture everything.

'There is a relative. You know, that one you've mentioned before,' Sheila said.

'What one?'

'That funny one.'

'Oh yes. That one.' Her mother's voice became louder as she spoke into the handset again. 'There's one I can think of. But if you do anything like shopping anyone I swear I'll find you, you little cow.'

'Name,' Nina snapped, holding a pen with trembling fingers. 'And address. Now.'

Caroline found a parking place for her car and braced herself against the wind on the way to her house. She was glad to get home. She hurried to her front door, and jumped in shock to find somebody on her doorstep.

'Oh God!' She put a hand to her chest. 'Brendan! It's only you. What are you doing, lurking about out here in the dark?'

He was in a thick coat and gloves, and in the dim light of the streetlamps, looked very cold.

'I was just about to leave. I'd rung the bell, but you weren't in.'

'Well no, obviously not. Here I am.' Caroline shivered as a few flurries of snow carried through the wind and landed on her face. 'Let me get the key in the door. It's freezing tonight.'

She got the door open, and Brendan followed her into the hall. She put on the lights, and was relieved to find that the central heating had already kicked in. The house felt pleasantly warm.

'Come through.' She hung her coat on the hook. She glanced at Brendan as he slipped off his coat and hung it up too. He was fairly subdued, for him. He was in olive chinos, a loose white shirt and dark green tie with a jacket over the top. He looked as if he'd come straight from work. It was probably about the time that he'd normally get home. 'Is everything all right?' she asked on her way to the kitchen to put the kettle on. 'It's not Lizzy or David, is it?'

'Nah, everything's fine with them,' he said and followed her through to the kitchen. He sat down at her white table and gazed distractedly at the shiny, clean surface.

'You're obviously staying, then,' she quipped, looking at him curiously. 'Tea, coffee? I'd offer you something stronger, but Lizzy drank my last bottle of wine and I haven't replaced it yet.'

'Ah no, coffee's fine.' He stood up, then sat down again.

'I've just had the drink-after-work-in-the-pub from hell,' Caroline told him, making coffee. 'Some old codger from school started pontificating at my expense, and you won't believe what I did. I can't believe it myself.' She shook her head at the memory. 'I threw my drink in his face. Can you believe that? Me? I'll have to apologise to him tomorrow. A well-chosen insult would have been quite adequate.'

Brendan scratched at the surface of the table with his nails, and nodded briefly. Caroline added milk to the coffee, one sugar for Brendan, knowing by now how he liked it, and put a mug under his nose. She sat down opposite him and saw him wince to himself, as if he was watching some private video in his brain.

'And then I ran around the pub naked with a beer mat clenched between my buttocks, and everyone clapped. It was a bit chilly, but it was great to see the looks on their faces,' she added. Brendan nodded again. 'You're not listening to a word I'm saying, are you?'

'Hmmn?' He looked up. She was transfixed for a moment by those deep, dark brown eyes. She had to admit that she sometimes felt a shiver of sexual attraction when he stared at her. It was no wonder that he never had a shortage of girlfriends, even if he wasn't the settling-down type. Well, that was his business. Everyone had a right to live exactly how they wanted, even Brendan.

'Earth to Brendan?'

He had that brisk, cold, man-just-come-in-from-the-night scent about him this evening. His eyebrows met in a frown. 'What did you say?'

Caroline shook her head at him, smiling. 'What's up? You're off with the fairies.'

'Your house,' Brendan said, looking around him. 'It's so clean and neat, it should feel strange. But it doesn't. It's comfortable being here. I've always thought so. I like it.'

'Aw that's nice. Anything else you wanted to come here in the snow to tell me?'

Brendan stood up, then sat down. Then he reached inside his jacket. He took out an envelope and put it on the table. He stared at the envelope, and Caroline stared at it too. She waited for him to say something, but he didn't. He sipped his coffee, and looked at her meaningfully. She was perplexed.

'What is it? Your marching orders?' As Brendan kept a totally straight face, Caroline felt a horrible thud of disappointment. What if it was his marching orders? What if this was the moment when he declared he was going back to Australia? She slid the envelope towards herself and picked it up, swallowing a lump in her throat. 'Brendan?'

He nodded towards the envelope, making it clear he wanted her to open it. She undid the flap and peered inside. She saw the edges of a thin booklet inside, looking very much like an air ticket. Caroline let the envelope droop back to the table and gazed into Brendan's eyes sadly.

'You're going home then?'

'Take out what's inside.' He seemed very jittery, for him. He smoothed a hand over his black hair as far as his ponytail, and let his hand fall to his lap. Caroline pulled out the contents of the envelope. She examined what was in front of her and looked back at him in confusion.

'What's this? Eurostar tickets?'

'Yes.'

'To Paris?'

'Yes.'

'Why are you showing me?'

Brendan cleared his throat and sat up straighter. 'I want you to know this, Caroline. I have never been so bloody nervous in my life.'

Caroline stared at him. 'Why?'

'Because those two tickets are for us. To go to Paris.'

She knew that her mouth had dropped open, but she couldn't do anything about it. She examined the tickets again. They were still the same tickets. She turned her eyes back to Brendan's. Her astonishment must have been smeared all over her face.

'Brendan,' she managed faintly.

'One night in a plush hotel in the city of love. You and me. We go Friday evening, come back Saturday afternoon, so you can't even pretend you've got too much work to do over the weekend.'

'But . . .' her voice died. She swallowed again. The lump seemed to have got bigger. 'But Brendan, why?'

'Because,' he said firmly, 'if we don't, and I go back to Australia, we will never know.'

Chapter Eight

It was eight o'clock when Antonia finally got home. She slammed the front door behind her and heaved several shaky breaths. The smell of something delicious wafted through the hall towards her.

'Zat you Mum?'

She found Sonia hunched over the kitchen table with Daniel opposite her. They were both tucking into pancakes curled around some kind of tomato filling. Daniel gave Antonia what she imagined to be a sympathetic look, and said in a tone that she assumed was meant to be heartening, 'Back at last! There's sauce in the pan, and I can whip you up a pancake when you're ready.'

'Thanks Daniel. I need a glass of wine right now.'

Antonia poured herself a drink from the cold bottle in the fridge, and studied Sonia carefully. 'Was Imogen's mum happy about giving you a lift home from gym?'

'Course.'

'And she brought you right home, to the door, and saw you inside?'

Sonia sighed. 'Mum, I've got a key, and I do let myself in at times when you're not back before me. It wasn't a great event.'

'How's the car? Sonia told me what had happened,' Daniel said to Antonia tentatively.

Antonia flashed him an annoyed glance.

'Buggered, thank you. The A21 is not the perfect place to break down. And it was bloody cold waiting for the breakdown guys to turn up.'

'Yeah, what were you doing on the A21 anyway?' Sonia asked with a mouthful. 'When you phoned me you said you'd been to a pub in the town first, so why would you go that way to pick me up from gym?'

'I was burning rubber.'

'You were what?'

'I've just told you.'

'Well, excuse me for asking.' Sonia pulled a face.

'Did they come and collect it then?' Daniel asked with concern.

'Collected it, disappeared with it. I am now car-less for the time being. Which I personally thought added to the Good News database.' Antonia couldn't help it. She was utterly pissed off.

'How did you get home? You know, I could have come and picked you up, if you'd rung.'

'Thanks Daniel, but they dropped me off.'

Antonia crashed a few pans around on the draining board, and began to clear up. She needed to do something with her hands. Any minute now she was going to shout, and she knew that if she did it would be the kind of shout that would have everybody backing up towards the nearest wall.

When she'd left the pub, she had felt a thread of burning anger in her veins. Gerry had been the catalyst with his inane comments about good health and marriage, neither of which she was celebrating at that moment. But the anger had been brewing inside her for days.

She had to visit the hospital soon for further

154

investigation. She was scared, but she was fighting the fear with defiance. All that pent-up adrenaline had resulted in her screaming backwards and forwards on the A21, blasting her ageing car pointlessly up and down miles of tarmac just to gain the feeling of being in control of something. She'd wrenched the gearstick as if it was Gerry's throat. Somebody had to be a scapegoat. She didn't give a damn who it was, as long as the idea made her feel better about her life.

Then steam had started to erupt from the bonnet, along with a violent knocking sound, and the car had died on her. She'd steered it onto the hard shoulder, caught Sonia on her mobile to arrange her lift home from gym and got hold of the emergency breakdown service she subscribed to. This had to be an act of God. Someone up there was taking it out on her.

Now Antonia was wondering what on earth she was going to do about it. She'd got home, but the car had been dragged off to the garage. How was she going to get to her hospital appointment? Why would the car choose this moment to die on her?

A bowl she was gripping slipped through her fingers, flew into the air, and hit the floor. It smashed. Antonia jumped visibly.

'Christ, Mum!' Sonia put her hand to her chest. 'You nearly gave me a heart attack.'

'Sonia, go upstairs,' Antonia said under her breath. She didn't want to yell at her daughter. None of this was her fault. But she couldn't stomach teenage flippancy this evening.

'What? Me? What have I done?'

'Probably best to disappear for an hour or so,' Daniel intervened with a wink at Sonia. 'Why don't you go and

155

dig out that S Club Seven track you thought I'd like. I'll come and find you later.'

Sonia pulled a face at her mother. 'Don't break all the crockery. It's not like we're Greek or anything.'

'Go!' Antonia instructed, pointing at the door.

Sonia skulked off. Antonia smoothed her hair back, and stood up straight again. She took another large sip from her wine. 'Daniel, thank you for doing dinner for Sonia. I appreciate it very much. I realise it's not part of our agreement for you to step in when I'm otherwise detained.'

'Antonia . . . you can drop the formality,' he said. 'You've had a bastard of a day. You sit yourself down, and let me clear up this mess.'

'No, I—'

'Come on, chill out. Drink your wine, then have another glass, and by the time you look up it'll be spotless again.'

Too tired to argue, Antonia sank into the chair that Sonia had been occupying. While she sipped her wine and took deep breaths to calm herself, Daniel worked away quietly. He cleared the table, washed up, stacked the plates, and swept up the broken china with a dustpan and brush, while Antonia gazed at him from time to time, or ahead, or out of the kitchen window at the stark twigs of the rosebush swaying in the cold wind.

'Mind if I join you?' Daniel said at last.

'Thank you so much for doing that, Daniel,' she sighed. 'I'm sorry to be such a tyrant.'

'Can we talk like normal people?'

Antonia glanced around. 'You mean, normal for someone older than thirteen? I'm not a monolith, you

156

know, despite my job, but I've got a young daughter and inevitably it does affect the way I am at times.'

'She's not in earshot now,' Daniel said. 'So what the hell is wrong at the moment? Since I've lived here you've changed, and only in the last couple of weeks. Is there anything I can do?'

'There's nothing,' Antonia assured him.

He laughed. 'Can I sit down for a minute?'

'Yes, of course. I've got work to do in the other room in a bit anyway. Help yourself to a glass of wine.'

'No thanks on the wine, but can I say something?'

'Whatever.'

'You've got something on your mind. Something big, I'd say, something other than cars breaking down. You want to talk to me about it?'

'No, Daniel.'

He shrugged pleasantly. 'Fine with me.' He sat down at the chair opposite hers. 'So are they going to lend you another car while yours is in the garage?'

'Er, no. That's not part of the policy I took out.' She gave a short smile. 'I went for the economy insurance package, you see. And now I want to kick myself for being such an idiot. It's an old car. I should have known it'd blow up at some point.'

'Hmmn. Well, you're going to need transport to get yourself around.'

'Thanks Daniel, I know that. It's one of the things I'm going to think about this evening.'

'You can use my car.'

Antonia looked at him cautiously over the rim of her glass while she took another sip. The alcohol had relaxed her throat and chest, and was now settling pleasantly in her stomach. Daniel seemed to be quite serious.

'That's impossible. You wouldn't be able to get to work.'

'Not true.' He raised an eyebrow and put up a finger. 'Someone I work with lives just around the corner. We always arrive and leave at about the same time. I know he'd give me a lift in for a week or two while your car gets sorted. And when I go to London, I can get the train, and as it's not that often, I can just get a taxi to the station. Besides, I'm not planning to go up there for the next couple of weeks.'

'Oh, that's . . .' Antonia was embarrassed. She wasn't used to people doing her favours. Her husband never had been particularly inclined to, and certainly nobody had since her divorce. She didn't need favours, or ask for them, and she wasn't quite sure what to do when one was offered. 'That's silly. I can get to work from here. No need for you to put yourself out.'

'Right.' Daniel gave a low laugh. 'So, we're what, an hour's walk from the station? Then you get the train to work with all your bags full of a thousand folders, exercise books and textbooks and God knows what else, and an hour's walk when you get home. Then you need to be able to drive Sonia about at times. And you need a car for whatever else you normally do, when you're off doing out-of-school things in the evenings.'

'I know all that,' she said.

'You need a car.'

'Well I'll . . . I guess I'll hire one.'

'Hmmn.' Daniel drummed his fingers on the surface of the kitchen table thoughtfully. 'That's expensive.'

'Yes, but there's no alternative, is there?'

'Yes,' Daniel said steadily, 'there is. You can borrow my car.'

Antonia fingered the stem of her glass in agitation. 'I'm not insured for it anyway.'

'It's insured for any driver,' Daniel replied with a slight smile.

'Is it? Why is it?'

'Because when I lived in London my mum used to drive it too, and I wanted it to be available for a couple of my friends. I haven't changed the insurance policy. Simple as that. You can drive it without us even needing to inform anyone. All covered.'

'And what does your mum do for a car, now that you're down here?' Antonia asked curiously.

'My brother Emile sorted her out. I think I mentioned him. He's making some money. He's in IT, a consultant now. He bought my mum a neat little Polo. She loves it.'

'Lucky Mum. Lucky Emile,' Antonia murmured under her breath.

'Emile's Natalie's dad,' Daniel informed her. 'My thirteen-year-old niece, remember?'

'The one who worships you,' Antonia said drily. 'Yes, I remember you saying. Sounds like quite a houseful.'

Daniel scratched his head and fixed his eyes on the swaying rosebush. 'Well, it's not that full. Natalie's mother went back to live in Dominica. Didn't rate it here much. Emile visits her, when he's over there on business. But Natalie wanted to stay here. She loves her dad.' He paused, then added, 'Although Emile's got his own flat in Kensington. He's a busy guy, he's single, what the heck. Nat's happy, and she sees him whenever she wants.'

Antonia hadn't really been planning on asking Daniel for his family tree, but it was interesting, and it was a blessed relief to take her mind off her immediate

159

problems for a second. And the wine had now succeeded in making her feel much more mellow. She
stretched her legs out under the table and cradled her
glass in her hand.

'Doesn't sound as if you and Emile are much alike.'

Daniel smiled. He obviously wasn't going to say
anything in the least critical about his older brother.
Antonia hadn't been able to treat her own mother to
much. Just as she and Rick appeared to be making head-
way with their finances, he'd run off with a younger
woman, and that was that. He wasn't on a big income
himself, and she hadn't wanted Sonia to be caught in the
middle of a bitter alimony battle, so she had very little in
the way of maintenance. They mainly lived off what she
earned, and now Daniel's rent, and it left hardly anything to buy presents for anyone else. But then her
mother had become so negative in recent years, she'd
have probably turned her nose up at any present
Antonia might have offered her. She seemed intent on
being unhappy with the world. Even Christmas was a
nightmare, trying to find a gift for her that she wouldn't
verbally rip to shreds the minute she opened it.

Antonia felt a prod of guilt. What was she doing for
her own mother, in real terms? And life was slipping by.
Not just her mother's life, but now maybe her own too.
At the thought, tears suddenly pricked at her eyes, and
before she knew it, a dribble had run down her cheek.
She brushed it away quickly, standing up and tightening the hairclip at the back of her head.

'Phone,' Daniel said, putting his head to one side to
listen. Antonia glanced at him and found him studying
her face with interest. He'd seen the stray tear. So what?
She was human. It wouldn't happen again.

160

'I'll get it, it might be the garage,' she said. 'And thanks for your offer of a car, but I'm sure I can get a cheap hire for a short while.'

Antonia went to answer the phone before Daniel could argue about it any further. He stayed in the kitchen while she took the call in the hall.

It wasn't the garage. It was the hospital.

'Your mother has had a fall,' the charge nurse informed her. 'She's fine, we've strapped her up, but I'm afraid she's broken her wrist. She tells me that she lives alone. Will it be possible for you to come and pick her up?'

Antonia leaned back against the hall wall, staring at her pale face reflected in the mirror.

'Oh dear God, I wasn't expecting this. How is she?'

'The wrist is broken in two places. Apparently she slipped on an icy path at a parade of shops near her house. They called for an ambulance and she was brought straight here – that's why you weren't informed earlier. She said there was no need to cause a fuss. But I'm afraid we can't release her if she's going home to an empty house. She's not in a fit state to cope at this stage.'

'No, of course, I understand.' Antonia swallowed. 'Of course I'll come and pick her up. Please tell her not to worry. And I'll . . . we'll . . . I'll sort something out.'

David slipped his arms around Lizzy's waist as she was standing over the kitchen unit, prodding her home-made chocolate mousse with the back of a serving spoon. Bubbles of laughter drifted through to them from the dining room, where their four friends were carrying on happily without them. The sudden clinch made her jump, and the spoon shot into the mousse and flipped out again, sending a lump of it flying towards the sink. Lizzy giggled.

'Aww, now you've ruined my work of art.'

'Give me a kiss you sexy beast,' David growled into her neck, nibbling the sensitive skin there. He turned her around in his arms.

'You're pissed,' she laughed at him.

'Not nearly enough. I want to make love to my wife. When do you think we can politely tell this lot to shove off?'

'Not till we've given them mousse. They'll resent us for ever if we chuck them out without dessert. What are you in here for, anyway? You're meant to be playing the gracious host while I work my poor fingers to the bone in the kitchen.'

'Came to get some brandy.'

'We haven't got any brandy,' Lizzy replied.

'Oh yes we have. I bought some on the way home from work. Really good stuff too.'

Lizzy bit her lip. 'David, you shouldn't have done that,' she said in a hushed voice. 'We broke the bank buying nice wine. We can't afford brandy too.'

David drew back and studied Lizzy affably. His complexion, always robust and healthy, became a little flushed when he'd had a drink, and it made his eyes glitter like sapphires. Her knees weakened. But she was worried about the amount they'd spent on this dinner party. The people they'd had round were good friends, but they all knew each other well enough not to go crazy just for friendly dinners. None of them were rolling in money. And the boys were young, and there was so much to pay for. Jacob grew out of his clothes as quickly as Michael grew into them. It seemed they were always buying shoes for them, or trousers, or new coats. And that was before they bought them anything else.

'Why can't we afford it?' David countered. 'We've got to live, Lizzy.'

'Live, yes, but we can't go bonkers. What about the bikes we wanted to get them this year? Their birthdays come round so quickly, and I'm not earning anything to add to the coffers. We've got to be careful, David.'

'We are careful,' David said. He removed his arms from around her waist and rested them on his hips. 'How much more careful could we be?'

'By not buying brandy, and by buying cheaper wine,' she said. 'We could have had one or two nice ones to start off, but for the last hour, nobody's cared if it was Tesco's one ninety-nine or something you'd bought at auction for a thousand quid. We just have to be sensible, David.'

'We can't be so sensible that we're miserable all the bloody time,' he said, his cheeks reddening.

'We're not miserable,' Lizzy gasped back at him. 'How can you say that?'

'No, we're not,' he said carefully, taking her hand and squeezing it. He kissed her cheek for good measure. 'No, we're not miserable, I take that back and I'm sorry I said it. I just mean we could become miserable if we don't enjoy ourselves. We have to live.'

'I just want the boys to have the best. I thought that's what you wanted too.'

'Lizzy, I do.' David pushed a hand through his brown hair. It sprang back into neat little tufts that made Lizzy's heart soften. 'But we can't sacrifice our lives for them. We'll only end up resenting it.'

'I know, David, but if we're going to spend more, we need to earn more.'

'I do my best. I really do try, and you know I might be up for promotion next year. I know it's next year, but . . .'

'We could earn more money between us,' Lizzy suggested tentatively. 'I know we could. I could go out to work again, and we could maybe get a childminder. Mum or Aunt Stephanie might help us out if it got tricky . . .' she tailed away. David was frowning, and even as she uttered the words, she felt uncomfortable herself. Everybody made their own choices about such a difficult issue, but she and David had been mutually adamant about how they were going to approach the first few years of the boys' upbringing. She felt as if she was breaking their agreement in even suggesting an alternative.

'We said we didn't want to do that until they were older and settled in the first stages of school. Both of them. And until they were at an age where an hour or two with a childminder wouldn't mean so much to them.'

'I know,' she said quietly. 'It was just an idea.'

There was a pause. Lizzy felt the pull of conflicting emotions. She acknowledged the pact they had made when Michael was born, but that was four years ago. Her feelings were changing. At the same time she didn't want to row with David. By the way he looked down at the lino, he also felt awkward about their exchange.

'Are you unhappy, Lizzy?' he asked her quietly. 'Are you missing work? Is that it? Because I thought this was what you wanted.'

He looked so forlorn that Lizzy wanted to take his

pain away as quickly as possible. She put her arms around his neck and looked into his lovely eyes. 'No, David, I am not unhappy. Not in any way. I love my life, I love the boys, and I love you.' He looked so relieved that she tightened her grip on him and kissed him on the lips. 'There, see?'

'I believe you,' he smiled.

They stood interlocked for a moment, then Lizzy disentangled herself. 'I'd better sort out this mousse.' She went back to the unit and smoothed the spoon over the top of the mousse to cover up the big dent. She heard David opening one of the cupboards. 'Oh, and David?' She glanced at him.

He had the bottle of brandy in one hand. On instinct perhaps, he hid it behind his back. Then he seemed to realise that it was a daft thing to do, and held it in front of him again.

'I'm going to take the brandy in,' he said defensively.

What concerned Lizzy, apart from David's shifty reflex action of hiding his expensive bottle of brandy behind his back, was the expression on his face. It was one of extreme guilt. It stopped her in her tracks, appalled that she'd made him feel like that.

'It's not about the brandy,' she said.

'Oh?'

'No, it's about Brendan.'

'What about Brendan?' David relaxed.

'Brendan and Caroline,' Lizzy hinted, peering at him out of the corner of her eye while she dabbed at the mousse. 'It seems Caroline had a visitation from him this evening. She rang me earlier to tell me about it, but everyone was about to come round so we couldn't really talk. It seems that he's made her an offer she can't refuse.

Something that involves Paris. I wondered if you knew anything about it?'

A corner of David's mouth lifted into a smile. 'And if I did?'

She turned on him in mock indignation. 'If you did, why didn't you tell me, you horrible man?'

David shrugged, then, as Lizzy glared at him, began to laugh. 'Brendan's my best mate. If I told you what he was up to, you'd have told Caroline and ruined it for him.'

'So you did know?'

'I might have done.' David looked insouciant. 'Or I might not.'

'Oh bugger off and drink your brandy then,' Lizzy said, and, tutting to herself, set about finding the dessert bowls.

'Thank you again for doing this,' Antonia said to Daniel, as they left the car in the hospital car park and walked over the tarmac towards the main entrance.

'It's no problem.'

'I suppose we need to go in here.' Antonia indicated the entrance.

Daniel stopped before they went into the hospital, and touched Antonia's arm to stop her too.

'What is it?' she asked.

'I was just thinking,' he said. He looked cold, standing in the gloom, partially illuminated by sporadic lights on the Victorian hospital building. 'This changes things, from your point of view. If your mum's broken her wrist and she can't manage on her own, I guess you're going to have to bring her home with you.'

Antonia let go a breath that she'd been holding in,

166

probably since she'd got the phone call. 'Yes Daniel, I can't see any other way. I'm her only daughter, and there's nobody else. She'll have to come home with us. It's the least I can do to help her.'

'Okay, I'd figured that, but I'd also figured that it's not just going to be one night.'

Antonia felt her cheeks tighten. A chill wind ruffled her hair. 'Probably not.'

Daniel smiled at her, and patted her arm in a friendly way. 'Hey, don't get stressed out. I'm not trying to worry you, just to say that I know you'll need the spare room. So I can try and find somewhere else, that's all.'

'Don't be noble right now, Daniel. The last thing I want to think about at this moment is you taking off and me losing the income that comes from your rent. I didn't take a lodger out of sheer devilment, you know.'

'Sure, I know that. But where are you going to put your mum? It's a bit tricky.'

Antonia gave a sharp sigh. This was all too much to take in over one night. She wanted to collapse in a warm bed and not think about anything apart from her worrying smear test. That had been enough. But a broken-down car, and an elderly mother with a buggered wrist on top of that? It wasn't fair, that was all there was to it.

But Antonia knew that nothing was fair, no novelty there. Her husband leaping off with a sexy young woman and abandoning the family hadn't been fair. Their relationship not working, and him finding true love with a woman who made her feel haggard and past it when she was only forty-two and still attractive was not fair. The fact that Rick had probably, if she was agonisingly honest, now found the right woman for himself, whereas she was alone bringing up her daughter was not fair. But what could she do about things not being fair? Make a sacrifice to the God of Not Fairness? Expect to wake up tomorrow and find she was miraculously healthy, happy, and wealthy? Nope, this was life. It was reality. There was no time for self-pity. It had to be dealt with.

But as she studied Daniel another thought crossed Antonia's mind. The poor man had enough to cope with, lodging in a house with two moody females, fond of their own privacy and both adept at sarcastic quips. So far, he'd held up well. Add to that equation Antonia's irascible mother, and what man in his right mind would want to lodge in such a house?

'Oh I see. Oh, of course, I'm so sorry,' she said quickly. 'Of course this changes things for you. What a gruesome house to have to live in.' She rubbed at her forehead, trying to think clearly. Now she needed to make decisions. It was expected of her.

'No, no,' Daniel laughed. How could he laugh, standing there in the freezing cold, outside this grim hospital, knowing he was about to pick up a miserable old lady with a broken wrist? Antonia stared at him in amazement. 'I'm used to full houses,' he said. 'I've been brought up in one. My grandparents lived with us too, only sadly they passed away within a year of each other. I'm not worried about your mum coming to stay, I just don't know where you're going to put her.'

Antonia's shoulders dropped. She'd been hunching them, and hadn't realised it. She'd been thinking of the extra expense of looking after her mum and the bill that would inevitably arrive from the garage, on the back of losing Daniel's lodging money. At least if he stayed, she should just be able to manage the garage bill, and look after her mother. But she didn't want him to be swayed out of pity for her.

'Daniel, I can manage if you move out,' she said firmly. 'And I can imagine that you'd want to. I would, if I were you. I promise you there's no problem with that at all. This isn't a situation you expected when you moved in, and it's perfectly fair for you to find some-where more . . . peaceful.'

'I don't want to move out unless you need the room, in which case of course I will,' Daniel said, equally firmly. 'But I don't want to go. It suits me. Sonia and me like liming together.'

'Liming?' Antonia shot at him, startled.

He put back his head and laughed into the air. 'Limin'. Hanging out. Chilling. And I like you, I like my room, and it's great. Good rent, close to work.'

Antonia scrutinised him. 'I won't let you stay because you think I need you to.'

'You going to throw me out on the street?' Daniel pulled up his collar. 'In this weather? You're a hard woman, Antonia, to do that to a poor civil servant.'

She felt her lips twitch, despite her stress. 'We'll suck it and see, then. But if at any time you find this too much you have to promise me you'll tell me and we'll part on very friendly terms. Okay?'

'Besides, you don't know how long your mum's going to need to stay with you. You don't want to throw me out and find you've got an empty room again a few weeks later. You'll be sorry you cast me into the gutter then.'

'That's possible. I don't know how long broken wrists take to heal. I've never broken anything.'

'You don't count hearts then,' Daniel bantered as they started to walk towards the entrance.

169

'Huh. Not for a very long time, my boy.'

Audrey was sitting on a plastic chair in Casualty, her arm in a sling. Antonia spotted her mother as soon as they entered the area and paced up to her quickly. For the moment, all thoughts of room-shifting, expense and inconvenience flew from her head. Her mother looked small, vulnerable and very frightened. Audrey was a slight woman anyway, but she appeared to be shrinking into the chair, the bones on her face prominent, the strip light overhead making her scalp shine under the thin mesh of grey curled hair. She seemed to be off in a sad reverie, gazing through the walls and beyond.

'Mum!' Antonia said loudly, putting a hand on her shoulder. 'Why didn't you get them to ring me as soon as it happened? I'm very cross with you. I could have been here much earlier.' In fact, Antonia knew she couldn't have been there earlier due to spending nearly three hours sorting out a broken-down car on the A21, but her conscience made her fervently wish she'd been at the hospital with her mother from the first moment.

Audrey looked up with pale eyes that were once very blue but now seemed more grey. 'I've been here for hours,' she said. 'They put me on a trolley. Then they took me off and X-rayed me. Then they strapped me up in plaster.'

Antonia perched on the seat next to her and took her good hand. 'I wish you'd phoned me earlier, Mum.'

'It wouldn't have made any difference. I had to wait for hours anyway. You'd have only got fed up.'

'No, I wouldn't. I'd have liked to be here, to help you.'

'Yes, you would have got fed up. I know you. You'd have been bored,' Audrey said.

They stared into each other's eyes for a while, as if it

took a moment or two just to recognise each other in an alien environment. Knowing her mother's expressions so well, Antonia immediately saw a passivity there that wasn't characteristic.

'You didn't have any sort of anaesthetic, did you?'

'I don't know what happens next,' Audrey said.

Antonia bit her lip. 'Have they given you painkillers, or a sedative or something, Mum?'

'You never know when you're going to go,' Audrey went on. 'I thought my time was up. One minute I was outside the chemists. I'd just picked up my prescription for my blood pressure. I thought that would carry me off, you know, but I was there with those pills in my handbag, then boof! I went down like a ton of bricks.'

'You poor thing.' Antonia patted her hand and kissed her cheek. 'I'm sorry that happened to you.'

'And now I've got a smashed-up wrist.'

'Does it hurt?'

'Like hell,' Audrey nodded.

Antonia stood up. 'I'm just going to chat with a doctor about it, then we'll get home.'

'Oh good. I want to go home now.'

'My home,' Antonia asserted. 'I'm taking you back with me.'

'There's no need for that.' Audrey's forehead crumpled like a fan. 'I want to go to my home. Just drop me off, I'll be all right. I'm used to being by myself now. It's what I'm used to. Take me home, will you Antonia?'

Antonia looked at Daniel, who was standing near them but gazing across the room as if he didn't want to eavesdrop. Audrey wasn't being herself at all. She was never usually this benign. Would this be a good time to introduce her to Daniel? Her mother knew she'd taken a

171

lodger, but she'd never met him. In recent months, every time Antonia or Sonia had seen Audrey, it had been at Audrey's house.

'Mum, this is Daniel. He lives in the house with us too. You remember I said we'd taken a lodger? Daniel, this is my mother, Audrey Jackson.'

'Hello Mrs Jackson,' Daniel said. 'I'd shake your hand, but it looks far too painful and swollen for anyone to touch it. What a bit of bad luck you've had.'

'It's these icy pavements,' Audrey complained, looking up into Daniel's face. 'They don't salt them, you see. They don't have an obligation to salt them any more. That's what they said, the people from the shops, when they picked me up.'

Daniel slipped into the seat that Antonia had vacated when she'd stood up, and nodded earnestly at her mother. 'It's terrible, isn't it? My grandmother had a fall, a few years back, and broke her arm. A clean break, it was. That was on an icy pavement too.'

'She did?' Audrey seemed alert again. 'And did she have a sling?'

'Yep. Plaster like you, and a big sling. And she was in awful pain for a little while, but you know what? After it healed up, she could use it again as if it had never happened.'

'And how long did that take?' Audrey turned to face him anxiously.

'A lot less time than she thought when she first did it. She thought she'd never be the same again. She was so upset, I can remember her howling at night in her room. She felt so helpless. It was her right arm she broke, just like you've broken your right wrist. And you're a right-handed lady?'

172

Audrey nodded, drinking in every word. Daniel looked sympathetic.

'That's a really tough thing to happen when you're an independent woman. And by God, my grandmother was an independent woman. Hated to have a thing done for her. She wanted to be out there, blazing her trail, without any help from anyone. Then suddenly, bang, broken arm. She found it tough, let me tell you. She was a warhorse, that woman. Had six children, never was ill in her life, never complained – well, not much anyway – but when she broke her arm? I can tell you, I was living with the family, and we were all ready to move out.' Daniel stopped to laugh. 'But bit by bit, we understood. Because, she used to say, if someone took off your right arm, how would you feel?'

Audrey nodded vigorously. 'What did you say your name was again?'

'I'll just go and check the situation with the doctor,' Antonia said to them both, and headed off, only glancing behind her once to see that Audrey had taken Daniel's hand and was holding it.

Chapter Nine

Heather Martin closed the door behind Caroline, indicated the chair in front of her desk and briskly walked around it to stand at her office window. Beyond, energetic calls echoed from the netball courts and bounced out across the grounds to the fields.

'Please, do sit down and make yourself comfortable,' she reiterated.

'Thank you.' Caroline sat, feeling embarrassed.

Sitting in the headmistress's office took Caroline back to their first encounter. Weary of teaching at the further education college in south-east London where she'd been for some years, she had leapt at the chance to apply for a teaching post down in Kent, so near to her home and her beloved family. It was a grammar school, one of the last to hang on, and on walking into the school Caroline had instantly been struck by how well-behaved most of the girls seemed to be. Not the stuff of docusoaps and sitcoms at all. Then she'd wondered if Heather Martin would be from the traditional, tweedy mould, but she'd found her to be dashing, in her mid-forties, with a forward-looking agenda for the school which emphasized the importance of science and technology.

She'd bonded with Heather instantly. The head-mistress's short hair was cut into feminine flicks around her cheeks, she wore make-up well but not ostentatiously, and was dressed that day in a smart suit with the addition of a stylish pashmina around her shoulders. Heather had taken Caroline on a tour of the new science block, showing her the physics lab where she might have a chance to work. Perhaps it was the sparkle in Caroline's eyes as she wandered around the lab that had clinched the job for her. She'd never tried to hide her passion for her subject.

'All the physics teachers since I've been Head here have been men,' Heather had observed, her eyes smiling. 'I've got nothing against good male teachers in a girls' school. I think it's a healthy balance for the students. But it would help to inspire them in science to have a talented, enthusiastic physics teacher who was also a woman. That's my view. They need role models in this area. Somebody passionate, someone they'll remember as they make their way on in life.'

Caroline had started that September and had loved every minute of her job ever since. It made her feel all the more awkward to find herself summoned to the headmistress's office.

Now Heather adjusted the lavender silk scarf around her neck and cleared her throat. Usually they greeted each other with warm smiles, even if there was no time to talk, but today Heather was unsmiling and Caroline had a feeling that she knew why.

'I'll get straight to the point as I know you're busy. I've had a complaint from a member of staff regarding your conduct in a public place. The way it was put to me was that you were "bringing the school into disrepute". Not my words, but so that you know what the issue is. I'm obliged to bring it up with you as a result.'

Caroline's mouth dropped open. She closed it again,

175

her cheeks reddening. Of course she knew what this was about. 'I'm so sorry, Heather,' she said sincerely. 'I promise you it won't happen again.'

Heather turned from the window and met Caroline's eye squarely. She had strong features and a steady gaze. It was impossible to tell from that inscrutable look what she might have been thinking. 'Do you have something to apologise for, then?'

'I – I lost my temper with Gerry Bream in a pub. I'm well aware that there were no older girls from the school present, nor any parents that I knew. I'd thought the matter was resolved but apparently not. I'm very sorry he felt that he had to report it. I can only say that it was out of character on my part, and that I was as surprised as he was by my reaction.'

'I'll say.' Heather snorted suddenly, causing Caroline to look up. 'Anyone on my staff, practically anyone at all, might have thrown a glass of wine over Gerry Bream, but not you. What on earth did he do to provoke you?'

'I'd rather not go into details unless I have to,' she replied hesitantly. 'I put a note of apology into Gerry's tray and I had thought it was a private matter between the two of us.'

Heather let out a loud sigh and sank into her swivel chair, her cheeks dimpling. 'Which is all quite proper and how I'd rather it was dealt with. Gerry, Gerry, Gerry. I'm afraid he's the one who's decided it shouldn't be a private matter. I wonder why that is. Have you any idea?'

Caroline shook her head. 'All I will say is that he made some very personal comments about me that were uncalled for.'

176

'Hmmn, that's rather an understatement, I think.' Heather picked up a pen and twirled it between her fingers. 'From what Greg told me, I think he's lucky he got the drink without the glass. Yes, Gerry unwittingly let slip that Greg Watts was there, so I spoke to him. I trust him to be honest. So I think we can safely say that I've spoken to you about it, I'm quite satisfied that you were placed in a situation of extreme provocation and for that reason it was a one-off that won't be repeated. Okay, that's enough time wasted on Mr Bream's election tactics.' Suddenly Heather flashed Caroline a broad, knowing smile. 'Try not to let any friction show in front of the girls.'

'Of course not.' Caroline was horrified by the thought. 'I wouldn't dream of it.'

'I know that. You can go now.'

In the lunch break, in the staffroom, Caroline felt awkward when Gerry walked her way. Antonia was relaxing in one of the easy chairs drinking coffee and reading a paper, and Caroline had been trying to retrieve her beef and salad roll to take back to the science block with her. The last thing she wanted was a show-down. She had seen that her note of apology had gone from Gerry's tray, so he'd obviously read it. But there was no friendly acknowledgement from him.

Eventually Caroline had felt so uneasy about him standing so close to her, his breath whistling in and out of his nostrils as he ostensibly read the notice board, that she felt obliged to speak to him in a low voice.

'Gerry, I've seen Heather. I had hoped we'd keep this between us but at least you'll have got my note by now. I hope I've made it clear that I'm sorry for what happened in the pub.'

Gerry rocked on his heels, his chin in the air, refusing to meet Caroline's eye. 'My opinion is that cream rises to the top, Caroline. Detritus sinks to the bottom.'

She sighed. 'I'm not bidding for the Head of Science job. If that's what this is about, rest assured that I'm not interested in competitions.'

Gerry looked around, beady eyes hopeful. 'Can I quote you on that?'

'You can quote me on whatever you like. I just want to do my job well.'

He was already walking away with more of a spring in his step, and had left the staffroom before Caroline could consider ramming her beef roll into his face which, on balance, she considered just as well.

'What an arse.' It was Antonia who spoke up from her low chair. She'd obviously heard the exchange, although Caroline had been as subdued as possible.

'Oh it's nothing.' She tried to smooth things over.

'Nothing?' Antonia stood up and dropped the paper onto the seat of the chair. She raised an ironic eyebrow at Caroline. 'In my opinion I'd have been bringing the school into disrepute if I *hadn't* told him to fuck off for what he said, and I gather it got a lot worse after I'd left. I wish I'd thought of throwing my drink at him. I think that's inspired. Yes, word gets around, but you shouldn't worry about it. There's not a single member of staff who doesn't wish they'd had the chance to do what you did, and I think that includes Heather.'

As an early wintry twilight descended, Nina had been driving to Kent. The sky had faded from pale grey to dark grey, and finally to an inky black. It had been comforting in the car with the heater and some music on, and the engine humming in the background. Nina loved driving, which was partly why she'd been so happy to take on the job of a rep that involved driving all day. It made her feel more in control of her life. It also gave her the sense of moving on all the time, to something better. Just the sound of the engine revving cheered her up when she was down. Sometimes she wished she could just live in her car. She was safe and secure here. She didn't have to focus on what she had, or didn't have. There was a sense of belonging in a car. It was warm and cosy and transitory, and in a car you were the same as anybody else in their car. No homes, houses, relatives, connections. You could be whoever you wanted to be.

It was nice not to go straight back from work to the mouldy smell of the motel room. Now she had left the A21 behind her and was climbing a hill with a map open on the passenger seat and an address scribbled on a piece of paper on the dashboard. It was a pretty town, even prettier this evening as a mist was lingering and the streetlamps were glowing mutedly. It had a distinctly Tudor feel, with gabled houses and shops to either side. She had no phone number to go with the name and address, and when she'd rung directory enquiries she'd found that the person wasn't listed. She'd deduced that one of three things was possible. First, her relative had died. Second, her relative had moved. Third, her relative was very antisocial.

From the garbled description her mother had given her, Nina had at first thought that it was an elaborate wind-up. But it seemed her mother was determined to get her daughter out of her hair by giving her an answer to her ultimatum, and it also seemed that this was one of the few people she could remember being related to. Nina was quietly convinced that this couldn't be the only relative that her mother could remember, but perhaps it was the only one she could remember after a bottle of vodka. Perhaps it was because it was a very memorable person. Perhaps it was because it was one of the few people she had written down in an old address book, which also lent more credibility to the possibilities that the person had since either moved or died. Her mother seemed to have jotted down the address in one of her more lucid moments about twenty years ago, and from what Nina could glean, it was more that she needed to remember it if she ran short of cash than out of any fondness.

Well, she told herself, she wasn't intending to descend like a sack of flour and make a nuisance of herself. She just wanted to see who else was out there. It was preferable to admitting that she was to all intents and purposes an orphan, adrift in life with no attachments to anyone. At that thought, she took a very deep breath, and slowed to consult her map again. She'd bought a street map at a Tesco's garage on the outskirts of the town and had located the road she was aiming for, which at least assured her it was real. She'd also bought a bunch of flowers and some cakes. It was best not to turn up empty-handed, even if it was only to smile at someone and let them know that you existed before driving away again. She rechecked the name of the street she was on. Just ahead was a turning to the right. She located her position on the map and –

'Bingo!'

She turned off from the main road and followed a narrower road for a short distance before turning off again, this time onto what looked like a private road with a ribbed, concrete surface speckled with beige and brown shingle. The houses to either side were set back on rising slopes that drifted naturally up from the road like riverbanks from a stream. Each house seemed to be large and individual, amid thick clusters of swaying evergreen trees and burgeoning, mature bushes and shrubs. Perhaps night made them look more daunting, with the craggy black silhouettes stark against the evening sky and the lamps burning confidently outside as if declaring that each residence was a mansion.

Nina began to feel a little nervous. This did rather look like a rich relative who was probably very pleased to have become detached from her mother's side of the family. She was aware that her mother had gone wrong somewhere along the way, but how wrong she hadn't been able to tell, as there'd never been any contact with her mother's family since the death of her grandparents. She'd long resigned herself to there being no possibility of any relationship with her father's side of the family, as he'd fallen out with his remaining relatives before she was born. As her mother had told her on the phone that he'd gone to Spain on a driving job two years ago and had not been seen since, she was now certain that both he and his relatives were lost to her.

She slowed the car to a crawl and edged along the road, reading the names of the houses as she passed them. Then she hit upon it. Corona. It was a pretty name for a house. She steered her car up the slope of the driveway to the top, where there was a flat plateau of shingle in front of a garage, and stilled the engine.

'Don't be a wimp,' she urged herself, prodding the button to silence her music and reaching for the flowers and cakes. It was seven o'clock. Not late enough to be alarming. Not early enough to be presumptuous. She pressed the overhead light, flipped down the sunblind and checked her face in the mirror. She looked pale, but then she was pale anyway. Her hair was more frizzy than usual, which was annoying. A little more lipstick and blusher made her feel better, but she didn't attempt to drag a brush through her hair. The car heater had been blasting warm air at her and any attempt to brush her hair now would turn her into a human dandelion.

There were a couple of lights on downstairs in the house, which hopefully meant that somebody was in. If nothing else, she assured herself, it had been a pleasant drive that kept her away from the motel until she could get back and fall asleep. She took her flowers and box of cakes, locked up the car and crunched across the gravel to the front door. There was a diamond-shaped window in the door, with panes of varied colours. The name of the house was woven in wrought iron and attached to the wall. Above the porch was a yellowed light shaped like a lantern. It illuminated a press bell of the old-fashioned kind, with a domed button and round brass setting. Nina held her breath and pushed it, then stood back and practised her apologies.

'I'm sorry to bother you,' she rehearsed. 'I'm sorry to call on you like this. I'm sorry to surprise you. I'm sorry but you weren't in the phone book. I'm sorry but I'm afraid that I'm related to you. I'm sorry but my relative used to live here, it's obviously not you. I'm sorry for breathing.' She swallowed.

Time passed. Then she heard noises coming from inside the house and felt encouraged. She pressed the bell again, this time for a little longer. A shadowy figure loomed closer to the door and the nasal drawl of a Siamese cat emerged. There was some muttering on the other side and she felt very awkward. Then, suddenly, the door was opened.

'Yes?'

Nina stared at the old man, all words failing her. He took a few steps closer to the doormat and peered out at her. 'Hello,' she managed.

'Yes?'

'I'm – I'm Nina.' Her heart pounded inside her chest. What was she doing here? Why had she done this? She obviously wasn't welcome. She should go.

'Is it the church?' He wrinkled his nose.

'No.'

'I see.' They stared at each other for a moment longer. 'Well thank you for calling,' he finished politely.

'It's no problem.'

'Goodnight then.'

'Oh, hang on. I brought these for you.' She handed him the flowers and the box of cakes. He didn't take them. He seemed displeased.

'Is this some Harvest Festival type thing?'

'Sorry?'

'Harvest Festival.' He raised his voice, evidently convinced she'd been unable to hear. Perhaps he was a little deaf himself. Didn't people who were hard of hearing often shout? 'They always bring me strange things, like tins of apricot halves. I never eat apricot halves, and Perseus certainly doesn't.' He nodded down at the cat, sitting obediently by his slippered feet and eyeing her. 'I can't stand apricots. Never could, doesn't matter if they're dried, fresh or tinned. But they don't care. They think you want generic food in a tin, regardless of what it is. It's as if you should be grateful for any kind of nourishment once you're on the Harvest Festival list. I look forward to the day when the process of digestion is completed with a pill. That'll take the shine off Harvest Festival, won't it?'

Nina nodded obligingly as she attempted to regain her senses. 'Are you Roderick Vinnicombe?'

He craned his neck and squinted at her. 'Yes. Have I won something?'

'Well,' she laughed nervously. 'It depends on what you mean. I think you were my grandmother's brother.'

'Yes?'

'And – and that would make you my great-uncle.'

There was a very long silence, during which the Siamese cat wound itself round and around Roderick Vinnicombe's legs in such an insistent figure of eight that Nina felt as if she'd been watching a sparkler weaving a pattern in the night and was left with a burnt image on her retinas.

'Oh I see,' Roderick said finally. 'I see why you've brought the cakes now.' Although his words were very polite, Nina could see by his expression that he was at an utter loss as to why she'd called by.

'I just wanted to say hello. Here I am. I'm your – your great-niece.' Her smile probably looked strained but she couldn't help it.

'Well I'm not in the directory so you'd have to ring the bell if you wanted to say anything to my face. That's logical enough, I think.' He opened his eyes wide and took a big step back into his hall. 'You'd better come in for a cup of tea then, hadn't you.'

Nina entered into her great-uncle's house, acutely aware that her newly found relative was wonderfully

184

well-mannered, but had neither looked nor sounded the least bit happy to have met her.

Lizzy finally arrived, and Caroline let her in.

'Help! You've got to tell me what to do with Brendan,' Caroline appealed.

Caroline had rung Lizzy after Brendan had left her house. They'd had a hurried conversation as Lizzy was expecting some friends round and was trying to clean the children and get them filed away between the sheets before the doorbell rang, but Caroline had managed to put over the gist of it.

'I'm so sorry we're in a rush,' Lizzy had said. 'I'd call you back later, but I think we're going to be late finishing up here tonight. How about if I come round to you tomorrow night? After dinner, about eight? You can spill the beans all over me then. And,' she vowed, 'I'll torture David and see if he knows anything about this. I have vays of making him talk.'

'Okay, but make sure you do come round,' Caroline had said. 'I mean, of all things, this was not what I was expecting.'

It was now half past eight. For the last half-hour Caroline had been restlessly awaiting her cousin's arrival. She'd logged onto the Internet, checked out her regular astronomy web sites, scanned the SETI home page for updates, bookmarked a few other good sites, and all this had been done feverishly. What she really wanted to know was, why had Brendan suddenly sprung this on her? And what the hell was she going to do about it? She'd been pacing the hall when Lizzy had rung the doorbell and made her jump.

'I got some wine in,' Caroline said, leading Lizzy

towards the kitchen. 'Boy, do I need your advice. I'm in a complete dither which isn't like me at all.'

Lizzy followed Caroline through the house, and stood in the kitchen in her furry hat and coat. 'We're not staying in. I'm taking you out.'

'Out?'

'Yep. You're presentable enough. You might want to put some lippy on. And grab your coat.'

'Out where?'

'It's a surprise,' Lizzy said, reaching for her own lipstick in her handbag and handing it to Caroline. 'Humour me for an hour or so. I just need to get away from kitchens.'

'I can't wear this colour.' Caroline handed back the coral pink lipstick. 'All right, give me five minutes, I'll dash up and sort my hair out. But can we come back and talk here later? I don't really want to be overheard.'

'We'll only go out for a bit, then we can come back. Deal?'

Caroline changed into some khaki trousers she was comfortable in, boots, and a loose green sweater. She'd obediently fluffed her hair, put a dark lipstick on which suited her colouring far better than Lizzy's sweet-shop pinks (although they looked fabulous with Lizzy's golden hair), and a flick of mascara for good measure. They left the house together.

'Where are you parked?' Caroline asked.

'Oh, we're walking,' Lizzy said.

'Good idea. Maybe a few large drinks is what I really need. And it is nice to walk, even if it's freezing. The sky's more promising tonight.' It was dark, but the road was well lit with streetlamps. Caroline glanced up at the thin cloud cover over the stars. 'No snow

186

today. Maybe it'll even be clear for viewing over the weekend.'

Lizzy slipped her arm through Caroline's as she nudged her into a side road. Caroline walked with her. 'This way,' Lizzy said.

'There's nothing up here.' Caroline stopped. 'If you go for miles up here you get to a pub over the brow of the hill, but there are nicer pubs closer.'

'Just do as you're told, will you?' Lizzy urged Caroline on.

'What is this, Lizzy?' Caroline shot her a puzzled look. Lizzy kept her eyes straight ahead. 'Come on, you're being very mysterious.'

'Down here,' Lizzy said.

'Randolph Road? But this only leads back down to the main road. Unless you're desperate to pick something up from the newsagents, but he's probably closed by now.'

'God, you are difficult to boss about,' Lizzy laughed. 'Just keep walking.'

Lizzy stopped. They were only halfway along Randolph Road. Caroline watched her peer at a couple of front doors. 'Yes, this is it.' She took Caroline's arm and squeezed it tightly. 'I want you to promise me one thing, Caro.'

'What?' Caroline was beyond bewilderment. Lizzy was acting very strangely.

'Promise me that whatever happens, you won't be rude.'

Caroline frowned at Lizzy. Her brain ticked over quietly. They were in Randolph Road. The gardens of the houses in this street backed onto gardens of the row of houses she lived in. Lizzy had been looking for a house she'd been to before. They were now standing on the short front path. Then, at last, it fell into place.

'Oh, no, no, no!' Caroline retreated down the path. Lizzy sprinted after her, took hold of her arm with surprising force and dragged her back.

'Caroline, please. I've booked it. I want you to do this. Something really unexpected has happened and you need to consider all angles of it. You don't even need to be specific about it. You need to spend some time thinking about yourself and your life. Just an hour, here, then we'll go back and talk.'

'This isn't going to answer the bloody question for me, Lizzy. I'm big and ugly enough to make my own decisions.'

'I know that,' Lizzy assured her. 'Look at it as a bit of fun. Or maybe you might be able to put things in perspective. Even if you can't, it can't hurt, can it?'

'I am *not* about to have my love life decided for me by a hippy in big earrings and a headscarf with a fetish for joss sticks.' Caroline raised her voice assertively.

'He isn't like that!' Lizzy pleaded, half-laughing and half-growling under her breath as she bodily heaved Caroline back up the path towards the door. 'He's normal, you'll see. No earrings, no gimmicks. Just him, his jeans, a cup of tea and a chat. What on earth can be wrong with that?'

'Everything!' Caroline protested, wriggling out of Lizzy's grip. 'And besides, what have you told him about me already? If he knows we're cousins anything else will just be deduction from meeting you. It's pointless.'

'He knows nothing about you at all,' Lizzy stated. 'I merely rang him and said that I wanted to bring a friend along to meet him. That's all he knows. He doesn't even know you're my cousin. He wondered why my friend wanted to see him, so I told him you were really interested in astrology.'

'*Astronomy*, Lizzy. There is a slight difference. One involves the pursuit of knowledge, the other's complete and utter bollocks.'

'Sounds like a lost cause to me,' came a male voice.

Caroline turned around on the path. Lizzy had a firm grip on her cousin's scarf and had been heaving her towards the door by it. Neither of them had seen the door open. The fortune-teller seemed more of a shadow in the dim light of the doorway. Caroline swallowed, embarrassed.

'I'm sorry I said astrology was bollocks so loudly outside your house,' she said to him quickly, as Lizzy fixed her with a very severe look. 'As you see, Lizzy is determined that I should visit you, and I'm equally determined that I won't.'

Tom gave a low chuckle. 'Well since you're both here, perhaps you'd like a cup of tea anyway?'

Caroline crept up the path, closer to the door. That voice was familiar.

'Do I know you?' She squinted at the figure in the doorway.

'I wouldn't say you know me at all, no.'

'Tom, this is Caroline,' Lizzy interposed in a sweet voice. 'And we'd both love a cup of tea, thank you.'

'Tom?'

'Come in,' Tom said. 'Birdbrain, how did you get out?' He picked up a heavy-looking black cat and flopped it comfortably over his shoulder. He stepped right back into his hall and stood under the light. Lizzy

189

hopped inside, gesturing for Caroline to do the same. With the light on him, Tom's features were revealed. The dishevelled dark-reddish-blond hair, wide shoulders, quizzical eyes. Him again.

'You?' she said faintly. 'You're the fortune-teller?'

'And you're Lizzy's booking. Well, we just keep running into each other, don't we?'

Too dazed to do anything else, Caroline followed Lizzy into the hall.

'Could you close the door behind you?' Tom said. 'It's the cats. They go darting out towards the main road if it's left open.'

Caroline obliged, noticing as she turned round a stack of books lining one of the hall walls, framed paintings and etchings on the other. Some photographs too, but she didn't get a chance for a close look. He had a lot of things, far more than she did – or perhaps it was that he chose to display more of them than she did. As if he was less shy about sharing his tastes than she was, or perhaps he wanted more of a chance to savour them.

'Look, Tom,' she said, turning around again, but Tom had vanished, and she could hear noises in the kitchen.

'In here,' Lizzy called from the room that ran off the hall.

Caroline marched into the living room. 'Lizzy, don't make yourself at home here, please. We can't stay. You don't understand.'

'Look around. Isn't it lovely here?' Lizzy smiled, rubbing the head of a furry grey cat who was settled on a chair in the corner. It purred like a dialling tone in response.

Caroline glanced around the room. She saw an illuminated fish tank of pretty tropical fish. Books

190

everywhere, wall to ceiling in dark oak bookcases, in heaps around the chairs. An ornate rug. Magazines strewn across a sofa, itself covered with a throw. A lot of clutter. A handful of large globes, one very large one placed on the floor. The globes at least were interesting. Everything else was a complete mess.

'It's dark in here,' Caroline stated gruffly. 'And I swear I can smell joss sticks.'

Lizzy sniffed the air. 'I can't.'

'Well I can.'

'Curious. I wonder if he's trying to be more of a professional.'

'A professional what?' Caroline said, as damningly as she could.

'Keep your voice down,' Lizzy hissed. 'You promised not to be rude. You've already said that what he does is bollocks. Don't make it worse.'

'I didn't promise,' Caroline whispered back. 'But you don't understand, Lizzy. This man can't read my fortune. I mean, I know there are lots of Toms in this world. But, the thing is – this is Tom.'

'Yes, Tom, I told you—'

'This one,' Caroline hissed, 'is the same Tom as the Tom I thought—'

'Tea,' Tom said, arriving in the room. 'And please sit down. Somewhere. Anywhere. If you get rid of Zsa Zsa you could sit on that comfy chair in the far corner, Lizzy. Caroline, you might want to sit at the table?'

'The thing is—' Caroline began.

'Sit down,' Tom said assertively. Caroline looked at him in surprise. His eyes were smiling at her. 'I think Lizzy would like you to sit down. And so would I. This mug is hot and I can't hold it all night.'

Caroline sat. She accepted the mug of tea he offered and took a small sip. White with no sugar, how she liked it. Nothing psychic about that. He'd seen them all drink coffee at the hall. He knew she didn't take sugar. Although she had to admit that it was surprising that he'd remembered. But then, of course, he had an excellent memory. How else could he conduct 'psychic' readings, without remembering clearly his clients' reactions to what he said as he went along, and drawing obvious conclusions from them?

This evening with Lizzy was meant to be about discussing Brendan's bizarre invitation to Paris. What were they doing here? Caroline peered at Lizzy resentfully as she relaxed on the chair in the corner with the grey fluffy cat, who fell lazily over her lap.

For the moment, Caroline was trapped in Tom's house. By Lizzy's generosity in thinking it might help her, by a simple cup of tea, by the desire, despite her ruffled feelings, not to offend anybody. And, this was Tom. The last time she had seen him had been in the pub. Her eyes had been drawn to him. She'd allowed herself to acknowledge that he was a very striking male. Now she was in his house. She was, at least, curious to see how he lived, but somehow not surprised to see it was chaotic. It went with the hair, and with the tone of his voice. He probably didn't even notice the mess. Ostentatiously Caroline brushed an invisible cat hair from her trousers as Lizzy talked to him about the fish.

But if Lizzy was going to insist on this, and if Caroline didn't want to upset her, perhaps it was best to get it over with as quickly as possible, so they could go home and talk about the real issues? Caroline decided that the wisest option was to play along for a bit.

192

She sat up straight, rested her hands on the table and cleared her throat. 'I'm ready,' she told them.

'You'll do it then?' Lizzy said. 'Great. Do you want me in the room, or shall I wait outside?'

'Stay in the room, Lizzy.' Caroline glanced over her shoulder at her. She seemed very comfortable in the corner with the cat flaked out on her lap.

Tom sat down opposite Caroline. He'd brought his mug of tea with him. It was a Big Gay Al mug, from *South Park*. Caroline had raised her eyebrows at it before she could stop herself. Tom smiled.

'I thought you'd rather have Miss Piggy.'

Caroline looked at her mug, not too happy about his choice for her. 'Well go on then. Tell me things.'

Tom sat silently for a while. He sipped his tea. He looked at Caroline, assessing her from the tips of her hair to the ends of her fingers. It wasn't a personal look. It was rather like being X-rayed by a dispassionate machine.

'You're difficult to read,' he said under his breath. She looked at him sceptically in return, but bit her tongue. Lizzy maintained total silence and for the moment it was easy for Caroline to forget that she was there at all.

'So . . .' Caroline prompted after a few more minutes of silence.

Tom leaned back in his chair, and raked his hands through his hair. It flopped back into place instantly. 'I don't think I want to use the tarot. I'd like to see your hand.'

Caroline pulled her hands into her lap. 'Why?'

'So that I can see your palm. If you're comfortable with that.'

193

'And if I'm not?' Her gaze faltered. 'Does it involve you touching me?'

He looked straight into her eyes. Caroline drew back in her chair, a subconscious movement. Now it felt as if he was giving her a personal look, one that reached right down into her soul.

'Would that bother you?' he asked quietly.

She didn't answer. It was disconcerting. The more Tom looked at her, the more she felt she was giving personal information about herself away. She averted her eyes to stop it happening. But she found herself voicing a random thought. 'Have we met before? I mean, before the newsagents and the astronomy club. I've just got a vague idea that I know you from the past, but I'm probably wrong.'

'I wanted to ask you that.' A smile lifted one corner of his mouth.

'It wasn't meant to be anything profound,' she said curtly. 'I just wondered.'

'It's fine. I didn't think it was profound either. I just had the same impression.'

'Well that's normal,' Caroline said, rattled. 'People often have that sort of misguided feeling that they've met before, maybe because the person they're talking to reminds them of somebody they know, and the brain reacts, but the person can't place it. It's totally chemical.'

'Sure.'

'It's like déjà vu. People used to think it was completely spiritual, but more and more evidence points to the brain failing to place things in the conscious memory, but then drawing on the subconscious memory without the individual realising it. It seems like a vision, but it's not, it's a split-second memory of

194

something you saw only moments ago. You saw it, you just don't remember that you saw it, then you think it's a psychic experience.'

'Okay.'

'There is absolutely nothing that can't be analysed, and laid to rest as a unique action of the brain. Do you realise that diseases of the brain could cause people to behave suddenly and dramatically in a way that is totally out of character?'

Tom nodded.

'Caroline!' Lizzy issued in a reprimanding whisper from the back of the room.

Tom put a hand out across the table and rested it there, the palm upwards. Caroline looked at it. It was a hand with a wide span, with long, firm fingers, the knuckles marginally swollen.

'Would you like to show me your palm now?'

Caroline took a sip of her tea. It helped to break the spell. There was something that was really getting under her skin about him. His eyes were disturbing her too. They were peaceful, but, at the same time, very probing.

'And the point of me showing you my palm would be . . .?' she quizzed.

'That I want to see it.'

'Right. I'll show you mine, you show me yours,' she parried.

'Is that a challenge?'

'If you like.' Caroline pulled her chair close to the table, as Tom still rested his hand, palm up, there. 'Let me see. You have a curious mind, and you like to read a lot. You're fond of animals, particularly cats and fish. You've got a dog who likes to eat newspapers, and you're impulsive. You're the kind of guy who'd buy ten newspapers in one go, rather than one that you'll actually read all the way through, and a guy like you would turn up unannounced at astronomy club meetings. You have a friend with short dark hair, who drinks bitter in pints. And you've done a lot of manual work in your life, which is why your hands look a little red. How am I doing?'

Tom gave Caroline a whimsical smile. 'Not too bad.'

'Well there you are then!' Caroline said triumphantly. 'That's all there is to it. A few chance meetings, a few observations, and it's as easy as that. You actually get paid for this? Simple, but brilliant, if you ask me.'

If Tom had a retort for her, he didn't show it. He chuckled, drank some tea and looked very relaxed. 'May I see yours now?'

'Sure.' Caroline felt she was on very strong ground. No harm in showing him her hand and shooting him down for his trite observations. She put her hand out on the table top, uncurled her fingers, and revealed her palm for him to see.

'May I touch your hand? I need to get it in the right position, and in the right light.'

Caroline hesitated. She took another sip of tea to distract herself from her uncertainty. Then she set her mug down and putting on a bright voice, said, 'Yes, why not?'

'You need to relax it. Let your arm go loose. From the shoulder. That's it.'

Tom placed a hand under hers, so that hers was cradled in his. With his other hand he gently touched her, moving her fingers and running his thumb along the lines in her palm. His hair fell over his brow as he concentrated. She watched him probe the soft pads of her fingertips.

A sensation began to build in her skin where Tom was touching her. Her hand felt warm. It tingled in every area where his skin made contact with hers. The warmth began to creep up her forearm, to her elbow. She felt goose pimples rising right up to her shoulder.

'Well?' she said, pushing back the odd sensations, and finding a need to speak to break the spell once more.

'You're a very passionate woman.'

Caroline stared at him, astounded. Then she covered the fact that he had thrown her off balance with a quip. 'I bet you say that to all the girls.'

Tom gave a slight smile. 'I need to go a little deeper. Can I touch you again?'

Caroline nodded, compressing her lips. It felt extraordinary, being touched by him. Tom rested his right hand completely over hers, his left below it, so that her smaller hand was encased between his. He still seemed to be concentrating.

The heat shot into Caroline's body from her shoulder. It spread across her stomach, and into her solar plexus. Then suddenly her stomach did a flip, seeming to leap off into the air and leave her body behind, before it rejoined it. It was like a falling dream, where you stepped over the edge of a cliff. But it wasn't unpleasant at all. It was more like a ride in a funfair, where the cart did an unexpected dive up and over a peak, but left you wanting to scream and laugh at the same time. But Caroline, once she regained her senses, was alarmed by it. She pulled back her hand quickly. 'I think that's enough.'

Tom looked up at her intensely. 'What did you feel?'

197

'Nothing,' Caroline lied. She stood up, then not wanting to be dramatic, drained her mug of tea, and hesitantly sat down again, careful to edge her chair away from the table.

'Nothing?' Tom said.

'No, I just felt you'd held my hand for long enough. And if you haven't got anything to tell me, we'd better call it quits. Don't you think?'

Tom drew in a very deep breath and let it out slowly. He gave her a self-conscious look, more poignant, as if they'd shared something private but both were too embarrassed to discuss it.

'Caroline,' he sighed. Then he relaxed in his chair and crossed one knee over the other. 'If you really want to go now, then of course, do.'

'Yes, I will. Thanks for . . . everything.' Caroline stood up, on edge. She darted glances to the fish in the tank, to the globes, the table, back to Tom sitting watching her. 'I still don't know why you're interested in the astronomy club. Seeing this, knowing you're Lizzy's fortune-teller, why would you come to our club? It doesn't make any sense.'

Tom looked surprised. 'I'd have thought that was obvious. Because I want to understand.'

'Understand what?'

'Many things.' He paused before adding, 'Everything.'

'Well . . .' Caroline struggled, pulling the belt of her coat around her waist in a gesture of finality. 'I'm not sure you've told me anything, but thank you for your time.'

Tom looked uncomfortable. He fingered the ends of his twisted mop of dark blond hair. 'You've got something on your mind that's very personal and you need to talk about it, but you can't discuss it with me.'

'Why couldn't I discuss it with you?'

'There are choices you have to make for yourself. That's the way of things.'

'What choices?'

'Please don't push me on this. It's not something I've dealt with before.'

She was trying hard not to get into schoolteacher mode, but this was like trying to extract a confession from a difficult pupil. She pushed him further. 'Tom, you can't just hint at things in this vague, mysterious way without explaining them.'

'You've got a fork in the road. You have to choose which way to go. One way will make you happy.'

'And the other?'

'The other won't.'

Caroline absorbed this, but was further confused by it. 'And why on earth couldn't I have talked to you about that? This is your speciality, isn't it? Forks in roads?'

'This is different,' Tom said. He stood up and opened the living-room door for her, making it clear that he was showing her the way out. When they were close to each other, she glanced at him.

'How is this different?' she asked him under her breath.

He returned her gaze for a few seconds, but he seemed to have drawn a blind down over his expression. She could see light, but no detail there. 'Aren't you going to take Lizzy with you?' he asked.

Caroline was astonished to realise that she had forgotten that Lizzy was there.

'Yes, of course.' She covered her disquiet smoothly.

Lizzy was perched on the edge of her chair, staring at Caroline and Tom with wide eyes and an open mouth. The cat was splayed out upside down on her lap. 'Lizzy? I think it's time to go?'

'Yes,' Lizzy said in an automatic voice, standing up in a daze and heading out of the room. She passed Caroline and Tom and opened the front door before either of them could get there.

'Goodbye, Caroline,' Tom said.

Lizzy and Caroline wandered home in silence. When they got into the kitchen, Lizzy said vaguely, 'What happened there?'

Caroline poured them both a glass of wine. 'I'm really not sure.'

'That was nothing like my session with him. Nothing like it at all.'

'It's not what I expected either,' Caroline said.

'When he touched you,' Lizzy said as she slid into a chair, 'you jumped away, as if you'd had an electric shock or something. It was so strange to watch. What happened?'

'I just . . .' Caroline took a sip of wine. 'Probably just that I'm not used to my hand being gripped by strange men.'

'But it wasn't as if you were strangers. The way you talked, the way you looked at each other. Do you think you have met him before, then? Years ago, when we were at school down here, or something?'

Caroline pondered, imposing rational thoughts where she could, but struggling. 'No Lizzy, I haven't met him until very recently. I'm quite sure of that.'

'But you said—'

'I haven't met him before, Lizzy,' Caroline said firmly. 'That is certain. There was a brief moment where it felt like I had.'

'You know who he reminds me of?' Lizzy pondered, taking off her furry hat at last and laying it carefully on Caroline's clean table.

Caroline sat up briskly. 'Well, not Brendan, that's for sure, and that was what tonight was supposed to be about. I can't believe Tom's just taken over our evening like this. It's really annoying.'

'Ah yes, Brendan. Yes.' Lizzy sipped her wine. 'No, it's Granddad.'

'What is?'

'Who Tom reminds me of. But I can't think why. And I was going to give him the wind chimes as a present, I thought he'd like them, but I completely forgot. So he's done it for free again. Poor guy. I'll drop them round.'

'He is nothing like Granddad,' Caroline interjected emotionally. 'Nothing at all.'

Lizzy put out a placatory hand. 'No, I'm sure you're right. So . . . Brendan, then. Brendan and Paris. Brendan and you. What to do?'

Chapter Ten

'There is no point in you helping to put things away with only one hand,' Antonia said, taking a plate from her mother and directing her out of the kitchen. 'Go and sit down while I clear up.'

'I can't just sit around.' Audrey wandered back into the kitchen as soon as her daughter had turned back to the draining board. 'I'm restless. I don't sleep well in your bed. It reeks of that strong perfume you wear. It makes me cough.'

'Should sleep in my room with me then, Gran,' Sonia said, leaning into the freezer and pulling out a tub of ice cream.

'Sonia, that's for later,' Antonia ordered. 'Put it back.'

'I'm hungry!'

'We've only just eaten lunch.'

'You snore, Mum,' Sonia said with impeccable timing as Daniel arrived to peer into the kitchen and offer Antonia a friendly smile. 'I thought it was bad enough through the wall, but you nearly knocked my ears off. I hope you're not going to be in my room for long. I'll never get any sleep.'

'I will be in your room for as long as Gran needs my room.' Antonia took the ice cream forcibly from Sonia, as she had opened it and stuck a spoon in the top, and put it back into the freezer. 'And seeing as I'm letting you have the bed and taking a mattress on the floor, I think you'd better thank your lucky stars, or I'll change my mind.'

'If we swap and I sleep on the floor, do you promise to stop snoring?'

'Is it time for my pills again yet?' Audrey said, reaching for a cup from the draining board.

'You can't dry up with one hand, Mum, please just sit down,' Antonia said firmly. 'And you've just had your pills. You don't have any more until this evening.'

'Look at my blue fingers.' Audrey eyed her fingertips morosely. 'Sonia, look. The blood supply's completely cut off.'

'Shit, they're going purple.'

'Language!' Antonia barked. 'Watch what you say, Sonia.'

Antonia edged around her mother and daughter as they stood beside the sink and compared fingertips. The kitchen was small anyway, so trying to get to cupboards when everyone was intent on standing in her way was impossible. Daniel chose that moment to sneak in and attempt to get to the counter at the far end.

'Oh well, I'll tell you what,' Antonia declared, slamming down the frying pan she had been washing and sending splashes of warm water up the tiles. 'Why don't we all try and get in the bathroom? No, there must be a smaller room in the house that we can all squeeze into. I know, the cupboard under the stairs. And let's get Norris McWhirter down here to witness our world-record attempt.'

Daniel looked apologetic. 'It's my mobile phone. I left it over there.' He pointed gingerly at the counter. 'Then I'll get out of your way.'

'I can't go to bed again. I can't sleep anyway,' Audrey said, her lips turning down. 'I'm in shock.'

'Course she's in shock, Mum,' Sonia defended her grandmother boisterously. 'And stop being such a bitch to her. You're not the one with a broken wrist.'

'Don't use that word to me, Sonia,' Antonia advised her with steel in her voice. 'If you want a birthday party, you'd better be on your best behaviour.'

'I'm not a child, Mum.' Sonia's cheeks flushed an angry red. She cast a self-conscious look in Daniel's direction. 'I'm nearly fourteen. Don't talk to me as if I was a little kid.'

'All right, other room, now,' Antonia instructed. She left the washing-up and walked calmly through to the living room. It was a command her daughter was used to. Ever since Daniel had entered the house Antonia had been attempting to keep their private squabbles as private as possible, for everyone's sake. Sonia was at a sensitive age and didn't like to be shown up. Antonia didn't like any scenes to take place that would make Daniel feel uncomfortable. Sometimes it couldn't be helped, but she tried her best to avoid them.

Sonia joined her in the living room, her eyes glowing. 'Don't talk to me like that in front of everyone,' she stated in her defence. 'It's totally humiliating.'

'Sonia . . .' Antonia took a deep breath and let it out in a measured way. She composed herself, and offered a smile. 'All right, here's the deal. Nothing's fair at the moment. We're all on edge. It's our first weekend together in the same house. For Gran's sake, and mine, and Daniel's, and yours, we all need to keep a cool head.'

'Yeah, and we all are, apart from you,' Sonia pointed out.

'Do you know what my first thoughts were when I brought Gran back here to stay with us?' Antonia quizzed her daughter, who looked flushed. 'I thought, damn, this is going to upset Sonia's birthday plans. And I want my daughter to have a lovely birthday. I didn't think Gran would be able to cope.'

'She can cope. She's said so. She wants us to have the party.'

'Yes, I know,' Antonia soothed. 'What I'm trying to explain is that my first thoughts were for you.'

Sonia looked down at the carpet and sniffed.

'So,' Antonia continued, 'we're going ahead with the party tomorrow night, and I want it to be fun. But you've said yourself that you're not a child. You're a young woman now. Nearly fourteen. I need you to act responsibly, and to help me keep things under control.'

Sonia offered a shy smile. 'I'll be fifteen next year.'

'It'll follow soon enough.' Antonia put out her arms. 'Come here.' They hugged, Antonia touching Sonia's soft hair and ruffling it gently. 'You know I love you, and I'm sorry if I embarrassed you. It's all been a bit unexpected, and I'm trying to deal with it, just as everyone else is.'

'You don't like Gran much, do you?' Sonia said into Antonia's chest.

Antonia paused in her hair-ruffling. 'Yes, of course I do. I love her, she's my mum. Why would you say that?'

'You're not very nice to her.'

Antonia sighed, rocking her daughter in her arms. There was so much that Sonia didn't know, that she didn't particularly want to dig up and explain. Audrey had caused Antonia a lot of hurt, at a time when Antonia had needed her to be there for her with open arms and a

205

hug. Instead, she'd found her mother harsh, distant, didactic in her opinions. She and Audrey had never been close, but Antonia had felt more alone than ever at that time. She'd never got over it.

'I don't mean to be unkind to her. She's not well and she's had a nasty shock.'

'Gran says you drove Dad away,' Sonia said quietly.

Antonia closed her eyes so that she could think before she reacted. Audrey had adored Rick. She'd shown more loyalty to Rick during their difficulties, and ultimately their split, than she had towards her own daughter. Antonia thought she knew why. Rick was the ideal husband. The ideal husband that Audrey had never had for herself.

'Sonia, there's one thing you'll understand a lot better as you get older. Relationships are unique experiences between two people. Whatever other people think they see on the outside, they can never know what the private situation is. What happens within a relationship is personal, and only the man and woman involved understand what's really going on.'

'Fine.' Sonia rested her cheek on Antonia's shoulder. 'So what does that all mean?'

'It means that Gran doesn't know what happened between your dad and me.'

'I do. I used to hear you through the walls, or when I was in bed.'

Antonia tutted. 'No, you don't know. Even the things we said to each other weren't true, we were just trying to hurt each other. The fact was that we just weren't right for each other. That's what it came down to.'

'Did you push him away? I heard you say that once.

Go and live with her then, or something like that, and he did.'

Antonia swallowed back the hurt. The rejection had been hard to take. What does a woman do when a man she's forged a life with falls desperately in love with someone else? His mind is already made up. Rick had already mentally left the house, got in his car and driven away before he even told Antonia about his feelings for the woman he'd met. She'd known, even as he'd confessed to his awkward situation, that she was looking at the tyre marks he'd left behind.

And the truth was, she'd known the relationship to be lacking even from the beginning. They'd never found the spark that she heard others speak of. She'd thought it wouldn't matter. They had things in common, they liked each other, at times had fun, and then they had a daughter. It was comfortable, pleasant, easy and warm. But they weren't in love. She knew it, he knew it, and all it took was for Rick to discover that magic with some-body else for their marriage to pale into insignificance. At least he'd been honourable about it, she believed that. Rick was an honourable man, the last person she'd thought would ever have an affair – and he never did. He did something much worse. He found the love of his life.

Whatever anger, pain, resentment or shock Antonia had felt when the reality was thrust in front of her, she had found a way to deal with over time. She found it hard to be offensive to Tasha, or even about her in her absence. She'd just turned up and provided the answer to all of Rick's prayers. They were happy together, and they'd been solid ever since their relationship had blossomed openly, and since their subsequent marriage.

207

God dammit, Antonia even quite liked Tasha. She could certainly see how happy she made Rick, not just once in a while, but all the time. There was nothing Antonia could do about it then, or now, even if she'd wanted to.

'Hey, you get on with Tasha well enough, don't you?' she asked Sonia.

'Yeah, she's fine. She tries hard. Too hard, sometimes, it gets on my nerves. But she's quite good fun. It's not like it's you and Dad though. That would have been much better.'

'But not to be, my love. That's what it comes down to.'

'Okay.' Sonia pulled away, and smoothed down her hair. 'Do you think you'll ever meet anyone else, or are you going to be a spinster like Gran?'

Antonia's lips twitched despite the bleak imagery placed before her. 'Gran's not a spinster, she's been widowed, and I'm not a spinster either.'

'What about Daniel?' Sonia's brown eyes probed her. 'Mind you, I did hear him talking about some woman in London. I reckon you have got competition after all. I think he might be shagging about a bit in his spare time.'

Antonia laughed. 'Don't use that language in front of Gran, for heaven's sake. Daniel is young. And he has his own life. Don't you dare try to match me up, young lady, I'll make up my own mind about things.'

'It's a shame though, isn't it? Daniel but sort of bigger would be good.'

'If I ever meet someone else it'll happen naturally. And if I don't, I really won't mind,' Antonia said with absolute honesty. 'I've really got enough to think about at the moment. Whatever might happen, I can tell you for sure, Sonia, that it's not going to happen any time soon.'

The hotel was about ten minutes' walk from St Germain des Prés. The narrow lanes were dotted with curious shop windows. Bookshops, antique maps, cafes, more cafes, simple restaurants, foreign restaurants, some quite standard stores. Caroline spotted a tiny branch of Dorothy Perkins. All seemed happy to be hunched up against each other. They fitted together, each component unique and with a personality all of its own, like individual pieces of a complex jigsaw. The smell of Paris was everywhere. Crêpes, coffee, a sort of burnt-rubber aroma that Caroline still had in her nostrils from their journey from Gare du Nord on the metro. It was somewhere between nine and ten at night and the restaurants and bars were bustling.

Caroline could hardly believe it. She was here, in Paris, with Brendan. How Lizzy had finally managed to talk her into doing this she wasn't sure. She and Brendan fancied each other, Lizzy had starkly pointed out. That much was apparent to everybody. They were consenting adults, both single, nobody was going to get hurt. What the hell was stopping them from fulfilling themselves? Plus, Lizzy had said airily, it would seem daft to turn down the opportunity of a free night in Paris. A change of scene was just what Caroline needed. Having sex with a man as attractive as Brendan was just a bonus, had she looked at it that way?

The thought gave Caroline a thrill of anticipation. When she pictured the reality of sleeping in the same bed as Brendan, her skin prickled. But on the other hand, so far she'd been much less apprehensive than she'd anticipated.

Their Eurostar journey had felt more as if they were

gliding towards Paris than arriving on a train. Brendan had bought a bottle of champagne and they'd drunk it, chatting amiably, the fun of the impulsive trip so far dominating any feelings of panic on Caroline's part. There was an advantage in having known each other for so long. There were no secrets, no surprises, they were friendly with many of the same people and conversation had been easy and unforced.

Now they were strolling through the streets and Caroline still wasn't alarmed. Perhaps there were just too many distractions. Brendan stopped outside a smart but cosy-looking hotel, with window boxes crowded with diminutive shrubs and pretty plants. It looked friendly and full of character.

'I wasn't sure if you were expecting the Paris Ritz.' He eyed her uncertainly. 'In the end I was convinced it was the Left Bank for you.'

'Definitely.' He was right on that count. It was by far her favourite part of Paris.

The foyer was neat, laid out with comfortable arm-chairs and plants, with a sparklingly clean marble floor. It was even smarter on the inside than it had looked on the outside, and Caroline noticed as they stood at the reception desk that the hotel notepaper laid out there had four stars on it. The receptionist greeted them instantly. Caroline's eyes grew wider as the young woman rattled away at them in French. She realised with horror that her own French was much rustier than she'd thought. Hopefully Brendan would now point out that they both spoke English, and as she could hear another receptionist further down the counter having a conversation into the phone in impeccable English, that obviously wouldn't be a problem.

But instead, Brendan answered her in French. Brilliant French, from what Caroline's fuddled understanding could identify. She stood, dumbstruck, while Brendan joked away – what he was saying was anyone's guess – the receptionist laughed, and seemed to say, *'D'accord, Monsieur Morrant,'* a great deal. He signed something and she handed them a key, smiling broadly at Caroline.

Then Brendan led Caroline away, around a corner, and towards a lift. There was a soft ping and the lift arrived.

'So you just forgot to say that you speak fluent French then,' she teased.

He laughed, took Caroline's bag, and they got into the lift. 'My French is awful. I never got to grips with the grammar. But I can talk, yes. I do *l'argot* quite well.'

'Is that something with snails in it?'

'Slang.' The lift stopped at the third floor, and they got out. They walked along a corridor, up a few steps, along a bit, around a corner, and stopped at a door. The carpet was plush, the corridor tastefully lit, and there were watercolours hanging on the walls. Brendan opened the door to their room.

'I never knew you were an expert on French slang.' Caroline drifted into the room, still too amazed by this revelation to register that she was now, without worrying about it, doing what she'd avoided doing for seven years. Walking into a bedroom with Brendan. 'Where did you learn it?'

He put down his bag, then threw himself on the bed, landing with a thump and laughing up to the ceiling. 'Don't ask unless you really want to know.' He put his hands behind his head and gave a contented sigh.

'I do want to know. I'm curious,' she said, putting her

bag down too, and stopping to look around the room. It was very big. It had a double bed, a television on the wall, a minibar, a table, an en suite bathroom, and a sofa. There was a tall window, and they were at the front of the hotel, which would mean they'd have a view over the street. She had to admire his taste. 'Is this place a Tardis? It didn't look this big on the outside.'

Brendan lay on his side, and propped his head on his hand. 'I learnt the French I speak from an ex-girlfriend.'

'Oh. That's okay,' she said. He was giving her a searching look as she pulled aside the net curtains, glanced at the street, and turned back to him. 'What? Did you think I'd be worried that you'd had a French girlfriend?'

'Well, it didn't strike me, until you asked that. I've never thought twice about mentioning an ex to you before.'

'Then why should you be worried about it now?'

'I don't know.' Brendan pulled himself up, and sat on the edge of the bed. 'I honestly don't know. I just hesitated before answering you.'

'Well, you shouldn't.' And yet, answering him confidently, Caroline did feel odd. Not so much odd that he'd mentioned an ex-girlfriend, but odd that he'd felt awkward about it. 'Look, there's very little that I don't know about you already. It's – well – it's quite unusual in these sort of circumstances. So you mustn't start making up reasons to feel awkward.'

'There's a lot you don't know about me.' He stood up, and gave her an admonishing look. 'Now, I'm cold, and you look cold too, after that walk, so I suggest we both warm up with a shower, or bath, or whatever you want, and then get out to somewhere cosy for a slap-up dinner.'

'Both in the shower?' Caroline heard a slight quaver in her voice. 'Would you mind if I dash in first?'

He shook his head at her, any tension he may have felt disappearing from his face. He laughed. 'I wouldn't have dreamt of inviting you into the shower with me.'

'Okay then.' She slipped off her jacket, threw it on the bed, and jauntily grabbed her bag and headed for the bathroom.

'Yet,' he added. And turning round, she saw that he was winking at her.

They walked all around the Left Bank, being beckoned into the Greek restaurants opposite Notre Dame, pondering over Spanish and Italian fare, their mouths watering at the Lebanese and Moroccan menus on another lane, finding a restaurant for whatever food fancy they could possibly nurture.

'We really should eat soon, I suppose,' Caroline commented as they both eagerly headed off down yet another cobbled alleyway in search of second-hand bookshops for more window-shopping. 'I just can't stop exploring. One night's so little time.'

'I guess a one-night trip's meant to be more about exploring *inside* the hotel room.'

Caroline slapped his arm playfully, her cheeks warming. 'And yet how could you do that, knowing you were in Paris?'

'Well, I probably could force myself,' Brendan said, but she was already shaking open the street map and showing him where she wanted to go next.

They found themselves at the Panthéon and from there, Caroline was aglow with ideas. 'The Sorbonne's all around here. It's surrounding us,' she enthused, leading Brendan off down a series of long roads as he wrestled with his own pop-up map he'd brought along to make her laugh. 'Look at it. Faculties everywhere, and the ornate face of this building. *Astronomie*,' she found, reading the lists of disciplines carved into the magnificent stonework.

'I hate to hurry things,' Brendan said, rubbing his fingers together. 'But if we don't eat soon everywhere will start closing. And I'm flipping freezing.'

They retraced their steps as far as they could, Brendan grabbing Caroline's arm as she threatened to disappear down yet another undiscovered alleyway, and finally found a restaurant on a sloped lane behind the Panthéon that wasn't overflowing with students.

They ate a four-course meal and drank wine liberally. Try as she could, Caroline could not stare meaningfully into Brendan's eyes, although she kept feeling she ought to. Every time he touched her hand or smiled at her, she found herself thinking of something else to say about Paris, and before long they'd got out maps and notebooks and were plotting what to do the next day before they were due back at Gare du Nord. It had ended up with a confused but good-natured verbal wrestling match, Brendan bidding for Montmartre over the Louvre and Caroline finally conceding that they couldn't do both in the time they had, not if they wanted to take a river boat too.

'It wasn't quite the romantic meal I had in mind,' Brendan said with a laugh under his breath as they paid the bill to the yawning waiter and left.

'But you enjoyed it, didn't you?' Caroline shot him a concerned look. 'I did. Wonderful steak, and the mussels were out of this world.'

'Had a fantastic time.' He took her arm and threaded

it through his as they set about a long, brisk walk back to their hotel. 'I could only ever have a good time with you, you know that.'

Caroline was talking so much all the way back to the hotel, in the lift and as they let themselves back into their room that, once again, she forgot to be nervous. They both huddled over the radiator, giggling, and rubbing their fingers to get warm.

'Now I know why people normally wait till the spring to come to Paris.' Caroline shivered.

'I can think of a way to get warm,' Brendan said, giving her a coy look.

So this was it, she thought. Any moment now she and Brendan would be making love. Her stomach jumped at the thought. And now, for the first time since she'd decided to come with him to Paris, she felt a strange reluctance. It went beyond embarrassment. She suddenly wanted to preserve the innocence of their friendship for a little while longer and treasure its simplicity.

'Brendan, I –'

'Shh.'

He approached her and kissed her lips gently. His skin felt cold upon hers, and she shrieked when he slipped a hand under her jumper and touched the warmer skin of her waist.

'I'm sorry. Your hands are just too cold.'

'I'll go and warm them up in the bathroom.' He gave her a world-weary look. 'Don't run away.'

'I won't.'

Brendan closed the door after him, and Caroline eyed the soft bed covetously. Her legs were aching from all the walking, her limbs stiff with cold. The duvet looked so large and enveloping. She slipped off her clothes, down to her underwear, and edged herself into bed. The moment she had, she closed her eyes in ecstasy. Her head touched the pillow.

'Caroline?' she heard a soft voice some moments later. 'Hmmn?'

'Caroline, it's half past eight in the morning. If we want breakfast we need to go and grab it now.'

'You're back again?' Roderick said as he opened the door.

Perhaps he didn't mean it to come out quite so bluntly. On the other hand, perhaps he did. He was dressed in a heavy woollen coat and a long scarf, looped several times around his neck and dangling unevenly to the floor. A black furry hat was perched on his head, giving him the debonair appearance of an ageing cold war spy. It seemed he was either just about to go out, or had just come in.

'I was just passing,' Nina said. 'You remember I said I drive with my job? That I'm down this way a lot?'

He looked aghast. 'Yes?'

'Well I just wanted to say thank you for the tea the other night. I enjoyed talking to you very much and it was good of you to invite me in.'

'Yes?' He was obviously nervously anticipating more.

'Well, and I brought you these.' Nina held out a tin of apricot halves.

Roderick took the tin and examined it, his eyebrows bristling, while Nina stood clenching and unclenching her fingers inside her gloves. It was an achingly cold night. He turned the tin over in his hands, then looked at her bleakly. 'These are for me?'

'Yes, but they're not really apricot halves. It's actually a cat food treat for Perseus. A gourmet meal, no less. I just took the label off and put this label on from another tin instead.' Roderick seemed baffled by this. 'With Pritt,' she went on lamely. 'As a joke.'

'Oh. Oh, a joke, I see.'

'It was because of what you said about hating the Harvest Festival people for giving you apricot halves.'

'Yes, yes, I see.' Was there a glimmer of a smile there? She waited in hope. 'Thank you. Perseus will be delighted.'

'Right, well.' She pressed her fingertips together. 'And it was really just to say that I'm staying near here at the moment. I was staying in Berkshire you see, at a motel but it wasn't a very nice one, and I liked it around here so I thought I'd change hotels, and I've found one that isn't too bad. It's only temporary because things are a little uncertain for me at the moment but it's not as bad as it sounds and I'll get settled somewhere soon, I'm sure of it.' She nodded at him, hoping for a response. 'It's gorgeous in Kent, isn't it? I hadn't got to know it around this way before, but I like it.'

'I see,' he said politely.

'So that's it really. And I've got a card here with the name and phone number of the hotel on it. I've written my room number there.' She pressed it into his hand. 'So that's for you and if you ever need anything at all, you just give me a call. And here's my business card too. That's got my mobile number on it and I'm always available on my mobile. Or you can just leave a message and I'm always picking those up so I'd be back to you in an instant. That's if you need anything, you know.'

Roderick looked very puzzled. 'I'm not likely to need

anything, my dear. I appreciate you are trying to be kind, but I am very self-sufficient.'

'Of course you are. I realise that,' she assured him.

There was a long silence. Perseus yowled from inside the house and appeared in the hall, picking his way over the carpet like a ballerina.

'Well if you'll excuse me then, I'm just about to do some viewing and I need to make the most of the time.'

'Of course,' Nina agreed, confused. Viewing what? 'I – if you're going out, would you like me to give you a lift? My car's just here. I mean, obviously it is, I didn't walk here.' She should stop trying so hard, she winced to herself. She sounded idiotic.

'I'm going into my garden,' he explained loudly. 'To do some viewing.'

'Viewing?'

He squinted at her and she remembered her impression that he was hard of hearing. 'The winter Milky Way,' he told her, watching her face for a sign of understanding.

'Oh, that kind of viewing! Stars and things. How. . . how . . .' He waited for her verdict. She wished she hadn't started a sentence she couldn't finish. She knew nothing about stars and things. 'How . . . pretty.'

'How what?' He shuffled forward and cupped an ear.

'Pretty.'

'I don't know about pretty.' There was another pause and he said, 'You're not very scientific, are you dear?'

'Not really. I do read a lot though. Especially novels.'

'Ah, I see. Novels. Yes.' He checked his watch. 'Forgive me, I would ask you in but it is peak viewing time for the work I want to do this evening and things will be at their best.'

'Oh that's no problem.' Nina started to back away, smiling. 'I completely understand. I'd be just the same if I was viewing. You wrap up warm and don't get cold. I mean, I don't mind hanging about and watching if it wouldn't bother you . . . but I'm sure it would bother you. I'd upset your concentration I'm sure and I wouldn't want to do that.' He didn't respond to her plea so she let it die on the chill air and enthused on. 'That's so – so great that you have a hobby like this. Something you're passionate about. Lovely. A nice hobby. I'll have to think about that. Just what I need, in fact, to take my mind off things. Or rather to put my mind on things that are more worthwhile. You've got me thinking now.'

'Hobby, did you say?' He craned his neck, somewhat offended, then drew himself up tall, even his furry hat seeming to bristle with pride. 'I'm the founder member and president of the astronomy club.'

'Oh, you are?' Nina was suitably impressed and nodded vigorously to demonstrate that fact. At the same time she found her car keys in her handbag and jingled them at him to assure him she was on her way. 'The local club, that is?'

'Just here, in the town. That's our club. It's small but it's very good. Our people are very good.'

'That's lovely.'

'And I am the president.'

'Oh yes, I see.'

'Well goodnight then, my dear.'

Nina walked back to her car, waving. 'I hope Perseus enjoys his gourmet meal.'

'And please don't think you have to keep dropping by like this. I'm quite all right. Have a safe journey home.'

He'd already closed his front door by the time Nina

was back in the driver's seat. She fired up the engine, twisted the heating button to full and put her music back on. A safe journey home. Such a simple expression that people said to each other all the time. As she drove away from the house, she was quite convinced that Roderick, delightful as he was, hadn't listened to a single word she'd said.

By late Saturday evening, Caroline was sitting with Greg in the Raj Bari.

'So let me get this straight,' Greg said. 'You've been to Paris and back since I last saw you.'

'Yes.'

'With an attractive man who you like, who you shared a bed with and yet you *still* didn't manage to have sex with him.'

'I'm hopeless, I know.' Caroline dunked a lump of naan into some chutney and picked at her meal again. She still couldn't quite believe what had happened herself. She felt refreshed, invigorated, and as if her batteries had been jump-started by their whistle-stop tour, but despite everything they had not even come close to having sex.

'You couldn't do it in the morning?'

'We had to go to Montmartre, the Rue de Rivoli, and to Notre Dame to find a river boat before we picked our bags up from the hotel again in time to get the Eurostar.' It seemed obvious to Caroline.

'What's any of that got to do with having sex with Brendan?'

'Well,' she struggled. 'There wasn't time.'

Greg snorted. 'Only you could go to Paris and say that there wasn't time to make love.'

Caroline sighed loudly. 'And the fortune-teller said I was passionate. I think he's completely wrong.'

'Whoa! Hold up,' Greg laughed. 'What fortune-teller? You saw a fortune-teller? Tell me I need my ears syringing.'

Caroline pondered. 'Actually, he was in the pub that evening we were there with Gerry.' They both paused to shudder at the mention of Gerry's name. 'You wouldn't have noticed him but—'

'Not the tall blond good-looking one you kept staring at?'

Caroline frowned. 'I didn't keep staring at him.'

'You did actually. He's the fortune-teller? How come you went to see him?'

'It was Lizzy's idea. You know my cousin? Well, it was a nice thought, but completely misguided,' she said, finishing off her tikka masala. 'Lizzy and I think so differently about things at times, you wouldn't believe we could be related. This man has half a dozen cats and some sort of enigmatic dog that I've never seen.' Caroline sought for words, gazing around the Indian restaurant for inspiration. Her eyes alighted on an illuminated fish tank partitioning the two spacious dining areas. 'And he's got fish,' she told Greg, nodding meaningfully.

'Brendan's got fish? Makes a change from thrush I suppose.'

'No, not Brendan.' She shook her head. 'Tom the fortune-teller. He's got a huge tropical fish tank in his front room with loads of tiny electric blue fish darting about, and one big fat yellow one with frilly fins. And there was some crab thing with spindly legs crawling along the bottom.'

Greg dabbed his mouth with his napkin. He gave Caroline a funny look. 'And what did you deduce from the presence of tropical fish, Sherlock?'

Caroline put out a hand expressively and tried to think of the right phrase. 'It's the sort of meticulous, vaguely inappropriate attention to detail that your average psychopath displays.'

'Or perhaps he likes beautiful things,' Greg suggested helpfully. 'Or, as you said he's got cats and a very shy dog, perhaps he just loves animals.'

'Fish aren't exactly animals.'

'No, Caroline, but neither are they suspension bridges. They're animate, alive, and vital. I can understand keeping fish. I had a goldfish when I was about ten. Loved it.'

Caroline abandoned her angle on tropical fish, scooping up the last of the bhindi bhaji with a piece of naan. 'All right then, globes. Lizzy went on about the globes, just because he has quite a few, and I've got one or two. Doesn't everyone have a globe somewhere in their house? It's just normal, isn't it? My mum and dad have got one, upstairs. I kept seeing second-hand shops on the Left Bank displaying antique globes. I suppose Tom would have been in there like a shot, buying them all up. Okay, there was one I rather liked but we didn't have time to go back. You see? Everyone's got a globe.'

Greg laid down his knife and fork, took a sip of his Coke, then rested his elbows on the table. 'I haven't got a globe.'

'Exactly.' Caroline put down her cutlery with an air of finality. 'So what's Lizzy talking about?'

'More to the point, what are *you* talking about? I guess the whole business of seeing a fortune-teller really agitated you, eh? Or perhaps it's the stimulation of Paris. Must be a bit of a shock to be whisked there and dragged back again all in the space of twenty-four hours.'

'Well I do have a fair bit of momentum now, even though I'm knackered,' Caroline nodded. She shuffled back in the cushioned seat and relaxed a little. 'Yes, it did agitate me.' She fell into private musings.

'And I suppose the Brendan proposition was quite enough to handle, without tropical fish to deal with as well,' Greg said in a deeply sympathetic voice. 'I mean, tropical fish. Just when the world's turning upside down, that's what you get. I can just imagine how you felt when you saw those fish. Like, "Oh great, I could have guessed. Just my luck, a fish tank." It's too much, isn't it?'

Caroline shot Greg a look. His eyes were dancing with amusement. He covered his mouth but it was too late, and he snorted with laughter. 'I'm sorry, it's just so unusual to see you rambling on like this, I don't quite know how to handle it. And you're not even drunk.'

Caroline watched Greg laugh at her, shifting uncomfortably in her seat. She fiddled with her cutlery, placed it back neatly where it was, and considered him again.

'Let's talk about your love life, then. I think we've done my situation to death.'

'No.' Greg was firm. 'Brendan. What are you going to do?'

Caroline tried to fix an image of Brendan in her mind. She could remember the intensity of his dark eyes, the questioning expression on his face in their hotel bedroom when he'd said he was going to warm his hands, his rueful smile the next day when she'd got her map and notebook out over breakfast, the kiss they'd shared back home in Kent. A warm kiss, not a passionate one.

'Well?'

'Brendan, Brendan, Brendan,' she muttered, scratching her head.

'You know, Caroline,' Greg said, his eyes serious, 'I think this stream of consciousness about the fortune-telling guy has been some kind of denial about how much this trip to Paris has set you off balance. I think it's because you like Brendan a lot. I hope I'm not out of place in saying that.'

Caroline gazed at Greg over the pink tablecloth and empty plates while the noise of the restaurant buzzed around them. She did like Brendan. Very much. 'It's okay.'

'I mean, obviously you've mentioned him before a few times, when you've been talking about Lizzy, or something you've been up to. I feel I know a bit about him already, and about how you feel about him.'

'You do?'

'It's the sort of thing a friend notices. It's been clear to me you quite fancy him. That's why you get frustrated with him being a womaniser.'

'Well, I –' Caroline was going to deny it. What was the point? What was the merit in spending the evening taking up Greg's time telling him about her Paris trip if she wasn't honest about a few small things? 'Yes, I do quite fancy him. There, said it. Don't tell Lizzy, or anyone else if you meet them, for God's sake.'

'Because you don't want to look like an idiot if he loses interest in you, as he does with most women after five minutes.'

Caroline bit her lip. 'Correct.'

'And you'd like to have got passionate with him in Paris, but you think he might use and abuse you.'

'Well, not abuse exactly.' Caroline wriggled uncomfortably. 'I mean, two consenting adults with no expectations can't exactly use *or* abuse each other, can they? And it is true that there wasn't time.'

'So what's the problem?'

Caroline sighed. 'The problem is, I don't want to lose a friendship.'

'Not scared you might fall in love with him, are you?'

She frowned. She put her elbows on the table, her chin in her hands, stared at Greg, and frowned even more severely. 'I don't think so. Do you think that's what it is?'

'No,' Greg laughed. 'Absolutely not.'

Caroline sat back, relieved, but bemused too. 'Really? How can you be so sure?'

'You're not in love with Brendan, Caro, nor are you ever likely to be.'

'And why not?' she laughed at him, feeling a weight lift from her body, like a rain cloud being sucked away, up into the sky out of sight. 'How do you know I'll never be in love with Brendan?'

Greg chuckled as the bill arrived. He swiped it from Caroline, and threw his Visa card onto the saucer. 'My treat – a reward for all the entertainment you've given me this evening. It's been riveting.'

'Okay, thanks,' Caroline conceded. 'I'll get it next time. But you still haven't answered my question.'

'Call it instinct,' Greg said. 'Tell you what, if I'm wrong, and you do fall for him, you can blame me for giving you rotten advice, okay?'

225

'Okay,' Caroline said uncertainly. 'So what's your rotten advice?'

'Next time he whisks you away, make sure you actually have sex.'

Chapter Eleven

Lizzy was in the spare room, delicately placing a tiny triangle of balsa wood into her complex picture. She had tweezers in one hand, angling the insert towards her masterpiece, the fine nozzle of the tube of wood-glue in the other.

The door burst open and made her jump. The glue blobbed onto one of the little wooden figures she'd made, turning its face into a glutinous dome.

'Oh *bugger.'* She glanced up in irritation at the intruder. It was Jacob, his eyes round at her outburst. She softened instantly. 'Come here, darling. Let me show you something.'

Jacob crawled up onto her lap and looped an arm around her neck. He hung there like a chimpanzee.

'See what I'm making? A picture. You know when you're drawing, you hate it when I tell you to clear up, because you just want to get on with it? I'm a bit the same. So you have to just knock on the door, or yell, "Can I come in" or something so that you don't make me jump. Can you remember that?'

Jacob obediently hollered, 'Can I come in!' into Lizzy's ear.

'Ideal. So is Brendan here yet?'

'He's just got here. Daddy says we're going now.'

'Okay, I'm coming down. You go right ahead.'

Lizzy cleared her tools carefully to one side, sure to

227

lock any sharp implements into a small metal box she'd bought for the purpose. The kids were about to go out with David and Brendan for the afternoon, but she was in the habit now of putting everything away whenever she left the room. All it would take was for Jacob or Michael to lunge in here when she was on the loo, or downstairs making a quick cup of tea. She'd already had the appropriate cold sweats at the thought of either of them grabbing something she was working with and perforating themselves with it. David was usually very attentive when he was in charge of the kids, but it was impossible to watch them every single second.

It had been David's idea to take the children off her hands, leaving her a Sunday afternoon to herself. It turned out that he and Brendan had planned to spend the afternoon up at the Biggin Hill airbase, wandering around. They usually made it to the annual air show, but there were plenty of light aircraft and flying schools up there to fascinate anybody with an interest. And it was only a few miles up the road. Lizzy knew of David's passion for planes, of course. It was a boys and toys thing. He'd been watching his fighter-pilot videos, playing out his fantasies, lusting after the flight-simulation computer games, for years. It was another thing he and Brendan had in common. They could talk for hours about Messerschmidts and Spitfires. It meant nothing to Lizzy, but it was great that she and David had their own enthusiasms that they could enjoy independently. She'd never thought that having every interest in common would have made their relationship any better.

She went downstairs and found David and Brendan helping the kids into their coats and boots. She stopped to admire the image Brendan created for a moment. He was sitting on the hall chair, in his jeans, a chunky suede jacket and DMs, with Michael balanced on his lap. He was carefully edging a little red wellington boot onto Michael's foot.

She knew that he and Caroline had been away, but when she'd phoned her cousin last night she'd got the answerphone. Today she was waiting for Caroline to call her and give her the low-down when she was ready. Lizzy was optimistic. He and Caroline could have fun together. And deducing what she could from the scene she was looking at right now, Brendan turning his fingers into a spider to run down Michael's leg while he shrieked with delight, Lizzy guessed that thoughts of fatherhood couldn't be far away either. Caroline would be such a fantastic mother, if only she got the chance to be one. It would be such a perfect resolution, for Caroline and Brendan to hit it off.

However, she had promised David faithfully that she wouldn't let on that she knew anything about the Paris situation to Brendan. David had insisted that Brendan needed his private space, to woo Caroline if that was his desire, without Lizzy's ham-fisted, if sweetly meant, interference. So Lizzy greeted Brendan warmly as usual, and tried very hard not to let it show in her eyes that she knew perfectly well that he'd been away for a dirty weekend.

'Hey there, Lizzy,' Brendan said, lifting Michael up and turning him upside down while he squealed and giggled. 'How are you, gorgeous?'

'Good, and yourself?'

'Pretty good. Has Caroline told you about Paris yet?'

Lizzy looked straight at David. He smiled at her, and shrugged. 'I guess that's direct enough. We probably all

229

know you and Caro far too well. You tell each other everything.'

Lizzy sat down on the stairs and gave Brendan an impish grin. 'Well, I might know something about it.'

'Course you do. Has she phoned you since she got back?'

Lizzy shook her head. 'She was out last night, but I'll call her later today.'

'Right.'

'Did it go . . .' Lizzy began tentatively. 'Okay?'

'We packed a lot into twenty-four hours. The calves of my legs feel like they've been pulverised.'

'That sounds promising.' She raised her eyebrows.

'By which I mean we did a lot of walking,' Brendan said philosophically, but his eyes seemed full of disappointment to Lizzy.

'Oh,' she breathed. 'She didn't get all logical on you, did she?'

'She certainly applied logic to her map of Paris. Allrighty.' He turned towards the front door. 'I hope you don't mind me borrowing your husband for a couple of hours.'

'Of course I don't,' Lizzy laughed. 'I want to get back upstairs and make my funny cards, as you call them. It'll give me a few hours of peace. Just don't lose my children in a hangar somewhere.'

'Scout's honour,' Brendan smiled. 'Okay Davey boy, shall we make tracks? I want to get up there and poke around while the light's still good.'

They bundled out of the door with the children, Brendan carrying a chortling Michael over his shoulder like a sack. Jacob's hand was gripped by David's as he trotted alongside his dad. She shut the front door, and watched their shadowy figures through the frosted glass as they disappeared. The car doors slammed, the engine started, and they were off.

For a moment Lizzy felt left out. The house was suddenly eerily silent. The children's coats hung like mementoes on the hooks, a few stray pieces of Lego were strewn around the hall carpet. A chewed-up plastic aeroplane, a football nudged into the corner, under the coats. Boys' things. She really was utterly surrounded by boys. How might things have been different, if her little girl had survived? David was such a straightforward sort of man, who loved his straight-forward male pursuits. Could he help it if he wanted to share them with the boys? She had her own input too. She was trying to make sure it was all balanced. Would David have run off to Biggin Hill with their little Elizabeth?

She considered for a moment, waiting for the sadness in her stomach to grow, as it usually did. But as she stood still, the feeling evened out. It was as if her spirit normally did a bungee jump when she thought of the little girl they'd lost, but now, for the first time in ages, the piece of elastic was shorter, and it took less time for it to spring back into place. And of course David would have taken his little girl to see the aeroplanes. It was just that she hadn't got the evidence in front of her eyes. But he would have done, with just as much enthusiasm.

But this silence, it was so hard to cope with, and she wanted to do something to break it.

'You're going to need to borrow my car,' Daniel said, as he appeared downstairs. Antonia was in the kitchen, Sonia drifting around, peering into the fridge and various cupboards. Audrey was watching television in the living room. 'I've arranged to go out with some friends for a bit this afternoon, but they're going to pick me up and drop me off. I'll leave the keys here for you.'

'Oh?' Antonia looked at him in surprise.

'You'll have things to get. For the party later. You're bound to have forgotten something.'

'That's kind of you, but I think we've got most things here, and if not, there's always the local shop.'

'But Mum, it's all rubbish,' Sonia said. She flopped into a kitchen chair disconsolately. 'I know you said I could make a chilli, and you've got all the stuff, but what about dips and nibbles and things? There's nothing exciting.'

'We're not having dips,' Antonia said firmly, thinking of the estimate she'd just received from the garage. The amount had shocked her. She'd politely asked them if they were planning to pull her car apart and rebuild it as an Aston Martin.

'What about drinks?' Sonia pouted. 'We've only got Coke and a couple of other boring fizzy things.'

'What else do you want, Sonia?' Antonia quizzed her.

'Punch? Or beer, or cider. At least something with a bit of kick. I mean, we might as well all play pass the parcel and go home with a bit of cake and a balloon. I'll just put my frilly frock and my shiny shoes on, shall I?'

'I'll hazard a guess you don't even own a frilly frock.' Daniel raised his eyebrows teasingly at her, and Sonia smiled, squeaking the toes of her trainers on the floor.

'You're thirteen,' Antonia told her gently. 'And so are your friends. I'm not exactly about to set up an open bar, am I? And when I asked you about chilli last week, you said that was great, and that you wanted to make it, and we agreed on it. I'm going to do that topping with mashed avocado and soured cream you like for it as a treat. I've had the avocados ripening on the window sill all week. How about that for planning?'

The avocado relish was one of the things Antonia had thought might make her economy party meal seem a little more exotic. That and the fortune-teller she'd booked. He sounded all right on the phone. Pleasant enough, a bit distant, but she'd expected that. She'd been quite surprised when all the girls' parents had thought the idea of the fortune-teller theme would be fun. She'd thought at least one or two of them might baulk at it, but it seemed the girls had been working hard on their parents, assuring them it was all in jest, so the result was a win for Sonia. Fortune-teller it was – on the condition that it was all public, all light-hearted, and that Antonia kept a close eye on the proceedings. Anything too deep, and he'd be out the door. The parents trusted her, she knew, in the knowledge that she was a teacher of teenagers herself. She took that responsibility seriously.

'I'm fourteen on Tuesday.' Sonia slid her arms onto the table and rested her chin on the surface. She let out a long sigh. 'I want Daniel to be at the party, but he won't be,' she said at last.

Antonia glanced at Daniel. She'd been assuming that he'd be around that evening, not least because he and Sonia got on so well, and Sonia had hinted that a couple of her friends fancied him. She'd left him alone to decide for himself whether he'd be there, knowing it would have come up during the one-to-ones he and Sonia often shared. He looked apologetic.

'Sorry,' he said softly. 'I've promised to visit Emile and Nat this evening.'

233

'Daniel, please don't worry about it,' Antonia said. 'I never expected you to be at Sonia's party, and neither did she.'

'I did,' Sonia whispered. 'Mum, I really want Natalie to come to my party.'

There was a silence. Antonia fiddled with some things she'd been organising on the kitchen counter ready for Sonia to make her chilli. She leaned back against it, folded her arms, and gave her daughter a knowing look. 'Do you, now?'

'Yes.' Sonia sat up straight, wide-eyed. 'You don't know everything that goes on here, you know. Daniel's told me all about Natalie, and I'd love to meet her. She's only a bit younger than me too. She'd really like the party. Why can't she come?'

Antonia appealed to Daniel with her eyes. 'Help me out here.'

Daniel chuckled, rubbing his hands over his head with an air of weary resignation. 'Well, it's a fact that Sonia's been telling me she'd love to meet Nat. I can't say that isn't true. But tonight's not the right night, I'm sure. You've got, what, six girls coming round? And your mum? And some sort of prophet?'

Despite herself, Antonia smiled. Sonia was canny. And it seemed as if Daniel really did regret that he wasn't going to be at her party. It was, knowing him, entirely possible that he was planning to slink away purely out of consideration for Antonia. She'd have quite liked him to be there. He was good with the girls, didn't have the responsibility of being a parent, and it took some of the pressure off. Especially as Audrey's mood that evening was going to be an unknown quantity.

'Daniel, you know that you and your niece would be welcome to join in. That's not a problem at all, I just didn't think of it. But it's such short notice.'

''S'not,' Sonia said. 'All he's got to do is ring Emile up and tell them to come. Not as if it's miles away.'

'Emile?' Antonia said. Of course, Natalie was Daniel's niece, and for her to get here would involve his brother driving her down. That was putting another person out at short notice.

'Forget it,' Daniel smiled. 'It's complicated, Sonia. The last thing your mum needs right now is to be introduced to strangers. There's enough going on at the moment.'

'But if they don't come, you won't come,' Sonia complained.

'All right.' Antonia put a hand to her forehead. 'Here is my executive decision. If, for any reason that I can't imagine, your brother and niece are masochistic enough to want to come to my loopy daughter's birthday party, they are genuinely welcome. But as for the logistics of it, that's something I'll leave you two to sort out. If they show, they show. If they don't, another time. Is that fair?'

'Antonia . . .' Daniel looked worried, as if he'd imposed on her.

'Trust me,' she said earnestly, 'it won't make any difference to me. We're making a huge chilli, the fortune-teller's booked for a group, we've got enough fizzy stuff, and if we haven't I can send Sonia out this afternoon to pick up some more. I've got a couple of bottles of wine to soothe adult nerves, and I'm expecting it all to be over by at about ten, half past ten at the latest. If you want to organise it, please do. I honestly do not mind at all.' Then, as Daniel still looked unsure, she added, 'Really.'

'Magic,' Sonia breathed, getting up from her chair. She put her arms around Antonia's waist and squeezed her. 'You're a star, Mum. I knew you'd come round.'

The doorbell rang. Daniel put the car keys on the kitchen table, and pulled up the collar on his coat. 'That'll be my buddies. Use the car if you need to.'

He left. Antonia took a long breath, put the kettle on for the sustenance of strong coffee while they got stuck into the cooking, and handed Sonia her chilli recipe. 'We'd better get started.'

'Who's that at the door?' Audrey hovered palely in the doorway. Antonia's stomach buckled. Her mother really did look unwell. She went up to her, and touched her shoulder gently.

'Just friends of Daniel's, Mum, he's gone out. You go and snuggle up on the sofa, and I'll bring you a cup of tea.'

'Haven't you done the cooking yet?' Audrey said, eyeing the kitchen surfaces. 'You won't get it done in time.'

'We will,' Antonia assured her brightly. 'We're going to throw it all together now, and it'll be nicely stewed by the time everyone's hungry.'

'Not without mince it won't.'

'We've got mince.'

'No, you haven't.'

'Yes, we have,' Antonia insisted, throwing open the freezer to display the large amount of mince she'd mentally ticked off and was completely sure she'd bought, that should have been sitting there, on the bottom shelf. She pointed at a pack of chicken kievs instead. 'Sonia, where's the mince?'

'Don't know.' Sonia hid her expression. Antonia

narrowed her eyes. Was this a ruse to ensure that they had to go to the supermarket again?

'You'll have to go and get some,' Audrey said insouciantly, and wandered away, fiddling with the knot on the corner of her sling. 'This thing bites into my shoulder. It isn't half sore.'

In essence, this was Antonia's worst nightmare. Sainsbury's on a busy Sunday afternoon. No, there was more. Sainsbury's with her daughter on a busy Sunday afternoon. No, wait, it was even better. Sainsbury's with her daughter *and* her mother on a busy Sunday afternoon.

Sonia had insisted on coming. She'd reasoned that she couldn't get the food started without the mince anyway, and they might see something else they wanted. Antonia knew that meant that she thought she might be able to persuade Antonia to buy things at the last minute. And Antonia didn't want to leave her mother in the house by herself. Audrey had taken to rearranging things and trying to make herself cups of tea with one hand. She was normally a very self-sufficient woman, and Antonia never worried about her doing herself any damage in her own house. But it was as if she was in a state of defiance, constantly trying to do things that she simply couldn't. The more confounded she was, the more she tried. She'd already poured boiling water all over the floor. So Antonia had ordered them both out of the door and the three of them had climbed awkwardly into Daniel's Peugeot and headed off to the supermarket with only two engine stalls and a couple of grating gear changes en route.

Reaching a traffic jam of trolleys at the end of the fruit

and veg aisle, Antonia was sorely tempted to ram her way through.

'We've only got a basket, all we want is mince,' she muttered. Sonia appeared to her left and slid a pot of hummus into the basket. 'What's that for?'

'Oh Mum, it's so gorgeous. Pringles dipped in hummus. I always have that round at Imogen's. It's orgasmic.'

'Put it back.'

'Where's Gran gone?' Sonia glanced around.

Audrey was lingering over some new potatoes. A young couple were holding a plastic bag for her and nodding sympathetically while she tentatively put individual potatoes inside one by one, holding them gingerly with fingers like pincers. They helped her along the aisle, then Audrey looked up, spotted Antonia and gestured to her with a plaintive look on her face. The young couple fixed their eyes on Antonia as if she was heartless.

'Oh for fuck's sake,' Antonia muttered. Beside her Sonia exploded with laughter.

'Mum!'

'Sonia, don't you ever say that yourself or you'll be in mightily big trouble. Go and get Gran and bring her to red meats, minus the new potatoes. I'm going to get the mince.'

'Rendezvous at the mince. Understood.' Sonia saluted, sucking in her cheeks. Antonia headed off around the corner to find the beef counter.

She stood with the mince in her basket for more than five minutes. Time passed. Then she went off in search of her missing relatives, banging into them as she reached the drinks section. Sonia had a basket over one arm which was crowded with purchases, including a number of exotic fruit juice cartons.

'What's that?' Antonia pointed. 'I've been waiting at the beef counter for you.'

'Gran says I can have anything I like.' Sonia raised her eyebrows. 'So we're just getting some things we really want.'

'And who's paying?' Antonia snapped.

'I am,' Audrey said. 'Bleedin' hell, you can't resent me buying my own granddaughter a few treats on her birthday, can you? And let's get on with it. No point in standing around gassing.'

'Mum, why don't we see you back at the car,' Sonia said, with more authority than Antonia was used to. 'Seriously, you look bushed. You get the mince, we'll just finish off and see you in the car park. Gran says she wants to get me some sort of birthday thing.'

'I do.' Audrey stuck out her chin. 'Go and buy your mince. We'll see you at the car.'

'I'm not losing you both again.'

'Trust me, Mum, we'll be five minutes, but you look so ratty, and your cheeks are all pink, and you're ruining this for me with your bad mood. Please go back to the car. Put the radio on and chill out or something.'

Antonia checked her watch. Her face did feel warm. Perhaps it was best if she went ahead and calmed down.

'If you're not at the car by two thirty, I'm going without you,' she instructed, and stalked away with her mince and a pot of hummus sliding about in her basket.

By five, the house was filled with the aroma of stewing chilli and assorted shampoos and perfumes, and resonated to the sound of cantering footsteps, banging doors and Sonia's music, throbbing from her bedroom while she got herself ready. Sonia had advised her friends to turn up some time after six. The fortune-teller was arriving at seven, Antonia was anticipating food at about eight thirty, by ten-ish she hoped everyone would be thinking about disappearing.

Sonia had initially pleaded for her party to be held on a Saturday night, with her friends all staying over. Until Audrey had broken her wrist, this was something Antonia had considered. Daniel could possibly have gone back to London for the night if he'd found the idea a bit overwhelming. But with Audrey taking over Antonia's bedroom, and Antonia sleeping on Sonia's floor for the time being, the thought of half a dozen lively teenagers staying late had just been too much. And Antonia was very conscious of her mother's delicate state too. She'd been quite amazed when Audrey had insisted that the party should take place. That had been generous of her, but Antonia didn't want to push her mother's nerves further than they could stretch.

So the compromise had been: same weekend, but Sunday evening, and not a late night. The fortune-teller had been amenable and as Antonia had pointed out to Sonia, she often had Friday night sleepovers, and she would again. So this was just a themed evening, something different to do that they'd hopefully all enjoy and remember. But it certainly wasn't going to be boisterous, and it wasn't going to be a late night.

Antonia was back in her own bedroom trying to find something to wear. Audrey, who had been wandering around the house, came in.

'Are you going to change, Mum?' Antonia asked,

240

sorting out a pair of soft tailored trousers for herself with a loose, silky blouse to wear on top.

Audrey sat on the edge of the bed, hoisted her feet up and lay back, her head on the pillows. She stared at the ceiling. 'I've got nothing to wear. All my clothes are at my house.'

'That's not true.' Antonia fastened her blouse in front of her full-length mirror. 'We collected a lot of things from your house. You said they were the clothes you liked to wear.'

'I'm all right in a skirt and jumper, aren't I? Are you ashamed of me, or something?'

Antonia turned round, disguising the hurt she felt. 'Of course I'm not ashamed. You can wear the *TV Times* if you like. I just thought you might – just whatever. Everyone's changing, it seemed like the thing to do, but you look lovely as you are.'

'I never brought you up on silk blouses,' Audrey said, eyeing Antonia's outfit. 'You always had airs and graces.'

Antonia bit her lip and turned back to the mirror as she buttoned her trousers. 'Would you rather I got ready in the bathroom?' she asked neutrally.

'Just don't squirt that stuff in here. It makes me cough.'

'I've already put my perfume on in Sonia's room. She likes the smell.'

Audrey wrinkled her nose and lay still, staring upwards again. Antonia brushed her hair roughly, and put it back in a gold-plated clip. She sat at her dressing table to rummage through her jewellery. A pair of bold earrings would be good with trousers. Confident, poised, in control. Exactly the opposite of how she actually felt. In the reflection of the mirror, over her shoulder, she could see her mother. Audrey lay there, her sling prominent as it rested over her chest, her face bleak, her eyes pointed to the heavens. She looked like an effigy on the tomb of a humourless medieval dignitary. Antonia softened. She twisted around on her stool.

'Mum?'

'What.'

'Are you in pain?'

'A bit.'

'So you need a painkiller?'

'No.'

'Then what is it? Can I get you a cup of tea? A cushion for your arm? Is there anything you'd like to borrow?'

Audrey swallowed loudly. She let out a long, depressed breath. 'I feel dirty,' she said.

'What do you mean?' Antonia stood up and walked to the bed. 'Dirty? I helped you wash this morning. Would you like a bath?'

'My hair.' Audrey pressed her lips together. 'My hair hasn't been washed. I don't see how I can do it.'

'Oh, Mum.' Antonia sank onto the side of the bed, and took her mother's good hand. She squeezed it. As she did, she noticed how bruised and swollen the fingers of the other hand looked, poking out from the plaster cast around her wrist. And Audrey had been surprisingly strong in Sainsbury's that afternoon. She hadn't wilted, as Antonia had feared. She really was trying hard in some ways to carry on as if nothing had happened. Antonia wasn't giving her enough credit, and she realised it. 'I'm so sorry. I thought you'd say if you wanted anything done. No, that's not it. I just didn't think about your hair. It's my fault.'

242

'Because you washed me, like one of those withered old things in a home. They get sponged, don't they? Why does everyone think older people like being dabbed with sponges? I don't want to be sponged. I'm not old. Don't you ever dab me with a sponge, Antonia, I won't stand for it. The minute someone dabs you with a sponge you might as well order up your headstone.'

'I promise,' Antonia said. She was a little daunted. She hadn't realised Audrey had been nurturing these feelings. 'Just tell me what you want.'

'I want clean hair. I want to be clean all over.'

'Then we'll go and wash your hair now,' Antonia said firmly.

Antonia helped Audrey into the bath, and adjusted the water temperature on the shower head so that it was nicely warm, taking care to avoid the sling and the plaster cast. She knelt on the bath mat and leant over the bath. Gently, she pointed the jet at her mother's body, squirting some of her all-over hair and body shampoo into the palm of her mother's good hand so that she could rub it into her own skin. Then when Audrey consented, Antonia told her to put her head back, and she sprayed the soft jet of warm water over the top of her head, and carefully shampooed her fine hair. She rinsed the bubbles away, wiping the stray streaks of foam that slid down her mother's face with her finger.

'Does that feel better?' she asked her gently.

'Yes. Thank God for that.'

'Enough yet?'

'Yes. At least your bathroom's warm, I'll give you that. Though Lord knows what you spend on heating bills.'

'Let me help you out.'

Once she had towelled her mother down, and draped her own thick towelling robe around her, and pulled the belt together, Antonia saw that Audrey was staring at her clothes in fascination.

'You've ruined that blouse. You've got water all over it. And the knees of those trousers are soaked.'

'Not to worry.'

'You're not going to go downstairs like that, are you?' Audrey's cheeks twitched with a hint of malicious humour.

'No, I'm going to take you back to your room, and get changed. So come on.'

In the bedroom, Antonia helped Audrey back into the skirt and top she was determined to wear, and dried her hair gently with her hairdryer. Then she turned her attention to herself as Audrey sat back on the bed. She had just pulled on a pair of grey wool trousers, together with a red cowl-necked sweater, when Sonia walked in.

'Got a glass of fruit punch for Gran – Mum! You haven't done your hair or face or anything!'

'It's all right Sonia, just relax. It's only . . .' She looked at her watch. Ten to six. 'There's still ten minutes before the first people might show up.'

'Go on!' Sonia urged. 'Now! All your stuff's in my room, or in the bathroom.'

'All right, Sonia. If the doorbell goes, you have to answer it, okay? I'll just be a couple of minutes.'

'Just bugger off, Mum. I want to give Gran a glass of this wonderful fruit punch she paid for, and I'm going to spruce her up a bit. Gran, you don't want to wear this old outfit, do you? Can't we find you something more glam? Or are you really sold on the Littlewoods look?'

'Not really,' Audrey said to Sonia in a pale voice. 'Have you got anything I can borrow?'

'No, but Mum will have.'

'Sonia,' Antonia interjected, as she loped towards the door with a few items of jewellery in her hand. 'Gran doesn't want to borrow anything of mine. Let her—'

'Just leave us alone will you, Mum?' Sonia pulled an irritated face. 'I've put a glass of wine in my bedroom for you, it's next to your make-up bag.'

'You didn't – I haven't –'

'Just get ready. God, what's up with you?'

'Where's Daniel?' Antonia managed. 'I've lost track of him.'

'He's gone to get Natalie from London. He'll be back soon. So will you just get ready.' She added in a much louder voice, 'Please?'

Chapter Twelve

Sunday evening in a small town. Perhaps it had the same feeling no matter which town you were in. It was already dark as Caroline drove back from an afternoon dinner party in Dulwich. She was full to bursting with a late Sunday lunch which seemed to go on for ever. The hosts were a couple, both of whom she'd trained with, and there had been several faces there she knew and had kept in touch with over the years. It hadn't been wild, but it was a pleasant distraction. When she'd left, a handful of the guests who lived in London had been getting stuck into the wine in the kitchen, claiming they only had to climb on trains or into taxis to get home.

She half-wished she'd taken the train up to London so that she could drink too. But over the years she'd learned that a Monday morning hangover in her profession was a complete killer. It wasn't as if you could slink away to the office canteen and nod off in the corner, or hide in the toilets and have a quick snooze while nobody was looking, or put your head in your hands and pretend to be reading something with close concentration while you actually drifted off. Recovering from a hangover, if you were a teacher in a busy school, had to be endured in broad daylight and very publicly. It was best avoided. Apart from anything, the older ones *knew* when you were hung-over, because they recognised the symptoms so well. Nowhere to run, nowhere to hide, it was a life under a spotlight. She wondered as she drove if Greg's life in his northern, richer, smaller school would be better or worse. She didn't really doubt that he'd take the job now. He'd talk to her about it again, when he was ready.

A heavy mist lay close to the ground, the streetlamps glowing eerily on the approach to the town. The rangy public school was perched to her right as she wound the car around a tight S bend. St Nicholas's church was emptying itself of its evening congregation. She slowed as the car in front stopped to allow a young family to cross the narrow road. Did people still go to church? Caroline absently watched the crowds spilling out of the old building. There wasn't much dwindling about this local congregation. There were handful upon handful of groups, young, old, single, in families, walking away from the church towards the High Street. They all seemed very lively and chatty. Caroline peered up at St Nicholas's, its yellow ochre stone slabs illuminated in the mist. It was a big church for a small town, with a solid square tower, and a large round clock. Fairly typical. It had some sort of medieval foundation, she remembered. She'd heard that John Donne had even preached there once.

She'd never been a church-goer, and couldn't envisage herself ever becoming one, but she was covetous of the contentment she could see. It would be wonderful to put your faith in something so much bigger than yourself, to have all those difficult questions answered. She popped a peppermint into her mouth and crunched it.

Where did they think God was hiding, Caroline mused, as a flow of people crossed the road in front of her. She scanned the sky on a regular basis. She knew all about compounds, elements, particles, atoms, quarks. So did they, she decided, as what looked like a family of stockbrockers jogged past her headlamps and jumped onto the opposite curb. These days, people watched *Horizon*. There were wonderful documentary series put out on television – things like *The Planets* and *Space*. Such dutiful, respectable middle-class families as these would be sure to have the children lined up on the sofa at nine o'clock on a Sunday evening, ready for a good hour of educational programming before bed. So how did they reconcile coming to church to sing hymns about God creating everything with going home and huddling on the sofa, munching Hobnobs and learning about the Big Bang?

It made her think about Tom again. He'd said he wanted to understand *everything*. He'd stressed it as if it was of great significance. The expression in his eyes had been one of hungry curiosity. She could understand that much. That was the way she'd always been. It was the creative force that dictated the direction of her life. But how did he ratify that with sending bolts of electricity up her arm and making her jump?

Caroline thought about this for a while longer. Then she realised that the car behind her was flashing its lights, that she was stationary even though nobody was crossing the road any more and to all intents and purposes it looked as if she'd decided to park there. She put the car into first gear and moved off quickly, only to find her head swivelling and her foot reaching for the brake again as she spotted a furry hat with curly golden blonde hair under it coming out of the church gates and moving towards the town.

'Lizzy?'

She jammed on the brake and pressed a button to zip down the passenger window. She leaned over the gearstick and yelled.

'Lizzy!' It certainly was Lizzy. She turned, saw Caroline, and looked very uncomfortable for a moment. 'Lizzy, come here!'

Lizzy appeared at the car window. Her nose was pink at the end as if she was very cold. 'Hello Caro.' She didn't sound particularly welcoming.

'What the hell are you doing here?' Caroline asked.

'I've left messages on your answerphone.' Lizzy evaded the question. 'I wanted to catch up on your Paris trip.'

'Nothing to report. No sex, lots of cobbled streets, very cold. That's about it.'

'No sex at all?' Lizzy seemed disconcerted. There was a brief silence, and for some reason Caroline felt awkward. Lizzy went on, 'Have you been out all day then?'

'Yep, I've been in Dulwich, seeing some friends. Where's your car? I'll drop you at it.'

'I walked,' Lizzy said abruptly.

Caroline nodded as Lizzy was silent again. She didn't look particularly happy, or unhappy, but her face was strange. It was usually so expressive, but it was as if she was deliberately keeping it blank.

'That's quite a walk.'

'Yes. I wanted a long walk.'

'So, did I dream it, or did you just come out of the church?'

Lizzy gazed behind Caroline's car. 'Oh, look out.'

Caroline turned. A man was thumping on her car

window. Was this going to be a horribly bloody case of road rage? Caroline pulled a meek and apologetic face quickly, and cagily lowered her window.

'It's like this,' the man said, not unreasonably. 'All I want is to go home. Could you practise your parking skills on an empty bit of road? There's about twenty cars behind you.'

'I'm so sorry.' Caroline flushed. 'I'll move off the road straight away.'

'Thank you,' he said testily, and went back to his car.

Caroline pulled a face at Lizzy. 'You'd better hop in.'

'Oh I'm – I'm just going to walk home again. I want the fresh air. Can I ring you when I get home? I really do need the walk.'

'Where's David? And the boys?'

'At home. He was out all afternoon, so I thought I'd go out this evening. He's putting them to bed.'

Caroline nodded. 'Get in then.'

'Caro, I really—' The horn of the car behind blasted, and remained blasting. 'I'll just get in then,' Lizzy muttered.

Caroline moved away quickly, waving a hand out of the window in apology to the car behind. She saw in her rear-view mirror that he waved his hand back, two fingers very clearly outstretched. Lizzy was quiet. Caroline glanced at her as she fiddled with her gloves.

'Shall I take you straight home? I don't suppose you fancy a quick drink somewhere?'

'Oh, no drink thanks. I'm bushed. It's been a long day, and I'm extremely tired. You must be too. I saw Brendan earlier today.'

'You did?' Caroline smiled politely. She realised she

wasn't aching to know what he'd said. She wasn't sure that it mattered.

'He seemed pretty flat.'

'We had a good time, Lizzy, just not romantic.'

'Fine.'

Caroline glanced sideways at her cousin. She seemed very intense, as if she was burying something deep inside.

'Are you all right?'

'Can you just take me straight home, please?'

'Sure.' A little further on, as she negotiated a series of turnings to take her back around the town and up towards Lizzy's house, Caroline asked, 'So I did see you come out of the church then?'

'Yes,' Lizzy said, her eyes ahead.

'Blimey.' Caroline couldn't keep the smile from her voice. 'Why on earth would you do that? Have they got a special offer for new recruits?'

Lizzy cleared her throat. 'I'd rather you didn't mention it to David.'

Caroline looked at Lizzy again. She did seem tense. 'Sure, if you want to be a closet Christian, that's none of my business,' she teased, but Lizzy did not laugh along with her. 'Seriously, what's all this about?'

'Actually it won't matter if you mention it to David or not. I'd just rather you weren't so ready to take the piss. You don't know what I was doing, or why, so please let's just drop it.'

Caroline pulled the car over outside Lizzy's house. In the dark, each window glowed with a different colour, reflecting Lizzy's taste in curtains and blinds. It was the sort of house you'd see from the road and want to go in to, knowing whoever was in there would smile when

251

they opened the door. But Lizzy wasn't smiling at all now. She looked, if anything, rather angry, and it took Caroline completely by surprise.

'I wasn't taking the piss,' Caroline defended. 'I just didn't think you were a Christian. You only had the boys christened because so many people seemed to expect it. I remember you saying what a sham it was.'

'That's the thing about you, Caroline.' Lizzy turned in her seat. 'You're the only one who's allowed to ask questions, and your questions are the only ones that are valid. There's no way you'd understand what I was doing tonight, but the point is, it doesn't matter if you understand it or not. Because I do.'

Caroline put out a hand. She could feel tears stinging in her eyes. The sort of tears that rise up the moment you know that it's no joke, and that you are getting a good telling-off. The tears came from indignation, and from the sheer pain. 'Lizzy . . . Has this got something to do with Tom? What's he done to you?'

'Nothing!' Lizzy slapped her gloved hands onto her lap. 'He's made a difference to me, that's all, but you'd never understand. You've been far too busy trying to ridicule him.'

'Did he suggest you started going to church? Is that where it's come from? You can tell me.'

'Oh, I give up. Not only do you box everyone in, you don't even listen to what they say.'

'Of course I listen. I do, I have to. I'm a teacher for God's sake.'

'That makes you good at talking, not listening.'

'Lizzy!'

'You think you're always right, Caroline. Always.'

'I – I don't.'

'You do. And I don't think you are always right.' Lizzy opened the car door and climbed out. She put her head back in. 'Thank you for giving me a lift home even though I told you I wanted to walk.'

Lizzy shut the door and Caroline sat as still as a statue in the car. She watched Lizzy find her keys and let herself into the house, closing the door behind her. Then she turned and put her hands on the wheel, staring ahead at the empty road while the heater sent wisps of warm air over her white face.

'Oh my God, he's gorgeous!' Sonia burst into the kitchen, slammed the door behind her and pulled a stunned face for her mother's benefit.

'Who is?'

Antonia was hurriedly squeezing lemons with the juice squeezer and picking out the pips. She'd forgotten to add the lemon juice to the avocado topping for the chilli, so had dashed into the kitchen to rectify it. She stood back and had a good look at Sonia. Her eyes were glowing like torches, her cheeks bright red. She'd put more eyeliner on than usual this evening – although she did always go for that panda look – and her hair was twisted into a cross between ringlets and dreadlocks which stuck out of the sides of her head like turkey drumsticks. The resulting image was a little startling.

'He is fu— freaking heaven on a stick. You've got to come and have a look, Mum. Where's your wine? You look irritable again. I don't want you being grumpy. Even Gran's not being grumpy.'

'My wine's there.' Antonia pointed.

Sonia deftly topped it up and handed her the full glass. 'Drink.'

'Sonia, I've got to—'

'Drink, Mother. Do as you're told. We've pulled out the table in the sitting room, as you said, so there's two chairs at the table, and lots of room for everyone else to sit round and listen.'

'So the fortune-teller's gorgeous?' Antonia deduced. The only other possibility for the burst of hysteria was Daniel, but Daniel had arrived back from London with Natalie a good three quarters of an hour ago. Sonia had taken to Natalie immediately, introduced her to her other friends, and they'd all disappeared upstairs to try out the heated hair tongs that Antonia had given Sonia as a birthday present. Hence the turkey-drumstick look.

'Not half. He didn't sound gorgeous on the phone. Just sort of spaced-out. But he hasn't got spaced-out eyes. They're really zingy.'

'Zingy.'

'Yeah. Those kind of eyes that make you go phwoar.'

'That's a very earthy noise for you.' Antonia felt a mother's pang of worry. It was bad enough teasing their emotions with this fortune-telling session. He wasn't allowed to tease their hormones too.

'He's a very earthy man. I'm getting him a glass of wine.'

'Oh no. I don't think so. I don't want a drunk fortune-teller in my house.'

'I've said I'll get him one. I can't go back and tell him you said no, can I?'

'All right, but just one. I don't want any – any mutual titillation going on in there.'

'Aren't you coming in? I thought you said you'd be there for the readings?'

'Yes, I wouldn't let him loose on you lot without

watching what goes on. I'm just finishing the relish. I don't think we should give him much to drink, Sonia, you should have asked me first before offering him wine.'

'I couldn't exactly offer him fruit juice could I? He's a bloke. Why don't you just trust me to be the gracious hostess while you hide in the kitchen?' Sonia filled the glass anyway.

'Where's Gran?'

'In the front room. We're all in the front room now. Apart from you.'

'Has everyone got punch? You'd better top them up.' Antonia had to admit her mother's interference on the fruit-punch front had turned out well. There was a huge vat of it in the dining room, and the girls seemed to love it.

'Everyone's helping themselves. Oh, unless you wanted us to put our hands up if we wanted a refill.' Sonia snorted. Antonia snorted back at her.

'All right madam, I'm coming through. I'd better see this miraculous vision of masculinity for myself.' Antonia turned round and found the miraculous vision of masculinity standing in the kitchen doorway. 'How long have you been standing there?' She recovered herself with a bright smile.

'About three fifths of a second,' replied the fortune-teller. He put out his hand. 'Hello, I'm Tom. Nice to meet you. I thought I'd better introduce myself rather than hang about in the front room there. No doubt you're a bit unsure of what's going to happen, so I thought I'd explain.'

Antonia was impressed with his forthright manner. She didn't want to be. She wanted to be everything a mother should be. Suspicious, unsure, sceptical, scathing, probably a bit mocking too. She should be laughing behind her hand by now. But Tom had an aura of honesty about him. She felt her fears dissolve.

'Sonia, go into the front room, I'll be through with Tom in a minute.'

'What are you going to do with him in here?' Sonia asked, with the most expressive eyes she could muster.

'Go.'

'Take this.' Sonia pressed into Tom's hand the glass of wine she'd poured. 'You'll need it. My mum's a teacher.'

Sonia slunk away. Antonia assessed Tom properly. Sonia was right – he was gorgeous. Pretty tall, with a strange nose because it was so straight. That's what a true Roman nose was. His skin was striking, a golden colour in the middle of winter, but not through a tan by the looks of it. One of those rare naturally healthy looks. His hair was an auburn-blond combination of straggles. That would depend on the light. Very clear eyes of a kind of aquamarine. Even from across the kitchen Antonia could see how arresting they were. What had Sonia said? Zingy. Yes, that would do. He was in jeans, and some sort of decorated waistcoat that gave him a slightly hippyish look. He had a thin navy blue scarf casually looped around his neck. Under his waistcoat he was wearing a collarless shirt, open at the neck. Between the scarf and the opened neck of the shirt was a small triangle of skin with a few golden hairs visible.

Antonia could, in fact, have pulled up a chair and spent the evening just looking at him, whilst sipping at her wine. It was aesthetic appreciation rather than personal interest, but she could understand why a flurry of squeals and giggles was drifting through the house.

He put his glass of wine down on the unit, untouched. 'Maybe later. Lively crowd out there. You'd better tell me what you'd like me to do.'

'Keep it simple. They're teenagers, and impressionable. No dastardly predictions please.'

'I wouldn't do that.'

'Nothing to get them hysterical, either through joy or grief, obviously. Nothing too personal. I have a host of parents to reassure.'

'Of course.'

'And I guess – nothing embarrassing.'

'For you, or them?' he smiled. 'Okay, got you.'

'How do you do it?'

'I've got the tarot, but some people don't like that. I can do palms if you like, or tarot. I brought the crystal ball for effect, but I don't see much that way.'

'They all seem to be hoping for tarot readings. If that's okay.' He nodded. 'But keep them fairly simple if you can. There are seven of them and they all want your undivided attention. But I'd like to kick them all out by at least half past ten, and once you've finished, I've got to feed them.'

'Okay,' he laughed. 'What about you? Your mother? Or Daniel, who I've just met through there? Do you want readings?'

'I thought – we've just arranged a fee for the girls, haven't we?'

'Oh, the fee. Well, don't worry too much about that, what we fixed up is fine. I'll talk to anyone who wants to see me.'

'It doesn't seem a lot for your Sunday evening. I mean, I know from talking to friends, or just from what I read, you people are normally very expensive. Suspiciously expensive, I'd say usually. But you're not charging much at all. You have accounted for seven of them?'

'Sure. Or whatever. If the adults fancy a shot afterwards, that's okay by me too. Whatever there's time for. I don't mind. Let's see how long my inspiration lasts out tonight.'

'Inspiration?'

'Yeah, it's usually fine, but it can burn out a bit after a few hours if things get really intense. But I can't imagine it'll be intense tonight. Not for a birthday party like this.' And he smiled again, as if reminding himself as well as reassuring her.

Antonia narrowed her eyes thoughtfully. 'Are you for real? I mean, I assumed this was all just show?'

Tom paused before answering. 'It's just a show,' he said.

'I wondered if you had Romany blood. You've got that look about your eyes.'

Tom laughed. 'What, shifty?'

'Not at all. Quite the reverse actually. They're very expressive. Excuse me for speaking my mind. I do teach English and it's a habit. It's nothing really, just a feeling.'

'My grandmother used to say there was Romany blood in our family,' he said, but stopped short of revealing anything more.

Antonia nodded. He was an interesting man. 'Shall we go through, if you're ready?'

'Sure.'

Seven teenage girls – Sonia, five of her best friends, and Natalie looking very shy but pleased to be there – were squashed into the two sofas in the front room. Audrey was perched in an armchair near the window, looking decidedly mellow. Sonia had dressed her in one of Antonia's long coat-dresses, something she hadn't worn for years. It was a fish-finger-coloured brushed cotton, with a jagged collar and buttons right down to the shins. Although it was big on Audrey, it was a definite improvement on the skirt and jumper. Her slippers stuck out a bit incongruously under the full hem. Sonia had put make-up on her too. Some smears of grey and brown, and some mascara even. How she'd managed to persuade Audrey to sit still long enough to do that, Antonia couldn't imagine. It did make her eyes look a bit demonic, and together with a blood-red lipstick, there was a definite aura of the werewolf about her, but Antonia was pleased she seemed content. She sat with a large tumbler of Sonia's punch, her sling resting in her lap, making observations about every-thing and anything to the girls, who talked to her as if she was one of their own. Odd, that, given Audrey's lack of earrings, beads, baggy trousers, trainers, vest tops or dreadlocks. But she had perfected the ability to produce from nowhere, on demand, the resentful pout. They had bolshiness in common, and that seemed to be sufficient reason to bond.

Daniel perched on the arm of the sofa with a glass of wine. He grinned at Antonia as she walked in. She rolled her eyes at him. She couldn't fail to notice that seven pairs of eyelashes were being batted between Daniel and Tom, and that a few bosoms were heaving.

'Right then,' Antonia said brightly. 'What do we do?'

'I'll get set up,' Tom said.

From a battered canvas bag, he produced a box of tarot cards. From another box, after unwrapping a dark

259

silk scarf, he delicately took out an immaculately polished crystal ball about the size of an orange. He set it up on the table, on a stand. He sat down.

'I always thought they were bigger,' Sonia said, wide-eyed.

'So who's first?' He smiled around the room, and a blush spread from face to face, like a Mexican wave.

'Birthday girl?' Antonia suggested.

'All right,' Sonia sniffed. She bounded into the chair opposite Tom's, stuck her hands under her thighs and fixed him with a look of concentration.

'So,' Tom said, still smiling. 'You shuffle these cards then hand them back to me . . .'

Nina dumped the last of her bags on the carpet, then lovingly closed her flat door. It was only a studio, but it had been empty, fully furnished and in a good position for the town and she was thrilled to have been able to rent it so quickly. It was on the top floor of a rambling Georgian building on a lane that looped around the old spa centre at the bottom of the hill in Tunbridge Wells. She had one wide living space with a high French window that opened out to a balcony that she could take one step onto and one step back from. So it was essentially a one-roomed studio on the top floor, but it afforded her a view of the grassy slopes of the common even if she couldn't squeeze a chair out onto her tiny balcony. No doubt in the summer the windows flung wide would produce a stirring breeze. The room was furnished with a sofa bed, single wardrobe and chest of drawers, desk, chair, armchair and a couple of coffee tables. There was no television or video, but she could set herself up with those as she could afford them. Off from the living area was a small kitchenette and a shower room.

When she'd come to see the flat the first thing that had struck her on walking into it was that it was warm. It was as much due to the colours as the well-functioning heating. The walls were painted a spicy shade of burnt-chilli red, the curtains were bold splashes of orange and cinnamon, the carpet an earthy rust colour. Perhaps in six months she'd be screaming at the sight of it, but for now it reminded her of mulled wine. Just what she wanted to come home to after a long day out racing around under the white sky of an English winter.

She clasped her new, strange keys in her hands. At the moment they were on a key ring with the name and address of the letting agents on it. She replaced it with her own key ring, a four-leafed clover encased in plastic that she'd found on a market stall. Then she wandered over to her long window, pulled back the curtains and gazed out into the blankness of the night.

A shiver rippled over her stomach as the silence of the room descended like a feather duvet and enveloped everything. She had no stereo of her own. She'd listened to music at home on Graham's stereo that he'd had for years, or otherwise in her car. She had a Walkman, though, and to keep her spirits up and stop the panic from spreading, she found it quickly and put it on. The CD that she'd previously left inside was a Lightning Seeds album, one that Graham had given her for Christmas two years ago. She wrenched off her earphones and quickly put her Walkman back in her bag, only to remember that she'd moved in now and didn't have to live out of her bag any more. She spent the next five minutes walking around the room opening drawers and trying to decide where it should go, before throwing it on the sofa.

Then she stopped, sat down and took a deep breath. It was time to take stock of where she was, and what she had done. If that involved silence and loneliness at first, then it was only what she should expect. She'd fled from a dysfunctional home, first into the arms and house of Paul, a boyfriend who was gentle but utterly uninterested in her, then to the arms and house of Graham, becoming a spare piece of furniture in the process. Now she'd discovered this pretty corner of Kent with a relative, albeit one who wasn't interested in getting to know her, a few miles up the road. It was a reason of sorts to base herself here. She'd marked her spot on the map and she would have to find her own way forward from here. She was twenty-six now and nobody had done this to her. She had done it to herself. For the first time in her life, she had taken control of the direction she was going in and was truly independent. Nobody had ever said that being independent didn't also involve being lonely at times.

She pulled on a suede jacket with warm, fake fur around the neck, and her boots, and decided to go out and get her bearings. Perhaps the flat would feel more like hers if she went out, bought milk, bread, tea and the usual essentials ready for the morning, and came back to it as if she lived there.

She was three floors up, and as she pounded her way down the wide staircase and passed the other flat doors, she wondered about the occupants. The sound of a television came from inside one. Voices of a couple laughing from another. Classical music could vaguely be heard from a flat on the ground floor. These were very subtle sounds though, and it was remarkable how solid the walls were. Perhaps the people in the flat below her were out at the moment, or perhaps the sound never carried. She found herself hoping that the sound did carry sometimes. It would be nice to know that other people were alive in the house.

At the bottom of the hill that the town was built on, also the lively, fashionable hub of evening activity there, Nina walked around and assessed her late-night shops. On her long circuit she spotted a supermarket for a fuller shop at a later date, and found an all-purpose news-agents and stocked up on her essentials. Then she strolled down past the designer clothes stores and antiques shops whose dark windows were studded with little white lights that contrasted with the more colourful bulbs of the wine bars and restaurants. Outside a Caffé Uno Nina pondered the customers meekly through the window, deciding eventually to take herself in and have a cup of coffee before she went back. She had a local paper and wanted to look at it, but not all by herself at home. It would be nice to have people around her.

An hour later, uncomfortable with the looks she'd received from couples and groups of friends who, with no malignant intent she was sure, had not been able to prevent themselves from glancing at her sitting reading the small adverts on her own, she decided to go back to her flat. She paid the bill and left, the waitress giving her a sympathetic smile as she walked out alone. Perhaps people had been wondering if she was waiting for someone, or if she'd been stood up, or if she was lonely. But she put her chin up as she strode up the uneven pavement to her new home. She would join an evening class. She would go to a gym or a sports centre, and maybe play netball or badminton. Perhaps there were social clubs in the town or nearby that she could become involved in. And then she stopped at the steps to her house and stared up at the sky, struck by the beauty of a ghostly cloud wisped by the breeze across the sad face of the moon. Perhaps she would even find out more about Roderick's astronomy club.

Chapter Thirteen

'That really wasn't too bad at all,' Antonia said to Daniel as they sorted out baked potatoes and chilli in the kitchen.

'Quite a laugh.' He topped up her wine for her.

There was a buzz like a hive of bees coming from the front room. Tom had done the round of all seven girls. He'd been gentle, funny, at times perhaps a little personal but never in a way that Antonia felt was inappropriate. He'd talked about their families, home life, ambitions, strengths, and it seemed to Antonia he'd kept it mostly vague and consistently positive. She'd been surprised to see several of the girls put their hands to their mouths and breathe, 'How do you know that?' He'd delighted them all, and now that he'd finished and had made a move to leave they'd refused to let him go home, and he was facing an excitable interrogation. But Antonia could hear him chuckling, and shouts of laughter coming from the girls. It had been a successful evening. Daniel smiled as another burst of giggles erupted from the front room.

'Pretty amazing. Not what I expected at all. They love him. He's a funny guy.'

'Peculiar or ha ha?'

'Well, both, I'd say.' Daniel stirred the chilli and turned the heat up a notch.

'Yes, that's what I'd say. Thanks for helping me out

here. Sonia swore she wanted to do all the preparation and serving herself, but she's pretty distracted.'

'She's got better things to do right now. I have to say they've been great to Nat. I did wonder. I mean, Sonia's a gem, not an unkind bone in her body, but when you get girls together in packs they can sniff out an outsider fairly quickly if they're of a mind. But there's been no chance of that here.'

'I always think I've been lucky with Sonia. Given the circumstances she could have gone a bit wild. But she's a good girl. It's a wonder, really.'

'Nat's had a great time.'

'You can tell that? She's very quiet. Understandable, of course, surrounded by six shouting girls who all know each other.'

'She's shy all right. Always been that way. Prefers to have her nose in a book than to talk, but she loves people who talk. She brightens up inside, you can see it in her eyes. She likes Sonia a lot, I can tell you that.'

'Sonia likes her too.'

'Nat's in awe of you,' Daniel laughed. 'She loves English, you know. It's her favourite subject. I should never have told her you were an English teacher. She won't say a word to you now, but she's been watching you with that sort of look in her eye. A respectful look, I'd say. Or it might be fear. She looks at my own mother that way a lot.'

'You never mentioned she loved English so much before.' Antonia was intrigued.

'I suppose it never came up. I never thought you'd get to meet Nat, I guess. But I'm glad you let her come. Thanks.'

'She's welcome any time,' Antonia said. She threw

another baked potato towards the bowl. 'Okay, let's take this lot through. I think I'd better ask Tom if he wants to eat with us too. I don't think the girls are going to let him go home yet, and he can't exactly sit there while we all stuff our faces.'

They laid the supper out in the dining room, with a pile of plates and napkins so that everyone could help themselves. The girls' shrieking seemed to get louder and louder. Antonia attempted to enter a few gentle words of complaint, to the effect that her eardrums were bursting, but Sonia had now put music on in the front room and they all dived back there with food.

'I'll take the punch through,' Sonia said, coming back for the king-sized pan.

'Leave it in here, it'll spill everywhere,' Antonia said. She was perched on a dining chair eating at the edge of the dining table, leaving the girls to annex the front room on their own now.

'No, I'll take it through,' Sonia said, disappearing with it. 'It's nearly finished anyway. Oops.' She crashed into the door frame with it, giggled, and staggered on.

Antonia shook her head at Daniel, who was eating at the opposite side of the table. 'I give up tonight. They're a thousand times more noisy than normal. I don't know what's got into them.'

'I'm going through there, with them,' Audrey announced, shuffling away with her food.

'Mum! Do you want me to cut it for you?'

Audrey flounced away. The door of the front room shut behind her, sealing her in with the party girls.

'Apparently not,' Daniel said.

'I don't understand it,' Antonia said. 'I'd have thought my mother would absolutely hate their music and their noise. But she seems to prefer it to sitting out here with us.'

Daniel smiled with his eyes but said nothing.

'Where's Tom now?' Antonia added, looking round.

'Just freshening up,' Tom said, arriving back in the dining room. 'It's very kind of you to offer me supper, but I think I'll go now.'

Antonia stood up. 'Only if you're sure. You've done such a fantastic job. Thanks so much, Tom. You've entertained them all brilliantly.'

'It's been great fun,' Daniel added. 'Really good act. They loved it.'

Daniel stood up and put out his hand. Tom took it. They shook hands. A cloud seemed to cross Tom's face as he held Daniel's hand. He seemed lost to them for the moment, a frown over his brow. Then he released Daniel's hand quickly. 'Sorry, I was miles away.'

'You need to come into the kitchen and we'll settle up. I've done you a cheque, I hope that's all right. God that music's loud,' Antonia said, leading Tom into the kitchen. She handed him an envelope into which she'd already put a cheque.

'Thanks a lot.' He laughed under his breath. 'I can't believe I'm getting paid.'

'Don't you normally get paid?'

'I do, in principle. I just sometimes forget to collect. People get carried away. I get carried away. You know how it is.'

Antonia nodded slowly. Yes, she was practical. Yes, she was a mother, and a busy woman with a lot on her mind. But she was spiritual too. It was what had always drawn her to literature, and nourished her love of words

268

and expression. She had a gut feeling for things where other people didn't have a gut feeling for things. An instinct, her university professor had told her happily. Her instinct for life had just been smothered with layers and layers of practicality, like a varnish. Years of having to do boring chores had nailed her spirituality into a box and sealed it down.

'It's not all an act, is it, Tom?'

'That's hard to say.' He smiled again.

Through the open kitchen door, Antonia could see Daniel leaving the dining room and knocking on the door of the front room. Ignoring the yelled 'Get lost, Mum', he went inside and shut the door after him. Antonia looked at Tom again.

'Well, thank you, Tom. It really has been interesting, and you've given the girls a great evening.'

Antonia saw him to the door. There was a low mist outside. She rubbed at her upper arms. 'You've got a car?'

'Yes, just parked there. So thanks, Mrs Clarke, and thanks for the cheque.'

'Oh, call me Antonia. Not that I'm likely to see you again, but no need for formality. Goodbye, Tom.'

They shook hands. Tom let her hand drop and pushed his fingers through his hair. It instantly fell back into place. Very silky, Antonia noticed, wondering why she didn't fancy this man at all. She should. He was lovely. But to her it was like the pleasure of studying a fine painting or a well-constructed poem. Perhaps she'd never feel lust for a man again? That was something she'd rather not think about.

'Maybe you will see me again. You could come round some time, if you wanted to,' Tom said. 'On your own, for some private time to do a reading and talk about things. Only if you wanted to.'

'Well, I'm not sure,' Antonia smiled. Tom was now on the path and she stood in the hall, edging the door closed to keep the cold out. 'But I have your number.'

'Fine,' he said easily. 'I haven't done healing for a long time, and it's all a bit haphazard, but bear it in mind if you'd like me to try. Goodnight.'

Antonia nodded, shut the door, then stopped. She stared at her fingers holding the door handle. Healing?

She opened the door again, but Tom had already climbed into his car and was starting the engine. She couldn't go racing down her front path like a lunatic to try to stop him and get him to repeat what he'd said. She'd probably misheard. Hadn't she? Tom's car moved away, the headlamps disappearing up the lane and into the night.

She ran his words through her head again as she shut the door slowly. *I haven't done healing for a long time . . .*

How did he know? Nobody knew. Absolutely nobody. Not Sonia, not her own mother, not Daniel, nobody at work, nobody in this house. Nobody knew about her health problem except Antonia herself, and she had not told a soul about it.

Caroline rapped her knuckles firmly on the front door. She was deliberately ignoring the fact that there was a bell. She wanted to make a loud banging noise. She stamped her feet in the cold until the door was answered. Then she took a step forward.

'I want to know what you've done to Lizzy.'

Tom blinked back at her. He had a hot dog in one

hand, and appeared to have just taken a bite out of it. He stopped in mid-chew.

'Pardon?'

'Lizzy.' Caroline stepped inside his hall. She wanted some answers. She was burning inside with the blasting she'd received from Lizzy tonight. She'd gone home and paced around her house and garden for some time, fighting back tears, beating back her emotions. She'd thought it through and decided that Tom was the link. She hadn't dared to ring Lizzy. She didn't want to get a repeat of her dressing-down over the phone and besides, she was far too hurt to speak to Lizzy again until she'd sorted herself out. She wanted to know now what was going on, and Tom was going to tell her.

'Come in,' he said as Caroline walked past him. He shut the front door as a cat scampered towards it. 'Do you want to go through?'

Caroline marched into his sitting room. Moments later she marched out again. Tom was still standing in the hall chewing pensively.

'There's a goat in your sitting room,' she said.

'I know.'

She put her hands on her hips. 'Why is there a goat in your sitting room?'

'She lives here,' he answered. He took another bite from his hot dog.

'So you have a goat that lives in your house,' she stated flatly.

'Yes.' As Caroline didn't speak Tom went on after a pause, 'She lives in the kitchen or the conservatory or the outhouse, or in the garden when it's not so cold. When it's cold like it is at the moment she lives in the house. Her name's Daisy.'

'Daisy.'

Tom took another bite of his hot dog. 'I thought you'd met Daisy. I was taking her for a walk that day I saw you in the newsagents.'

'I assumed that was a dog,' she declared, too confused to be polite.

Tom laughed under his breath. 'Caroline, I don't know what this is about, but I'm pleased to see you anyway. Would you like a cup of tea or something? And I'll introduce you to Daisy properly.'

Caroline stood tensely in his hall. She curled her fingers into her palms. She was still forcing back a damned good cry after her argument with Lizzy that evening. She was not equipped to deal with more shocks, like walking into a room and finding a goat sitting on a rug.

'Did you tell Lizzy to start going to church?' she asked accusingly.

He looked completely astonished. He seemed unable to reply.

'All right, let me try another, what is it that you've done to Lizzy? She used to be happy, carefree, good old Lizzy, getting on with everything, always smiling, always laughing. And suddenly, she's getting emotional, saying strange things and going to church. And on top of that she's being aggressive. So what have you done to her?'

'Perhaps her mood has nothing to do with me.' He blinked at her. 'It's just a thought.'

'And perhaps it has a lot to do with you.' Caroline rubbed at her forearms in agitation, fighting down the tears.

'Speaking of aggressive, will you please go into the front room and sit down? I'll make us tea.'

'I don't want tea, thank you.'

'Fine,' Tom said. He pushed his hands through his hair, looking a little more agitated. 'Fine, Caroline, so will you please take a seat in there, and I'll get some whisky, because I think I need a slug of it before I have any more of this conversation.'

Caroline glared at him indignantly, but stalked back to his sitting room. She sat on a sofa, and shied away from the fish zipping about in the tank, the three cats that were secreted about the room like furry cushions with eyes. And the goat.

The goat, hooves tucked in, head down, was evidently trying to snooze on the rug in front of the gas fire. It was clearly disturbed by Caroline's presence. It kept looking round at her. Caroline had never met a goat before and as much as she counted herself an animal lover, or at least an animal supporter if it came to taking sides, she had no idea what to do or say to appease it in Tom's absence. Was it better to make eye contact, or avoid eye contact?

'Hello Daisy,' she whispered pathetically.

Then she spotted a set of wind chimes on the table where she had sat before. They looked like the ones that her father had binned and her mother had subsequently given to Lizzy. If they were, it would show that Lizzy had been back to see Tom again, on her own. In fact, it was forensic evidence of his continued influence.

She stood up and went over to the table to look at them more closely. She picked them up, the bamboo tubes smooth against her fingers. They were definitely the wind chimes from her parents' house and there was only one way they could have made their way here. The goat stood up too. It followed her to the table. It came up to her thigh and set about sniffing her coat noisily. It seemed to want to lick the wool.

'Shoo, shoo, shoo.' Caroline darted back across the room to the sofa and the goat cantered with her. She curled up on the sofa and drew her ankle boots right up under her body onto the fabric. She hoped Tom wouldn't mind her putting her boots on the throw. But then, she didn't care at that moment.

Daisy sniffed at her knees and around the hem of her coat. She seemed to like the smell of this coat particularly. She began to lick it again. Caroline pulled back as far as she could on the sofa. The goat leaned further over her and bit at her coat.

'Tom?' Caroline called weakly.

There was no reply and Caroline, normally calm, rational and well in control, found herself at the edge of a very big panic. The goat's eyes studied her sombrely. The pupils were strange, like slitty cat's eyes that had been rotated by ninety degrees. They put her on edge. She slid from the sofa and moved cautiously across the room with her back to the fish tank. The goat followed. A cushion that had been black and furry uncoiled itself and jumped down from a rocking chair. Both animals seemed intent upon pursuing her as she backed out of the sitting room towards the hall.

It was a black cat with startlingly clear green eyes. It looked just like a witch's familiar. But the goat? She'd never read of a witch having a goat as a familiar. It would weigh down a broomstick fairly comprehensively. Daisy nudged Caroline's thigh with her forehead and she backed away, towards the foot of the stairs. Knowing nothing of goats and their body language she was now genuinely frightened. Although it was a small

274

animal, it was sinewy and more importantly, it looked pissed off.

'Tom,' Caroline uttered in a strangled breath.

This was ludicrous. She hadn't thought of herself as somebody who was easily scared by animals. She wasn't scared of anything. But Tom shouldn't have left her in a room by herself with a goat when she'd never met one before. It wasn't fair. She tried to back away from it further and found her foot making contact with the bottom stair. The goat stuck its neck out swiftly and made a grab for her hand with its teeth.

'Oh my God.'

Her panic fuelled, Caroline turned and ran up the stairs. Towards what, she had absolutely no idea. She thought she heard footsteps thundering up the staircase after her. Adrenaline surging, she found herself on the landing and grabbed at the first door handle she saw. She cast herself on the other side of the door and slammed it behind her.

'Ridiculous woman.' Her forehead lolled against the gloss of the door. She closed her eyes while the world became normal again and the adrenaline receded. Then she glanced over her shoulder to see where she was and her face dropped.

She was in Tom's bedroom.

A solid wooden bed with a mahogany headboard dominated the room. It was draped with a woven throw of a design that seemed Moorish. Two silk cushions of dark wine lay on wide square lace pillows. A gnarled lamp stood on each side of the bed, the iron of the decorative stands wrought into teasing designs that seemed to be floral patterns but became crouching goblins when you stared at them. One of the lamps had been left on, casting a soft light over the room. A heavy oak wardrobe was wedged into one corner. Next to it was a cabinet carved out of a dark wood with an intricate original painted finish which glinted red, green and gold like an extravagant Asian wall-hanging. On top of it, an ancient chessboard, the marble pieces worn down to stumps. By the position of the pieces it looked as if a game was in progress. Two vast Asian rugs that were fine and old were spread across the floor, one of china blue and faded orange, another of tints of green and brown that almost smelt of wild herbs and fertile earth.

Over and around this were signs of Tom's everyday life. Several pairs of jeans were strewn over the ajar wardrobe door, along with a sweater. A drawer in the dresser was half open and a thick sock hung over the rim. There were books everywhere. On the carpets, on a carved table next to the bed, stacked at all angles in a bookcase set against one of the walls, in a heap on the cabinet next to the chessboard.

Caroline stood still and drank in the detail of the room she had escaped into. There were bite-sized tastes of such antique exoticism downstairs, but nothing like this explosion of sensuality. It was as if Tom had saved the best of everything he had, filled this room with it and turned it into an experience. A hint of musk sat in the air and as she moved her head she thought she could smell lilac. From the candles, no doubt, or perhaps some aromatic oil he used in here. It was intoxicating and she felt heady. Drawn further in she could read some of the titles of his books too. There was a Koran in the heap next to a sculpted Buddha head. A copy of Kant. Maupassant. Tolstoy. Plato. She touched the goblin on the lamp and it seemed to curl a lip at her.

Thus, she was standing right next to Tom's bed and had hardly realised how she had got there, when the door opened and he walked in.

He stopped inside the door and their eyes met.

'I wondered where you were,' he said.

She knew that she should pinch herself to become fully awake again.

'It was Daisy,' she told him.

'I heard footsteps on the stairs. Daisy's in the kitchen now. It's quite safe to come down.'

'I will,' she said. But she didn't move straight away. Then she followed Tom's eyes and realised she was still fingering the clawed hand of the wrought-iron goblin on the stand of the lamp. 'I . . .' She couldn't think of anything else to say.

'It's African,' he said.

'It's . . .' Not lovely. But engrossing. 'It's fascinating. And I noticed your chess set. It looks unusual.'

'It is. It's Persian. Ninth century.'

'It should be in a museum,' she admonished, forgetting for a moment that she was an intruder into his bedroom.

'It was a gift, and I don't like to pass on gifts.'

There was a pause. The musk seemed more honeyed now, as if standing closer to the yellow light cast out by the goblin lamp had influenced the smell. 'I didn't mean to snoop,' she said.

'I know.'

'Who do you play chess with, then? You seem to be mid-game.'

'Do you play?' Tom's eyes brightened, as if he was drawn from behind a mask that he'd been wearing.

'Of course. But knowing how to play is one thing,

enjoying it is another thing. Most people know the moves. Do you enjoy playing?' she asked him.

'Yes. Very much. It's never the same. There's always something you hadn't seen. Do you enjoy playing?'

She paused before saying, 'Yes.'

'Well.' Tom crossed his arms loosely in front of his chest and a smile flitted about his lips. 'We should play sometime, then. Shouldn't we?'

'Not with a ninth-century Persian set. I'd be too scared to touch it.'

'I have others.'

'So, you're a bit of an antiques buff. I hadn't realised.'

'Not at all.' He shook his head. 'Gifts, mostly.'

'Gifts,' she sighed under her breath. 'Tom, people don't dish out gifts like this. Not unless you've donated them a kidney or cleared their country's national debt. How on earth could you acquire such exquisite objects as gifts?'

He surveyed his room. 'In many parts of the world old traditions still survive. Strangers are rewarded for their contributions.' He added, as Caroline was silent, 'It's completely voluntary. It wouldn't be a gift otherwise, would it?'

'I don't understand.'

'I know.'

She frowned, breathing the lilac over the honey and sweeping her eyes around his room again. He leant against the wall as if he were completely comfortable at that moment with Caroline standing by his bed, firing questions at him. She was perplexed. The more questions she asked him, the more questions she wanted to ask. 'All of this,' she put out her hand to his room, 'I

278

know I wasn't meant to be in here at all, but it's just – it's beautiful.'

He stayed by the door as if moving further into the room would be impertinent. 'You suit this room,' he said.

'Me?' She was surprised. 'I'm so ordinary, what could I have to do with things like this? Those plates, that mask, those designs, even those wine-dark cushions.'

'From over the wine-dark sea. I love that description,' he said, and added as she looked blankly at him, 'it's Homer.'

Caroline found herself wordless again. 'Homer,' she repeated.

'It's just there, under your elbow.'

She glanced down. The *Odyssey* lay on top of the other books on the carved bedside table. She picked it up and opened it but it wasn't a translation, it was printed in ancient Greek. She recognised the letters. 'You can read this, in the original?' she queried.

'It has more impact that way.'

She closed the book and laid it down carefully. The Spinning Fate. Tom the fortune-teller. Tom the stranger at the astronomy club. A man with an insatiable lust for learning, and more knowledge than she had possibly imagined. And yet she'd come here to challenge him for his influence, not welcome it. Certainly not to identify with it. What had happened?

'Have you bewitched me?' she asked starkly.

'Absolutely not. Scout's honour.' His mundane phrase brought her closer to reality.

'It must be the scent in here. Oil or something, it's making me feeling quite giddy. And it's nice of you to say I suit this room, but I couldn't be more out of place.'

She thought of her *Star Trek* duvet and practical white geometric furniture which could easily be wiped down. The Berber carpet spread throughout the downstairs of her house because it allowed her to traipse in and out to the observing shed without panicking about leaving shoe marks on it. Her matching kitchen utensil set from Argos in white and yellow plastic.

He laughed softly. 'You could be Moorish, or Spanish with your colouring. That's why you look right in here.'

'Me? God no. English bog standard – stick insect. That's me.'

'You do yourself down with no reason.'

'Well I'm not exotic, Tom, whatever I am.' The image of that yellow and white utensil set would not go away. The end of the spatula was ridged from where she'd left it lying on the side of the pan and it had melted. She'd left something cooking while she'd been downloading some new observing software from the Internet.

'Have you seen the black olives on the market stalls in southern Europe? Glossy, dark, pungent, completely mesmerising. You have those eyes.'

'I've got eyes like olives?' The lilac wafted again but she had no idea where it had come from. Tom gave a half-smile.

'And Merino cherries. So deeply red that they're almost black.' He took a step into the room.

Caroline fingered the goblin on the lampstand. She should move, really. She would, any moment now.

'My . . . ears?'

'Your lips,' Tom said, but this time he didn't smile. He walked steadily towards her. She heard herself swallow. A warmth spread up into her chest and around her neck, then restricted her breathing as he moved closer to her.

Her eyes stung as she watched his without daring to blink – pale, green, insolent. She had no idea what she was doing, or what was going to happen next. She was completely paralysed. It was agonisingly exciting.

He took her hand and her pulse surged as if she'd been jump-started.

'What?' she said in a hoarse whisper.

'Let's go downstairs,' he said.

She stood still as he gently tugged at her hand. Enchantment. It had to be. Why would she be reluctant to leave his bedroom, when she'd merely flown into it while escaping the menacing teeth of his bad-tempered goat? And this was a man whom she suspected of corrupting her much-loved cousin into changing the rubric of her life and subsequently throwing unpleasant accusations at her.

'Tom?' She heard her own voice, a whisper, throaty, thick with curiosity, as they reached his bedroom door. She didn't want to leave. She had no understanding of why she was resisting being ejected from his bedroom. Her stomach felt hot and a threading sensation had snaked its way up her legs. Was this sexual attraction to him? All over her skin felt alert, as if she had lost an outer layer and was aching for the new skin to be touched, just so that she could be assured of its sensitivity.

He turned round and put his hands to her face, cupping her chin.

'Not yet,' he said.

'I don't understand. What not yet? What . . .?'

They looked at each other for a long time. Caroline couldn't understand why the smell of lilacs had gone now. They were at the bedroom door. Probably the through breeze. She thought he was going to kiss her. He lowered his head to hers and she closed her eyes.

He spoke onto her lips, brushing them with the softness of his. 'Not yet.'

When he pulled away again she felt groggy, as if she'd been dozing. He led the way back down the stairs. The black cat was sitting in the hall, washing itself. It winked a green eye at Caroline.

Birdbrain. She remembered that cat's name now. It was a cute cat, very furry, fond of purring. She put out a hand to it and it rubbed a cold wet nose on her fingers, tickling her palm with its whiskers. It seemed very ordinary under the plain light cast by the bright bulb in the hall. Not witchlike at all, just an everyday moggy in search of attention.

'So Lizzy . . .' Caroline tried to concentrate as she stood in the hall, ready to leave.

'You'll have to talk to Lizzy about Lizzy,' he said.

'Right. So this is like the Hippocratic oath or something? Psychic, magic-type people don't let on about what their customers tell them?' She twisted the latch on the front door and a blast of cold air shot into the hall. The last shroud of fog left her brain. She couldn't smell musk, honey or lilac any more. Only the sharp, metallic stab of an icy cold wind.

'Goodnight,' he said.

'Tom.' She touched his arm, already angry with herself for thinking that he might have kissed her earlier. Or perhaps he was forgetting it already. Perhaps she would forget it soon. It had been very vague and was becoming less distinct with every gust of this winter wind ravaging her warm face. 'I just want to know. Did you do this to Lizzy?'

'Do what?' He seemed genuinely unsure of her meaning.

'Did Lizzy— she didn't see that room, did she?'

He seemed uncomprehending, then shook his head. 'Nobody's seen that room.'

Caroline sailed down his path in a cloud of confusion. She waved a hand without looking behind her, passed through his gate, then turned and walked away from his house. She was several yards down the road before she heard his front door close.

Caroline sat on her sofa for a long time when she got home, gazing weakly at her framed poster of the horse-head nebula on the wall. At one point she thought she was going to cry, then she realised that she was too tired to cry. Some time after this she felt very positive and her spirits rose so much that she sat smiling to herself. Her mood was definitely untrustworthy. She poured herself a glass of wine and felt relaxed by it, but no sharper in purpose.

The more she tried to remember what had happened in Tom's house, the more the memory eluded her. It was like trying to capture sand in a sieve. The small amount that she could remember clearly was very clear indeed. He seemed to be saying that whatever feelings might have been evoked by being in his house were natural. They weren't about him, they were about herself. Perhaps she should explore them, somewhere else. She had to make her own decisions.

Above all, as she sat quietly on her own, Caroline's image of Lizzy castigating her would not leave her. As she was about to go to bed she decided to risk it. One last phone call to Lizzy, to say sorry.

Lizzy picked up the phone which, thank heavens, avoided any false jollity with David.

'Lizzy, I'm so sorry,' Caroline sniffed. 'I'm sorry for everything I said and for not listening to you. Are you all right?'

'Yes, I'm fine, Caro. You just need to chill out.'

That wasn't what Caroline was expecting at all. She'd expected a mutual apology. Caroline prostrates herself, so then Lizzy prostrates herself. On the very few occasions when they'd fallen out before, that had been the way that the conflict had been resolved.

'But – are you all right, Lizzy? I'm worried about you. If you need to tell me anything, you know I'm here. I'll try to understand.'

There was a pause, then Lizzy said more gently, 'Thanks, but I'm fine, really, and I'm sorry I ripped your head off. But you have been a bit like a bull in a china shop recently. You've got a lot of pent-up tension inside you, and it's pretty hard to be around. Why don't you ring Brendan up, have sex with him, and put us all out of our misery?'

Chapter Fourteen

As one by one the girls were picked up by parents or older siblings, Antonia did notice that they were shrieking much more than usual and that there were a lot of glowing eyes and red faces. She put this down to the unusually high pheromone count brought about by both Tom and Daniel's presence earlier. But it was, typically, when the squarest parent of them all, Imogen's mother Jill – a woman with fawn hair, fawn eyes and fawn freckles, who bore a marked resemblance to Boris Johnson – arrived to collect Imogen, that Sonia produced projectile vomit in the hall, slid down the wall, and it started to make sense.

'She's drunk,' Jill said factually and turned to her own daughter, who was attempting to slide along the hall wall towards the front door. 'Imogen? Look at me.'

Then Antonia could see clearly that Imogen was also drunk, as she staggered past her mother and down the path towards the car, somersaulting over a rose bush on her way.

'Good God!' Antonia declared, squatting down to pat Sonia's cheeks, probably a little harder than necessary. 'Sonia! What have you done? What have you been drinking?'

'At least,' Jill said, eyeing the liquid splashes Sonia had left on the wallpaper, 'I hope it is drink and not drugs.'

'Look, Jill, please come in for a second. I knew nothing of this. I can't imagine where they might have got alcohol from. There was only wine in the house, and we've been drinking that in the kitchen.'

'While the girls got slaughtered somewhere else?'

'They're not toddlers. I can't watch them every second. I can only say that I'm shocked and disgusted with Sonia. It's her house, and she should have been in control.'

'Yes, she should.'

'Please, come in. Let me close the front door.'

'Actually I think I'll take my thirteen-year-old paralytic daughter home,' Jill said frostily. 'There is such a thing as alcohol poisoning, and my first thought is to make sure she lives through the night.'

'I'm sure she'll be fine. I can't imagine what they drank.' She slapped Sonia again for good measure. 'Sonia!'

A pair of brown, bleary eyes rotated in front of her. 'I need to go to bed,' Sonia chanted. 'Have to go to bed.' She curled up on the carpet.

'I think the first thing you should do is ring the other parents. Have the other girls all gone home now?'

'Yes,' Antonia said. Apart from Natalie, that was. As soon as she'd got rid of Jill, she'd have to find Natalie and make sure she wasn't throwing up too. She felt horribly out of control of the proceedings. She was the teacher. She was the one trained to control teenagers. Jill was telling her what to do. She was agreeing. The natural order of things was upset.

'I can ring Carolyn and Kathleen if you like,' Jill offered, as they both heard the guttural sound of Imogen throwing up on the front lawn on her way to the car.

'No, no, I must ring everybody myself.' Antonia put her cold palm on her hot forehead, tears of sheer frustration stinging her eyes. 'I think perhaps you'd better bring Imogen in. We'll wash her down and give her some water. I'm worried about her.'

'Home, bath and bed is what Imogen needs,' Jill said, turning on her heel. 'And just how I'm going to explain this to my husband is quite another matter. Peter's not very understanding about these things.'

The smug look in Jill's eye suddenly turned the situation for Antonia. How dare she be so ready to blame Sonia for it all? How did Jill know that it wasn't her own precious offshoot who'd got them all pissed? A mother's instinct for loyalty erupted.

'Well perhaps if Peter was more understanding about Imogen, she wouldn't have gone on a bender,' she muttered, but it was too late. She'd been heard.

'And perhaps if your household was more balanced, Antonia, Sonia wouldn't have been so keen to get drunk herself.'

'She's fourteen next week. It's what they do at that age.'

'You may have done, I didn't.'

'It's experimentation.'

'Well it's fairly clear that Sonia's as experimented as a newt. I hope she'll be ashamed of doing this to them all when she comes round.'

'Assuming that it is all Sonia's fault, which is far from apparent,' Antonia defended. The sitting-room door banged, and she glanced over her shoulder to see Audrey headed at high speed for the kitchen with the empty vat that had held the fruit punch.

'This is a pointless discussion. I'm taking Imogen

home. Until we get to the bottom of this you can assume that Imogen and Sonia will no longer be friends.'

'Mother?' Antonia was yelling simultaneously, but as she turned to look out into the blackness of the night again she could see Jill heaving Imogen up, supporting her in her arms and dragging her towards the car. She called down the garden path, 'I don't choose my daughter's friends for her.' It was a futile last word, but she felt it made a point.

Antonia glanced down at Sonia again, curled up and by the looks of things already headed off into deep sleep. She pulled her up as far as she could by her arms but she slumped back onto the floor again. Daniel came down the stairs.

'Antonia?'

'What?' she said without ceremony as she struggled once more to get Sonia to stand. She couldn't even get past her to shut the front door, and a cold blast of air was assaulting them all.

'Oh,' Daniel said. 'You've found out for yourself.'

'Jesus, is Natalie all right?'

'Passed out on my bed for now. I took her up there to show her a new game I've got on my laptop. I thought it was weird she was grinning so much, then pow, out for the count.'

'Oh God,' Antonia said. 'How are we going to get her home?'

A crash and a squeal from the kitchen caught their attention. There was a hollow metallic sound, very loud. It sounded as if the empty vat had been dropped and possibly as if Audrey had gone down with it.

'What's that?' Daniel said.

Antonia sprinted towards the kitchen, yelling over

her shoulder, 'Just make sure Sonia doesn't throw up again, if you can, Daniel. Mum!'

Audrey was at an odd angle, having evidently fallen, ending up wedged between a wine rack and the washing machine. Her plaster cast was sticking out and she had a wild look about her face.

'I was just washing up,' she declared.

Antonia pulled her up straight, firmly but carefully, then stared her in the eyes. 'Mum, I told you to leave the washing-up all the time you are here. You might have broken your other wrist, or an ankle.'

'I'm all right,' Audrey said. Antonia caught a whiff of something on her breath. Booze. But she thought she'd only drunk fruit punch all night.

'Did you have any wine tonight? It's no wonder you're falling about.'

'No,' Audrey defended. 'I didn't touch your bleedin' wine. I stayed on the fruit punch.'

It clicked. Antonia looked from the vat, which Audrey had keenly soaked in washing-up liquid and hot water, back to her mother's expression. Her breath stank of it. Her eyes were darting about and she seemed to be disguising an urge to laugh. When Audrey did drink at home her tipple was vodka. It made perfect sense. Antonia gripped her good arm and gave her an even harder stare.

'You put vodka in the punch.'

'I didn't,' Audrey lied.

'Where's the bottle?'

Audrey pursed her lips together.

'Right,' Antonia said, breathing hard and pushing back her hair. 'I have to find the bottle, Mother, because I have to know how much they've drunk, and if they're in any danger. I have several sets of parents to ring this evening, and at least one of them, who happens to be a doctor, will ask me questions in milligrams. And I have to try to explain it away to Daniel. Thank you *so* much.'

She opened the swing bin, and rifled through it. There was no empty vodka bottle there. Antonia stormed from the kitchen. She heard her mother's weak voice behind her. 'It was only a bit of fun.'

'Look at me bloody laughing,' Antonia said with sharpened daggers in her voice.

At the front of the house in the pitch dark, Antonia went through the last bin bag to be deposited out there. She managed to untie the knots.

'Daniel? Can you open the front door wider? I can't see out here.'

Daniel, in the hall with Sonia propped up on his lap, obliged, pulling the door wide open. Antonia dragged the bin bag to the path, where the light slanted out clearly from the hall. The bin bag clunked. 'Ah, here we are. Evidence.'

'It was only meant to be a bit of fun, Daniel,' Audrey slurred, arriving in the hall and clinging to the wall. 'Tell her for me. She listens to you.'

Daniel pulled himself up, dragging Sonia with him, and tried to put out a hand across the hallway to stop Audrey from heading outside. 'I think you'd better leave her to it.'

'Is the vodka bottle in here?' Antonia barked at her mother from the garden path.

Audrey put one hand up over one eye, as if she was trying to focus. 'In where?'

'Forget it,' Daniel said, nudging Audrey back along

the wall. 'Why don't you go and sit down, Audrey? We'll take it from here.'

Audrey ignored Daniel, turned around again, and headed back out the front door. She began to cry. There was a loud sob in her voice which seemed to echo in the still, cold night. 'Antonia? Don't be hard on me. Don't be hard.'

'I think I'd better get Sonia upstairs to the bathroom,' Daniel said, as Sonia let out a loud belch.

'Don't be hard,' Audrey wept, getting past Daniel as he peered at Sonia's green face with concern, and making for the doorstep. 'Antonia? I only wanted us to have some fun.'

'Fun? Fun? I'll give you a bottle of bloody fun,' Antonia said, and turned the bin bag upside down on the path. The mess spread everywhere. 'Aha!' she exclaimed in utter triumph, as she spotted the bottle amongst the rubbish.

It seemed to Antonia in the few moments that followed that everything happened at once. Just as she dived upon the empty vodka bottle and held it up in the air in vindication, Audrey fell out of the door, over the doorstep and onto the lawn. She lay there on her back, her plastered arm sticking out. Simultaneously, Antonia heard Daniel say gently, 'Oh dear, too late,' and Sonia threw up again all over the hall. Then, as her mother lay prostrate on the grass crying with her sling in the air, the front door wide open with all the lights full on, her daughter visibly being ill in her lodger's lap on the hall carpet and herself standing like the Statue of Liberty holding an empty bottle of vodka over her head, she heard a voice behind her.

'I'd love to but I can't thanks, I'm driving.'

Antonia turned around numbly.

A man was standing on her path, his hands in his pockets. He took a couple of steps forward so that he stood in the light cast by the hall and she could see him more clearly. He maintained a moment of seriousness, then, as if he couldn't contain himself, let out a low rumble of laughter. She let the arm and the vodka bottle fall to her side.

'Hello?' she said.

'Bit dull round here, isn't it?' he quipped, nodding from the old lady with her arm in plaster who now seemed to be falling asleep on the lawn, to the emptied bin bag on the path, to the groaning teenager in the hall, and back to the empty bottle of vodka Antonia was clutching in her hand. 'What on earth does one do for kicks on a Sunday night?'

Antonia suddenly wanted to laugh loudly. At that moment, the absurdity of everything, the pressure, the frustration, the lack of control, her illness, her mother, her daughter, her job, her ex-husband's happy life – all of it seemed funny. But far greater than that was the frisson this man sent over her, like a breeze rippling the surface of a lake. She gazed at him, equally confused and elated. He looked back at her, his quips swallowed for a moment or two.

'Bro!' Daniel called from the hall. 'Hey there.'

'Bro?' Antonia looked from Daniel, who was again trying to heave Sonia up the stairs, to the man on her path. 'Emile? Are you Emile?'

'I most certainly am. I assume you must be Antonia.' He put out his hand to her. She automatically extended her hand in return, then retracted it when she realised it still grasped the empty vodka bottle.

She offered him her other hand. They shook politely.

But of course. Emile, Natalie. This man's thirteen-year-old daughter was upstairs, on Daniel's bed, as pissed as a fart. And it had happened in her house. Politely shaking hands was a good start but it was all about to go downhill.

'Oh my God, Emile,' Antonia said quickly, leading him towards the house. 'Please pick your way over the litter – yes avoid that patch there, somebody was – somebody was sick there, just behind the rosebush I'm afraid. Mum, get up now. Mum! Sorry, Emile, please do come in.'

Antonia made it inside the front door. The pale wallpaper was splashed all over with Sonia's liquid ejections. There were stark damp patches on the hall carpet.

'She doesn't look too well,' Emile noted.

'Who? My mother or my daughter?'

'Well, neither really,' Emile said.

'Okay, can you hold tight for a sec and I'll just get my mother in? I don't think she should sleep out there. It gets very frosty in the morning this time of year. Look, would you like to go through?'

'Through . . . where?' Emile said, continuing his air of politeness. Now he was under the bulb of the hall light, Antonia stopped again and blinked at him. There was something strange that she just couldn't pin down. He wasn't more handsome than Daniel. In some ways you might argue he was less handsome. A little taller perhaps, or maybe it was because he was broader. His face was different. More interesting, more worldly, more . . . what was it? There was the same humour there that was often dancing in Daniel's eyes. But it was

different. More dry? More subtle? More cynical perhaps? No, he wasn't more handsome than Daniel.
Certainly not. He was simply more attractive.

'Through – to the living room? Or the kitchen? There's
a table you can sit at there. Or the dining room.
Wherever you like, Emile, and we'll just . . .' She looked
at Daniel, who widened his eyes. What could she say?
We'll just get my comatose mother in from the lawn.
We'll just get my vomiting daughter up the stairs so she
can't ruin your trousers. We'll just let you know in due
course that your innocent daughter is drunk and out like
a light. 'Daniel?' she said, hating herself for needing him
to mediate with his brother.

'Let's get Audrey in first,' Daniel said, backed up
against the wall with Sonia draped in his arms. 'But I've
got to get this girl into a bathroom before she strips any
more of your wallpaper. Emile?'

Emile offered an easy smile. 'Anything I can do.'

'Your help in getting my mother inside would be
appreciated,' Antonia said.

Between them, they brought Audrey in. Emile at the
head, Antonia at the legs. Once they were in the hall,
Antonia kicked the door shut behind them.

'The rubbish?' Emile quizzed.

'Not tonight. It'll be a quicker job tomorrow morning
in the daylight.'

'Good thinking.'

'Thanks.'

'She really does seem to be out of it,' Emile observed
of Audrey. 'Which way now?'

'If you don't mind, can we get her right up the stairs
and into bed?'

'Sure.' Emile took the head, and the weight, and they

294

carried Audrey up the stairs and Antonia pointed towards her bedroom door.

'In here.'

'Are you quite sure she hasn't done herself any further injury?'

'I'm sure,' Antonia said.

They laid Audrey on Antonia's bed and Antonia pulled off her shoes but otherwise left her intact for now. She draped a cover over her. She was snoring loudly. Antonia perched on the side of the bed and felt over her mother's arms and the parts of her legs that were showing, just to reassure herself that the tumble onto the soft lawn hadn't caused more damage. 'I'm sure she's fine. She may have one or two small bruises but thank heavens I saw her fall onto the boggy part of the lawn, and she did it via her knees, and had enough time to put her bad wrist out of the way.'

Antonia gazed over her mother's hunched form under the bedclothes. She was off in her own world of sleep, content with the knowledge that she had livened things up and caused a rumpus, and with it a certain amount of happiness. Was she so heinously wrong? After the hangovers and the recriminations, would she still be blamed for a terrible act of corruption? When all these girls were thirty, wouldn't they laugh over it? Sonia's dotty granny put vodka in the punch, and they all threw up? As long as it wasn't a serious amount, might they not learn from it? Antonia would never have welcomed it, but judging by the state of these girls they were going to have the hangovers from hell the next day. That would be a lesson.

Antonia stood up again, and turned to face Emile. She caught him gazing around her bedroom. She thought he might look a little embarrassed when his eyes came back to meet hers, but he didn't. And of course, she remembered, he was not Daniel's age, he was older. More like her own age, although she couldn't remember ever asking Daniel exactly how old. It didn't really matter. They looked at each other, then they both looked away. Emile let himself out of the bedroom and Antonia followed.

'I hope Sonia's going to be all right.' Emile sounded concerned as they stood on the landing.

Sonia was retching in the bathroom and Daniel was uttering soothing noises to her. 'There, there.'

'I have to get in there and do this,' Antonia said to Emile. 'This isn't Daniel's job. She's my daughter, and seeing her through times like this is part of being a parent. And there's something you have to know, Emile,' she said with sudden urgency.

Emile put out a hand. It landed on Antonia's arm. She looked down at the brown skin, holding hers. His hands were large. The frisson danced over her again.

'I know,' Emile said simply.

'No, you don't,' Antonia said, not listening and not knowing why he'd said that, but now needing to interpose between Emile and Daniel, and take responsibility herself for the drunken orgy that was her daughter's birthday party. 'It's about Natalie.'

'Daniel called me. On the mobile,' Emile said. 'I'll check her in a minute. We had more important things to do.'

'We have to see if she's all right,' Antonia insisted.

'Daniel told me she was all right,' he said. 'I trust him. He told me she was drowsy and was sleeping it off.'

'But she's your daughter.'

'And this is your mother, and *your* daughter and from what I could see, that was a more urgent situation to resolve. Nat, I'm pretty sure, is dreaming of *Gulliver's Travels* and whatever boy band member she's fixated on at the moment.'

'*Gulliver's Travels*?'

'It's her favourite book. That and anything by Patrick Leigh Fermor.'

Antonia was silenced. A thirteen-year-old girl who had discovered that exquisite travel writer? 'How did she – ?'

'Public library. She reads everything, and if she likes something, she reads more of it.'

Not quite knowing what to say, Antonia gestured towards Daniel's room. 'We really should see if she's all right.'

They propped open the door, Antonia feeling awkward as she had not been in Daniel's room since he'd moved in. They spotted a soundly sleeping form on the bed. Emile went in, and Antonia waited on the landing until he returned. When he did, he shut the door behind him. She looked at him quizzically.

'You don't want to whisk her out of here at high speed, in utter horror? You amaze me.'

'Daniel told me she was fine but sleeping, and would have a bad head tomorrow and would have learned a lot from the experience. That's exactly the case. I'll get her up when I'm headed out through the door. Until then, she should sleep.'

Antonia looked at Emile again. Every time she looked at him he became more interesting and more attractive. 'You should be blowing my head off. She's only thirteen.'

'She'll be fourteen in September. And perhaps if you were a stranger, I would be blowing your head off. But you're not.'

'To you I am.'

'Not at all. I talk to my brother a lot.'

'I thought you were always away?'

'Have you heard of the Internet? This e-mail thing. I know, it's new, it's scary, it's the death of the sharpened quill and soft clay tablet . . .' He laughed. 'Natalie talks to me too, almost every night while I'm away. I bought her a computer to make sure we could.'

'Phones too boring for you?'

'We express more to each other on e-mail. Natalie's not very forthcoming verbally, but she's great at writing things down.'

The sound of Sonia retching echoed along the landing. 'I have to go and relieve Daniel of my daughter now. I do really need to see her through this.'

'Sure, check it out,' Emile said.

Antonia showered Sonia down in the bath. She realised as she did that she'd been doing exactly the same thing to her mother only a few hours ago. The idea of her seeing either her mother or her daughter stark naked would have been absurd until this evening. They were all distinctly sensitive about being observed in the raw, and Antonia had no desire whatever to intrude on their privacy. Antonia herself was embarrassed about being seen by either her mother or her daughter in anything less than her underwear. A woman either side of her, one old, one young, both in need of her help and protection. She felt like the pivot on a see-saw, holding it together in the middle.

Once she'd got Sonia into bed, Antonia was utterly

dishevelled. By now, Emile would have taken Natalie away and Daniel would probably have gone to his own bed. It was Sunday night, and getting late. Now Sonia was settled, she had to quickly ring round the parents before they went to bed. She was sure she'd heard the phone ringing distantly while she was blasting hot water at Sonia in the bath, but first things came first.

Emerging from the bedroom where Sonia was tucked up and breathing heavily, Antonia mentally planned the cleaning-up job that would follow as soon as she'd made all of her explanatory phone calls. First in the hall where Sonia had been ill, next the rubbish that was spilled over the path. Although she had claimed that she'd sort it out in the daylight, she felt obligated to put everything right tonight before she went to bed.

As she descended the stairs, she could clearly smell disinfectant. In the hall downstairs, she could see that the mess had been cleared up.

'Daniel?' He was the only option. Her mother and daughter were blotto.

'In here,' Daniel's voice came from the kitchen.

Antonia wandered through, tired, her once attractive outfit blotchy with water, still in a state of disbelief as to how wrong it had all gone. 'Daniel, thank you so much for doing that. I think . . .'

Emile was still there, seated at the kitchen table with Daniel. He stood up straight away and pushed a mug of coffee towards her. They had a coffee each, so they'd obviously made that one especially for her.

She felt as dishevelled as she ever had, her clothes wet from showering Sonia, her hair all over the place, her face – God knew what her face looked like. Tired, numb, pained, worried. And also, finally, just very faintly amused.

'Emile, I don't know how to explain it to you, or how to apologise . . .'

'Neither would I, if I were you. It all seems to have gone a bit unscripted tonight. Not your fault, as I can see.'

Antonia hesitated before answering. 'I should have realised. Ultimately, it's my fault. I was supposed to be the responsible adult in charge.'

'Have a cup of coffee.'

'Thank you. Who cleared up the hall?'

'I did,' both men said at once, then laughed.

'I did the path,' Daniel said, now stifling a yawn.

'I did your hall,' Emile said, his eyes enigmatic. 'And now you're downstairs, I think I should take Nat back to London. You have phone calls to make, and it's better you make them without an audience.'

'Oh yes, you should take the poor girl home, and listen guys, I can't imagine why you took it upon yourselves to clean up but I'm really grateful. That isn't what I expected. And let me just once again apologise for what's been a very odd happening.'

Daniel headed out towards the stairs. He waved a hand in good humour. 'It's cool. I'm gone.'

'But Natalie's not his daughter,' Antonia said to Emile, who'd stood up in the kitchen, and had put his hands in his trouser pockets again, and was looking at her.

'No, she's mine, but don't be misled into thinking I don't care about her as much as anybody else does,' he said.

'No, I wouldn't do that.' Antonia scraped back her

hair and tried once more to clip it neatly. It seemed to be determined to escape, as wild as her clothes, her eyes, the whole evening. Nothing was under control that night, least of all her blonde hair. What would Emile think of this human disaster in front of him? He was watching her as she struggled to get her hairclip back into place, where it belonged.

'You couldn't be more beautiful if you tried,' he said softly.

Antonia watched Emile as he walked out of the kitchen, through the dining room and out into the hall. She heard his footsteps on the stairs. She stood still while muted voices retrieving Natalie came from Daniel's room. Then she heard them coming back down the stairs and the sounds of farewells being said in the hall. It was better, for now, to try to forget that wonderful remark. But it had filled her up, like air filling up a balloon and swelling it. She just didn't know what to say.

She walked out into the hall. Daniel kissed a tired Natalie on the forehead. She was leaning on Emile's shoulder.

'I'm off to bed,' Daniel told Antonia. 'Goodnight.'

He'd bounded up the stairs before she could say anything to his face. She called after him, 'You've been a complete hero, Daniel, and I'll make it up to you.'

Emile rubbed his hand over Natalie's hair and stroked her face. 'If only my daughter could know all the things I know now, but she doesn't and there's nothing I can do about that.'

'Thank you, you've been amazingly understanding.' She looked away. He'd said that she couldn't be more beautiful if she tried. For the moment, she felt embarrassed, but she also felt hot and as if every nerve in her body was reaching out and waving in the air like live coral in a tropical ocean current.

'Goodnight Antonia,' he said, as he walked out of her front door with Natalie carefully protected under his arm.

'Goodnight Emile,' she said.

She watched him walk halfway down her path, then she closed the front door.

Nina wasn't quite sure what she'd expected on that chill evening in the week when she first turned up at the astronomy club. A hut on a hill, perhaps. A smaller version of Greenwich Observatory, which she'd once seen on a television programme. She'd imagined at least there'd be a telescope and lots of people dressed in scarves and hats, waving their arms around like Patrick Moore, enthusing wildly about solar systems or something similar. She was right about the winter apparel at least.

What she found was a small gathering of people dotted about several rows of chairs inside a Methodist hall, which was situated in a back lane of the town where Roderick lived. The hall was freezing, only loud clunking noises coming from the old, peeling radiators lining the walls indicating that there would be heat at some juncture. A woman, probably a little older than Nina, with short black hair and bold dark eyes was standing up and addressing the group, who were firing lively comments at her and making up in spirit for their lack of numbers. Next to the dark-haired woman sat Roderick, bound up in a long scarf and eyeing the speaker eagerly, and a middle-aged man of large build with a friendly face and big eyebrows which he raised at Nina as she slipped into the back of the room.

'Caroline, dear,' he said, standing and touching her arm. 'Just a mo, we've got a new member.'

'We have?' The woman called Caroline turned around and instantly delivered a wide smile. 'Hello, welcome, take a seat anywhere. Help yourself to a coffee from the table at the side. Carl? Can you do the honours?'

'I'm Nina,' she whispered, a little overwhelmed by this vigorously energetic woman with her seemingly abundant confidence. She noticed too that she was setting up a projector and a portable screen. She was evidently the speaker for the evening. What sort of brain must she have to be able to understand all the intricacies of her subject? Nina was awed.

A huge man in biking leathers with a red, beaming face and long fair hair appeared from nowhere and made Nina jump. She'd had such an image in her head beforehand of small, pixie-like boys in cagoules that he seemed even bigger and more startling. It was like running into Meatloaf. But he was grinning cheerily at her as he poured her a cup of coffee and handed it to her.

'I'm Carl,' he said in a lowered voice to her as Caroline continued to set up her equipment and exchange comments with the others. 'We can do all the honours with the rest of the group later. And we always go to the pub after too, so I hope you'll join us and get to know everyone. There's a seat next to me if you fancy it. Caroline's about to wax lyrical about modifying her shed and setting up her garden tele-scope, so I hope the subject of amateur observatories is up your street.'

303

'Oh.' Nina felt as if her eyes were growing by the second. 'It sounds fascinating, although I don't know anything about it.'

'Beginner?'

Nina nodded so hard her head nearly fell off. How could she get over just how much of a beginner she was? She didn't know a single star in the sky. She wasn't even sure what a star was. She certainly couldn't name all the planets. 'I know nothing,' she told him.

'I know *nah-thing*,' Carl laughed back at her. 'Sorry, you sounded like Manuel there for a minute. I believe you. Don't worry about it, we all have to start somewhere. Great that you're taking an interest.'

She followed him back to the chairs and as he slid along the row, took the empty seat at the end and heaved a relieved breath. So far so good. Nobody had laughed her out of the room. Nobody had grilled her about what she knew and made it clear that at least an elementary knowledge was essential before one should dare to make a personal appearance at a club. She clutched her cup and saucer, took a sip of the coffee (which was surprisingly good with the exception of the lumps of dried milk powder floating in it) and sat still, wondering what she should be doing as far as Roderick was concerned.

Her relative had given her a cursory glance as she'd walked in and settled herself, but Nina wasn't entirely convinced that he'd realised who she was. He seemed to squint around the room from time to time, as if getting his bearings, but his focus was otherwise on Caroline, who was talking and arranging some slides on a small table between the blocks of chairs. A smart, older man in a suit, his winged black hair edged with grey, swivelled round on his chair, stuck out a hand and said, 'Hi, I'm William.'

'Nina,' she'd told him.

There was one other woman present, probably of about her own age. She didn't look very well, or perhaps she was naturally very pale. She gave Nina a shy smile then looked away. A couple of other men glanced at her, smiled encouragingly, and turned back to the slides. She still felt like an impostor, but she pursed her lips together, held onto her courage, and sat tight.

The slides that Caroline showed seemed very technical to Nina, but beyond the detail that the others picked up on, she found to her surprise that she could understand some elements of what was being discussed.

'This is what I call my flip-top observatory,' Caroline was saying. 'As you can see from this series of photos, the roof slides off on bracketed arms made of aluminium and rests alongside the outside wall during observing. I flip it back up again when I've finished. And here, my beloved ten-inch LX two hundred, which most of you have seen by now. It's remotely controlled by the computer and here,' she changed slides, 'you can see better the control system. The desk's a bit temporary but there's room for the computer there, a comfy chair, a bit of gadgetry, and handwritten notes. So the shed has proved to be big enough so far, which was one of my doubts when setting it up.'

'I'm curious to see how you set up the permanent mounting,' Carl contributed. 'I'm thinking of rigging something like this up in my own garden in the summer. It's heavy work doing the building though, isn't it?'

'Luckily my family all mucked in.' Caroline smiled,

and Nina stared at her in fascination. 'In fact, that's my mum's hand there, in the side of the shot, giving me a cup of tea. My dad helped with cementing in the mounting and it was tricky, yes. I can go on to that in a minute. I would advise you to get family and friends to help you out with it.'

She did look like the sort of woman who would have an abundance of family and friends, Nina mused, gazing at another slide where Caroline's mother appeared to be about to walk across the shot just as it was taken.

'You've still got that same telescope you had last year haven't you, Carl?' asked the robust man whom others had called Dylan, sitting at the front of the room.

'Sure. My ETX one two five, it's done me proud. Nice and portable.' He winked at Nina. 'Specially good for star parties.'

'Well, that's good,' Caroline contributed. 'Because one of the other things I meant to remind you of tonight is the meteor showers which are just coming up, and to see if you all wanted to get together for some photographs and some viewing.'

'Count me in.' Carl stuck up a hand. The others nodded their assent.

'I'll be videoing this,' Dylan said. 'I'm going to try anyway.'

'Good. And I'll try to get some photographs, though it's not easy with those buggers.'

'Meteors?' Nina asked in a soft voice, but she had been heard and all seemed to turn towards her, making her cheeks glow red.

'There's a period of activity which should last, for us here in the south-east of England, perhaps two to three days, but by far the best night will be the Saturday.' There was a pause as Nina felt totally stupid. Meteors? All she could think of was *Armageddon*.

'Will they be dangerous?'

Dylan chuckled pleasantly. 'Unfortunately it's not at all as exciting as that, although the light show will be spectacular, if we get a clear night.' The group groaned as one at that thought. 'Really it's just a trail of dust and debris which the earth passes through. As we go by, the small bits – most no larger than a grain of sand – burn up in the atmosphere and create shooting stars.'

Nina listened, her head filling with picturesque images. A swell of excitement rose in her chest that went far beyond the warm welcome she'd received and the pleasure of seeing Roderick again. One minute she'd been in her tiny flat all by herself, wondering if it was worth the drive, the risk, the cold, to gatecrash the astronomy club. Now a new world had opened up to her, one which contained language of amazing resonance. Meteors. Shooting stars. It seemed as if something extraordinary had happened to her that evening. Even, she reasoned to take the edge off her disappointment, if Roderick had failed to notice that she was there. But just as she was combating that thought, Roderick suddenly sat up and put his hand in the air to draw attention to himself, and the room fell silent.

'I suggest that we meet in my garden for the viewing of the meteor shower. I'm at the top of the hill, my garden is domed and as you all know, looks out over a fine view of the Weald by day, and a wide, unpolluted sky by night. We could go and sit in a field again, of course, but my garden is such a tremendous vantage point. What do people think?'

'Good plan,' Caroline nodded. 'Everyone agree?'

'Sure,' Carl said. 'We'll be close to a power source too, which will help my car batteries. I don't want to get stranded like last time. Plugged it into the ciggie lighter,' he turned to Nina in explanation. 'And when we came to leave, couldn't.'

'But Patrick saved you on his white charger,' Caroline teased. 'Yes, thank you Roderick, that will be excellent.'

'Nina, my dear,' Roderick suddenly said across the heads of the gathering, causing her heart to beat fast with pleasure. 'I think you'll find the display very,' he hesitated, then she saw him smile for the first time, 'pretty.'

'Sure I can't walk you home, Roderick?' Caroline asked. The members had all departed and headed on up to the pub. Only she, Dylan and Roderick were left as they had been dawdling, enjoying some last-minute discussions about the coming meteor shower.

'My dear, you ask me every time and I always give you the same answer. I was born alone, I shall die alone. It is the way I am.'

'If you're sure. We'll see you for the shower, then. And I hope that new girl turns up too.'

'Nina?' Roderick looked puzzled as he looped his scarf around his neck so many times that Caroline felt that he was about to disappear inside it completely. 'Yes. Quite strange, really. She's some relative of mine and she won't go away.'

Caroline raised her eyebrows and said nothing. She hadn't thought that Roderick had any relatives at all, even distant ones. But Nina had been an interesting addition to their evening. Aside from the fact that she was blonde and pretty, which had enlivened the male element of the gathering considerably – and especially Carl, Caroline had thought – she'd been bright and wasn't scared to ask questions. She'd be a good member to have along. Sometimes it was easy to go too fast in a burst of enthusiasm and leave people behind. You needed somebody asking obvious questions and keeping the pace manageable for everyone.

'Sounds like she wants to get to know you, Roderick,' Dylan opined as he donned his furry hat and pulled the earpieces down.

'I don't appreciate being stalked,' Roderick said as he shuffled away. He turned at the door and stared back at Caroline and Dylan, who'd been rather startled by the idea that this sweet-faced willowy blonde creature could stalk the eccentric old man, and hadn't been able to think of a thing to say in reply. 'Although I will say that she has the potential to be a fine woman. Unlike her mother or grandmother before her who were, as they say in the vernacular, sauce monsters. I bid you good-night.'

'Good grief,' Caroline said after Roderick had left, pulling on her coat and gloves. 'I'm hoping Nina will turn up for the meteor evening now. This story's starting to intrigue me.'

'So,' Dylan said, flapping his arms against the bite of the air on the doorstep as Caroline locked up. 'No Tom then.'

'Tom?' The mention of his name sent goosebumps up and down Caroline's arms. She found herself standing perfectly still, staring at Dylan, her mouth open. Her head was instantly flooded with images of his house, his bedroom, his face.

'Your funny bloke. I had wondered if we might see him again. Rather a shame really. I found him pleasantly provocative. Well goodnight, Caroline. I'm going to give the pub a miss tonight as I've had rather a long day.'

'Oh, yes. Bye Dylan.'

Dylan trudged off to his car, leaving Caroline waving and pretending that his casual mention of that name hadn't thrown her thoughts into confusion. But her mobile trilled at her as she was walking out of the car park and turning up towards the pub to meet the others. It pulled her from her reverie.

'Caroline.'

'Brendan!' Images of Tom were now replaced by images of Brendan. She had to smile. All they'd wanted was a dirty weekend, but they hadn't even been able to manage that. Caroline stopped in her tracks and pushed the phone to her cold ear. 'What's up?'

'I know our Paris mission wasn't exactly successful. The thing is, I've booked a luxury hotel for next Friday night. Swimming pool, sauna, top-class restaurant.'

'Let me guess. Big springy bed?' she said wryly. Was trying to have sex this contrived normally?

'Well, it wasn't really so much about the bed.' His voice softened. 'I actually wondered if we could just get away from here and talk to each other. See how we feel. You know, just try and work out whether we want to take things further. Does that make any sense to you?'

Caroline blinked. It made a surprising amount of sense.

Chapter Fifteen

Lizzy's stomach was groaning like a rusty oil tanker. If only her period would start, rather than hovering over her. Once every other month she suffered like this. It would last about thirty-six hours then move on, like a tornado making a strike on her body then calmly going about its business, invisibly heading for some other poor female's ovaries. She felt as if she was floating through a fog, her feet plodding along like the prancing shoes of a Thunderbird puppet, her arms outstretched, pushing the baby buggy (that Michael was attempting to do a headstand in) ahead of her.

Lizzy was in Tunbridge Wells for a reason this morning. She had a plan, something she hadn't told anyone about, not even David. She and David were having an odd few days of it. He'd been very withdrawn when he'd got back from Biggin Hill. She'd asked him plenty of questions about the afternoon he'd spent up there looking at the planes with Brendan and the boys, but it was as if the more she asked, the more he pulled away, like a cuttlefish covering itself in sand the more it sensed intrusion.

Ever since they'd had that minor incident over the brandy he'd bought for the dinner party, something had changed in him. Or perhaps it had been there before, but the brandy argument had suddenly made her notice a problem. Was it her imagination, or could she sense a boredom in him? A restlessness with the situation they'd established together? Only last week he'd started going on about mountaineering, of all things, and how he wished he'd learned to climb before they'd settled down. She'd caught him watching *Survivor* in a very odd frame of mind, and he'd slammed out of the room without speaking when she'd cracked a joke. He'd cherished his day out with the aeroplanes, which she'd expected as he had a passion for anything that flew, but she sensed too he'd craved it on another level. It was as if he'd seen it as an opportunity to escape from something. Her? The house? His identity as a family man? She felt as if she was living with a man who was in the throes of a silent rebellion, and it made her very uncomfortable.

Whatever it was, they had certainly been withdrawing from each other recently, and that had made her secretive about her own plans. Money was tight and Lizzy wanted to do something about it. There were things they couldn't afford, things she wanted for her family. Bikes for the boys to skid about on. Going out to the cinema and maybe for a meal afterwards. A few exciting Christmas or birthday presents. A few changes of shoes for all of them, and occasionally some new clothes for herself or David. Things that weren't around when she was a child, such as a good computer and Internet access. And, once in a while, a weekend away somewhere wonderful. She knew they couldn't have all of those things, but at least if she made some money they might be able to aspire to some of them.

Tunbridge Wells was as busy as usual, especially at the crown of the hill where the major roads met in a thick cluster of popular shops. She'd parked her car in

312

the central multi-storey and was now careering down the steep hill on foot with the pushchair, away from the chain stores and towards the rustic quaintness of the Pantiles. She wove the pushchair past the station, Michael peeping questions at her which she answered on automatic pilot, Jacob trotting obediently beside her, much quieter than usual. At times she thought he could sense when she felt under the weather. He'd look at her with huge, soulful eyes and for a moment she'd imagine she could see David's adult understanding there. But it was probably a lot more simple than that. She'd grouched at Jacob when he'd run over to the Pay and Display machine before she'd got Michael out of the car. Self-preservation was no doubt telling him to keep his mouth shut for the time being.

She stopped the pushchair on an uneven stretch of paving beyond the window of a crafts shop, and inhaled a bracing lungful of cold air.

'I'm all right, Jacob,' she assured him, as his blue eyes grew watchful of her. 'I'm just not feeling very well today. But I'll be fine and we'll have a burger for lunch. How does that sound?'

Jacob's grin reassured her that she hadn't lost another friend, and feeling a little better, Lizzy took stock of her location. She was in the intriguing cobbled lane that led through to the Pantiles. The pavement was uneven, the small shops housed within curiously shaped old buildings, each shopfront unique. The road itself was on a horizontal slope, one side higher than the other. This was where the antiques shops, crafts shops, exclusive designer boutiques and gift shops were to be found. Lizzy headed for Criss-Cross.

She hesitated at the door and peered through the

glass. It was a very smart shop, mainly selling cards but also small unusual gifts, mostly handcrafted. There were pots of reeds in the corners, hessian on the walls, dried flowers forming a window display. 'Arty-crafty,' David would have said with a derisory snort. Although he appreciated something beautiful and handmade when Lizzy created it herself, he didn't seem to see the connection between her hobby and any shop which sold such things.

Taking a deep breath, Lizzy nudged the door with the pushchair and tried to get inside. A sleek, wealthy-looking woman of late middle age was trying to leave as Lizzy was trying to enter the small shop, but Lizzy hadn't seen her. The woman tutted loudly, tucking a Criss-Cross paper bag into her handbag as she scowled at Lizzy.

'That's the thing about pushchairs,' she said archly. 'They're a little like bulldozers.'

'I'm so sorry, I'll back out again. I didn't see you there.'

'No, women with pushchairs never do see anyone else. I think the shops at the top of the town are better able to cope with the paraphernalia of children.'

Lizzy obligingly backed away, her lips pursed, her face red. What the woman meant, clearly, was 'stick to the chain stores and leave the exclusive shops to us exclusive women.' Lizzy could see a smart woman behind the counter inside the shop glancing over. This was not the first impression she'd wanted to create. The disgruntled customer trying to leave the shop followed Lizzy as she retreated, step by step, then as soon as Lizzy was outside on the pavement, almost up against the trunk of one of the trees planted there, she marched off, her heels resounding against the stone slabs.

Lizzy swallowed, feeling small. She clutched Jacob's hand tightly.

'Why did that lady tell us off, Mummy?'

'Because I got in her way, darling.'

'She said we should go to the other shops.'

Lizzy stared at the window of Criss-Cross, at the expensive price tags, the finely made goods, the original Georgian window and door. Was she out of her league? The clientele at this lower end of the town had the distinctive aura of ladies who lunch. Some of the major designer labels had boutiques along this road. The Persian rugs in the window next door started at four figures, and that was for something that was so small it might just cover a coffee stain. Lizzy bit her lip, trying to regain her failing courage. Her belly was aching, her blood was warm, and she had a stupid urge to have a good cry. But Jacob was still looking up at her, waiting for a reaction.

'We're going in here, darling, because I'm going to show them my drawings.'

Jacob raised his eyebrows, and without waiting for further approval, Lizzy once again pushed the buggy into the shop.

Half an hour later, Lizzy floated out of Criss-Cross with the boys. The sun had appeared and was making a thin effort to warm the wintry morning air. It looked as if it might rain later, but for the moment it seemed to Lizzy as if the sun had never been so warming. Jacob danced beside the pushchair as they made their way back up the steeply sloped pavement. She was hardly aware of the twinges in her stomach now. She felt lighter, brighter,

315

feathery, as if she could sail home on a cloud without the need to negotiate the petrol-stained gloom of the multi-storey.

Cassie Grey, the manager of Criss-Cross, had bought her designs. She'd taken them to display in the shop and had promised to be back in touch to let Lizzy know how things went.

'Perhaps the posh cross lady will buy one,' she told the boys, grinning.

They enjoyed a burger in the town before getting some mundane shopping chores done. Lizzy picked up some things at the chemist, some new knickers from Marks, they took a pile of books back to the library and they went to get some new shoes for Jacob. Now that both the boys were tired they began to whine and their reedy voices uniting in complaint began to wear Lizzy down too. Finally, late in the afternoon, they headed back to the car and climbed into it with relief. Lizzy sat at the steering wheel after she'd strapped the boys into the back and had succeeded in getting the buggy into the boot. Michael was already asleep in his chair. He could sleep anywhere. Jacob's eyes were drooping, his cheeks ruddy from the extended shoe-trying-on session which had left them all wanting to sink to the floor and weep with sheer exhaustion, including the shop assistant

'I sold my cards,' Lizzy said under her breath, fingering the car keys. 'I sold my flipping cards.'

It was a dreamlike drive home. The boys slept soundly in the back, and Lizzy flicked the radio on to stop her eyelids from becoming heavy. Every so often a contented smile spread across her face, then she would feel less tired and more excited. Then she would remember that she hadn't actually sold a card yet, and feel less excited. Would she tell David? What would he think?

It was so tempting. She knew that the moment he came home from work she'd want to run at him and tell him. But what if it all ended up as a failed venture? And what sort of 'Yeah, but,' questions might he pose to her now? She'd been pointing out that they couldn't afford to spend money regularly on luxuries. He might equally observe that she was spending money on making cards and pictures which might not sell at all. And he was so moody at the moment. She didn't want to be brought down. She hadn't felt this good about herself since Michael was born.

No, she decided. She wouldn't tell David anything just yet. Not unless the cards actually sold. And then only if he wasn't going to be judgemental about her spending time making cards upstairs in the spare room rather than washing fruit squash beakers, or ironing shorts, or clearing up plastic dinosaurs, or listening to the boys reading.

Back at home, Lizzy got everything out of the car and safely up to the front door without anything (it was usually Jacob) having a burst of high spirits and racing off down the road in the direction of the playground. As she pushed the door open the phone was ringing.

'Everyone inside,' she instructed the boys, who trotted in. She piled everything onto the hall carpet and glanced at her watch. It was gone five o'clock. No wonder they were all knackered. The boys would be wanting their tea. She picked up the phone.

'Hello?' she said wearily.

'Lizzy, it's Cassie.'

317

'Cassie!' Lizzy injected life into her voice. 'Is everything all right?'

'I think it's time you got some business cards made,' Cassie said with a smile in her voice. 'I've sold all but one of your designs this afternoon. How soon can you provide me with some more?'

Antonia wandered towards the front door when the bell rang. It sounded as if Daniel was upstairs in the bathroom. Sonia was flipping hot toast around in the kitchen and had retuned the radio from the *Today* programme to Radio One the minute she'd seen her mother leave the room. Antonia was ready for work, and had a hot cup of coffee in one hand. Audrey was still in bed. All week, Daniel had been kindly allowing Antonia to borrow his car while the garage continued repairs on her own, and he'd been picked up and dropped off by a colleague who lived nearby. Today was the first day that Daniel hadn't just flown out of the door when the bell had rung. Antonia hesitated at the bottom of the stairs.

'Daniel? I think it's your lift. Daniel?' she called. The whooshing of water was the response from the bathroom. Antonia decided she'd better answer the door.

There was a good-looking man standing there, in his early thirties she'd estimate, with light brown hair and striking blue eyes. He wore a contagiously cheerful expression on his face for a cold morning. He had good colour in his cheeks, which made him look robust. He was wearing a trench coat over a smart, dark suit. She wondered idly what his job up at the MOD was. She'd never really probed Daniel about what he did either. Whatever it was, it paid the rent and he seemed to enjoy it.

'Hi,' she said. 'I'm Antonia. I've called Daniel but I think he's still in the bathroom. Would you like to step in for a moment?'

'Oh, hi.' He put out his hand. 'I'm David. Daniel and I work together.'

'Yes, he told me.'

'You're a teacher, aren't you?'

'That's right.'

'My cousin teaches locally too. Or rather, my wife's cousin.'

Antonia nodded politely as Daniel bounded down the stairs looking very dashing in a dark suit, his overcoat slung over his arm. 'Sorry, Antonia, running a bit late this morning.'

'That's fine,' she smiled. 'Nice of you to lend me the car. I hope very much to have mine back from the garage any day now. And nice of you too, David, to help out.'

'No problem at all.' David raised his eyebrows affably. 'I pretty much come by this way anyway, and it's not as if it's a long journey to work. I don't have to suffer Daniel's appalling jokes for too long.'

Daniel looked indignant. 'Bad jokes? Right. You were the one who mentioned Douglas Bader at Biggin Hill.'

'Ah, but excuse me, you were the one who told me I hadn't got a leg to stand on.'

Daniel gave Antonia an apologetic look as he went out of the door. 'Light aircraft bore. Don't ask him about it, whatever you do.'

Antonia laughed as the two men left. 'Have a good day, nice to meet you, David.'

Sonia wandered into the hall chewing toast as Antonia was still smiling and tucking her hair behind her ears, studying her reflection in the hall mirror.

319

'Was that the guy Daniel went to Biggin Hill with the other day?'

'Probably, he said something about light aircraft. Is Daniel into planes too then?'

The phone rang, interrupting them. Antonia dived on it first. It was the garage saying that the car was ready for collection. Antonia made an arrangement to pick it up and rang off.

'Great,' she said, taking her coffee mug back to the kitchen, where Sonia was now reading *New Woman*. 'Car's ready. So we're independent again, as from this afternoon. Daniel will be pleased.'

'How are you going to get it?' Sonia peered at her. She'd got a lot of eyeliner on this morning. Antonia wasn't sure whether to say anything or not.

'I'm going to pick it up. Obviously.'

'Yeah, but I heard you say you'd be there at one thirty. So are you going to skive off school, or what?'

Antonia filled the kettle again to give herself time to think.

The fact was that she had a further appointment at the hospital this afternoon. She had told them at school that she needed the afternoon off for dental treatment. But she didn't want Sonia to know about any of it.

'As you would say, my love, I've got a free period,' Antonia said, rinsing out her mug so as not to meet Sonia's eye. 'I've just got time early afternoon to get a bus down to the garage and collect it.'

'What about Daniel's car? How will you get that from the school back here?'

'I'll think about that.'

'What, you going to drive two cars at once?' Sonia

raised an eyebrow. 'I didn't realise just how talented you were.'

'I'm going to sort it out later, all right Sonia?' Antonia raised her voice. In fact she had been planning to come home at lunchtime, spruce herself up and have a shower, in the knowledge that she was going to be invaded by medical instruments. Then she was planning to drive from home to her appointment. Then she was intending to head home at the normal time. Now she could leave Daniel's car at home when she got here, take a bus or taxi up to the garage, and go straight to her hospital appointment from there. That way, Daniel's car would be at home and her own car would be successfully collected and paid for, and her investigative appointment could be honoured. In actual fact, it worked out very well. Apart from Sonia's staring face and the uncomprehending downturned arc of her mouth.

'But you'll end up with both cars at school,' Sonia persisted.

'Close your mouth, Sonia, you look as if you're catching flies.'

'Unless you leave Daniel's car here this morning, but then, why didn't he take it to work?'

'Well maybe I'll get Greg to give me a lift down to the garage.'

'Has he got a free period as well then?'

'I don't know.' Antonia studied her watch avidly. 'Maybe.'

'But you'll still end up with two cars at school,' Sonia said.

'Sonia, you've got far too much eyeliner on. You look like you've been punched. Go and sort it out,' Antonia snapped, to Sonia's surprise. 'And if you don't leave in five minutes you'll miss your bus.'

Hours later that same day, Antonia pulled shut her car door and huddled in the driver's seat. She couldn't stop shivering. Slivers of freezing rain filled the air, spattering the clear glass of the windscreen. With trembling fingers, she pushed the key into the ignition and turned it one click, twisting the heater switch and turning the heat on full. The blast of dry air filled the car. She sat with hunched shoulders, listening to the white noise of the heater, waiting for the warmth to be absorbed by her coat, her clothes, her body. Beyond the windscreen, the hospital car park was full. A mesh of multicoloured cars, all belonging to someone, everyone with their own story. Beyond the car park the red-brick hospital outbuildings ranged untidily in random directions, like Sticklebricks stuck on experimentally by a winsome child. She had just been inside one of the buildings. She shifted in the car seat, reclaiming the sensations between her legs.

Apparently her cervical cells were 'on the turn'. She'd had some kind of liquid brushed onto her cells which showed up patches of abnormal growth. All of this she had watched, as if it was happening to someone else, on a television screen fixed to the wall above the couch she'd been lying on. She'd seen the patches of cells show up fluorescently, and the look of satisfaction on the young doctor's face to have identified her target.

'There! Can you see?' she'd said to Antonia, then, turning to the nurse as if Antonia wasn't there, 'I think we have CIN two to three there. The other patch there, right on the entry to the uterus? That's a definite CIN three. Mark it on the chart at three possible plus.'

Antonia had blinked at the young woman's clear eyes, hopeful of elucidation. 'What?'

'What that means,' the doctor said, easing a long metal instrument inside Antonia and clipping a sample from each of the affected areas, apparently failing to notice Antonia's strong wince each time, 'is that you're here just in time. We hope. You're on the turn.'

Tomatoes were on the turn as they went red. Avocados were on the turn as they became edible. Milk was on the turn as it went sour. Antonia's cells were on the turn as they went –

'Cancerous?'

'We'll see when we get the results of the biopsies. That'll be quick, so you won't be left hanging about too long. But I can tell you from what I can see that we'll be doing further work on you.' She grinned inappropriately.

'Further work? I'm not the M25. Can you be more specific?' As the doctor looked slightly alarmed at the sudden command in the tone, Antonia added from her position on her back with her legs hoisted into the stirrups, 'And a little less euphemistic. I am a secondary school teacher. In a grammar school. You may speak to me as if I have a brain cell.'

'What I mean is, you're almost certainly coming back for loop diathermy. I would hope that's all we'll need to do.'

'And that is what exactly?' It was hard to be intimidating on your back with your legs in the air, to somebody who had a hand stuck up your vagina. It would be fairly clear, even to the most impartial of observers who was in control.

'We give you local anaesthetic in the affected area. Then it's just a question of running a hot wire over the problem patches on the cervix. If you like, it's like skimming off the cells that are causing the trouble on the surface, and in the process cauterizing what remains. You feel nothing at all. It's very successful and causes minimum intrusion to the patient.'

'Minimum intrusion,' Antonia repeated in disbelief, wondering what on earth the alternatives could be.

'Patients are in for perhaps an hour or two. We like you to sit tight and have a couple of cups of tea before you leave, then you can go home.'

'Out the same day?'

'Absolutely,' the doctor said in triumph. 'Although you'd probably want to go to bed when you got home, and perhaps for a day or two afterwards. The products are a little messy.'

'Products?' Antonia swallowed.

'Leakage afterwards. It can last several weeks, but can be controlled with king-sized pads after a few days.'

This was joyous. The images in Antonia's head were becoming more gruesome by the minute. 'Oh God.'

'But think of it this way.' The doctor withdrew all her implements and set about putting things in specimen containers. Antonia decided not to watch her so closely. 'You had no idea whatsoever that you had pre-cancerous cells on your cervix until you had your smear. You haven't felt a thing. You wouldn't. In the old days, by the time you'd felt it, it would have been too late. The silent killer, they call it. You're lucky, Antonia. It'll be a bit of hassle, but it's almost certain that we've caught it and controlled it. You can get up now.'

Antonia struggled to a sitting position and tried to

look dignified as the nurse handed her her knickers and a pad to stick inside them. She slipped them back on and stood up.

'Hang on. What do you mean by "almost certain"? Almost?'

The doctor's eyes widened. 'We'll get the results of the biopsy very soon. Then we'll know how much surgery we'll have to do. But it looks highly likely to me that it'll just be loop diathermy. I can't imagine we'll have to go further.'

But one of the problems with being a teacher, Antonia thought as she placed her hands over the car ventilators and felt the warmth gradually sink into her fingers, was that you just had to know everything. So she had sat at a side table with the doctor, and they had talked about every single possibility. Every worst-case scenario. Every possible thing that could go wrong. And it was when the young doctor asked her in a fake-casual voice, 'You have had your children, haven't you?' that the real bottom line began to whisper itself to Antonia.

This was it. This was the moment when her decisions were wrenched out of her hands. She would be lucky if she came out of this process and still had a womb. She would be very lucky indeed if she still had more than half a cervix left. In other words, from this moment on, the option of being a fully functioning woman in every sense of the word was in doubt. She was forty-two. She hadn't had any serious signs of menopause and the knowledge that she was probably still fertile had played around in her mind at times. But it was time to face up to the truth. This situation meant that there was serious doubt that she would ever have another child.

She turned the windscreen wipers on, pressed

325

buttons, made things happen, cleaning the back and front windscreens. Then she sat perfectly still. For the first time, Antonia could understand how her own mother felt about her broken wrist. Used to being the one in control, but now being controlled, her independence wrenched away from her. Perhaps that was why her mother had taken to completely rearranging Antonia's house every time she looked the other way. Perhaps that was why she had suddenly, madly, inexplicably got a houseful of teenagers drunk. Maybe she just needed to feel in control of something, however ridiculous and insignificant it was.

Antonia stared dazedly at the spattering drops on the windscreen. She couldn't move. She couldn't cry. She just felt very, very quiet.

Caroline sat very still in her kitchen. Beside her on the floor was her packed bag. Underneath her suede trousers she was wearing a pair of red silky knickers that had tie-ups on the hips.

The reason for the sexy knickers was this. She and Brendan had talked some things through on the phone. It was probably the most open and honest conversation she'd ever had with him. The more he'd assured her that sex didn't have to come into another trip away together, the more she believed him. But it was perverse. The more he let her go, the more she wanted him to draw her in. Brendan was a gorgeous-looking man. So was Tom, and Tom had been clouding her thoughts a little too much recently. He was strange and unsuitable. And hadn't Tom shown her the door when they'd been about to kiss? At least Brendan was, as they say, a sure thing. She was a woman, after all. Her feelings had been awakened.

326

But, having readied herself for him to come and collect her, saucy knickers and all, she found herself swamped by last-minute doubts. She could imagine Brendan in a sweaty Australian bar, somewhere in the outback. It'd be full of men in stained vests and unkempt stubble, with hats surrounded by corks, beating away flies with barbecued chicken legs.

'Aw, strewth mate, you mean you didn't give her one? And you had seven years to get yer strides off?'

Caroline was as sexually curious about Brendan as he was about her, that much was obvious. But what happened next? How would she feel when he disappeared into the void on a Qantas flight, never to be seen again, filled with intimate knowledge of her inner thighs? The closer they got to the experience, the more doubts she began to have. So when the doorbell rang Caroline sat perfectly still, unable to move, aware that she was like a horse refusing at a fence it recognised. She waited for a few minutes and the ringing came again. She'd have to tell him she wasn't going to spend a night with him in the hotel after all. That was only fair.

She got up and went into the hall, stopping to smooth down her hair before she opened the door. Brendan was on the doorstep and a taxi was waiting at the curbside. As soon as she met his eyes Caroline was further stricken with indecision. He handed her a single red rose.

'For you.'

She took it, and then stood awkwardly, wondering how to let him down gently.

'Are you ready?' he asked. His face was very uncertain. He didn't look as if he was expecting her to say yes. 'Your body language tells me conflicting things.

You've got a jacket on and you've done your hair, and that tells me you're coming. But your eyes are telling me to go to hell. Is that about right?'

'Yes.'

He nodded, and gave a self-deprecating smile. 'I guess you've packed an overnight bag, but that was before you changed your mind.'

'Yes,' she breathed, feeling awful as disappointment fell over his face.

'Ah well.' He pulled his collar up, as the wind was still whipping sharply. 'Can't blame a guy for trying, can you? I guess I'll head off.'

He gave her another smile and walked back to the waiting taxi. Watching Brendan's back as he ambled away, Caroline felt a sharp stab of regret. He opened the taxi door without looking back.

'Brendan! Wait!' she called.

He glanced back at her. 'Don't worry, Caro. It's what I expected.'

'I'm coming,' she yelled, amazing herself. 'Wait there, I'll get my bag.'

So, this was it. She was taking off with Brendan for a night of passion, and this time there would be no Paris to distract them. Caroline's heart did a little leap. She was going to have rampant sex. The truth was, she couldn't wait to get physical with someone. Brendan would do very nicely.

She hopped into the taxi and the driver set off. Just as she had turned to say something to Brendan, the car screeched to a halt and both she and Brendan were thrown forward.

'Bloody hell,' Brendan said. 'Sorted out which one's the brake now?'

'It's that rival company, Roadline.' The driver pointed at a car that had swerved across them to park. 'Cut me right up and stopped in front of me he did.'

'Well we've managed about a yard so far,' Caroline said drily. 'It's progress of a sort.'

'Someone you know?' the driver said as he was about to attempt to pull away from the curb again, nodding at the passenger from the cab in front, who had climbed out and was waving frantically at them through the window.

'Who's that?' Brendan said, leaning across for a better look.

Caroline crouched forward, then sat bolt upright. 'Oh my God!'

'Oh my God,' Brendan echoed. 'I don't believe it.'

Caroline yanked open the taxi door and threw herself out. 'Phil! What the hell are you doing here?'

'Who's Phil?' the driver asked Brendan.

'Her brother,' Brendan said with a sigh. 'This obviously isn't meant to be. You might as well drop me here too.'

Chapter Sixteen

Phil looked as astonished to find himself in England as Caroline was to see him there. She sat him down at her kitchen table and filled him with tea. Brendan leaned against a wall, his arms loosely folded, watching the scene bemusedly.

'Explain yourself,' Caroline demanded eventually, sitting opposite Phil.

Phil gulped another mouthful of tea. He looked exhausted. His brown hair was ruffled, his normally animated blue eyes hollow. He'd either been crying or rubbing them in frustration. His cheeks were flushed, and there was the oaty smell of beer on his breath. He'd obviously been making the most of airline freebies.

'I've left Luzie.'

'You've what?'

'Left. Gone. It's all kaput.'

'That's not possible.'

'It's made us both so miserable. It's just not working and we've got to do something about it before we both go mad.'

Caroline thought fast. 'A break may be good for you. You can stay here tonight, of course, then you can go back again and talk things through.'

'Forget it. It's over.'

'You can't tell Mum and Dad that things are so bad you've flown home.' Caroline chewed her lip. 'They'll get too upset. You know how they are. We'll keep it between us.'

'I don't care who knows.'

'Mum and Dad won't take it well. They've really warmed to Luzie.'

'Luzie's not married to my mum and dad. She's married to me, and I say it's over.'

'It can't be.'

'Run that one past me again, Caro?'

'Phil, you can't leave Luzie. She's your wife.'

'Marriages break up all the time.'

'Not in our family they don't,' Caroline stated.

Phil raised tired blue eyes to hers. 'Doesn't hearing yourself say that piss you off?'

'What do you mean?' Caroline frowned at him.

'Our fucking family. Fucking perfect. Or fucking else.'

'Phil!'

'Oh forget it. I knew I'd get this. I should never have come home. Complete fucking waste of time.'

'Phil, stop saying "fucking" to me. I'm your sister. I'm listening to you. You don't have to swear your head off.'

'What if I want to swear my head off? Or is that down on the list with divorces and separations? Not an integral part of the Blake repertoire. See also taboo language.'

'Phil!' she repeated, unnerved by his aggressive energy.

'He's right, Caroline.' Brendan spoke in a soft voice. 'Your family can be oppressive without meaning to. I know what Phil means.'

'Oppressive? What, my poor scatty mother and my gentle, eccentric father? Who could they possibly oppress, even if they tried their best? They can't even

331

oppress the Hope-Potters next door and they are really obnoxious, so how could they oppress all the people they love? Which actually includes you, Brendan, even though you're certainly not a part of this family,' Caroline said very precisely. 'And I think they would be gutted to hear you talk like this.'

'Oh Caro for God's sake, Brendan's practically been adopted.' Phil was rifling through her fridge. He found a bottle of wine, a corkscrew and set about opening it.

'What are you doing?'

'Getting smashed. What does it look like?'

'Phil, I'd rather we talked about this sensibly.'

'You've never been married, Caroline,' Brendan said, giving her a slight smile that could be interpreted as either apologetic or smug, depending on what mood you were in. Caroline decided he was being smug.

'So what?'

'So you've never been through a marital separation either. Let alone a divorce.'

'And?' Caroline said to Brendan, red-faced.

'I have,' Brendan said. 'And I got pissed too. Sensible comes later. A little bit after rebound.'

'Oh yes, I forgot you're the expert on dysfunctional relationships,' Caroline bit at Brendan, suddenly resentful of his alliance with Phil. Phil was *her* brother. Part of *her* family. Why were they ganging up on her?

'Well, Caroline,' Brendan said slowly. 'At least I *have* relationships.'

She blanched. The kitchen was silent, apart from a loud pop as the cork sprang from the bottle. Phil splashed wine into two glasses, handed one to Brendan and kept one for himself, muttering to Caroline, 'I'm assuming you don't want any.'

'And what point are you trying to make about relationships, Brendan?' Her veins turned chilly. She wasn't going to let it drop now, even though Brendan averted his eyes.

'My point is that you can't live up to your family's expectations either. You just show it in a different way.'

Phil raised a finger. 'That is a fucking good point.'

'Meaning what?' Caroline's stomach felt like lead.

'Look, everyone's emotions are obviously up at the moment. I don't want to make you feel uncomfortable,' Brendan said.

'Me? Hang on, it's Phil who's just turned up here with his life in a heap. None of this is my fault.'

'Sit down, Caro,' Phil said, sucking up a long mouthful of his wine and relaxing back into his chair as if it had done him instant good. 'I know what Brendan means.'

'Perhaps you'd both like to enlighten me. I must be stupid. I thought we should be talking about you and Luzie.'

'All Brendan's saying is that the pressure's too much. To be perfect. To have the same fairy-tale marriage as Granddad did with Gran, that Mum has with Dad. That Doe's got with Ron.'

'That Lizzy's got with David,' Brendan contributed.

'Yep, that too. They're all shining examples, don't you see? I can't live up to it, but at least I've tried. You're more sensible actually. You know in advance you'll never live up to it, so you've thrown in the towel before you've even started. You just don't go out with anyone, ever.'

Caroline slid, ashen-faced, into the chair opposite Phil. She'd never heard these things said before but a spear of truth jabbed at her insides. She wanted to cry, but she wanted to shout at Phil too. And at Brendan, nodding sagely from where he was leaning, propping up the door.

'I do go out with people,' she protested.

'When?' Brendan and Phil said at the same time.

'I – well, I went out with someone at my last college.'

'Not the divorced bloke with the bald patch and the chip on his shoulder about women earning more than him?'

Caroline blinked at Brendan. 'No, I mean Keith the geography tutor.'

'Okay, that's the same one,' Brendan explained.

'Oh.'

'And you ran out on that one after three months. It didn't even get physical.'

'Yes it did!' Caroline countered. 'Just not very – excitingly physical.'

'And before Keith with the bald patch it was years,' Phil said.

'And just how do you know that?'

'It was, Caroline. Years before Keith,' Brendan contributed. 'That's the only reason you went out with him. You'd obviously completely forgotten what a man looked like and mistook him for one.'

'And what makes you think you know that?' she asked Brendan indignantly.

'David's my best mate. Lizzy talks to David. I know things. Not intimate girl things, just fact things. Like it being years before Keith.'

'And what about since you've been back in Kent?' Phil asked. 'You're still putting off seeing anyone.'

'It's true there's been nobody since I've been here, but that's because nobody's been right.'

334

'Gee thanks,' Brendan muttered.

'I mean, nobody's jumped up and hit me in the face as the perfect date. Sorry, Brendan, but that includes you, given your record with women over the last God knows how many years. And if I haven't been out with anyone I'm so bloody sorry but I thought it was my decision.'

'It is your decision, Caro,' Phil said gently. 'But don't you think it's interesting that you never go out with anyone?'

'I'm happy being single.'

'Fine.' Phil put up his hands. 'Your prerogative. I just thought it was a normal human trait to like having relationships with members of the opposite sex.' Then he added, 'Or the same sex. Whatever.'

'I'm not gay,' Caroline stated stonily. 'Although at this moment I wish I was. It would bloody well shut you both up.'

'No, it wouldn't,' Phil said earnestly. 'Even if you were a carpet-muncher I'd like nothing better than to see you happy with someone.'

'A carpet-muncher?' Caroline blinked.

'The point being that I wouldn't give a stuff whether you were gay or not. I'd rather see you happy than unhappy.'

'Well I'm not unhappy. And you're the one who's left your wife, so why don't we talk about you instead? It seems a bit odd to me that you've come all the way from Germany to tell me what's wrong with me. You could have done that over the phone.'

'The point is that we've both been stymied by this idea of the perfect life.'

Caroline's chest heaved stormily. Phil was so dogmatic he was making her nervous. More than that, there was a ring of truth to everything he was saying, and that was putting her even further on edge. 'Even if you were right, where does it get us?'

'Perhaps it means we can start again on a different footing,' Phil said.

'What's that?' Caroline breathed.

'Well, before you try to force me back into a loveless marriage just because it is a marriage, you might consider the glass house and throwing stones analogy. I did it and failed, you didn't do it. Neither of us have achieved the ideal. We're quits. No moral high ground on either side.'

'Phil, I've never seen you like this,' Caroline said. 'But if that's the point you want to make, I heard you. All right?'

'I'm not even sure I would have married Luzie if everyone hadn't expected the first serious girlfriend I had to be my perfect partner for life. I'm not thirty yet. I don't even know who I am, let alone who she is and what we are together. I don't know anything.'

There was an awkward pause. 'I'm still listening,' Caroline said.

'And if this wasn't a marriage I was leaving, nobody would be having hysterics about breaking open a bottle of Tipp-Ex for the first time and ruining the family tree.'

'All right.'

'So let's go from here with the assumption that everyone in this room is a fallible human being, capable of making stupid mistakes. Shock horror, that means even you, Caro.'

There was a long silence. Then Brendan shifted.

'Look, I'm going to leave you guys to talk. I'll drop in again. Phil, you've got my number haven't you?'

'Yep. I'll call you tomorrow.'

'Goodbye, Caroline.'

'I'll see you to the door.' She got up. Vaguely she remembered that they'd been about to shoot off to a hotel to have passionate sex. Brendan had already gone out to the hall. She followed him. 'Brendan, can't you still go?'

'Where?'

'The hotel, of course. Have a sauna or something.'

'I've gone off the idea.'

'It's a waste if you've already booked the room.'

'It's only money, Caroline. It means so little. So very, very little.'

'But –'

'Phil will ring me tomorrow. We'll probably go out and talk. You're forgetting how much we used to go out when he lived in England.'

Yes, she probably was. Phil, David and Brendan. When Phil was around, he always hung about with them. She'd forgotten. 'Right.'

'He needs his mates around, and he'll want to talk to a bloke about it as well as his big sister. It may be a false alarm, but he may be right. It may be over. And as much as you hate me for it, I have been married and seen it fall apart under my nose. I can probably be a good listener just because I've been through something similar, if for no other reason.'

He was right. Caroline nodded. He went on, 'I can't bugger off to a hotel as if nothing's happening. He's like a little brother to me.'

As Caroline was opening the door for Brendan she said, 'I'm sorry for what I said. About you not being a part of this family. You are.'

'That'd make this incestuous then, wouldn't it?'

Caroline didn't answer, and Brendan walked away without even attempting to peck her on the cheek or give her a more intimate goodbye than a final 'See ya.' She closed the door, her emotions rolling around like clothes in a tumble-dryer.

Antonia was astonished when she got to Tom Grainger's door to discover that there was a queue outside. She'd parked the car in the only space she could find further up the road, and walked back to see two young women loitering on his path, chatting to each other.

'Excuse me,' she said, edging past them and wondering what they were doing.

'You here to see Tom?' the blonde one asked.

Antonia didn't answer. She wasn't about to discuss her business in the street.

'This is the queue,' the brunette added. 'There's three people in there already, and he said he couldn't have more inside because it wouldn't be private enough for sittings.'

'So we're waiting out here.' The blonde woman lit a cigarette and exhaled blue smoke into the twilight. 'Want one?' She held out the packet to Antonia.

'No thank you.'

The two young women exchanged glances. 'Right then.'

'If you'll excuse me, I'll knock. He's expecting me. If you've just dropped by no doubt he'll see you afterwards.'

What on earth was she doing here, Antonia yelled at herself as the two women blinked iridescent eye make-up at her. She marched past them to Tom's door and rapped hard. It took a long while for him to answer.

'He's busy,' the blonde woman said. 'Like we told you.'

'I have an appointment,' Antonia gritted.

'Yeah but Tom doesn't live by rules,' the brunette said in a strange, soft voice. Antonia glanced at her sharply. Her eyes had become dreamy.

The door was opened at last, and Tom stood in the doorway. He had on a waistcoat studded with tiny mirrors. His hair looked wilder than before. Antonia peered at him closely. She was sure he had lipstick on his cheek. He followed the line of her stare and put his fingers to his cheek in embarrassment, and rubbed hard.

'Antonia!' he said. 'Hi.'

'You said to come round at six,' she said in a low voice. 'But you seem busy.'

'It's just,' he lowered his voice too and leaned towards her. His pupils seemed dilated, but whether out of excitement or alarm she couldn't tell. 'It's just that it's sort of mushroomed.'

'Mushroomed?'

He rubbed at his cheek again. 'A bit out of control,' he whispered, 'they keep turning up. These women.'

Antonia eyed the smear of lipstick and said with heavy irony, 'How terrible for you.'

'No, really. Come in, please. I've got a group session in the living room, but if you want to come through to the kitchen I'll finish up soon and we can spend time on our own. You won't mind sitting with Daisy, will you?'

'Who's Daisy?' Antonia asked, irritated and wondering if she should just go straight home.

339

'My goat. You don't look like somebody who'd mind goats.'

'I've never met one before.'

'Good. No history of trauma. Come in then.'

'Tom!' The blonde woman stuck out her hand. 'Do you want to see my palm?'

He scratched at his hair, looking agitated. 'Are you two still here? I'm not sure how long I'll be. Probably another couple of hours.'

'That's okay.' The brunette nodded at her friend. 'We'll go to the Castle for a couple of drinks then come back again. You did promise that you'd see to us tonight, didn't you?'

'Both of us,' the blonde said, and gave him an overt wink, before they turned and stalked away down the path. Antonia turned back to Tom in astonishment.

'What on earth are you running here?'

Tom rolled his eyes in despair. 'Just come in, please.'

Half an hour later, Tom came to find Antonia in his kitchen. She'd been sitting next to a warm Aga, resting her elbows on his rough oak table, admiring the earthy quality he'd created in the room, rubbing her hand absently over Daisy's head. When Tom had first led her in she'd found Daisy happily settled on a big blanket bunched up into bedding in the corner of the tiled floor. He'd made her a cup of coffee then rushed away, looking harassed, promising that he'd clear the house quickly and give her his undivided attention. Within seconds, Daisy had got up clumsily and wandered over to sniff Antonia. She hadn't had any experience with goats, but the animal looked more nervous of her than she was of it, so she'd put out a hand. Daisy had seemed happy since then to hover next to her chair and while she'd been lost in thought, Antonia had been fingering the wiry hair. The two of them seemed very much at peace with each other. Antonia found it strangely comforting.

'Right then,' Tom announced himself. 'Oh Antonia, Daisy's eating your coat. Didn't you notice?'

She looked down and found that Daisy was chewing contentedly on the corner of her overcoat. She yanked the soggy material from the goat's mouth, unfazed. 'Does she eat everything?'

'Oh yes. Everything. And I mean, absolutely everything.'

'She's gorgeous.' Antonia rubbed the goat's head again, and it put up its teeth in an attempt to nibble her.

'I'm glad you think so. Not everyone does.'

'How couldn't you fall in love with her?'

Tom laughed under his breath. 'Believe me, I've had some odd reactions to that goat.'

'Really?'

'You'd be amazed.'

'Why did you decide to get a goat? I see you've got a conservatory out there, but the garden's not that big. It's not the first thing you'd think of.'

'I didn't decide to get her. I found her. It's not a very happy story, but let's just say she was practically a baby, and she was starved. So I took her in. She's only a teenager now. She'll be bigger than that when she's fully grown. I only realised I didn't know anything about goats once I'd got her home, but I've found out a lot since then. She seems to prefer it inside to out there in the cold though, so I treat her pretty much like the others.'

'The others?'

341

'The cats,' he said, blushing slightly. 'They're probably all hiding if you haven't spotted any yet. They've all got their places to sleep.'

Antonia found herself thinking again that he was an interesting man, and now he was showing himself to be an enormously kind one. He was really quite rare. And that was before she put her mind to the spiritual quality in him that she just couldn't pin down. A mass of fluff swaggered past her at shin level. 'There's one of your cats. Did you rescue all of those too?'

Tom laughed. 'Actually, most of them, yes. You'd be amazed how often you find a stray in need if you're hopelessly soft like me.'

They fell silent while Antonia stroked the head of the fluffy grey cat by her feet. It meowed up at her, and she smiled at it. 'You must treat them well. They're very trusting.'

Tom eyed the grey cat indulgently for a second, then turned his attention back to Antonia.

'I think you're here for help, if I can jump in.' He pulled up a chair and sat with her at the table. 'I've cleared everyone out now, and I'm sorry you had to wait.'

'It's not a problem,' she said, wondering why it wasn't. Probably because sitting in his warm, cosy, cat-and goat-filled kitchen absorbing the aura of his house had surrounded her with a sense of well-being. She'd needed that half-hour to herself.

'So the living room's clear now. Do you want to go in there?'

'Do you know, I like it in here. Is that a problem?'

'Not at all.' He looked around, hooking his hair behind his ears. 'It's a bit messy. You're sure you don't mind?'

'I like it for being messy. It shows that you have more on your mind than pedantic, stupid details like, oh I don't know, washing up, and cleaning the cooker and clearing old newspapers off the table,' she indicated them, 'or brushing up every strand of cat hair.'

'Thanks,' Tom said ironically.

'No really. I mean it. Those details are stupid, pointless, repetitive, recycled chores that we spend far too much time worrying and arguing about. Who cares if nobody washes up? Or if my daughter leaves toast crumbs all over the unit, and puts empty cartons of milk back in the fridge? Or if she spills her nail varnish on the bath mat and doesn't tell me it's ruined. Who cares if my mother rearranges my kitchen every time I go out and has turned the house into a Chinese laundry? I mean, who gives a shit?'

Tom said after a diplomatic pause, 'Not you, obviously.'

'You're quite right. Not me. Because I know that life is not about those silly things any more. It's about – it's about your love for your animals, for example. Wanting to make a difference, however small. Easing the suffering of another being. That's what you do.'

'They don't exactly suffer,' Tom smiled, as his grey cat dived with noisy enthusiasm head first into a bowl full of biscuits.

'I didn't mean them,' Antonia said. 'I mean us. The people you see.'

'I don't . . . really.' His cheeks reddened and he looked away.

'Why did you offer to see me when you left my house? You said I could come here, on my own, because you did healing.'

'I haven't done healing for a while,' Tom hedged. There was reticence in his eyes.

'But why say it to me?'

He played with the corner of one of his old news-papers. 'You're here, aren't you?'

'You're not answering my question.'

'Because I can't. And if I did explain it in words, it wouldn't make any more sense to you than it does to me. I can try to help, but I can't promise anything.'

'What's wrong with me?' Antonia leaned forward. 'What do you know?'

'I don't know anything.' Tom pushed back his hair, avoiding her eye.

'I think you do.'

'Antonia, I want to help if I can. I'm not a scientist. I can't diagnose.'

'What can you see?'

'I can't see anything.'

'What can you feel?'

He turned his eyes straight to hers. 'I can't answer that.'

'Tell me.'

'It won't change anything.'

'Tell me!' Antonia thumped the table. 'Or you are a fraud and I'm wasting my time.'

'I'm not a fraud. I'm not trying to pretend to be anything I'm not.'

'Then bloody tell me what my bloody problem is,' Antonia yelled.

There was a silence. Antonia's voice echoed in her ears. She must have needed to yell like that. The minute it was out she began to feel better. It was like ejecting poison from a wound.

344

'All I can tell you is that there are images sometimes. Not always, just sometimes. When I touch people it happens. Just a frame, sometimes two, sometimes a smell or a sound. There was an image when I shook your hand at your house when we said goodbye. It was one I'd seen before. My grandmother was ill once, with a tumour. She recovered. It's milder with you, not so powerful. Low down, here.' He put a hand on his stomach.

Antonia sank right back in her chair with relief. She draped one arm over the back of it. She crossed one leg over the other, and gazed at him calmly.

'Well blow me down. You're the real thing.'

'You said you knew. I'm assuming you weren't bluffing.'

'Yes, I knew.' She took a long breath. 'I'm sorry to do that to you.'

'It's all right. I understand,' he said.

'Yes, you do. There's a lot you understand.' They gazed at each other peacefully for a while. 'Where did your grandmother come from?'

'I'm not really sure.'

'You don't know where your own grandma came from?'

'Well, here. There. Everywhere.'

'You have got gypsy blood, haven't you?' It gave Antonia an odd thrill. She knew she was right. If she'd been of Romany blood herself it would have been recognition, but it wasn't that. It was a perception.

He relaxed his shoulders. 'Gypsies aren't famous for their popularity.' He gave her a cryptic smile.

'You know, Tom, it's my job to analyse the hidden meanings in things and then attempt to express them.

345

It's what I do. Poetry, drama, literature, you name it. I interpret it. Words are my tool, you see. And I can say without any false modesty or undue egotism that I'm very good at it.'

He nodded. 'I can imagine.'

'But when it comes to you, I'm stuck.'

He gave her a full, warm smile that stretched right to his eyes. Then he put his hand out and indicated that she should offer one of her hands to him.

'What? This?'

'Yes, give me your left hand and let me hold it. And stop trying to explain things just for a moment. Just relax.'

Once her hand was in his, she noticed his reddened knuckles. His thumb seemed swollen. The warmth spread from his palm, across hers, and up her arm. It felt wonderful. But she couldn't help remarking on what she'd seen.

'Is it arthritis?' she asked starkly. He sat up straight, his face troubled. Her hand was still in his but it was clear that his concentration was broken.

'Yes,' he said simply.

'Is that why you do this – I mean, do you have another job?'

He stalled and blinked at her. 'Why do you ask?'

'Ah,' she said, smiling. 'You do all the asking normally, don't you.'

'No, I don't normally ask anything. I'm just very surprised you noticed. Nobody else has.'

'My father suffered from it. Your hands reminded me of that. But I'm sorry to jump in like that.'

'It's all right.' His expression indicated that it was far from all right.

'I'm aware that it can happen to younger people.' There was an uneasy silence. 'I mentioned my father and I know, I can imagine that's what you picture. Old people with stiff joints. But I'm not an uneducated woman. I know that arthritis isn't an old person's disease. I do know that,' she emphasised awkwardly, aware that images of the elderly were now hanging over them. She realised that she'd stumbled across a very sensitive issue.

He looked even more uncomfortable. 'If you say so.'

'Have you – has it been bad for you?'

'Bad enough for me to change my job.'

'What did . . .' Antonia thought better of it. Perhaps it wouldn't be helpful to quiz him. 'Whatever it was I presume you don't do it any more.'

'No.' He looked philosophical but she knew it was a mask.

'So what do you do now?' Antonia pressed.

He paused before answering, flicking his eyes around the room in a gesture of possession. 'I don't actually *have* to do anything.'

'But that wouldn't be interesting enough for you,' she said confidently.

'No.'

'So?'

'Do you mind if we don't talk about it just at the moment?' he asked, and Antonia nodded. 'Could you give me your hand again?'

She fed her hand back into his. There was hurt in his eyes, and as their palms touched and she seemed to float between her chair and his in the warm kitchen, it became harder to guess whether the hurt was on her account or his own. Her body felt light, and she closed

347

her eyes to enjoy the sensation. It was like a meditation session she'd gone to once with a friend from university. Just for a few moments, you lost yourself completely, and it was bliss. And once, when she was a child, she'd had two back teeth out. The dentist had given her a kind of gas through a mask to put her out, except she hadn't been completely unconscious and she'd been vaguely aware of what was going on without feeling a thing. It hadn't smelt of gas either. Wasn't it called twilight, or something similar? It had made every nerve ending tingle, and she'd forgotten everything that she'd ever worried about. And then when she'd woken up, it had been like sliding on velvet towards consciousness again.

'There,' Tom said.

Antonia opened her eyes, and blinked sharply. She felt as if somebody had opened a door to a warm room and let in cold air. He delicately untangled her fingers from his.

'What happened?'

'You relaxed,' Tom smiled. 'And it will have done you the world of good.'

Antonia sat up and patted at her hair. Her clip, her symbol of composure, was in place, her coat still on, but she felt as if she'd fallen asleep while someone was watching her. 'How long did you hold my hand for?'

'A few minutes. Nothing more.'

'Good grief.'

'You were very tired. Sometimes completely letting go is nature's best medicine. I think you might have done that. How do you feel now?'

Antonia considered. She curled her fingers into her numb palms and felt the sensation return. She hunched

348

her shoulders and let them drop. She rubbed her face, and wiggled her toes inside her boots. 'I feel as if I've had three days' sleep.'

'Never underestimate the power of sleep.'

'But I wasn't asleep. I was aware of everything happening in this room.'

'It amounts to the same thing. You're giving your body a chance to heal itself.' Tom stood up, and she reluctantly stood up too. But at the same time, she was quite keen to get home now. She wanted to see how Sonia was, and give her mother a kiss. Her poor mother, who was struggling with so many practical and emotional issues. And Daniel. She wanted to see him too. He was such a nice man. And Emile, Daniel's brother. Good grief, Emile had practically made a pass at her. Of course, he didn't know what was going on and she wouldn't do anything about it, but it was nice. He fancied her, and she fancied him. That hadn't happened for a very long time, and it felt lovely. A smile touched her lips.

'Who is he?' Tom said as they reached the hall.

Antonia hadn't realised she was still smiling. She straightened her face. 'Who?'

Tom laughed. 'Nobody.'

'Are you being weird again?'

'Not at all. I'm a human being, and I'm male remember, Antonia. I know that look on a woman's face.'

'Was it that obvious?'

'Yes.'

'Well.' They paused in the hall. 'Actually it's Daniel's brother. You remember Daniel, who you met at Sonia's party?'

'Yes, I remember Daniel.'

349

'Well, his brother Emile turned up after you'd left, and we met. That's it.' Tom nodded and didn't say a word. Antonia found herself laughing. How was this happening? How could she be laughing at Tom's expression, as if she hadn't got a care in the world? She put out a warning finger to him. 'Nothing's going to happen so there's no need for you to go all psychic on me.'

'I won't do that.'

'Tom, thank you for this. I'm not sure what you've done, or whether just being here's given me a chance to unwind. I feel a thousand times better, though. I can face my daughter and my mother without being morbid now. Thank you.'

'We all need our guardian angels, don't we?'

Antonia nodded and opened the door. Then she turned back to Tom. 'And who's yours? Or don't you have one?'

'Oh, I have one,' he said. 'She just doesn't know it yet.'

As Antonia started the car, she saw the two young women who had been queueing at the door earlier walking back towards Tom's house, leaning on each other and laughing loudly. It looked as if he was in for a boisterous evening. She put the car in gear and drove away. It was only when she was halfway home that she realised she hadn't even offered to pay him.

Chapter Seventeen

Caroline put a cup of tea on the floor next to the hunched, snoring form that was Phil. She had uncovered the Z-bed from under a neatly stacked pile of boxes in her spare room. Pushing all the junk to one side had revealed a stretch of carpet just big enough to set it up. In the process, she'd also found her old globe again. She'd held it up and turned it around fondly. Then she'd decided to take it downstairs so that she could see it all the time.

Phil had offered a weak joke about the faded solar-system duvet cover she'd found in the bottom of the airing cupboard, recognising it as the same one Caroline had used at university, but he'd been drunk enough to subside onto the thin mattress and fall asleep instantly. She hadn't made any further attempts to influence him. Brendan had been right. She had no idea how her brother felt. All she could see was that he was on an extended adrenaline surge. Phil normally swore as much as anyone, but not usually so much more that each sentence was doubled in length. She'd managed to make him eat half a Chinese takeaway and they'd talked until the early hours, at which point Phil's head had started to loll and she'd somehow coerced him up the stairs. It was ten o'clock now on a dull, grey Saturday morning and Caroline had been up for over two hours already.

On waking she'd felt a thrill when she'd remembered

that Phil was staying in the next room. Having him there took her back in time. Their bedrooms had been down the corridor from each other, with their parents in between. Caroline had smuggled Phil into her room on many an occasion, to put earphones on him and share with him the music she loved, or talk to him about her early boyfriends, or, later on when she was at university, to tell him all about the bars, the parties, the lectures, the societies. Especially the lectures and the astronomy society of course, which he'd want to gloss over in order to get on to the parties again, which she knew less about. She'd always been a cross between an auntie, a sister and a friend to him. Only in recent years had she started to feel that Phil had also given her the affectionate label of 'fuddy-duddy'. The age difference being what it was, it had been a subtle shift between Caroline being the cool, older one, allowed to do whatever she liked, and Phil overtaking her both in theory and in practice. She had been sharing a house with a group of fairly square women and getting her toes under the table in teaching when Phil had junked in university and first sped off to the Continent on one of his impulsive bids for adventure.

That morning Caroline had lain in bed, *Astronomy Now* propped open on her chest like a tent while she remembered such things with a smile. Then she'd reminded herself that Phil was only staying with her because his marriage was falling apart, and she'd felt dismayed again. So she'd got up, listened to the news on the radio sitting in her pyjamas at her kitchen table while she drank coffee, then showered and dressed.

She'd unpacked her overnight bag swiftly the previous night before she went to bed. She didn't particularly want Phil to know that she and Brendan had been off on a saucy jaunt when he'd turned up. His first reaction would probably have been to give a disbelieving snort. It was private and she was glad he hadn't asked her about it. He seemed to have forgotten that they'd been perched in a taxi about to shoot off somewhere when he'd descended on them. He was probably too distraught over his own situation to give it a second thought. She wasn't sure what she felt about it herself as she'd put her toothbrush and toothpaste back on her bathroom shelf, and the shampoo and conditioner back on the corner of the bath. Regret or relief? Poking her silky lingerie to the bottom of her underwear drawer and hanging her bag of cotton-wool balls back on the corner of her standing mirror, Caroline had felt an uncomfortable niggle, certainly, but whether that was because she felt guilty for upsetting Brendan's plans at the last minute, or as if she'd escaped a close shave just in the nick of time, she couldn't tell. Or perhaps it really was the sense that she'd missed a chance to be wild, impulsive, passionate and sexual with her old friend Brendan.

But the moment had passed. She couldn't imagine the circumstances arising again. Next time, if there was a next time, she'd have already thought of all the reasons why it wasn't a good idea to go away with Brendan. She'd had time to add a few since Phil had turned up the previous evening. His curiosity about her would have to remain unassuaged. And hers about him.

That morning, waiting for Phil to wake up, Caroline had applied herself vigorously to her mental passions instead. She'd been checking up on her astronomy web sites and had downloaded some new mapping software. She'd tried to do some marking from her A level group, which she normally enjoyed, but she'd eventually become too impatient to see Phil again. He was rolled up in the duvet with his hair sticking out at one end.

'Morning.'

Phil woke up with a yell of shock. 'I was dreaming.' He pushed himself up crookedly in the bed, his eyes bleary, his brown hair springing from his head in tufts. 'I dreamt Luzie told me I needed to have more sex and made me join a dating agency. So I went to one, and it specialised in sex orgies in disused tunnels. They told me the best one they'd had had lasted twelve months in a collapsed mining shaft.'

'Put that down to last night's sweet and sour sauce.' Caroline opened his curtains and scowled at the grey bank of cloud.

'Then I was conscripted and sent out to fight in a war. But when I got there, the only other people there were *Guardian* journalists.'

Caroline put his tea under his nose. 'Here you are. I thought you'd like to wake up slowly this morning, so I've put the hot-water booster on for another hour. Then you can use the phone if you like.'

Phil propped himself up on an elbow. 'Great tea, thanks. Why would I use the phone? Oh, to call Brendan.'

'You weren't thinking of ringing Germany?' Caroline hedged.

'No, not yet, Caro.' Phil squinted at her. 'I told you last night. She knows where I am, and we both need to think about this. The last time we shouted at each other was only yesterday morning. I'm not exactly in a hurry to be shouted at again.'

354

'Are you sure it's wise to let it fester?'

He slurped his tea noisily, then let out a long breath. 'Okay, let's have this conversation once more and get it over with. I'll ring Luzie if I want to, she'll ring me if she wants to. We both know we're married, and we both know that the other one isn't Satan. We'd just like to be left alone to work it out for ourselves. Can I be clearer than that?'

Caroline sat on the edge of his bed and touched his hand. 'No, that's clear. I guess I was just wondering how long you wanted to stay for.'

Phil wrinkled his nose. 'God Caro, I just don't know, do I? Why, are you expecting company? A coachload of comet-spotters arriving soon?'

'No, no. It's just – you know me. Always like to have things planned, to know where I am. It doesn't matter really.'

'I just don't want to stay at Mum and Dad's. Not right now.'

'Probably wise.'

'And I don't think staying with Brendan's a very good idea either. We'd spend the whole time watching videos. Therapeutic, but we'd never open the curtains. Anyhow, he's really busy.' And so am I, Caroline said with her eyes while she smiled. Phil went on, 'I mean, he's busy socially as well. You never know who he's going to bring home. I think I'd cramp his style.'

'You're welcome to stop here, you know that. I've got no style to cramp, after all.' She couldn't help her smile becoming slightly brittle.

'Oh don't start on that again, Caro. Give me a break. I feel like shit this morning.'

'All right, let's keep it all simple. Just tell me what to do and I'll try to get it right. I'd love you to stay here while you sort yourself out. You know that. I'd be offended if you went anywhere else. Just give me some pointers.'

'Number one, stop telling me to ring my wife.'

'Understood.'

'Number two, stop hinting that I should make it up with her.'

'All right.'

'Number three, stop looking at me as if I was about to die.'

'I'll try.'

'Number four, I don't suppose there's any breakfast is there?'

There was half a loaf of brown bread and some bacon in the fridge, but not enough to make a proper late Saturday morning breakfast. And she was running low on milk. Caroline decided to set off to the shops. She called up the stairs before she left.

'Phil? Will you be in for lunch?'

'No,' he croaked back as he headed for the shower. 'I'll be out getting pissed with Brendan.'

'Okay.'

'Which reminds me, can I have a spare key?'

'Help yourself. There's one in the kitchen drawer next to the fridge. Will you be here for dinner tonight?'

'No.'

Phil leaned over the banister, looking sleepy and adorable. He was so handsome. Caroline could only picture poor, sensible Luzie's heart breaking at the loss of him.

'You won't make dinner tonight?' Caroline quizzed.

'No, I'll be out getting pissed with Brendan,' he emphasised.

'Oh.'

'Don't say it like that,' Phil yawned as he pushed open the bathroom door.

'Like what?'

'Like Luzie does.'

Caroline took the car to Sainsbury's. It was on the verge of getting busy but still not overcrowded, so she decided to coast around the wide aisles and do a general shop. It would be a good time to stock up on food so that she could produce tasty suppers for the evenings Phil might be at home. He couldn't get pissed with Brendan every night, after all.

What was it about having a younger sibling to stay that brought out the maternal instinct in any big sister? Caroline knew for sure that Phil was quite capable of feeding himself. To add to that, she was the last woman who would normally go around worrying about men and their ability to look after themselves. Her mother, Stephanie, doted on her father, just as he doted on her, but she'd never looked after Howard in the traditional sense of the word. She was far too scatty. But as she wandered around the aisles Caroline found her trolley filling up with food that she guessed Phil might like.

She was entranced by all the items, floating from fresh vegetables to dairy and cheese, off to the delicatessen counter where intriguing hunks of ham and exotic sausages were on offer and on past the fresh fish counter where squiggles of seafood suddenly seemed nutritious and exciting. It was as if Phil's adventures clung to him, like the waft of somebody's strong perfume. You couldn't help but be turned on by it. Anything that had a hint of foreign travel about it went into the trolley. At the last minute, as its contents formed a range of hillocks

357

that even the most hardy Mediterranean donkey would curl a lip at crossing, she remembered that she was in Sainsbury's to buy Phil the ingredients for a cooked breakfast. And as she was sailing past the cold meats counter once more she spotted a selection of herby sausages that looked wonderful. She screeched to a halt and reached out to grab a ticket from the machine. As she did she knocked elbows with somebody else reaching out at the same time, and their fingers touched as she picked out her ticket. It made her jump. She withdrew her hand quickly.

'Oh, I'm sorry,' she said.

'Caroline. Hello again.'

She turned around and saw Tom. He was in a shirt and jeans with a scuffed brown leather jacket open to the waist. His greeting had been very casual and he now seemed preoccupied, turning his attention to the items on display in the glass cabinet before them.

'Hello Tom,' she said, slightly miffed that he wasn't paying her more attention. Their last encounter zoomed into her immediate memory.

He nodded without looking at her, then walked behind her to survey the range of meat cuts on the other side. It was as if he'd politely acknowledged her, but was too busy to chat.

'So what are you doing here?' She edged her trolley towards him.

'Hmn? I'm shopping. It's a Sainsbury's thing.' He smiled and turned his attention back to the food on display, bending down to examine it through the glass.

Caroline felt strange. When she'd recognised him she'd felt a rush of nerves and a widening of her eyes that she'd thought might show, but she couldn't quite take her gaze away from him. She'd forgotten just how charismatic he was. Under the bright lights of Sainsbury's he somehow seemed even more exceptional. In the background, couples and families mooched about with their trolleys, glum-faced and torpid. It was the usual mix of languorous weekend supermarket traffic. But Tom stood out somehow. He was too tall, too handsome, too much like – what? A musician, or a poet. He didn't seem to fit. But instead of this making him look out of place, it made everyone else look out of place. When he glanced up at her again, she realised that she was staring at him and tried to look away, but couldn't.

'I'm sorry about what happened,' she found herself saying. 'The last time I saw you.'

He walked up to her with his basket on his arm. He was smiling a gentle smile to himself. Perhaps he was laughing at her. She had behaved very strangely at his house, hadn't she? Why did she feel this need to ingratiate herself?

'It's okay, don't apologise.'

'Just to say that I think I overreacted,' she said under her breath. Images of ornate craftsmanship and the smell of something that she couldn't identify tiptoed across her memory.

'Maybe. And how are you?'

'Me? I'm fine. And how are you?'

'Very well.'

'Good.' She swallowed. It was dangerous to stare into his eyes for too long. She could feel herself drifting away on aquamarine waters. She could forget where she was. Hadn't she realised how intoxicating he was?

'How's Lizzy?' Tom asked.

Caroline didn't know. She hadn't spoken to her for days. She was still offended by Lizzy's harsh words to her when she'd dropped her off. She expected Lizzy to make it up to her at some point but she wasn't going to let Tom know that. Perhaps she'd been a little quick to assume that Tom had influenced Lizzy's behaviour, but until she could speak to Lizzy properly she couldn't be sure, and now that the wider family wasn't supposed to know that Phil was hiding out at her house, speaking to Lizzy was an even more distant proposition.

'She's doing brilliantly, thank you,' Caroline bluffed.

'Good. Not behaving out of character then.'

'Not at all. All sorted now. Just a little misunder-standing.' Caroline had the uncomfortable feeling again that Tom knew more about Lizzy than she did herself, and that wasn't allowed. Not in such a close-knit family as they had.

Tom nodded. 'Well, I'll let you get on with it. You're obviously expecting a siege.'

Caroline followed his nod down to her trolley. I've got somebody staying with me at the moment. So we're eating for two.' Maybe that would make him think that she had other romantic interests. A defensive stance was needed, that way she couldn't lose face.

'I was going to ask you out for dinner,' Tom said, as his number was called at the counter. 'But maybe you won't be hungry.'

Caroline gripped her trolley as Tom ordered some pâté. She knew she hadn't misheard that one.

'For dinner?' she echoed.

'I was going to,' Tom said.

Caroline stood very still, leaning on her trolley as shoppers bustled around her. The artificial lights blazed down on them. Tom calmly ordered some smoked ham as if Caroline wasn't there. Then he offered her another small smile.

'But – you didn't come to the astronomy club again,' she blurted out, confused.

Tom said, 'It's okay, Caroline. Don't be put out. I'll see you around.'

But suddenly she didn't want him to disappear again, leaving things vague between them. She found herself saying, 'We're meeting tonight, to observe the meteor shower. What's more, it looks as if it might be clear later.'

'You'd like to watch shooting stars with me?' He seemed very amused.

'Would you like to come along?' She gave him the address anyway. 'You remember Roderick, the president of the club? It's his house. And Dylan and the others will be there, and Carl's threatening to bring along a keg of his home-made beer too. That's if you wanted to watch it with us. You could see it from wherever you wanted to, obviously.'

'Yes, I could, couldn't I.' She had the horrible feeling he was teasing her, and enjoying every minute of it. Then he said, surprising her, 'I suppose you're not free tomorrow night?'

'Tomorrow night?'

'Yes.'

'Why, are you?' she asked him, rattled.

'Yes. Are you?'

Caroline swallowed, the panic feathering its way up and down her tight throat. Was she free? Phil was staying with her, but was obviously intent upon making his own plans. But had Phil not turned up unexpectedly, she might have been in a luxury hotel with Brendan last night and just waking up slowly with croissants and jam on a tray now. Was it unethical to be asked out by another man that same weekend? But now she was relieved that she wasn't having breakfast in bed with Brendan and was instead standing in Sainsbury's with Tom. That was an odd realisation. Luxury hotel, Sainsbury's. It wasn't much of a swap. Brendan, Tom. That was what made the difference. But dinner? A proper date? She was so out of practice. Time passed while Caroline's brain locked up.

'Are you free tomorrow night?' Tom repeated gently.

'Caroline!' It was Greg, hurrying past with a basket on his arm. He did a sharp U-turn and greeted her. She cursed inwardly, although she would normally have been delighted to run into him. 'I hardly saw you at all this week. How are you doing? You know what they say, never go shopping when you're hungry.' He nodded down at her trolley, laughing. 'I wouldn't mind swapping fridges with you for the next week.'

'Greg! Fancy seeing you here.' He was in a tracksuit, looking as sporty as ever, his skin glowing. 'Been out running?'

'Football training this morning. For the local club. Bloody knackering but fun.'

'So, Greg, this is a neighbour of mine . . .' Caroline turned to Tom to introduce him. He wasn't there. She looked around distractedly, but there was no sign of him. He must have disappeared just as Greg appeared.

'Really?' Greg raised his eyebrows. 'Who? Where?'

'He was just here.' The supermarket was full now, and it was huge enough to lose somebody very quickly if you didn't know which way they were headed. 'How weird.'

'Friend of yours, was it?'

'Oh . . .' Caroline opted for vague. She was too perplexed by Tom's disappearance to attempt to explain anything. 'Oh no, just a neighbour I banged into. It doesn't matter.'

'Are you in a hurry?' Greg asked. 'I wondered if you wanted a coffee or something before we head home.'

'What, here?'

'They've got a cafe over the back there somewhere.'

'The thing is, I'm supposed to be cooking breakfast for my brother.' Caroline glanced at her watch. 'Oh God, I've been gone for ages. He's probably got fed up with waiting and gone out by now. Damn it.'

'Your brother? Not Phil who's in Germany?'

'The same one. On an unexpected flying visit.'

'Wow. Well don't worry about it then. Another time.' Greg smiled, but behind his spectacles Caroline thought he looked troubled. He'd been a good friend to her in the past year and she owed him some listening time.

'I tell you what,' she suggested. 'If you've finished your shopping and can bear to wait while I get through the checkout with this lot, you can come and have a late breakfast with me and my brother at home. That's if you haven't eaten yet.'

'No, I haven't and I'm half-starved after footie practice. That'd be great. Are you sure I won't be intruding?'

'Not at all. We could both do with some light relief.'

The even more confusing thing was that though Caroline wandered up and down most of the aisles on her way to the checkouts, in the hope of spotting Tom again, she couldn't see him anywhere and his astonishing invitation to her was left hanging, tantalisingly, in the air.

Phil wasn't at home. Instead there was a note on the kitchen table, that read 'What breakfast?!!!!! Gone out. Don't wait up. Love P xxx'.

'Bugger,' Caroline said. 'Well, make yourself at home, Greg, and I'll put some coffee on and start cooking. We might as well have a slap-up brunch anyway.'

While Caroline busied herself with arranging in the pan half of the sausages she'd bought, Greg wandered around the downstairs of her house, occasionally flinging out comments to her.

'Is that the horse-head nebula? Ah yes,' he called. 'Lovely poster.'

'Thanks. I got it from Greenwich.'

'So neat, your house. Wish I could live like you.'

'You don't really,' she said.

'Are you online all the time then?' Greg called.

'Er, no? Why?' Caroline wandered through to her living room, where Greg had been looking at her computer. She checked and found that the computer was still connected up. Phil appeared to have left it logged into his Hotmail account where he'd obviously been checking or sending e-mails.

'Little brother problems?' Greg smiled.

'Well, not yet. Not exactly. But it is the weekend. Cheap rate. I'll give him a cuff round the ear when I see him.'

But Caroline couldn't fail to see the contents of the last e-mail that he'd picked up. She tried not to read it. Greg had gone back to the kitchen to take care of the sausages and make coffee. Caroline wouldn't have dreamt for all the world of reading her brother's private mail, but the first line of this one had caught her eye and before she knew it she'd skim-read it. The first line had been, 'I'm dying to see you. It feels like years since Brussels and I miss you so much.' The e-mail was not from Phil's wife. It was from somebody called Trixie, who was apparently in England. Having been frozen while she swiftly got the gist of the message, Caroline quickly clicked her way out of Phil's account and turned the computer off. She stood quietly for a moment by herself listening to Greg humming in the kitchen.

Phil was having an affair. The woman's message referred to previous meetings. She couldn't tell any more than that. Not whether it was frivolous, meaningful, whether any love was involved or whether it was all about sex and adrenaline. She wondered if Luzie had found out. Was that what they'd rowed about? Or had she guessed? Or had Phil engineered a split because he wanted to sleep with someone else? Caroline wandered back into the kitchen, concern tugging at her.

'Want to be breakfast monitor?' Greg asked. 'I'll do coffee.'

'Yes, sure.' Caroline laid bacon in strips alongside the sausages, keeping her thoughts about Phil to herself. Maybe she would talk to him about it later. She certainly couldn't involve Greg, so she tried to move things on. 'So tell me what's happening with you.'

'Well,' Greg said, piling coffee into mugs. 'The thing is, I've accepted the job in the north.'

Caroline paused in her bacon prodding and let out a sigh of dismay. 'So you're definitely leaving?'

He nodded ruefully. 'I've handed in my notice. I'm

making a clean break. New place, new faces. Maybe some new female faces.'

'Not running away?'

'No, no. Just that – well, I was seeing someone for a bit, then it didn't work out and I think the fact that it didn't work out made me see my life for what it was. Grey, boring, safe, predictable. I want new challenges. To break out for a bit.'

'You call going to work in a boys' public school breaking out?' Caroline quirked an eyebrow at him.

'It's breaking out from what people expect me to do. By earning more in the next year or two I can free myself up. I want to get off the track. It feels like I've been on the tramlines for years, and they've been established since so early on in my life that now I can't remember even who put them there, other people or me. That's the thing about tramlines. And if we're not careful we stick to them and roll down them in this inevitable, lurching, dull crawl towards . . . death or retirement or something.'

'That was a pretty epic speech.'

'I feel quite epic. I don't want to end up like sad old Gerry Bream. Hating my job and deserted by my wife. What's he got to show for anything?'

'His wife left him?' Caroline gasped. 'How do you know?'

'Apparently Hilary was quite friendly with her. She gave me the nod and told me to go easy on him for a few weeks.'

'Well I'll be blowed. Hilary didn't say anything to me.'

'He just might have specifically asked her not to. He wouldn't want you offering to lend him your Solos holiday brochures.'

'As if I'd do anything so tactless.' Caroline mused, feeling sorry for Gerry. 'Poor old thing. I'll be nice to him when I see him again.'

'You've got a bigger heart than him, then. Last I heard, he was telling everybody in the staffroom that you'd specifically said you didn't want the responsibility of Head of Science.'

Caroline felt a flutter of outrage but let it pass. 'It doesn't matter, Greg. He's got less to look forward to than me.'

'And that's exactly the point.' Greg's eyes lit up again. 'I don't want to reach that stage in life where I don't wake up every morning looking forward to the next twenty-four hours. I thought that when I made this decision to leave I'd be guilt-stricken and feel worse and worse with every disapproving look that I got. But I don't. I feel like sticking two fingers up at the world.'

'Me excepted, I hope.'

'Yes, you excepted. Because I want to get away from the predictable path,' Greg went on, stirring the coffee with such passion that it looked as if the spoon was wearing a hole in the bottom of the mug. 'I'll teach at this school for a year or two, then I'll do VSO. And I'll have a bit of a safety net of cash behind me. God knows where I'll go from there. Probably out of teaching completely.'

'VSO?' Caroline was further amazed. She'd thought she'd known Greg. Just like she thought she'd known Lizzy. Or Phil. Or Brendan. But people were getting into the habit of astonishing her. She wasn't sure she liked it, but then again, she couldn't do much about it. She didn't know where she was from one minute to the next. 'You want to teach abroad?'

'Yes, or for the British Council, or something. I always

wanted to travel in Africa or Asia, and do something different.'

Caroline stood with her yellow and white melted spatula in her hand, surrounded by her white, wipeable units, feeling pathetic by comparison. 'I had no idea you wanted to do that.'

'No. I haven't talked about it because the one thing I hate is teachers who sit around whining about what they would have done if things had been different. Or the ones that say, "I might teach abroad, I might work in Africa, I might get the Nobel Prize for legible hand-writing, I just don't feel like it today." I don't want to become like that, Caroline. Every staffroom's half-full of them. You know that.'

She gave each sausage a sharp stab with a fork. 'And for every one of those, there are just as many teachers who think it's a bloody good thing to do the job really well.'

'I know,' Greg said with exaggerated patience. 'And I know that it's worthwhile and meaningful. You inspire somebody else to do all the things you didn't have the courage to do yourself.'

'Greg! Christ, if I thought that, I'd give up now.'

'Isn't that what you do?'

'What?'

'Inspire other people to do what you'd have liked to have done yourself?' Greg probed.

'No! I love my job.'

'You've told me before you'd dreamed of working in pure astrophysics research. Wasn't that true when you said it?'

'Well, yes, I suppose I thought about it once some years ago.' She threw a handful of mushrooms in the

368

pan and stirred them roughly. 'But I adore my job. It's what I'm meant to do, and it's as simple as that.'

'But you'd have loved to have been a research scientist more?' Greg bantered.

'No.'

'Are you sure?'

'Yes.'

'So you don't regret the fact that you're not working with Jocelyn Bell-Burnell on the Mars Mission at all then? Or,' he eyed her provocatively, 'is it that you weren't really academic enough for post-grad?'

Caroline slapped the spatula down into the pan. 'I bloody was good enough. I had a master's place already in the bag when I changed my mind and went for teaching instead. Schools were crying out for science teachers, and I suddenly knew it was what I had to do.'

'Had to?'

'*Wanted* to.'

Greg smiled and clapped his hands together slowly. 'You pass with flying colours. You see, when I talk to you I can see what a vocation is.'

She realised he'd been playing devil's advocate with her and tutted at him in return. 'You annoying sod. I'm glad you're leaving.'

'Well, I know I don't have a vocation, but maybe it's as well that we're all different,' Greg said. 'I don't want to be able to turn around in years to come and know that I had a fantastic opportunity staring me in the face but didn't do anything about it. Coffee?'

369

Chapter Eighteen

'You're going out again?' Lizzy quizzed David in the hall as he put on his jacket and boots.

'Yup.'

'Who was that on the phone?'

'Brendan.'

'Brendan?' Lizzy frowned. 'That can't be right.'

'What do you mean, "That can't be right"?' He narrowed his eyes.

'I thought,' Lizzy said, her nerves becoming more brittle, 'that you'd said Brendan was whisking Caroline off to some smart hotel this weekend. I could ring her and find out what happened.'

'Why don't you do that then?' David suggested unsmilingly.

But Lizzy didn't want to ring Caroline. Not yet. She wasn't ready to talk to her again. She was still smarting from her crass comments and it was taking more time than she might have expected to get over them. Caroline could have no concept of the peace and comfort that Lizzy had found from sitting silently on her own in the company of strangers at the Sunday evening church service. She'd taken a pew at the back and spoken to nobody. It had been a private experience. Just Lizzy whispering a silent and loving prayer to her lost little girl, the baby she was supposed to have forgotten by now. Even David didn't know she'd gone to a church. Caroline had bruised her badly in her treatment of the whole affair, and Lizzy wasn't going to talk to her until she felt resilient again. Her threat to ring Caroline, she realised with a certain amount of secret alarm, was a way of pointing out to her husband that she could check up on him. That wasn't something she'd ever either wanted or needed to do. If David wasn't going to meet Brendan as he claimed, where else would he be going?

'So what is it that's so urgent you have to mess up all our plans for the day?' she insisted as he moved towards the front door. 'Brendan never used to ask you to do this. Just drop everything and go out with him. I'm not sure I want him to get into the habit of thinking that you're on call. You've got commitments that he hasn't got.'

'I know that,' David emphasised.

'So what's going on?'

'I don't know what the big deal is,' he said edgily. 'We hadn't got anything planned for today. We did the shopping in the week, the boys are busy pissing each other off, any moment now you'll go into your room to play with your cards and probably be in there all afternoon.'

'Play with my cards?' She should have told him about the sales to Criss-Cross. But they'd been in an odd, distanced state in recent days, and it was such a personal triumph for her. She didn't dare let anybody take it away from her. Not her husband, her cousin, her mother even. It was private until she knew how to present it in such a way that people would understand what she'd done and support her.

'Your pictures. Occupational therapy, creative

fulfilment. Whatever it is you do in there. It leaves me sitting downstairs, quietly saving money.'

'What do you mean?' She took a step towards him.

'Isn't that what you want me to do? Sit still, don't move, don't spend? I told you. I want to live as well as have a family. We both should. So I'm going to meet Brendan. It'll make me a more balanced individual, think of it that way. That can only be good.'

'Why can't Brendan come round here?' Lizzy protested, hating herself for pleading, but not looking forward to spending another long afternoon by herself with the children.

'Because what we are going to do involves being somewhere else.'

'David, why are you being so bloody cryptic?' Lizzy raised her voice as he was halfway out of the door.

'I'm not,' he said, and shut the front door behind him.

Lizzy pivoted around and yelled up the stairs. 'If you two don't shut up right now you'll both get a smack!'

Then she kicked her way back into the kitchen and crashed the plates around in the washing-up bowl. If her period had actually started instead of hovering over her like a malevolent hawk, perhaps she would feel a little calmer. As it was, the need to break something was growing.

She pulled herself away from the sink, dried her hands on a tea towel and went to her handbag. Inside, she found the small plastic box she'd collected from the printers earlier in the week. She removed the lid and gazed fondly at her new business cards. A swell rose in her throat. She was a businesswoman now. At the right time, she would explain it to David too.

*

'Oh, are you off out?' Antonia asked as Daniel retrieved his mobile from its recharging position on the kitchen unit and slipped it into the pocket of his leather jacket.

'Yeah,' he smiled. 'It's some sort of bloke gathering. Don't ask me what about.'

'Sounds frightening.'

'Well maybe. If so I'll come back early. I was planning to hop up to London this evening to see Emile.'

Antonia's ears pricked up at the mention of Emile. Her skin tingled. It was a pleasant sensation. 'Oh, Emile.' She casually flipped a blouse from the ironing board to its hanger.

'Uh-huh, then Dave rang me about some get-together today so I thought I'd turn up and see what's going on. I'm not really sure what it's all about, but they're good guys. Dave – David – he's the guy who gave me lifts in to work while your car was in the garage.'

'Nice to have friends,' Antonia said, then laughed at herself. 'I sound like I'm talking to Sonia.'

'I'll see you later then.' Daniel paused at the door. 'By the way, you look great today. Glad to see that. I was starting to think you weren't well.'

'Oh no, I'm fine. Just peachy,' Antonia replied. Daniel went out.

She hummed to herself as she finished the ironing, then went up the stairs to find Sonia, who was lying on her stomach on her bed with her Walkman on, flicking through a computer magazine. Sonia waved a hand indifferently, nodding her head in time to the music.

'Where's Gran?' Antonia mouthed. Sonia blinked dismissively in return.

Antonia found her mother in the master bedroom she'd given over to her. She was awkwardly folding clothes and laying them with painstaking care into a travelling case. She glanced up as Antonia entered the room but said nothing. Antonia sat on the edge of the bed.

'Are you going somewhere, Mum?'

'I'm going home.'

Antonia nodded and perched quietly on the duvet, watching her mother handle the clothes. It took her back to her childhood. Sitting at the kitchen table learning Latin or French verbs or scribbling away at an English essay while her mother did the washing, wound it through the mangle, then carefully arranged it on the dryer in front of the open oven.

'You can tell me off all you like,' Audrey announced. 'But I'm going home. I have to be at home, on my own. I can't hang around here like a spare pair of drawers any longer.'

'I understand.'

Audrey raised disbelieving eyes. 'I don't think you've thought for one minute how this is for me. You've put up with me, tolerated me very *nobly*.' She emphasised the word as if she was quoting royalty. 'You've done your duty. But I've been under your feet and in your way, and you wouldn't let me go home and be where I wanted to be. You just took control of me.'

'That was only because I didn't want you to hurt yourself while your wrist was bad.'

'Huh.' Audrey slapped a folded pair of corduroys into her case. 'Well it's much better now.'

'If you want to go, perhaps I can arrange for a nurse to come in during the day to check on you, and I can be there in the morning and evening. As long as you promise not to do any cooking or kettle-boiling when

374

I'm not around. I'm sure we could work it out now that your wrist's that much stronger. So if you're very unhappy here we could find a way for you to go back home again. That's what I'm trying to say.'

Audrey looked very surprised and paused in her packing. 'I might just do that.'

'I want to say sorry, Mum.' Antonia considered her mother affectionately as she attempted to roll a pair of tights with one hand. 'I'm sorry for not being more sensitive.'

'To what?' Audrey stabbed.

'For not realising how hard it was for you to have your independence taken away so suddenly like that.'

Audrey's light eyes hovered over her daughter suspiciously, but then she too sat down on the bed. She sighed loudly. 'I'm used to my own things. My own ways. I have my routines.'

'I know.'

'It's not that I don't love you.' Audrey suddenly shot Antonia a look. 'I do, you know. But your ways are so different from mine. Whenever I'm here, I feel like I just disappear. Like a ghost, hanging about and invisible while you get on with your life. I've always felt like that around you. You make me feel, what's the word you'd use, non-existent. Like I'm not really there.'

Antonia crept closer to her mother and took her hand. 'Mum, there's something I want to tell you. But before I do, you must swear to me that you won't tell anybody else about it. Not anybody at all. Sonia especially must not know.'

'Jesus, you're not preggers are you?'

Despite herself, Antonia smiled. 'No, I'm not preggers. Chance would be a fine thing.'

'Ah. I wondered if you and Daniel . . . Or that great big brother of his. No? You haven't?'

'Mum!' Antonia started to laugh. To her surprise, her mother gave a short laugh too.

'Daniel's a nice-looking boy. I wouldn't really blame you.'

'Well, I haven't. Never crossed my mind.'

'Brother's a bit scary. What's with *Emile* for a name? Where's that from then?'

'I think it's the Creole influence in the West Indies. Daniel said something along those lines.'

'What's that then? Creole?'

Antonia brushed her fingers over the top of her mother's bony hand. The papery skin looked pale, vulnerable, tired. She felt a surge of love. 'Mum, I need you.'

Audrey sat quietly for a moment, watching Antonia's fingers stroke her hand. Then she said, 'So, what is it that you want to tell me?'

Antonia told her mother about her illness, carefully picking the right words so that it wouldn't sound more alarming than it was, trying to put the emphasis on life-changing rather than life-threatening. After she'd finished speaking, the two women sat silently together on the bed, their hands entwined.

'You always could surprise me,' Audrey said at last. 'You realise it's not your turn.'

'My turn?'

'Things happen in a natural order. Me first, you next. Let's not mess about with that.'

'I'll try not to mess about with that.'

'No, Sonia mustn't know,' Audrey said, her voice firmer. 'And I won't go home just yet. I'll wait till you've had your op, then I'll go after that.'

Caroline went out to her shed wrapped up in several outer skins of sweaters, topped with a jacket lined with thick fleece. She had some equipment to collect to take to the meteor evening, some handouts she'd downloaded from a web site, and Carl had asked to borrow some sky-mapping software she'd recently bought. She'd collect this lot from her shed then head straight up to Roderick's house in the car.

Over the gardens came an unusual sound, and she stood still to hear it better before she went into the shed. A rattling, almost tuneful, almost rhythmic tattoo, gaining momentum with each gust of the wind. Like an echo of South America. What on earth was it? Then the puzzle clicked into shape and revealed itself. Wind chimes! No less than the wind chimes she'd seen on Tom's table, that Lizzy had given him, no doubt as some gesture of payment. Lizzy had rescued them from Caroline's parents, but in her mother's garden they'd sounded English. Now they sounded exotic and eerie. It was a strangeness that wasn't altogether unpleasant, like the guttural dip and curling rise of a new language.

She stood as the wind whipped her hair into strands and beat them across her forehead and listened a moment longer. Tom had obviously hung the chimes up in his garden. She couldn't see anything, the darkness staining everything apart from the random, comforting golden squares of windows at the backs of the houses. His wind chimes responded pertly to every probing of the wind. It was as if they were having a conversation with the elements. Caroline listened until there was a temporary lull. Then she let herself into the shed.

As the brusque evening wind had arrived, the grey-

377

ridged clouds were being harried across the sky and she was hopeful that they'd get to see something later. The temperature had dropped too. The rhododendron rustled against the wooden shed walls. The towering spruce swayed wildly each time the wind gusted, scratching at the tiny window. Then the wind dropped again, leaving the bushes only murmuring to each other. The problem with such erratic weather was that one could just position a good shot ready to log when a bank of cloud could be swept into the way. Patience would be needed. The spruce scraped persistently against the wooden walls as she collected the belongings she wanted to take with her and locked up the shed.

She was turning to go back to the house when she heard an odd noise in the bushes at the foot of the garden. Probably just the wind taking handfuls of twigs and hurling them at each other in mercurial squalls. She stood still and peered into the darkness, holding her breath and listening. The wind, the branches, the wind chimes rattling a native rhythm into the suburban air. Something else. Thud, thud, thud.

Tiptoeing down the garden path, Caroline held her breath. Thud, thud, thud. She reached the end of her garden, where the naked wands of bushes stripped of their leaves stuck out into the night like fingers. A thin wooden fence stretched high enough to maintain complete privacy from the garden beyond. It reached a height several inches above her head. Thud, thud, thud came from the other side of the fence, a scurrying accompanying the unearthly noise at ground level where the garden debris was amassed on her side of the fence.

'Hello?' she called a little weakly, images of urban

strains of wild animals with sharp teeth arriving just as she'd bent closer to try to see into the gloom.

The scuffling stopped, as did the thudding. The wind rose, threw her hair into chaos around her ears and sent the bushes leaning over dramatically to one side, then dropped with equal suddenness. In the brief interlude of calm that followed there was a plaintive animal sound, somewhere between a sheep and somebody coughing. Caroline crept closer to the fence and tried to see through one of the narrow cracks between the flat woven wooden strands.

'Daisy? Is that you?'

Daisy gave an affirmative bleat and Caroline dropped to her haunches, laughing under her breath in relief. It was only Tom's neurotic goat. What was she doing at the fence? Trying to head-butt it, by the sounds of it. So that confirmed it then, his garden backed directly onto hers. And when she listened again, Caroline could hear the pensive mutter of the wind chimes coming from a tree in his garden.

Putting her eye to the narrow gap she could see he had a conservatory of some kind at the back of the house. The lights from his kitchen spread into that area through open doors, but the door out to the garden seemed to be closed. She wondered again if he would come to watch the meteor shower with the club. He hadn't given any indication that he would.

Daisy seemed happily preoccupied with attempting to wear a hole through the fence that separated Caroline's garden from Tom's. Observing the endeavour, Caroline couldn't help feeling more amused by the symbolism of it than concerned for the well-being of her fence. It was strong enough.

379

'You're missing all the fun.'

It was Carl who opened Roderick's front door. He had a glass of dubious-looking beer in one hand, an object with a wire hanging from it that looked like a light meter or something of that ilk in the other. He grinned at Nina and stood back to let her in.

'I'm a bit late, I know. I had a phone call just before I left my flat. It held me up a bit, sorry about that.'

'Don't apologise.' He shook his head. 'Roderick's in the garden with everyone else, I was just getting myself a refill from the kitchen when I heard the bell. Good job, otherwise we wouldn't have realised you were there. Have you seen any of it on the way here?'

Nina blinked at him as she followed him through the huge, dusty house into the spartan but enormous kitchen. In fact, she hadn't noticed anything at all on the drive over. She'd been too preoccupied.

Earlier, she had been in her studio flat wrapping herself up in layers of jumpers and a thick coat, having been warned about the effects of the cold during these extended outdoor viewing sessions by everybody in the pub after the meeting, when her mobile phone had rung. As she found her car keys she answered it, not really thinking clearly about who it might be. Several of her friends had her number, she'd also given it to Roderick, and then to Carl in the pub just in case there was any change of plan before the meteor party, so that she could be kept informed. But it wasn't any of those people. It was Graham.

For a while she hadn't recognised the sounds coming out of his throat. They were so odd, like an animal grunting and making eerie, guttural appeals. But then

380

she'd realised that he was crying and that was why she'd never heard a noise like it coming from him before.

She'd pursed her lips, eyed her watch and fingered her car keys, hesitating at the door to her flat. She didn't want to take the call walking down the stairs. As Graham started to speak she realised that he was very drunk.

'When are you coming back?' he'd demanded. She'd gazed around her mulled-wine-flavoured studio flat, small and transitory and yet warm, homely and full of promise.

'I'm not coming back.'

'Of course you're coming back.' He seemed off in his own world, partly talking to her, partly to himself. 'What else would you do? Nowhere else to bloody go. And we're going to move to a bigger house and have a baby. It's all just starting.'

'I'm not ever coming back. Now I'm going out so I can't talk.'

'Where are you staying? I need your address.'

'I'm not giving you my address. Not yet.'

'But the bills?'

'I'm up to date on bills. I've posted you a cheque that will cover everything that I'm responsible for up to the day I left. From now on, you're on your own so there's no need to send me anything.'

'But Nina,' Graham squawked after a minute of gulping at her. 'You're so hard. You've changed. What's got into you?'

'I grew up,' she told him, and switched her mobile off.

She'd got through the conversation boldly, but as she tossed her phone away from her she leaned back against her dark red walls and trembled from head to foot. What had she done? Was she mad? Did other women dream of having a stable husband with colour-coded stickers on his bank statements? When she was forty-five would she look back upon this as her one and only chance of marriage and family?

She'd opened her eyes, tremulous tears spilling down her cheeks. It was a risk she would take. There was no going back now.

So as Carl handed her a small glass of a dark brown liquid he'd poured from a plastic barrel set up on Roderick's kitchen table, she was annoyed, but not very surprised, to see that her hands shook.

'Everything all right with you?' Carl breezed on cheerfully, after a slight pause.

'Everything's fine,' she nodded back, forcing her lips to arc upwards. 'I'm really glad to be here, to meet you all again, here in my . . .' She put her hands out to the kitchen, a laugh under her breath. 'Here in my great-uncle's house.'

'And it's a thrill to be here with you,' Carl responded equally theatrically, his pale blue eyes twinkling at her. He was a robust character, funny and unusual. She couldn't help liking him. 'And now let's get outside and see those shooting stars. Brace yourself. It's bloody windy.'

In the garden, Nina could make out most of the people she'd seen before at the meeting. Some were standing, some were gathered around a telescope set out on a patio, and, to her shock and delight, she saw that Roderick himself had a miniature observatory of his own complete with a white dome opened up to the elements. It was very small, perhaps would fit just one or two people, but it was such an interesting feature that she felt proud. What an unusual, thoughtful man he was. Perhaps there was a minuscule thread of his curiosity running in her family? She could hope. Maybe she'd discover abilities she'd never known she possessed? Who knew what she might have done in a different life. Perhaps not left school at sixteen. Perhaps not tried to build a home with either Paul or Graham. Perhaps had more confidence to get out there on her own.

At that thought, she looked around for Caroline, the tall black-haired woman who had made such an impression on her. Caroline had come along to the pub after the astronomy meeting, but Nina hadn't had a chance to speak to her. In the corner of the pub where they'd all been amassed around three tables pushed together, Nina had been itching to get up so that she could go over and say something, but Caroline had been caught up in a very involved conversation with the debonair man who'd called himself William. Then Caroline had stood up, waved a general goodbye and left, so in the end they hadn't managed to speak to each other at all.

But Nina felt drawn to Caroline. She wanted to speak to her. She moved that way over the garden, but stopped as she saw a tall blond man approach Caroline and touch her arm. By the look that was exchanged between them it seemed very clear to her that he was a boyfriend or lover of some kind. They talked together and the conversation appeared to be very intimate. Then a squall of wind nearly threw the entire company off balance and everybody exclaimed aloud.

'Nina, here!' Carl took her arm and pointed to the sky.

'You're missing it. Why don't you grab a seat on the rug here and remember, keep your eyes pointed upwards. I've got my camera on a tripod there, so I'm just behind you if you want to ask anything.'

'Is Yoda offering his services?' a voice quipped.

'Brain the size of a planet, me.'

Abandoning her pursuit of Caroline for now, Nina sat on the rug and obediently tilted her head so that she could stare upwards. She waited, wriggling her fingers in her gloves. Clouds were being pushed around by the strong wind. Beyond, a black void. Whatever was up there was a mystery to her, but it was unexpectedly wonderful just to sit still and look up at it. When had she ever done that? Never. Or perhaps only—

'Oh my God!' She clasped a hand to her mouth as a fast-moving streak of light darted across the sky. It took her breath away. She'd only ever seen anything like it in films. The reality was much more daunting, much more fantastic and much more exciting.

'Yaay!' came a group cry.

'A blue one,' the young woman whose name was Lesley called from across the rug.

'White.'

'Whitish-blue.'

'Definitely more blue than white.'

'Oh, hold up.' Carl fiddled frantically with the lens of his camera. 'I think we're in for a few fireworks now. Are you videoing, Dylan?'

'Got it,' Dylan said.

The group fell silent as the most wonderful show of lights emerged overhead. A streak of yellow light was followed some moments later by further streams of brilliant white or electric blue. Each experience lasted no more than a few seconds, but it seemed to Nina that they would stay in her mind for ever. Then she gasped and the others exchanged excitable comments as a flash of dazzlingly bright green shot over their heads.

'Wowee!' Carl whistled. 'Got you on film, baby. You get that, Dylan?'

'I hope so.'

'And where's Roderick?' Nina asked, having been unable to work it out.

'In the observatory.'

Nina got up stiffly, flexing her legs, and wandered over to it. The door was hooked open and he was seated, his head bent to the eyepiece of what looked to her like a very expensive piece of machinery. He was as still and silent as a stone.

'Don't move!' Roderick said without looking round. 'Don't cause any extra vibrations. I'm attempting to record the event.'

'I'm sorry,' Nina said in a low voice, turning carefully so that she could leave again.

'Is that Nina?' Roderick asked, his eye still fixed to his machine.

'Yes.'

'Are you enjoying yourself?'

'Yes.' Nina swallowed. 'You've shown me a whole new world and I'm so grateful to you.'

'The same world, through different eyes.'

'Yes. Yes, that is what I mean really.'

'You were right, dear. It is very pretty. I'd forgotten just how pretty it was. Thank you for reminding me.'

She stood still, pleased beyond words, then crept away from him to enjoy the rest of the evening.

*

'Why are you here?' Caroline breathed at Tom. Colours exploded over their heads as they examined each other's faces in the gloom of the night. The individual calls of the small crowd melted into an amorphous block of sound. Caroline had been so shocked to see him that for a full minute she was sure she'd done nothing but stare at him before she recovered herself.

'I'm here to make a point,' Tom said in a low voice.

'And what's your point?'

'My point is that I want to watch shooting stars with you by my side.'

She jammed her hands in her pockets. 'You're not watching the stars, you're watching me.'

'Actually, I'm doing both.'

'Well you can look through Carl's telescope that he's set up on the patio if you like. You're unlikely to be allowed into Roderick's observatory as I'm afraid he's a bit picky about who he ever lets in there. By which I mean he never lets anybody in there. Or you can grab a glass of Carl's very dodgy home-made beer, which I have to tell you isn't as strong as it looks but tastes of pickled onions, and you could sit on the rugs with the others and just look up and enjoy it.'

'Or I could just stand here with you.'

'Yes.'

'And ponder the conversation we had earlier today.'

'What about it?'

'I got the feeling you'd rather I were a part of this group activity, which has no undercurrents whatsoever, than sit opposite me in a romantic setting and look deeply into my eyes,' he said with a smile in his voice. 'I think.'

'Undercurrents?' she breathed, annoyed that her voice quavered.

'Undercurrents.' He put his mouth to her ear, so close that she could feel the warmth of his skin burning like a three-bar heater next to her cheek, and the tickle of his hair touching hers. 'Goodnight, Caroline.'

'You're not going?' She swung around a little too quickly and found his mouth close to hers. A whisper of his breath tantalised her mouth.

Then he was gone, walking away across the patio saying goodbye to the others, a cheerful farewell to Dylan who, she was curious to see, seemed to have taken a liking to him. He turned into the kitchen and disappeared from her sight.

'Oh what a bummer,' she heard Lesley's voice. 'The clouds are coming back. I think that's the best of the night.'

'I want a word with you,' Caroline told Phil when he staggered into the house at two in the morning. She'd been standing in the garden gazing upwards, trying to catch the last shards of light, but the clouds were now defiantly dense. She shut the back door firmly and gave Phil an unforgiving stare as he lolled against the fridge with a vacant smile on his face.

'What *were* you doing out there?'

'I was hoping to catch the last signs of the meteor shower,' she began, but stopped. Phil's eyes were rotating in different directions and he was giggling. There was no point in trying to explain it.

'Not spying on the neighbours, surely. Don't tell me there's a hunk over the back who does naked press-ups with the curtains open and all the lights on?' Phil was oblivious to the daggers in her eyes. 'Oh come on Caro, you're not going to nag me for being late are you? You're still up and dressed your-self.'

'I don't care how late you are. You've got a key. This isn't about that.'

'Well, what the frig's the problem then?'

'Who's Trixie?' Caroline shot at him. She was still rattled after her encounter with Tom that evening. She was further irked because Phil was so obviously plastered. She wouldn't have minded him being plastered normally, but at that moment she felt jittery and very sober. Firing the name *Trixie* at her brother had been easier than it should have been.

She watched his face turn pale and his eyes grow dark. A long silence elapsed between them, broken by Phil walking to her pedal bin, dropping an empty beer can inside, opening her fridge door and taking another out. The ring pull fizzed and he swallowed a mouthful. When his eyes met Caroline's again they were focused and accusatory.

'That's out of order,' he said eventually.

Caroline felt uncomfortable. She was meant to be his big sister. Understanding, comforting, tolerant, protective. She was messing it up every time she opened her mouth. Now she was throwing accusations at him. She didn't know what to do that would be good for him, but she was sure now that everything she was doing was wrong.

'I'm sorry, Phil, I saw the e-mail by accident. You left the computer on. It's just –'

'That you had to read it. Not your business, Caroline. Badly done, as Granddad used to say.'

Caroline was stalled by the sudden mention of her grandfather. It was if he'd walked into the room and shaken his head sadly at them both. In her imagination, he took a seat at the back of the room and waited for things to calm down. She could almost smell his pipe. Phil broke through the images.

'I should have stayed in Germany. It's just like being with Luzie, except –' He stopped and bit his lip.

'Except what?' she queried.

'Nothing.' He sipped his beer and swallowed loudly.

'No go on, what were you going to say? Come on, Phil.'

'I was going to say, except she's more normal than you.'

Caroline flinched.

'I mean, what has got into you, Caro? You were never exactly a wild child but I don't ever remember you being as uptight as this.'

'It's winter!' Caroline brought her hand down on the table. 'I hate winter. I can't do anything, everything's on hold. I hate it. I can't even follow my stars. You know me well enough to understand that.'

'Winter outside? Or winter inside?'

'Oh Phil, don't. Be careful what you say. You're drunk. You could say things you'll regret tomorrow.'

'Well perhaps I should.' He yanked at the top button of his shirt and spread the collar to refresh himself. 'This isn't what I expected from you. We could always talk, even though we were so different. I always thought it was because we were different. Brendan said you were on your way to a hotel for the night when I showed up. Is that what's hacked you off so much? That I foiled your plans for a shag?'

'No.' Caroline sank to a chair at the kitchen table. 'I'm glad you turned up.'

'So's Brendan,' he said, his eyes glittering with a hint of malice. Caroline hoped it was the drink talking. She shouldn't have mentioned Trixie. It was like lighting the slow-burning fuse to a firework.

'I only mentioned . . . the other woman because I'm worried about you. I'm so sorry I read your mail. It was a complete accident.'

'I'm not going to talk to you about it.'

'All right, all right.' She put out her hands. 'I understand if you'd rather talk to the guys about it. I just want to know you're okay.'

'I'm okay. But that's not what's really bothering you.'

'Of course it is.' She glanced up. 'I care.'

'You want to organise me and I won't let you, that's what's annoying you. You're wondering if Luzie knows. You've been working out how to talk me out of it all day. Forming words and phrases in your head that you think might be influential even though you haven't got a clue what's really going on or how I feel.'

'You're wrong.'

'Oh come on.' Phil swigged his beer disdainfully.

'I mean, you flatter yourself. I didn't spend all day thinking about you.' Caroline's blood began to rise. 'And the last thing I was going to do was raise it with you. I don't know why I did. It was a mistake. I'm sorry, Phil, it's your business. What more can I say?'

Phil maintained a brooding silence. He covered one eye with his hand, then the other. 'I really am pissed. Thank God for Shepherd Neame.'

'Do you want to talk to me about it?' Caroline ventured.

'Nope,' he said.

390

After a short silence, Caroline asked quietly, 'Why not?'

Phil sighed. 'Because you won't know what the hell I'm on about. I don't mean to hurt you, but you're not even having one relationship, let alone two. When you're sitting on the sidelines you can afford to be analytical about everything. You're safe. You're not emotionally entangled with anyone. You're cool, calm, rational.'

'That might make me a good listener,' she suggested hopefully.

'No, it makes you a know-all without any relevant experience.'

Caroline bit her bottom lip, heat rising in her cheeks. 'I'm sorry if that's what I am. If you tried to talk to me you might find I'm much more receptive than you expect.'

'I don't think so. David said you and Lizzy had some kind of bust up. He warned me that you were in full-blown "That's illogical, Captain" mode at the moment, and I'm sorry Caro but I can see his point.'

'He said that?' She was horrified. 'What else did he say?'

'Dunno. He didn't seem to know what was up between you and Lizzy and I'm not asking you. My point is, you don't really understand it when people get messed up emotionally. It's not your fault, it's just that it doesn't seem to happen to you. You can't imagine what it feels like to be caught in an emotional wind tunnel.'

The wind squalled, rattling the panes in the kitchen windows. The blind that Caroline had pulled down over the kitchen door flapped. Her vision of her grandfather in the corner of the room flickered in the breeze, like the flame of a candle. She certainly wasn't going to share any emotional agitation she felt with Phil when he was in this mood.

'Don't blame me for being single,' she said, hurt.

'I didn't do that.' He sounded exasperated.

'Well, just don't have a go at me for being fussy in my choice of partner,' she attempted, knowing it sounded lame as she didn't have one.

'We're all fussy.'

'Well, maybe I'm fussier than most people.' Caroline stood up with a hot face, her defences aroused to the full. 'And I'm not going to justify it any more. I'll either meet somebody special or not go out with anybody at all. I don't care if it sounds naïve, it's who I am. So you can stop expecting me to go out there and sleep with everything in button-fly Levis just to prove to the world that I'm *normal* and just so that members of my family feel that I've caught up with them and am finally worthy of their confidences. I'll wait for somebody exceptional, somebody different, somebody like Granddad if I have to wait all my life.'

There was a silence after she'd spoken, then the gazes of brother and sister met and they connected.

'For God's sake,' Phil muttered gently. 'Caro, you are not going to meet somebody like Granddad. Is that what you think?'

'You don't know that.' She'd been able to feel her grandfather's presence since Phil had summoned him. He was listening to them, like a sage, as they pecked at each other like a couple of mean chickens. He was averting his eyes, waiting for them to finish.

'Yes I do. He was a one-off,' Phil said more kindly. 'You always had your head way up there, above the earth. It's no wonder nobody can get to you. Gramps is dead. His like don't turn up every five minutes. You could try giving mere mortals a chance.'

'I do,' Caroline said in a strangled voice. 'I was going to give Brendan a chance.' Suddenly she wanted to choke on an upsurge of tears. No man like her grandfather, in her lifetime? She'd *always* known he was out there and that she'd recognise him on sight. That was why she'd never bothered to go out looking. She'd known that he would find her. Could she be wrong? She hadn't ever defined how she felt about her love life, real or potential, until Phil had arrived and placed it in sharp focus.

'I'm sorry, Caro,' Phil sighed, as if he felt guilty for telling a child the truth about Father Christmas.

'Perhaps it's an illusion,' she said, 'but I'm not going to plough my way through a load of meaningless relationships to pass the time before he turns up.'

'What makes you think I don't share that hope?' Phil said, sounding very sober. 'Don't you think I have a dream of a woman who's right for me, who makes my heart stop, who moves me so much that I can't breathe? Do you think either Luzie or Trixie have managed to make that happen?'

They looked at each other. Phil's lower lip gave a wobble and he wiped his eyes with the back of his hand.

'Oh Phil, come here.' Caroline took him in her arms and held him tight.

'I was too young to get married,' he said. 'We didn't know each other. I'm just not grown up enough, Caro.'

'Poor boy.' She rubbed his back.

'I don't love either of them. I don't.'

'It's all right.' Caroline kissed his cheek indulgently.

Such a handsome, flush-faced brother. No wonder he got confused about his love life. The more choice, the more complication. 'It'll be all right.'

'Luzie started seeing this old flame, supposedly just as a friend.' He spoke into her jacket and Caroline listened. 'I swear I was faithful at that time, although I wasn't happy. But then she started staying out late and stuff and he started gloating at me in a subtle way, so I just knew. It wasn't about sex, it was about the fact that he was closer to her than I could ever be.'

'Oh,' Caroline whispered, rubbing his hair.

'So I had a fling when the chance came up. And it didn't solve anything. Luzie and I just barked at each other. Neither of us had the courage to move out, but all that affection turned to disdain. We lived in the same apartment but we couldn't stand each other and spent every evening in separate rooms, or one of us went out. My fling just split us further apart, but we were apart anyway. Don't make me go back, Caro. Please don't. It's not right.'

Caroline didn't know about juggling lovers and fighting them off every time she left the house – an aspect of Phil's life he sometimes entertained her with in his lighter moods – but she knew when something wasn't right. He said it with conviction, and it changed the way she felt completely. She should have had more faith in him. He was a kind man at heart. He wouldn't knowingly cause pain to another individual if he could help it. She should have trusted him, but she could make up for it now.

'I won't,' she assured him. 'I promise you I won't. And I'm so sorry for not listening to you before. I'm here for you.'

''S'okay.' Phil stood up straight, his face streaky from the tears. 'I think I'm going to go to bed now. Is that all right? I'm really, really drunk, I'm just trying to pretend I'm not.'

Caroline laughed and kissed him again. 'That's okay. We can do something nice tomorrow. Anything you like.'

'Oh, I would.' He looked apologetic. 'But I can't. I've got a commitment with the guys again. We're going out and . . .'

'And what?' Caroline smiled at him, just pleased to have him in her arms and her friend again. She didn't care what he did. It was his business.

'I'm not supposed to tell you, or you'll tell Lizzy,' he said in a childlike way, reminding her of how drunk he was. 'So I can't tell you, but it'll be fun and I'll tell you afterwards.'

Caroline widened her eyes. 'Just assure me it doesn't involve loose women.'

'Absolutely not. Women are the last thing on my mind. It's much more fun than that. But we'll do something together soon, I promise. If not tomorrow, soon after. Okay?'

'Sure. Listen baby bro, I know we don't say this very often, but I love you. You know that, don't you?'

'Yes. I love you too, Spock.'

She smiled then frowned as Phil binned his empty beer can and poured himself a glass of water to take to bed.

'Spock?'

He glanced at her with pink-rimmed eyes. 'Yes, Spock. It's what we all call you behind your back.'

Caroline swallowed. 'All?'

395

'Me, David, Brendan. Mainly.' He gave her a good-natured smile. 'Goodnight then.'

Caroline followed him out to the stairs and watched him slowly walk up them, carefully clinging onto her stair rail. 'Since when?' she called up after him.

'Since – forever. They'll kill me for telling you. G'night.'

He let himself into the bathroom and closed the door. Caroline blinked after him, then went back into the kitchen to lock up.

It felt as if her grandfather was still there, in the corner, with something to say.

Chapter Nineteen

The cold air tasted of freshly cut coal and dry earth. Antonia negotiated the steep path which ran like a dried-up stream under a canopy of evergreens down into Knole Park. Her boots skidded on the twigs and she struggled to keep her balance as the path plunged towards a swing gate let into the tall wire fence. She fed herself through the gate, smiling politely at a young family who had paused on the other side to allow her through, and entered the park with a bouncing stride. She pushed her arms out in front of her, stretched expansively, then interlaced her gloved fingers in the air away from her chest. She probably looked as if she was practising the breast stroke. The space, the freedom, the nip of the country air was fantastic. She breathed deeply, ranging her eyes over the rust stains of the bracken-strewn slopes, the shapely hairpin branches of the ancient trees and the faint tracks of the fallow deer. She stopped at the top of a slope where a private drive cut through the parkland and peered out at her view, espying a deer herd alternately grazing and wandering in the direction of Knole House, whose crenellated hair-line was just visible over the brow of a hill. She decided to follow them.

She was taking time out, on her own, for herself today. Sonia was busy experimenting with a dessert that she'd seen made on the television and was adorning the kitchen with a combination of strawberries, melted chocolate and custard powder. Seeing that Antonia was heading off with the car keys and a purposeful expression, Audrey had promised to supervise Sonia's efforts.

'And no, I won't touch or break anything,' Audrey had stated bolshily, only the twinkle in her eyes revealing that the dynamic of their relationship had changed.

After five minutes of walking, Antonia caught up with the deer. All proudly displayed sleek coats as rich as warm honey, white flecks dabbed along their backs. They ranged in size from just over knee-high to one or two stags with elaborate antlers who would probably easily come up to her chest. The stags seemed preoccupied and at a safe distance, so she settled herself on the ground with her back to a solid oak trunk, her padded jacket providing sufficient cushioning underneath for her to be comfortable for a while. It also provided a protective buffer against the unpredictable squalls of the wind that were harrying thin clouds across the sky.

Once seated, Antonia watched the deer peacefully. They moved slowly, with a collective unconscious, over the pitted ground, chewing at tufts of grass as they went. It wasn't clear who was leading and who was following. It seemed to be a mutual decision, lacking competition or conflict. To be so close to such a gentle display of co-operation moved Antonia, and she drew her legs up to make herself less conspicuous to them. They seemed happy to graze around her, ignoring her presence apart from one or two curious looks. She sat quietly while they moved over the area of ground where she was seated and began to pass beyond her to a thick copse that studded the open land, blowing plumes of cloudy breath into the cold air from delicately rimmed nostrils.

As she was absorbing the tranquillity like a sponge sucking up water, Antonia's mobile phone suddenly shrilled its distinctive tune from her handbag. As Sonia had insisted that she install it with 'Hit Me Baby One More Time', it ensured that the moment of calm was well and truly lost. The deer raised their antlers as one and gave her offended looks. One or two of them quickly cantered on their way.

'Damn.' She retrieved the phone from the bottom of her bag hastily and stabbed at a button. Apologetic looks in the direction of the deer didn't seem to achieve much. Their expressions indicated that they didn't share her taste in music. 'Yes?'

'Antonia?'

She frowned. It was a familiar voice. The rustling of the branches above her head in the gusts was probably distorting her hearing, so she pressed one ear firmly against the phone and put a finger in the other to hear better.

'Daniel?' She'd seen Daniel go out earlier. He had her mobile number of course, but it would be very odd for him to call her unless something was wrong.

'No.' A slight chuckle.

'Rick?' Not her ex-husband today, when she felt so pleasantly drained of adrenaline. She didn't want to think about him just now.

'Wrong again, it's Emile,' he said, as if he wasn't that interested in playing games and wanted to get on with the business of talking to her.

'Oh.' She sat up straight, pressing her spine against the gnarled bark of the oak and removing from her hair

399

a dead acorn shell that had just decided to fall from above. She smiled. 'Oh, Emile. Hello.'

'You sound as if you're doing twenty knots in a force nine gale somewhere out in the Arctic Ocean.'

She laughed and turned to put her back to the wind. She pulled up the hood of her jacket, nestling the phone against her ear inside the padding. 'Is that better? I think the wind was blowing into the mouthpiece. It's astonishingly – ' She tried to think of another word but she couldn't. Her heart had started to beat rather fast. 'It's windy down here.'

'Are you outside? I could call again later if you're shopping or something.'

'No, I'm not shopping. At this moment I'm sitting in a pile of dry deer poo next to an oak tree in the middle of a beautiful natural park.'

'Really? Where is that?'

'Knole. Just on the outskirts of Sevenoaks. I was . . . I'm watching the deer.'

'What a fantastic way to spend a Sunday afternoon. I'm sitting in Kensington listening to the rumble of buses and the blast of taxis outside my flat window. I've got Hyde Park up the road I suppose, but I'm not in the mood to go jogger-dodging. I've got my computer on, and it's whining at me that I've got a load of work to do before tomorrow morning. A country park sounds like heaven.'

'That's what I thought,' she enthused, suddenly pleased that he had rung so that she could share the moment with somebody. 'It's so solitary up here. So – ' The oak swayed violently in another gust of wind and a smattering of twigs and acorn shells fell to the ground. 'So rustly.' She giggled like a girl. 'Windy and rustly. I

400

sound just like a teacher of English, don't I? It's very uplifting. I know why cats go silly in the wind now. It brings out your high spirits.'

'You sound like a woman who'd enjoy a monsoon.'

'As it happens I am just that kind of woman. I was in India once. I was a university student at the time and then, well the world was even smaller to me then than it is now. And my friend Sanjit and I hadn't timed it very well. We got caught in the monsoon as we went south. And you're right, I did love it. Apart from the disruption to the local people of course, that wasn't enjoyable, but it made me feel alive. I think it was . . .'

'The magnitude?'

'Yes, exactly,' she said with an affirming finger as if he could see it. 'That's just it. Well, you know what I mean then.'

'Yes, I do. Have you ever been to the West Indies?'

'I never have. I've often been curious about it, but I guess in recent years it's all been, well, just very busy. What with putting Sonia through education and making sure of the house so that she knows where she lives.'

'The way to see the West Indies,' he went on, as if they were sitting down together in the cosy corner of a pub and had all the time in the world to chat, 'is to stay with people who live there. None of this Sandals Hotels and nightclubs routine.'

'Yes, I'm sure. When we visited India we stayed with Sanjit's cousins at one point. Sanjit was a very good friend at college and she'd arranged for us to put up there for a night or two. I think that was the part I remember the most. They were wonderful.'

'And what happened to Sanjit?' he asked.

'Do you know, I can't remember.' Antonia felt a dip of

401

nostalgia in the pit of her stomach. Why had she lost touch with her old friends? She'd lived a cosmopolitan life then, one of travel, possibilities, adventures, excitement and laughter. When had she become nailed down in a small Kentish market town and started to turn into a static, English-bred, English-teaching, English-living-and-breathing middle-aged woman? How had that happened to her?

It had happened because she hadn't realised that life was short. She had been so busy building up solid foundations for herself and Sonia that she had been forgetting that living is what you do while you're alive. You can't shelve it for a later date.

'When did you and Sonia last take a holiday?' Emile asked, unwittingly voicing Antonia's internal query to herself.

'I was just wondering. A long while ago. We do day trips, and we've been on the Eurostar once or twice for long weekends.'

'I mean, a complete break. Two or three weeks somewhere completely different.'

'Oh well, that we haven't done. Not ever as far as I remember. At least, not since Sonia was very little so she wouldn't remember.' She shook her head and laughed to herself. 'No. But I don't think Sonia's noticed. How sad is that?'

Emile chuckled and there was a pause as Antonia watched the toffee backs of the deer wandering away over the hill. A thread of nervous energy snaked its way through her chest. She caught her breath.

'Emile, have you ever wanted to do something really wild? I mean, do you ever do impulsive things that nobody expects you to do?'

He laughed very loudly at that.

'I have a daughter but I've never been married. Ask me another.'

'Oh I'm sorry, I didn't mean to pry. Daniel had said –'

'Nat's mother and I are good friends but we don't have a relationship. But in answer to your question, I don't suppose you mean impulsive things like emptying bottles of vodka into fruit punch? I'd say you get that from your mother.' He found that very amusing.

Antonia had prostrated herself quite enough on her mother's behalf to all Sonia's friends' parents, and equally to Emile through Daniel. She'd also sent everybody, including Emile, a notelet with a written apology on it. She'd done that one to death.

'I'm not wearing a hair shirt for my mother any more,' she said firmly. 'I meant something more profound.'

'Like what?' He had a smile in his voice.

'I don't know.' Her voice was carried away on a blast of wind, along with a dry leaf that curled and twisted in front of her before being catapulted away.

'Antonia? Are you still there?'

'When all this is over,' she said aloud to the wind, not minding that Emile could hear her too, 'my life is going to be different. Sonia and I are going to live. I mean *live*.'

Her mind was full of images that were so tangible she could smell and touch them. She knew it was true. She didn't need reassurance or encouragement. Nothing anybody said or did would make any difference. It was as if she'd been given a privileged glimpse into her future, and been shown vibrancy and colour. It brought tears of relief to her eyes. She put a hand to her mouth, happier than she would have ever been able to explain. She was so in tune with her imagination at that moment that she didn't notice that Emile hadn't said a word in reply. Above her, the sky was majestic, like the vaulted roof of a magnificent cathedral. 'It's so beautiful,' she whispered as the wind ruffled the fur of her hood.

'Antonia, may I invite you to dinner?' Emile asked. His voice was full of warmth, and she felt it spread across her chest and stomach like a cup of spicy mulled wine spilled over a white tablecloth.

'In another life, Emile, perhaps you and I would have been kindred spirits,' she said with heart. 'In this life, I'm on a solitary journey. I have problems to sort out, things that I have to face on my own.'

' "But I have promises to keep," ', he quoted, astonishing her.

She shifted against the tree trunk and blinked at the lofty chimney stacks on the horizon. 'That's Robert Frost,' she told him. 'Do you like poetry, then?'

'It's amazing what you learn from your children.' His voice was still smiling. 'You are a unique person, Antonia. May I call you again?'

'Yes,' she said contentedly. 'Of course you can call me. Any time you like.'

He rang off and she put the phone back into her handbag thoughtfully. No awkwardness, no pressure. It was natural. It was how it was meant to be. They'd just talked for, she wasn't sure how long, about anything that came into their heads. She felt as if she knew him already. She felt buoyed, energised, happier than before he'd rung. She'd been allowed a glimpse of how it was when it was right.

She stood up and pulled off her hood, allowing the wind to rail against her sensitive ears, casting her blonde hair into confusion. She reached up to her hairclip behind her head. It was still there, but wonky. She pulled it from her hair and put it into her jacket pocket. Then she shook her head into the wind so that her hair flew freely in every direction. It made her laugh.

Then she walked over the hill in the direction that the deer had taken. As she reached the dense copse, she stopped.

> *The woods are lovely, dark and deep,*
> *But I have promises to keep,*
> *And miles to go before I sleep,*
> *And miles to go before I sleep.*

'I want a word with you,' Lizzy said in a low voice.

Brendan widened his black eyes at her as he followed her into the kitchen. She flicked the switch on the kettle in the absence of something else to do. She was ratty, temperamental and what was worse, the more she didn't want it to show, the more it did.

'What went on with Caroline?' she threw at him.

He drew a mask over his face. 'Nothing.'

'You're talking to me, not Debbie down at the Dog and Duck. I know you and Caro. One minute you were pursuing the idea in an optimistic kind of way and I'd really thought myself into it. The next minute you're trying to kill my husband with alcohol poisoning. Did she turn you down for good?'

Brendan pursed his lips and offered no reply.

'Are you on the rebound? Because if you are, you're forgetting just who it is who's nursed you through every frigging rebound you've been through since I've known you. I've even been known to hold your head over the loo on one or two occasions.'

'One,' Brendan clarified.

'Okay, one. I know about you and your rebounds, but normally you do them in this house, not out there somewhere.'

'Actually I normally do both.' Brendan picked up a plastic Thunderbird plane that was covered in jam and played with it between his fingers. 'This isn't about me, Lizzy. I can see why you'd think that but it isn't my binge.'

'Oh, what does that mean,' she said sarcastically, taking the toy off him and throwing it into a bowl full of warm washing-up water. 'Is it like being conscripted or something? Does somebody drop a pound into your pint as the whisper goes round? Binge coming up, be there or have your knackers chopped off?'

Brendan laughed, the worry lines over his forehead disappearing. 'It's not like that.'

'So what is it, Brendan? I hardly know David at the moment.'

'I can't . . .' He looked away. 'I can't answer for David.'

'All right.' She took a deep breath, heaving the air right into her lungs and out again. Calm. Start again. 'Okay, let's talk about Caroline. Why didn't you make it to this luxury hotel?'

'It just didn't happen. I'm sorry, Lizzy. I know you're angry with both me and Caroline for that, but there's the truth.'

She watched Brendan pretend to be interested in her spice rack for a while then a thought struck her. 'Why aren't you asking me if I've spoken to Caroline about it?'

'Oh, I just know she's busy this weekend. A lot going on. And David said you and she'd had a bit of a tiff. I didn't think you were as chatty with each other as you normally are.'

Lizzy nodded slowly. 'All right.' She sighed out loud as she pressed the switch on the kettle for the third time. 'Do you want a cup of tea or not?'

'Not really,' he admitted.

'What's odd to me is that you lot have closed off. Normally you all share things with me. I'm one of the boys. I mean, God, I have to be when I'm surrounded by three men, albeit two very little ones.'

'That'd be David and Michael.'

Lizzy stretched a smile. 'Don't joke about David being a little boy. It's a bit too close to the truth.'

'I wasn't joking,' Brendan said.

The door opened. It was a small, square kitchen. Lizzy had squeezed a diminutive Formica table into it for the boys to eat on their own at times, but as adults entered it, it was quickly full. David posed in the doorway with a towel slung around his waist. His eyes were bloodshot and he was smiling.

'Michelangelo eat your heart out.' He pointed a foot artistically.

Lizzy scowled at him where she normally would have laughed. 'Right.'

'Watcha sport!' He clasped Brendan's hand and shook it. 'Achtung that Spitfire.'

Lizzy spitefully prodded the button on the kettle again. 'Does anybody want a bloody cup of tea or not?'

'I'm just going to get my clothes on and we're going off for a bit,' David said, still smiling.

'Aren't you hung-over, David?' she asked.

'Nope,' he assured her cheerfully. 'I'm not in the least hung-over because I'm still drunk. That's why Brendan's driving. But we'll be back later, I promise.'

Lizzy raised her eyebrows as high as she could.

'So I presume you'll spend the afternoon making stacks of those wonderful cards of yours.' David rubbed the corner of his towel over his chest. The wind gusted and Lizzy quickly reached up to shut an upper window that had been ajar as the blast rattled the louvre blind into chaos.

'What do you reckon?' David looked enquiringly at Brendan, who remained poker-faced.

'I reckon you need to get your strides on,' he replied.

'That's the Dunkirk spirit.' David headed off.

'Why does he suddenly sound like an extra in a bad Battle of Britain film?' Lizzy asked Brendan testily.

'Dunno.' He wandered away too.

Lizzy stayed in the kitchen finding things to do so that she didn't have to speak to either of them. David got himself ready upstairs, Brendan hung about in the living room, fiddling with one of the boys' games. Upstairs in their bedroom, the boys were busy on the PlayStation that had been the major outlay she and David had made that year for them. That usually meant that Jacob was hogging it and Michael was complaining that he never got a go. At that moment, Lizzy couldn't have cared less whose turn it was. She thumped things around in the kitchen until David, in his jacket and solid DMs, stuck his head around the door.

'We're off, sweetheart.'

'Up the pub again?' Lizzy looked at David with concern. 'David, I get as squiffy as the next person, but what's with this bid for a liver transplant?'

She couldn't maintain the anger in her face for very long. They loved each other. What was going on? They were acting like a couple of strangers.

'Lizzy.' He took two steps towards her and held her

tightly. He kissed her cheek. 'Just don't ask.'

'Why not? What's the big secret?'

'That's the thing, my lover. You can't keep secrets. I can't tell you just yet, but I will.'

David left the kitchen and Lizzy screwed up the tea towel in her hand. She threw it at the floor as she heard the latch of the front door.

'Bastard,' she muttered, tears locking in her throat.

They both left. Lizzy stood silently on her own for a while, then was surprised to hear the key in the latch again. The door to the kitchen opened and it was Brendan's head that appeared, his black eyes assessing her.

'I've told him I've come back to get my gloves.'

Lizzy was bewildered. 'What is this about?'

'I can't say, but it's nothing for you to worry about.'

'You wanker. You could tell me.'

'You're my favourite woman. I luv ya, you know that. Hang loose and it'll all come boomeranging back.'

'You are just a walking cliché.'

He grinned. Lizzy stared unforgivingly at Brendan as he backed out of the room. He waved a hand around the door to her in farewell. She heard him retreat through the hall, yell a goodbye upstairs to the boys who sang out their goodbyes downstairs in return, then the front door slammed again.

Slowly, Lizzy mounted the stairs as she thought about it all. She reached the door to the bathroom and her stomach lurched again.

A blue sky. At last. Caroline couldn't believe it.

Her grandmother had owned a crockery set that was the colour of this sky. So pale blue that it was almost white. The sun was a clear, bright bulb. On the horizon the grasping branches were maroon in the sharp light. Overhead a few smudged vapour trails trawled over the blue, blown out of shape by an ardent wind, like an artist's sleeve carelessly wiped over a fresh line of paint. Somebody across the gardens was using a hedge strimmer. It droned sporadically, ensuring a Sunday afternoon ambience.

Caroline tilted herself back in her chair and gazed up through the opened gap in the shed roof. Up, up and into the distance. Acres and acres of water vapour. Beyond that, blackness. She thought of the Apollo space capsule. Why hadn't she been born in a hundred years' time? What would a hundred years' worth of advances bring? The problem was, she mused as she chewed on a sausage roll she'd brought out to the shed with her, that there just wasn't time to get around the universe within an individual lifespan. Humans would have to live longer. Or send out machines, relying on future generations to interpret the data. Once again she thought of the astrophysics department at Kent University, where she'd once held a place to study for a master's. What a different life it would have been. No kids, no noise, no fun. She smiled to herself in the knowledge that she had made the right choice.

A biplane droned overhead. Lolling on her chair with her head back, Caroline watched it weave its way from one side of her square viewpoint to the other. The engine fizzed and spluttered as the wind gusted the sound into distortion, then it ambled out of sight. The wind dropped into another lull and the plane purred smoothly on its way.

She stood up. Phil had been out since lunchtime so she

had the house to herself. It was chilly in the shed. She'd make another cup of coffee and come back with it. There was no real observing to be done in the daylight, but there was plenty of data that needed logging properly and organising. And if she was honest, she just loved being out there in her flip-top observatory, fiddling with all her gadgets, on her own. That's what Sunday afternoons were for.

As she got to the kitchen, Caroline realised that somebody was ringing her doorbell. She glanced at her watch. It was nearly three o'clock. Phil was likely to be gone for hours yet and as it seemed to be another boys' get-together, that would account for David and Brendan too. Perhaps Lizzy was dropping by?

With a light step of anticipation Caroline went through to the hall. In that swell of hope she realised just how much she was missing Lizzy, her impulsive visits and her regular phone calls. If this wasn't her at the door, she would definitely ring her this afternoon. Somebody had to take steps to put things right between them. And Phil's observations, harsh as they were, had made Caroline feel fairly sure that she'd been insensitive to people recently. She was the one who should make it up to Lizzy.

But it wasn't Lizzy at the door and Caroline gazed in astonishment at her caller.

'Tom.'

'I worked out that this one must be your house.'

Caroline flushed, pleasure teasing her into a smile. 'So, how are you?' she asked, cringing at her mundane query.

'I wondered if you wanted to go for a walk?'

The simplicity of his question threw her completely. It was a little like when he'd suggested they might have

411

dinner. It was so simple that she couldn't think of anything to say in response.

'A walk?' she echoed.

'It's the weather. The bluster of it, the energy in the trees and the bushes. And in the sky.' He peered upwards and she followed his gaze.

'Yes, it's – it's pretty windy.'

'You like the outdoors, don't you?' He nodded at her thick jacket. 'Anybody who spends half their life sitting in a shed with the roof pulled back has to be a bit of an outdoor girl. Not that I pay that much attention, you understand, but I can see into your garden from my back room upstairs. I could just about make out that you had a lot of technical equipment in there. When you have a light on in your shed it does tend to show up in the darkness. At first I thought you must be a radio ham,' he explained.

'What made you change your mind?'

'No aerial. And you take the roof off when you're in there at night. I don't think radio hams are forced to battle with the elements in the middle of the night if they don't want to.'

Caroline laughed under her breath. 'You saw how we were last night, and that was with Roderick's house to dive into to get warm. You should see the star parties. We spend our lives looking like walking sleeping bags. Give me Hawaii any day.'

'Have you ever observed the Southern sky?'

'No.' She'd always wanted to, though. 'Have you?'

'Yes. With my grandmother, years ago when I was very young. We went all around the Mediterranean and into North Africa too. It feels as if you can reach out and touch the stars there.'

Caroline watched him for a moment while he contemplated the harassed clouds in the sky. 'I was going to offer to lend you a star chart, but I get the feeling you're not the sort of guy who follows maps, are you?'

But they were still standing on the threshold of her house while they had this conversation, and she still hadn't answered his question. He asked it again.

'So are you coming for a walk?'

The truth was that Caroline didn't know what she was doing. She allowed herself to answer instinctively, and then found that it was incredibly easy to know what to say.

'Yes.'

Chapter Twenty

They walked to a nearby village. There, medieval cottages huddled in conspiratorial groups around a village pond. Behind the village, a footpath ran away over the fields and they decided to take it. Traffic from the motorway link stirred distantly in the background and sheep trotted ahead of them as they disturbed them. Others, bored, hung about at the edge of the field and chewed.

'I wonder what Wolsey would have made of the motorway,' Tom said.

'Wolsey?'

'The palace. The old ruin the other side of the village was his pad. This would have been a thriving community in the Tudor period. Funny how things turn out. Only four or five hundred years later and their grand centrepiece has turned into a cute little ornament.' He glanced back at the quaint cluster of gabled houses marking the village.

'Four or five hundred years is pretty relative.' Caroline removed a strand of hair from her eyes that the wind was playing with. 'In terms of what we know about the universe it's not even enough time to flutter an eyelash.'

'You think about it all the time, don't you?'

'Yes, all the time.' Caroline laughed, the wind catching in her throat. They both staggered against a daunting blast.

'God, this is a serious gale,' Tom said as they attempted to walk on in a zigzag but found their legs foundering, their coats mushrooming out behind them like sails. They looked like two galleons vying for position in a stormy sea, Caroline mused. A thin branch cracked and fell from a line of horse chestnuts to one side of them. As she turned to look, she was caught off balance again as the wind raged maliciously around her and left her gasping. She clutched at Tom's arm as she felt her ankle twist on the grass pocked by the incessant prodding of sheep hooves, then sank a knee into a dry dung cake.

'Oh lovely!' she exclaimed, as Tom pulled her upright again and they both looked at the brown smear across her jeans.

'Is your ankle all right?' He had a firm hold of her arm.

'Yes, yes.' She nodded cheerfully.

She found herself smiling at him again. A huge, quarter-orange of a beam. She just felt happy. It was a while since she'd felt as uncomplicated as this. It didn't make much sense, seeing as Tom was one of the reasons that she'd started to be complicated about things. Perhaps it was just too long since she'd been out marauding through the countryside on a windy day with such a good companion.

The thought made her smile stretch further while the wind turned her hair into a rolling mop. Tom *was* a good companion. He wasn't alarming, he *was* disarming. If she was honest with herself, being around him made her feel extraordinary.

Caroline was a teacher, and she was good at it. She was used to drawing responses from reticent people. She was an expert at making conversation where there wasn't any. All teachers learned over time how to hide an embarrassing silence in the classroom, and it was a handy skill to have tucked away in your back pocket so that you could reproduce it on social occasions. But, with Tom, Caroline didn't have a moment when she had to force the conversation. On the contrary, she only felt the questions she wanted to ask him piling up in her head like a great heap of novels with shiny covers, stacked so high now that they were slipping over each other. Almost every simple statement he made prompted her to want to ask, 'How did you . . .?' or 'Where did you . . .?' or 'What did you mean by . . .?' and even sometimes, 'Yes, I know! And have you thought . . .?' During their walk, she'd been quizzing him about his grandmother's method of reading the stars again, but he still wouldn't relinquish what he knew. She was determined to find out. And they'd talked about other things too. When she concentrated, it was hard to remember what exactly had been said, but her mind was buzzing.

As all these thoughts were running through Caroline's head she was standing in the middle of the muddy field, smiling at Tom, while he maintained a hand on her arm and they looked into each other's eyes.

'Caroline,' Tom said, his voice carrying strangely on the wind. It was almost as if he was reaching towards her from a greater distance than he was. 'Would you think again about having dinner with me?'

For some reason, in this field, in this gale with the trees all around rustling at her like cheerleaders, Caroline no longer had any doubts. 'Yes, I'd love to,' she said.

'Are you free tonight? I know that seems impulsive,

and if it's rushing you just tell me. Or next week or the week after?'

'Tonight would be lovely.'

Had Caroline ever been in love before? So far in her life, she would probably have estimated that she had been in love twice. Once in her teens, once at university. Everybody fell in love with someone on the school bus in their teens, and she'd been no exception. Everyone who made it to university also fell in love there and had at least one tragically unrequited relationship. Hers had been, predictably maybe, with the president of the astronomy society when she'd first laid eyes on him at the freshers' fair. In retrospect she'd decided that she'd turned up at the fair resigned to the fact that she would fall in love with the president of the astronomy society, whoever he was. The fact that he'd been tall, dark and very knowledgeable on the subject of pulsars had only fuelled her admiration. In her mature adult life, she couldn't say she'd ever been in love.

As she and Tom looked at each other she felt a sensation creeping up on her. It scampered up and down her arms like a nervous bird. It began again in her stomach and spread to her chest. It pricked at the skin on her legs and produced a surge of warmth that swept upwards to the tips of her hair. Where her breathing had been inhibited by the squalls of the wind, now it was subdued by a more profound experience. Tom's eyes were intent upon hers, a hue of aquamarine that suddenly seemed wonderful to her, his pupils wide and invigorated. Then she knew that he was going to kiss her and it seemed that every nerve in her body nodded assent at him like the fragile tips of a line of poplars in the breeze.

Tom bent his head to hers and kissed her lips. In moments, her hands were on his shoulders holding him closer, his arms were wound around her waist. In the midst of the violence of the gale, they were locked in a well of warmth and energy.

An ear-splitting crack forced them both to glance away. Ahead of them an old willow had parted in two, a moss-daubed branch crashing towards the field. Tom looked back into Caroline's eyes and in that moment, they exchanged information that didn't need to be spoken. Yes, he assured her in his look. I do feel that way about you. And yes, she replied, as much as it amazes me, I do feel this way about you too. Then after that was affirmed silently between them, they could react to the wind storm.

'We need to get inside,' Tom said.

'Agreed.'

'Take my arm, we'll go back.'

And so they plodded a tricky path back across the fields, exclaiming as twigs and full branches creaked and thrashed around them, sympathising with the sheep who were now much less bored, and talking where they could above the howl of a relentless wind that if anything seemed to be gaining in strength. Caroline's arm remained threaded through Tom's and his hand was placed over hers. They were like a couple promenading, displaying their partiality to their ovine audience. How amazing, Caroline thought, excited beyond measure, that an afternoon could start with so many questions and end with a simple answer.

They found themselves back at the door to Caroline's house. She pulled away from his arm reluctantly.

'May I pick you up this evening at eight?' Tom asked.

'Yes, you may.'

He inclined his head. 'Then I'll see you again at eight.'

She was loath to go inside. She didn't want the feeling to lessen in any way. Her fingers lingered in Tom's hand.

She was taken back to something that had happened when she was a very little girl. Her friends had told her she could buy real earth that had been brought back from other planets in the local shop. It was sold in a paper sachet and called Space Dust. The first time she'd ever bought it with her pocket money, she'd excitedly run to her grandfather with it.

'Tell me if it's real,' she'd demanded, pushing him by his legs towards his microscope where he always made slides of things of any interest to show the children.

'It's not real, love,' he'd told her.

'Then what is it?' Caroline had become distressed. How could she be sold something that wasn't real? What would be the point of it if it wasn't real?

'It's fun,' he'd said, his face crumpling into humour at her childish misunderstanding of what she'd bought.

'Fun?'

He'd put a couple of speckles of it on her tongue where it had fizzled and popped. Her grandfather had laughed at her surprise.

'Maybe when you're older, you'll find real space dust,' he'd said, stroking her hair.

And then, her humour failing to overcome her disappointment, she'd burst into tears. 'They said it was real!' she'd howled at him. 'They said it was the real thing.'

'My poor love,' he'd said to her. 'When you're a

woman you'll recognise the real thing when you see it.'

Tom's fingers were still touching hers, his gaze unwilling to leave her face. A puff of Woodbine smoke lingered in the air, then was shot away on the squall like a cannonball.

Caroline looked in vain up and down the street. Nobody was passing. 'Did you smell that? Pipe smoke?' Disconcerted by Tom's incomprehension, Caroline stepped out into the street again and gave it one further scan.

'Pipe smoke? Maybe it's a chimney?'

She shook her head. 'No, definitely not. It's my grandfather's smell.'

'Well,' Tom's face relaxed into a smile. 'I'll see you again at eight.'

'Yes,' she said, backing towards her front door with the unmistakable aroma of her grandfather's presence cloaking her like a blanket. 'Yes Tom, I'll see you then.'

Caroline showered, made her face up and squirted herself with perfume. She was at the stage of casting clothes about the bed when the phone rang.

She still had a couple of hours to go before Tom dropped by her house to collect her for dinner, but she wanted to get her outfit right so that she could relax. Work clothes were mingled with practical clothes and a few things that were more dressy but she had no idea what to choose. She had turned into the human equivalent of a pair of salad tongs, tossing the combination over her bed in the hope that something would stand out.

Normally Caroline never aligned herself slavishly with the idea that she had to look alluring whenever she left the house, but she liked to look good in her own, understated way. She hadn't wanted to seduce anybody for a very long time. She'd been busy, her thoughts and ideas exploding like an internal fireworks display, keeping her well occupied and stimulated without any need for external input.

But she felt excited about her physical appearance now. She sat on the edge of her *Star Trek* duvet and surveyed the mess that was her wardrobe, emptied onto her bed. The evidence gave her a pang of uncertainty. She'd tried trousers and decided that they were boring, then a selection of skirts but found that they looked even more boring. Then she'd attempted a couple of dresses that she preserved for special occasions. One was far too glitzy. Her most flattering option was probably a wool pencil skirt to the calves which went with a soft autumnal-shaded loose top she'd bought some time ago. It would go beautifully with a pair of leather boots which she sometimes wore to work. 'This is it,' she'd chanted to herself.

And now that there was a reason to dress up, she vowed to find time to go shopping for a few other things. It was amazing how her collection of clothes had gone from adequate to dreadful in the space of her afternoon's walk with Tom. Suddenly she wanted to look great. She wanted curves and legs again. She wanted new, sexy knickers and a bra that made her chest look enormous. She wanted skirts that made her legs look long, tops that brought out the best in her natural colouring. God, she missed Lizzy when putting this all together, but she'd restrained herself from ringing her and blurting it all out. She was enjoying herself so much that she didn't want to justify it or explain it. She'd ring Lizzy in the week. She could just imagine her cousin's shock at finding that after all the antagonism Caroline had shown towards Tom, she'd ended up having a romantic date with him. Yes, in time Lizzy would share this and they'd laugh and it would be fun. Just at the moment, though, it was too private for Caroline to breathe a word of it to anybody else.

And at that point, humming to herself along with the music that she'd put on, Caroline cocked an ear and found that the phone was ringing. In her green wool outfit and her soft brown boots that she'd been displaying in front of her mirror, her best underwear beneath, her face radiant, her eyes glowing and a cloud of her favourite perfume about her, she sidestepped to the phone and picked it up with impish good spirits.

'Well hello.'

'Caroline. Don't say a word until I've finished.'

'Brendan?'

'This is important and really urgent, so can you shut up and listen? I'm at Bromley General. Phil's in intensive care. A tree came down on the car and smashed through the window on the passenger's side. The others are shaken up and bruised but mainly all right. You need to get here now. They might need blood from a relative.'

In one day, Caroline's world had gone from black and white to colour, like the moment in *The Wizard of Oz* when Dorothy enters her magical world. Now, the same illusion being ripped from her, Caroline saw the colours melt away and the monotones emerge again. She felt her way to the sofa and sat on the arm to steady herself. She found herself echoing Brendan's words, skirting around the real issue that was frightening her. Phil.

'Caroline? Are you there?'

'Yes. Bromley? Why are you in Bromley?'

'It was the closest A and E. We were on our way back from Biggin Hill.'

'Biggin Hill?'

'I can explain all that when you get here. Do you know what blood group you are? Phil's is apparently rare and it might cause a problem. They asked me to ask you.'

'Phil's got the same blood group as Mum.' Her voice was a whisper. 'I'll ring her now.'

'You need to get here fast. I'll get off the line.'

For a moment everything seemed to be frozen. Sound, vision, movement, it even seemed as if the witter of her watch had ceased. It was like swimming underwater. Then an eruption of noise and activity took its place.

The first person Antonia saw when she arrived at Bromley General was Caroline. She was so used to brushing past Caroline at school as they shot from lesson to staffroom to canteen to lesson that at first she walked straight past her in the hospital corridor, nodded and hardly reacted. Then she stopped dead and turned around. Caroline had done the same.

'Caroline! How bizarre. This is the first time I've ever been to this hospital, and I bang into you. Are you all right?'

Caroline was clearly not all right. Her face was white, her eyes black and startled by contrast. Her lips were pale and dry. She had a lot of make-up on, for her, and she was wearing a pretty woollen outfit under an open coat. Perhaps she'd been out somewhere else before coming here? She looked beautiful, Antonia realised, having never thought of Caroline as a beautiful woman

423

before. But she looked ill and shocked beyond that.

'Antonia,' she said hoarsely. 'I'm sorry I can't stop. My brother's in intensive care.'

'You're headed the wrong way.' Antonia nodded at a board on the wall with arrows pointing in various directions. 'I'm picking somebody up from there anyway. It's this way, I think. Walk with me.'

'I just found out,' Caroline said, more to herself than anyone else it seemed. 'Brendan, my friend, phoned me. I don't know how bad he is. It could be awful. They need our blood. Or they think they might. It sounds bad.'

'Here, lean on me.' Antonia took a firm decision and linked Caroline's arm through hers just in case she felt faint. She was walking steadily but her face was so pale Antonia thought that she could go at any moment. 'Don't assume the worst. Let's just get there and find out.'

'What are you here for? Are you all right?' Caroline asked.

'My lodger. He's fine, fit enough to phone me himself, but he's had a car accident and messed up both the car and his ankle in the process. He sounded pretty shaken up, so I've come to make sure he's not worse than he sounds and take him home if he's well enough.' Antonia shook her head wryly. 'So that'll just make three invalids and one adolescent in my house. Sheer heaven it is.'

'Three?' Caroline repeated, but as they reached a T-junction in the corridors and each turned in a different direction Antonia was sure she wasn't listening.

'This way.' Antonia repositioned her.

'This is good of you,' Caroline muttered as they strode along, Antonia not relinquishing her grip on Caroline's arm. 'Are we lost?'

'Here.'

They both stopped in their tracks. There were a handful of people sitting on chairs and a bench beyond the ward in a wide part of the corridor. Antonia spotted Daniel instantly. He was seated, his elbows on his knees, his head in his hands. His foot was bandaged heavily. He stared down at the floor. Next to him was Emile, his arm around his brother's shoulders, talking quietly into his ear. Antonia's first reaction was amazement. How had Emile got down from London so fast? Daniel must have rung him almost immediately after the accident had happened. Her second reaction was a rush of joy to see Emile again, his shoulders stretching broadly under a tanned suede jacket, a strong hand on his brother's knee, offering guidance and support. Then she felt guilty to have been thinking of the pleasure of seeing Emile when Daniel was obviously in a bad state of shock. Then she wondered who the others were sitting with Daniel, and as a tall, angular man with bright blue eyes and ruddy cheeks turned round, she recognised the friend who had picked Daniel up for work during the time that her car had been in the garage.

David walked towards the two women, glancing at Antonia then at Caroline. As he looked at Caroline, his eyes filled with tears.

'It's David, isn't it?' Antonia asked politely, but David leaned past her and gathered Caroline in his arms. Antonia gazed at them both in surprise.

'Oh God, David. I'm so scared,' Caroline said into his shoulder.

'It's all right, love. It's going to be all right. Stephanie's already here. Your dad's with her. They're taking some blood from her now as a precaution.'

'Are you all right?' She touched his face. 'You're cut and bruised.'

'I was in the back of the car. I'm much better than the others.'

'Where's Brendan?'

'Here.'

A striking man with black eyes and black hair in a ponytail then gathered Caroline in his arms and they hugged. Emile looked over at them all and met Antonia's eye. He stood up and came towards her.

'Emile.' Antonia was confused. 'What's happened? Caroline?'

Caroline had raised her head, tears brimming in her eyes as she clasped the dark-haired man tightly to her. 'Antonia?' Caroline said. 'You know David?'

'Daniel was in the car,' David said to Caroline. They all looked at Daniel, sitting hunched, his head still rocking in his hands.

'Daniel's my lodger,' Antonia explained to Caroline. 'And David works with him, but I had no idea you knew each other.'

They gave each other curious glances. Such an event, involving all of them. And yet Antonia realised that she and Caroline knew so little about each other that she hadn't even known that she had a brother. She definitely hadn't known that the energetic, attractive man who'd been giving Daniel lifts could possibly be related to Caroline in any way. What separate lives they had been leading. Perhaps she could have been more of a friend to Caroline. When she thought about it, she didn't have a close female friend at all.

'If there's anything I can do,' Antonia said to her. Caroline nodded tensely.

426

'I'm pleased you're here.' Emile's eyes darkened as he considered Antonia.

'So am I.' They exchanged gentle smiles. Then she glanced over at Daniel again and felt a lurch of serious concern. He looked as if his spirit had been knocked out of him.

'I was driving the car,' Daniel said in a flat voice.

Antonia was still piecing the unwelcome news together when Caroline's voice rose again.

'I need to see my brother. I have to see him right now. Someone show me where he is.'

The tall dark man whom she'd called Brendan put a hand on her elbow. 'Come with me, Caro. I'll take you into the ward.'

Antonia watched the two of them go through the double doors and into the intensive care ward. Beside her, David heaved a harrowed breath.

'Phil's still in surgery. It's better they tell her than we do.'

'In surgery?' Antonia swallowed. 'Are you saying that this really is critical?' But she could see from the blur of tears in David's blue eyes that the situation was very serious. 'Poor, poor Caroline.'

'We managed to pull him from the car but he was still unconscious when the ambulance turned up. He went straight into the theatre from the ambulance. We don't know much more other than they needed more of his blood type.' David sniffed and edgily looked down the corridor. 'And I want to know where my wife is.'

'You absolute bastard!' Lizzy flew at David with her fists, thumping at his chest. 'How dare you, how could you? What the hell were you doing at Biggin Hill? How many lies are all caught up in this?'

'There weren't any lies.'

'What were you doing there?'

'We'd gone up for a helicopter trip, but it was cancelled because of the wind. We were driving back on some minor road afterwards when it happened.'

'Helicopter trip?' The knife twisted in Lizzy's chest. 'What helicopter trip? Who organised that?'

'I did.' David's eyes were wet as he explained in anguish. 'I arranged it. I paid for it. For all of us.'

They were standing separately from the group. David had told Lizzy in a short, tense phone call that they were at the intensive care ward. She had strode in and found a collection of people sitting or standing in the corridor in a state of anxiety. She'd instantly singled David out and taken him off, away from the others. Her fury was only second to the incredible pain she felt at being excluded from all of this. So many secrets. So much to unravel.

She'd driven the boys to her parents' house. A hospital was no place to try to keep control of them, and Doe and Ron were happy to have them at short notice. Then she'd steamed to Bromley on a blast of hurt, confusion and rage. She'd had such a staccato message from David. She'd known from his voice that he was ashamed. Of what exactly, she was still trying to uncover.

'But how could you afford that? Private plane trips, for God's sake? Who do you think you are? Madonna? Where were you going?' Her face was as tight as a drum.

'We were going to London. It was part of the package. We were going to be dropped there for lunch and then come back.'

'How long had that been planned for?'

'Just a few weeks.' David fixed miserable eyes on the floor.

Lizzy's mouth dropped open. Soon her husband might start saying words that she could understand. How could all of this have been going on without her knowledge?

'Do you know,' she said, trying to sound steady as the injustice exploded inside her ribcage, 'that I have been working my arse off, privately, without making a fuss, in that poxy little room upstairs, trying to earn an extra couple of pounds so that I can buy the boys the bikes they want.'

David looked up. His mouth was a downturned curve.

'I have taken my funny cards, as you all like to call them, to a shop in Tunbridge Wells and have sold them. For money. So that our sons can have some bikes to ride like we did when we were kids. And while,' she paused for breath, tears rising in her throat. 'And while I've been doing that, you have been blowing our money on a helicopter ride for your mates. Am I right so far?'

'Yes,' David said.

'Jesus Christ.' The bubble of tears rose further in Lizzy's throat. 'You're not even sorry.'

'There's something else you don't know, Lizzy.'

'Oh God, now what?'

'It's about – it's about Caroline and . . .' David's cheeks were red. 'And Phil.'

'Phil? What, Germany Phil?'

'He's just come back from surgery and he's still uncon-scious.' David inclined his head towards the swing doors. 'Caroline's in there with him now. Stephanie's given blood. She's in another ward being looked after, and Howard's with her.'

'Phil is in England?'

'Phil's through there.'

'Nobody told me that my cousin was in the country? You mean you knew, and you didn't tell me? My own cousin?' Her fists found David's chest again. 'My own bloody cousin, and you kept it from me? You're not even related to him except through me, you absolute, utter bastard. How dare you?'

Lizzy felt the blood drain from her head. David's voice became echoey and strange, and dark blotches imposed themselves on her vision. Oh blast it, she wasn't going to faint was she?

'Lizzy, are you all right?'

'I need to sit.'

David helped her to a chair that was set against the wall. She sank into it. Her skin prickled, then became cold and clammy. Time passed and the world came back into focus again. She swallowed, David becoming clear before her eyes once more and the warmth returning to her flesh.

'God, you're pale. You look as if you're going to be sick.'

'So you are telling me,' Lizzy said breathlessly as she recovered herself, 'that my cousin Phil was involved in this crash, and now he's through those doors in a critical condition.'

David nodded. 'I'm sorry,' he whispered.

'How long has he been back in England?' Lizzy felt a hot tear dribble down her waxy skin. Didn't anybody like her? Or trust her? What had been going on?

'Only a couple of days.'

'And where,' Lizzy struggled, 'has Phil been staying? Mum and Dad didn't mention anything when I dropped the boys off.'

'That's because they don't know yet. He didn't even want Steph and Howard to know. He didn't want hassle. That's why we couldn't tell you.'

Lizzy creased her eyes at her husband. A man she thought she knew. Her confusion was making her sound hard, she knew, but she had to get as much information as possible while she had this second wind and before the nausea struck again. 'Where has Phil been staying? Oh, don't tell me. With Caroline.'

David nodded.

'And Caroline didn't tell me.'

'Phil asked her not to. Not until he was ready to face everyone.'

'Why? What has he done, stolen the Crown Jewels?'

'He's left Luzie. The marriage is over.'

Lizzy took deep breaths and the world began to go fuzzy again. 'I need to find a ladies.' She stood up, swaying. David put a hand on her arm. She shook it away. 'Oh fuck off and leave me alone, David. I just want to find a loo.'

'It's just here. I'll show you.' A harmonious female voice had interposed itself. Lizzy swung round to stare. It was a blonde woman, immaculately dressed, with pale blue eyes that were for some reason flooded with concern.

'Who the hell are you?' Lizzy issued, her breath ragged.

'I'm Antonia, a friend of Caroline's.'

'Caroline's asked her friends along?' Lizzy felt sweat break out on her hairline and wiped it away clumsily.

'I'm here for another friend, Daniel. He was in the car too.'

'Oh.' Lizzy wanted to cry. To sink to the tiles and weep into her coat sleeves. What was going on? It was too confusing and she felt so weak. If she could just eat or drink something this grinding nausea would pass.

'Along here.' Antonia had a hand on her arm and was guiding her up the corridor. Everything seemed to be echoing. It was a horrible sensation.

They found a door and pushed into a tiny room with two cubicles, a dull and rusted mirror on the wall and a bin overflowing with paper towels.

'You look as if you need a drink and to sit down,' Antonia said. 'I was talking to David before you got here. I think it must be a horrible shock.'

'What did he tell you?' Lizzy asked suspiciously. Even this sophisticated stranger knew more about it all than she did.

'Only that you hadn't known that your cousin was back in the country, so it'd be startling for you to find out he was here and in such bad shape.'

'My cousin.' Lizzy let out a tearful 'huh'. 'So much for my cousins.' She leaned on the edge of the sink and ran the cold tap, splashing some water onto her lips.

The door to the ladies opened and both women looked up in annoyance at the intrusion. Then they both exclaimed.

'Caroline!'

Caroline's face was a mass of brown and black streaks where she had wept and wiped her skin, with her fingers by the looks of it. Antonia instantly found a tissue in her handbag and handed it to her. Caroline rubbed it over her face, then as she gazed at Lizzy, tears emerged and shot in streams down her cheeks again.

They embraced each other. Caroline, the taller woman, rested her head on her cousin's shoulder.

'Oh Lizzy, I've missed you so much.'

'And I've missed you.' They clung to each other tightly.

Lizzy was overwhelmed with love for her friend, her cousin, her confidante. What on earth had happened to them recently? Why hadn't they been sharing all the things they usually did? Had it been so desperately important to maintain this frosty, edgy silence just to prove the point that somebody had been in the wrong? Then she stepped back and examined Caroline's face. 'Any news on Phil?' she queried faintly.

'He's out of the theatre.' Caroline's eyes widened into black orbs. 'He may have to go back into surgery if the internal bleeding starts again but for the moment they think he's stable. I think that his face is going to be . . . a little different when he comes out of this.' She shuddered suddenly. Both Lizzy and Antonia reached out to touch her arm comfortingly. 'Thank you. Both of you. He looks like a mummy in there. Don't go in unless you're prepared for it.' Caroline gulped with shock again.

Lizzy felt the nausea rise from her stomach, up through her chest, spreading as a film of sweat across her neck and face. She knew she was going to be sick. She headed for a cubicle and shut herself inside just in time.

'Oh God, Lizzy,' she heard Caroline's gentle voice beyond the toilet door. 'You poor girl. Are you all right?'

'She needs some sustenance,' Antonia's practical voice contributed. 'And she shouldn't be standing so much in her condition. The last thing she needs is to put her body through more strain.'

The voices became background noise as Lizzy vomited several times. It felt as if the retching was coming right from the tops of her legs and through her body. It was as if somebody was trying to turn her inside out. Eventually she wiped her face and hands with tissues and leaned against the door. It was over. For now.

'I'm going to leave you two alone for a bit,' Antonia said. 'I'll go and get us all some hot drinks. I saw a machine a little further up the corridor.'

'Thank you.' Caroline put a hand on Antonia's arm. 'I appreciate your support.'

Antonia smiled at Caroline. Caroline smiled back at her. Lizzy watched this exchange in a daze of her own as she wiped cold water all around her face. Antonia left, the door swung shut, and Caroline and Lizzy were alone again. Caroline's sombre brown eyes met Lizzy's in the mirror.

'Why didn't you tell me Phil was back in England?' Lizzy asked plaintively.

'Why didn't you tell me you were pregnant?' Caroline replied.

Chapter Twenty-One

'I need to see you.'

Tom only hesitated for a second before standing back and opening his front door wide. It was nearly midnight but he didn't comment on the time. Caroline drifted into his house. The chaos, the explosion of colour, the furry creatures dotted about were welcoming and wonderful. She had parked her car at home and walked briskly to his street, but she was still shivering.

'I want to tell you why I wasn't in when you called for me this evening,' Caroline blundered on, then glanced at him for confirmation. 'Assuming that you did.'

'Yes, I did.' Tom offered a vaguely ironic look. 'Let me take your coat.' He helped her out of it and put it over his arm. 'And I'd suggest we go through to the kitchen. You're freezing and there's a warm Aga in there.'

'I didn't have time to write you a note. I didn't even think about it. I had to leave straight away. I'm sorry you would have found an empty house when you came round. You must have wondered what it all meant.'

'You need a glass of something. Brandy or a whisky, I'd suggest. Or I've got a Rioja in here. Let me open it.'

'Yes, I could really use a glass of wine. I'm exhausted, but my brain won't stand still.'

They'd arrived in the kitchen. There was the hint of an aroma in the air, of percolated coffee and something else, perhaps something that had been roasting earlier. It was a home. It was more of a home than her own practical set of surfaces crowned with her yellow and white set of kitchen utensils.

Caroline marvelled at how she felt in this room. Her experience of bachelor kitchens was confined to burnt baked beans and the contents of cupboards making their way to sinks and staying there. At least, any kitchen Phil had frequented prior to his marriage had evolved that way. At the thought of Phil, her stomach contracted painfully again. She tried to relax.

Daisy was curled up on a blanket in the corner. Caroline absently nodded a greeting to her, then sat at one of the scrubbed pine chairs. A spongy blue cushion made it more comfortable. The table top was strewn with Sunday papers, and a tumbler with a measure of whisky and melting ice stood next to an open colour supplement.

Tom opened the wine, poured Caroline a glass and handed it to her. She took several large sips straight away then put the glass on the table. A deep breath seemed to arrive from nowhere. She didn't think she'd cry again. She was all cried out. A tremulous sense of peace descended.

Tom sat at the chair to her right. He took a sip from his whisky and examined her face with concern.

'Bit better now?'

'Yes, the wine's helping.' Her hand threatened to tremble again so she put it into her lap.

'Tell me about it if you like.'

She crossed one knee over the other to get comfortable and was suddenly reminded that she was still in the soft brown boots, woollen skirt and top that she'd put on hours ago with the idea of impressing Tom with her femininity. And of the make-up she'd so carefully applied, now all wiped away. Not that it was important. Images of Phil haunted her.

'My brother,' she began in a low voice, trying to keep a steady rein on her emotions, 'who is staying with me at the moment is now in hospital after an accident.'

There was a pause. Daisy was emitting soft snores. A cat crawled onto the top of the Aga, lay down and formed the shape of a croissant. Caroline took a larger sip of wine.

'Go on.' Although Tom's voice was calm, his eyes were startled.

'He's such an incredibly good-looking, carefree guy. He was something of a flirt before he got married.' She shook her head sadly. 'And after he got married. I don't know how good-looking he's going to be after this. His face is badly hurt.'

'What happened?' Tom asked. He held the tumbler in his hand tensely.

'They'd been to Biggin Hill trying to get on a helicopter flight. One of these novelty day-trip things. They were meant to be flying into London somewhere, having lunch and flying back. They hadn't told anyone about it. It was cancelled because of the weather.'

Tom nodded slowly. 'I see.'

'They were driving back from the airport when a tree came down on the car. The windscreen shattered, but the others seemed to have got away with it. My brother –' Caroline stopped as her chest heaved. 'My brother got the worst of it. Daniel, a friend of theirs, was driving. It was his car.'

'Daniel.' Tom turned his glass around, placed it to the side of the newspaper and shook his head. 'Goddamn.'

437

'Daniel's in a very bad way about it. He blames himself.'

'I bet he does.'

'He's being too hard on himself.' She rested an elbow on the table. 'He was still at the hospital when I left. His brother was trying to persuade him that he couldn't do anything and that he should leave and get some sleep.'

Caroline's mobile shrilled, startling them both. She scrabbled in her handbag to retrieve it, glancing at Tom. 'I need to take this. I'll just go out into the hall where I can talk quietly.'

'Anywhere you like. You've seen most of the house anyway. Make yourself comfortable. And take the wine with you.' He pressed the glass into her hand. She nodded and nipped away through to the hall.

'Caro, it's Lizzy. Any more news since we left the hospital?'

'Nothing. Any news from your side?'

'No. I'm just picking the boys up from Mum's. I tried you at home first but got the answerphone. Where are you?'

'I'm . . .' Caroline hesitated. But there had been so many hidden truths between them recently that she couldn't bear to tell her a half-truth now.

In the past they had always maintained a pact, a united front in the face of any obstacles. Their mothers, Stephanie and Doe, had laughed about it. 'As unlike as cold brick and wet cement,' Doe used to say. 'That's why you can't get between them.' Even now Caroline was horrified that she hadn't told Lizzy that Phil was at home. If it hadn't been for their stupid spat, she would have done.

'I'm on my way home. I've stopped at Tom's house.'

There was a pause while Lizzy computed this. 'My fortune-teller, Tom?'

'Yes. The thing is that I quite like him.'

Lizzy paused. To her credit she didn't say anything to indicate that she'd been several steps ahead of Caroline in that area. She carried on breezily. 'Sounds like the perfect tonic. Just leave your mobile on in case anyone hears anything.'

'Of course I will. And you, are you feeling less sick?'

'Yes. It's always fine at night. Late afternoons and early evenings have always been the worst in the past. This one doesn't seem to be any different.'

'When will you tell David?' Caroline ventured hesitantly.

'He's a shit and tonight I hate him. He wants to play James Bond and I'm expecting another child. Doesn't augur too well, does it?'

'Oh Lizzy, I'm sorry.'

'He's been explaining to me how he had to let his hair down. To get out there, to live. It seems that two small children are a bit too restrictive for him. Who'd have guessed it? Not me. I'm the clown. Never saw this coming.'

Caroline winced at Lizzy's acidic tone. 'Nor me. I'm sure it'll pass.'

'You think his desire to run away from a young family will pass if I tell him I'm expecting another baby?'

There was a long, uncomfortable silence. Caroline absorbed Lizzy's anger. 'I love you, Lizzy,' she said finally.

'I have to ask you not to say a word about the pregnancy to anyone, Caroline. Not until I'm ready.'

'Of course.'

'I mean, you have to promise me. Not your mum, Phil, anybody. At the moment only your friend Antonia, you and I know. Only the three of us.'

'How did Antonia know?'

'Instinct. I like her. Perhaps another time the three of us should be friends, but not now. I just have to make sure that you and she are sworn to secrecy about this.'

'All right.' Caroline was perturbed by the darkness of Lizzy's tone.

'But we're not important tonight. I'm going to pray for Phil.'

'Me too.'

Lizzy tucked the boys in and watched with satisfaction as they both snuggled under their duvets and began to snore. She dimmed the overhead light and put on the night light which stood on the dresser between the two small beds. A honeyed tone fell across the room, dappling the walls and the bedlinen like petals.

Downstairs, David was slumped in his favourite armchair. He had opened a can of beer and half-filled a tall glass with it. It sat untouched on the coffee table in front of him. Lizzy followed his gaze as she leaned in the doorway. He had his eyes fixed on the video, television, music centre, and the organised stacks of videos and CDs that they owned. She was intending to have a very serious talk with him once she had ensured that the boys were asleep. She was burning with humiliation and hurt after the day's revelations and she wanted answers. Under those circumstances, there was no way she could tell him about her pregnancy. What she really wanted was to shout at him until she found out what she had done wrong to deserve this. However, looking at his gaunt face, she was struck by how exhausted he was. No doubt he was still in shock. She was shocked herself, at the thought of how close he had come to serious injury and survived, and at Phil's predicament, and at the fact that she had been kept ignorant of the whole affair. All because David wanted more for himself than they had agreed that they could afford.

'It's easy to forget what we've already got,' Lizzy said, walking into the room and sitting down.

David's expression was pensive. He probed at his skin with a fingertip. 'I'm going to look as if I've done seven rounds with Tyson tomorrow morning.'

'I'm amazed the hospital kicked you all out so promptly.' Lizzy was unable to sound as sympathetic as she probably should. She was still stunned at the way David had handled himself, and of what had been revealed.

'Neither Daniel nor Brendan would have slept a wink if they'd been kept in. They're not in a fit mental state. And Brendan's not up to our sofa. He needs some space,' David said blankly. He wouldn't look Lizzy in the eye.

'I wasn't happy with him going home on his own.'

'It's what he wants to do. He's knackered. He'll sleep as much as possible and I'll talk to him again tomorrow morning.'

'He won't attempt to go into work tomorrow, will he?'

'Of course not. None of us can go into work tomorrow. We have to be at the hospital.' David was wide-eyed. 'We have to see Phil through this.'

An uneasy silence fell. David was in a dazed state. Sitting on the sofa near him, Lizzy could feel her eyes glazing over too.

441

'It was my fault,' he said suddenly.

Lizzy watched him carefully. Then, as he didn't seem to be capable of drinking his beer, she had a sip of it instead. The bubbles prickled on her palate and the tense spring in her stomach uncoiled just a little. She didn't want to tell David it wasn't his fault, because somewhere inside she wanted to yell exactly the same thing at him. She loved Phil. She'd never been as close to him as she was to Caroline, but he was her cousin and had a special place in her heart. He had always been elusive to all of them, just that little bit out of reach. It was probably his wildness that had ensured they had a soft spot for him. They needed someone to blame for the patched-up wreck that was Phil. For the moment she was content to allow David to blame himself.

'It was all my idea, and I dragged them along with me. Brendan was into it too, almost as much as me. You know how we love the planes.'

'I know how you love the planes,' Lizzy repeated flatly. There was a stack of videos to prove it.

'But he advised me to wait a bit until the weather was better. He also told me to talk to you about it.'

'Good job you ignored that, then,' Lizzy muttered.

'The irony of it is,' David went on, 'that of all of us, Daniel and Phil were the least bothered about doing it and they're the two who've come off worst. Phil just wanted to have a good time and forget about Germany. He wouldn't have cared what we did. Daniel was as easy-going and fun as ever, but a bit bemused about the whole thing.'

Lizzy pursed her lips to avoid saying anything cruel.

'It's such a mess and it's all my fault.' David's voice broke with a loud sob. He put his hands over his eyes.

442

Lizzy stood up and went to her husband. Anger or no, some matters were dealt with on the pure instinct that came with love. She spread a hand gently over his back and kissed the top of his head.

'Phil will be all right.'

'I don't know.'

'It will be all right, David, you'll see. I'm as worried about Phil as you are, but they've told us he's stable. And we all know Phil. He'll come through this. He's a cocky bugger and he'll make it out the other side. In a few weeks he'll be out clubbing again.'

David let out a harrowed, shaky breath. 'Please take me to bed.'

'Come on.' Anything else would have to wait until David was stable enough to think more clearly. Until she was stable enough.

'Can you face another cup of tea, or would you like something stronger?' Antonia asked Emile.

'A sip of something stronger would be magic. Better only be a sip though. I'm not sure what my brother's going to want to do.' Emile rolled his eyes up at the ceiling and Antonia nodded.

'I don't have much in.' She opened the fridge. 'There's half a bottle of white in here, a bit of gin left in the cupboard I think. Pimm's without lemonade, oranges or mint? Although I do have some cucumber but it's no great shakes on its own. Oh, and an unopened bottle of Baileys. And ice, if you want it. My mother purged the house of vodka a little earlier in the month. You may remember.' She gave him a twisted smile and he laughed back at her.

'A Baileys with ice, if you can be bothered. Do you

443

mind if I sit down here at the kitchen table? I'm not sure I want to perch politely on a sofa after all that's happened this evening.'

'By all means. That's what kitchens are for. Just shove aside all of my daughter's beauty accessories. She says the light's better in the kitchen, and it probably is. The pop socks are my mother's.'

Antonia poured two measures of Baileys into tumblers and added ice. She delivered them to the table and slid into a chair opposite Emile.

It was a relief to sit down and relax at last. It had been a long, long haul at the hospital. Caroline had left just before they had, finally assured by her parents that they would stay on and see Phil through the night and contact her if there was any change. Her parents were apparently doing a night shift, Caroline relieving them in the morning. Antonia had liked the older couple instantly. Two rangy and unusual but perceptive people whom she had talked to when Daniel had insisted again on going into the ward to look at Phil. She could see where Caroline got her sense of individuality from. Both her parents were utterly charming, but neither of them were out of any mould. She'd particularly taken to Caroline's mother, Stephanie. What an intriguing woman. She was like a Russian doll with many layers. And she had a firm shape and a neat bun behind her head that became more loose and flyaway as she used her hands and head to express herself.

Finally they'd managed to persuade Daniel to leave the ward. When they got home both Audrey and Sonia were asleep. Antonia had told her mother what had happened as she was leaving the house and she'd also rung her once from her mobile to give her an update,

444

pleading with her to get Sonia to bed at the usual time. She'd been gratified to come into the house at gone midnight and find both mother and daughter in bed.

She drank some Baileys. 'Do you think it's better if Daniel goes back to London with you?'

Emile took off his suede jacket and hung it over the back of the chair while he thought about it. 'I think he's got to decide that. But aside from all the other implications of this accident, he's got a severely sprained ankle and he's going to be frustrated with loping about. I've got more space for him in my flat in Kensington than you have got here.'

'And you're his brother, of course. He'll probably want to be with you.'

'Let's try him again when he comes down.'

As soon as they'd got home, Daniel had insisted on going upstairs to take a bath. Antonia had been concerned about the logistics of doing this given that his foot was heavily strapped, but he'd protested that he'd manage.

'I was a bit surprised at how much Daniel's taken this upon himself. I mean, I know that it's a serious situation and it was his car. I'm not denying the psychology of it's very powerful.' Antonia fingered her glass thoughtfully. 'Having got to know Daniel in these past months, I was just a little surprised by how much it's knocked him for six. He really seems to think that he should be the one who's laid out on the hospital bed. I know about survivor syndrome, but Phil is alive and will soon be well as far as we know.'

Emile cast Antonia a look, then examined his glass again. 'I'll continue to talk to him about it. He was driving, and that's a pretty tough reality. And there's something else, about the boys' frame of mind at the time. I'm not sure what it is. I think they'll have to get together on it and sort it out themselves.'

Antonia glanced up to see her mother in the kitchen doorway in her nightgown.

'Mum!' Antonia stood up. 'We didn't want to wake you.'

'I was awake anyway. Sonia's talking to Daniel. She was awake too.'

'I thought she was asleep?'

'Course she wasn't. She was worried about Daniel.'

'But Daniel's in the bath.' Antonia frowned.

Audrey rolled her eyes and wiggled her eyebrows in such an expression of exasperation that Emile laughed out loud. 'And you think I'd let my fourteen-year-old granddaughter go and sit in the bathroom with the lodger while he washes his nadgers? Oh grow up, Antonia. Sonia and Daniel are talking in his bedroom.'

Antonia felt confused. The protective instinct of a mother was uncomfortably combined with the gratification of knowing that Daniel was obviously now considered a family friend by all of them, including her own mother. 'Well I hope she's dressed properly.'

'Head to toe in chain mail.' Audrey winked at Emile across the room. 'For a modern woman Antonia can be a bit square, don't you think?'

'Oh, I don't think anything,' Emile evaded.

'I'm not sure if that's wise,' Antonia hedged. 'Daniel's in a fragile state and he's just had a terrible shock.'

'If he's cheesed off she'll leave him alone and go back to her room,' Audrey said bluntly. 'But they're very good friends and for all you know she might be just the person he wants to talk to at the moment.'

446

'Maybe.' Antonia was unconvinced. 'Or she might be imposing on him and he might need time to himself.'

'Well, when I knocked and put my head round the door they both told me to get lost.'

Antonia stood up. 'I should probably check that he's not being bothered.'

'Leave them.' Audrey went to a cupboard and got out some cream crackers. She set about making herself a snack.

'Mum, you'll get cold.' Antonia took off her cardigan and wrapped it around her mother's thin shoulders. While she was there she gave her a hug.

'Cold? Not likely. I've pinched a pair of your thermal knickers. You'd never be able to see them from on top, would you? Probably because you've got those ones that come right up to the waist.'

Just as Antonia was torn between the desire to kiss her mother for looking so tired and small, and to punch her for telling Emile that she owned a pair of thermal knickers that came up to her waist, Daniel appeared, causing them all to face him with bright smiles.

'Daniel! How are you feeling now?' Antonia hoped she didn't sound overly hearty.

'I'll stay here tonight.' He tried to smile but ended up looking exhausted. 'That's if you don't mind, Antonia. I'd really like to be close to the hospital so that I can get there tomorrow morning.'

'How are you going to do that?' Emile stood up. It was amazing, Antonia thought, that Daniel seemed a strong and manly character until his big brother was in the room. Then he seemed to adopt the role of pupil to Emile's teacher. She could imagine that it had always been like that.

447

'I'll find a way to get there.'

'Daniel, think. Your car's a heap of scrap and you've got a gammy foot. You need someone to drive you. Antonia has to be at work in the morning. She can't ferry you about.'

'I'm afraid I do have to be at work as usual,' Antonia confirmed apologetically. 'But I could drop you there on my way and we could work something out after that.'

'It's not on your way,' Emile said.

'No, but it's no trouble to take a detour,' Antonia smiled. 'Daniel helped me when my car was off the road, and this is far more important. I can help.'

Emile pondered Antonia for a moment, then he looked back to his brother with an air of decisiveness. 'This is what's going to happen. I'll come down and pick you up tomorrow, and get you to the hospital. We'll take it from there. For the moment I think we'd better concentrate on getting through the next twenty-four hours in a way that ensures we've all got both our sanity and our careers intact at the end of it.'

'Thanks Emile.' Daniel looked wobbly again. 'If you all don't mind I'll go on up to bed now. Sonia's gone to bed, Antonia. She's fine so don't worry about her.'

Antonia nodded and Daniel hobbled away. They all watched him, Audrey wincing visibly, cream cracker poised in her hand. As he disappeared from view she took a big bite out of it.

'Bleedin' hell. I don't know what's the more tragic. Me and my wrist, him and his foot or you and your cancer. Hark at us lot . . .' Audrey's voice tailed away as if she sensed the flames leaping from Antonia's eyes. Without looking round she hunched her shoulders and headed out of the kitchen. 'I'm going to bed,' she muttered as she disappeared.

Antonia stood very still, looking at the empty space that her mother had filled.

'"But I have promises to keep"?' Emile had stood up and was walking towards her, his voice a gentle query. She looked away from him.

'My bloody mother.'

'Your mother is honest. She's no different from my mother. They say what they see.'

Antonia shook her head, her blood surging. This was going to be hard to forgive Audrey for. Something of the utmost privacy that she had entrusted her with, and she'd blurted it out in front of a complete stranger.

'It's unforgivable.' Antonia concentrated on the square toes of her boots contrasting against the white glare of the kitchen floor.

'I think it was a very deliberate mistake.' Emile touched his fingers to her chin and tilted her face up so that she couldn't avoid looking at him. 'I think your mother was trying to tell me something.'

'*Trying*?' She gave a hollow laugh. 'How much more trying would she have to do to actually get a result?'

'Is this the problem you have to sort out, the thing you have to face on your own?'

He seemed to have a good memory. She thought she'd put it to him in exactly those terms. 'Well, what do you think?' She tried to pull away but his fingers coaxed her back.

They were tense with each other. His hands holding her face, her body as taut as a peg. Then he smiled and it was as if the sun had come out and warmed her body from head to toe.

449

'I think that you want me to kiss you.' His thumb stroked her skin.

'I think you're a confident so-and-so.'

'I think I'm only confident when I know I'm right.' His lips were nearing hers.

'I have a problem with the early stages of cervical cancer.' Antonia tried to pull away as she forced the information out. 'It's probably only temporary, and they tell me that it can all be sorted and leave me as I was, but that's what my mother meant.'

Emile's expression softened towards her, into one of affection that she wasn't anticipating. 'Have you quite finished yelling information at me that I don't need to know?'

'Of course you need to know. My mother's just said something dramatic and I need to qualify it.'

He shook his head at her. 'Do you think it makes any difference to me whatsoever?'

'Well, it might do. And it makes a difference to me.'

'What difference does it make to you?' His breath was soft upon her lips.

'It makes . . . the difference to me is that . . .' Antonia struggled as Emile's scent engulfed her. 'I think that . . .'

'I think that you need to trust your instincts,' Emile said softly into her ear. 'And when your instincts tell you that a man has fallen madly in love with you, they are probably right.'

'But perhaps . . . maybe.' Her words were lost on her breath.

'Not another word.'

'My mother,' Antonia managed, 'is sleeping . . . in my bed.'

'You have a sofa, don't you?'

'It's . . . it's a little uncomfortable for sleeping on.'

'Who's talking about sleeping?' Emile responded.

'I'm sorry, I'm going to have to go back to the hospital,' Caroline said, setting down her glass with a jolt. 'I can't go home. I can't sleep. I can't see that I'm going to be able to do anything other than sit by Phil's bedside tonight.' She stood up and turned a full circle, her throat constricting with anxiety.

Tom was by her side in an instant. He laid his hands gently on her arms. 'Look at me, Caroline.'

'I need to get back there.' Her breath was coming in shallow gasps. Images of Phil in the hospital bed darted in and out of her head. Her muscles tensed. 'I have to go.'

'You can't drive like this. You're not calm enough to drive.'

'I have to go. Phil needs me.'

'Phil's asleep and he's got both your parents there. Stand still and look me in the eye.'

'I have to . . . Let me go.' Caroline scrambled for her handbag, tears arriving again and streaming down her face. 'I can't breathe. What's happening?'

'Look at me.' Tom took a firmer hold and forced her to face him. 'You're going to take a deep breath and let it out very gently.'

'I've got my bag,' Caroline mumbled. 'I'll just get my breath back. Oh God, what is it? My body's tingling all over and I . . . I can't breathe properly.'

Tom took her into his arms and held her. 'You're just having a moment of a panic. I'm not surprised after what you've been through today. It will pass. Just stay still for a moment and breathe slowly. Let your head rest on my shoulder and relax.'

His arms formed a band around her body, holding her inside as if he were protecting her. Little by little the dizziness began to subside and the soft hues of his kitchen came back into normal focus.

Tom's shirt was cool against her cheek. A provocative, musky aroma seemed to drift from his hair and mingle with his body smell. She rested her head against his neck and soft strands of her hair were caught up in his stubble. He stroked her arm through her clothes and uttered quiet, reassuring words into her ear. A long time passed. Perhaps five minutes, perhaps fifteen.

'I'm so sorry,' he said in a hushed voice. 'I wish I could have warned you. I'm so, so sorry.'

His hand spread over her back and filled her with warmth. 'I feel a little better now,' she whispered, closing her eyes.

'Shh. Take it gently. Keep breathing slowly.'

Caroline did. A warmth rose steadily through her body, like the smell of baking bread. As the feeling expanded within her chest she sighed with relief. Tiredness swamped her.

'All right. Keep your eyes closed.' Tom stroked her hair. It felt incredible. 'If you want me to I can drive you back to the hospital, but I think it's better if you let Phil rest tonight, and sleep well yourself.'

'Hmmn. Yes, you're right.'

'So when you're ready, I can walk you home.'

'I don't want to go home,' Caroline muttered sleepily.

Tom tightened his grip around her and she felt his lips on her hair. 'Take your time. Think about it.'

Caroline wound her arms around Tom's waist. The strength of his body under her touch was comforting and exciting at the same time. She pulled her head away from him so that she could look at him properly. 'Tom, I don't want to sleep alone tonight.'

'You need to sleep. You need rest.'

'Are you saying that if I stay here I won't get any sleep?'

Tom swallowed. She watched his Adam's apple rise and fall, and ran a fingertip along his throat. He caught her finger in his hands. 'Caroline, careful. You need gentle handling, but if you tease me I can't promise to be all that gentle.'

'Don't be gentle,' she said, her nerves bursting into life like a fountain.

'What are you saying?' He probed her cheek with his lips.

'I'm saying that I want to be here, with you.'

'Please think carefully. I'm sure I should walk you home and see you inside your house.'

'No.'

'Are you sure?' Tom's voice was low and throaty. It filled Caroline with newly awakened desire.

'I want you to take me upstairs, to your bed. I want you to make me feel alive.'

'Right, that's it,' Tom said. He hoisted her into his arms and carried her from the room. In the hall she shrank against his chest, hoping that he wasn't going to deposit her on the doormat and propel her out into the night, but at the bottom of the stairwell he swung around and began to mount the stairs. She pushed a hand inside his shirt and felt the warm, damp skin. The sexual tension mounting inside her made her dizzy again. She prayed that he was aiming straight for his bedroom.

He kicked the door open and the familiar heady scent

453

of the room returned. Then she was thrown onto the bed, her head on the Victorian square lace pillows she'd admired before. Tom put on a soft light and returned to her, leaning over the bed and kissing her lips.

'Don't go,' she begged him as he stood up again. 'Don't leave.'

'Oh don't worry,' Tom said, stripping off his shirt. 'Neither of us are going anywhere.'

In the morning, Caroline awoke to the aroma of fresh coffee and the sensation of a hand stroking her cheek. She opened her eyes slowly and her head was flooded with images. Phil in hospital. Tom over her body, his fullness inside her. Her mother's wiry hair, her tired eyes. Tom's lips over her breasts, filling her with joy. Her father's face, questioning her. Tom's stubble grazing her thighs, his tongue sliding over her. Lizzy's pale face, her knotted fists. Tom's stiffness arching inside her again, then again. The fulfilment of her climax, and his. Brendan's dark eyes, hollow and guilty. Tom's seed exploring her body.

She sat up, startled. 'What's the time?'

'Early. Not even seven.'

'Really? It feels so late.' She took a sip of coffee from the mug he handed her. The sun poured into the room energetically and fell over the bed. The covers glowed in the light like a field of corn ripening under a summer sky. Her spirits rose. Phil was going to be all right.

'You slept well?' Tom quizzed. He sat on the edge of the bed, a hand lazily draped on her stomach. He seemed troubled, then his eyes smiled at her, and her breath stopped again.

'Yes, amazingly well.' She smiled back at him, inviting him to return to bed.

'There isn't time. You have to get up,' he chided her.

'Yes I know.'

'Would you like me to run you a bath or shower here, or would you rather have one at home?'

'I'll probably be more organised at home.'

'Then drink your coffee and I'll walk you back.'

At her front door, Tom bent his head and touched Caroline's lips with his. Then he pulled back and gazed at her pensively. 'You take care of yourself, won't you?'

'And you.'

'I'm so sorry about Phil. I am just so sorry I was no help.' He tailed away and for a second she saw a tortured look in his eyes. Then it was gone. 'Goodbye, Caroline.'

'Bye Tom.'

He walked away while she put her key into the lock and let herself in. She stopped on the doorstep and turned back to look at the sky. The wind had dropped and it was a clear, untarnished blue.

Chapter Twenty-Two

From that day on, Caroline was overwhelmed with activity. Days passed in which she juggled her school commitments with visits to Phil in the hospital. She spent time with her confused parents, consoling and heartening them. She snatched time with Lizzy where they comforted and reassured each other.

She even went out for a drink with Antonia one evening, later on down the line when Phil was much improved and people who loved him were beginning to take the first tentative steps back into a normal routine. Now that Phil was talking and reacting normally again, albeit from his hospital bed, they needed time to reclaim some energy. This was nearly a month after Phil's accident. She wouldn't have thought to suggest it herself, but Antonia had passed her in the corridor just after Caroline had dropped a register and was on her knees pushing papers and notes back inside it. Antonia had lowered herself to her haunches, smiling.

'How are you? We've only managed rushed conversations recently. Why don't we get together over a glass of wine and talk properly?'

Caroline had noticed how good Antonia's colour was, how bright her eyes. And she never seemed to have a smile far from her face these days. Once Caroline had been in the women's toilet next to the staffroom and had actually heard Antonia in one of the cubicles, humming.

Caroline collected her papers into her register, stood up and smiled back. She'd felt a bit light-headed recently. All the hours spent at the hospital and with her family, essential though they were, had taken their toll. And she was today especially pallid, due to something that had happened the previous evening.

Caroline's night with Tom had been so special that she hadn't sought to see him again. It had felt so natural that she just knew in her heart that he would find her again without her needing to do anything at all. The glow that she'd been left with had carried her through the ensuing days as if she were floating through the shock on a magic carpet, observing everything but protected from it by a little bit of enchantment that he had lent her.

But as the days passed and became a couple of weeks, Caroline did start to feel somewhat puzzled. She continued her commitments to the astronomy club but Tom didn't reappear there. She asked Lizzy if she'd heard from him or contacted him at all, but Lizzy had shaken her head. Then Caroline had decided that perhaps he was being tactful, leaving her to sort out her problems in her own time, so had last night taken a walk around the back roads to his house to see if he was there. After all, it was now coming up to a month since they'd seen each other. Had she not had so much going on in her life, she wondered if so much time could have passed without her being as disconcerted as she was now.

She missed him. That was the fact of it, and she wanted to see him again. Just to talk, or go for a walk again, or go out for a drink or for dinner, or whatever they might do. And he had awoken a violent, exciting passion inside her that had been latent for a long time. She longed to make love with him again. With all of those upbeat thoughts in her head, she'd called at his house and waited, but there had been no answer. Then she'd noticed that the front room curtains were closed and an upstairs blind was down. There was no sign of life at all inside the house. Had he gone off on holiday or something?

As she was pondering this, a woman had arrived home at the neighbouring house, weighed down with a sleeping baby and a bulging bag of shopping. She was in jeans and a roll-necked sweater and smiled at Caroline as she reached her door.

'Excuse me?' Caroline ventured. 'I don't suppose you know whether Tom's gone away?'

'Tom?' The young woman had looked confused.

'Tom who lives here?'

'Oh, the good-looking bloke? I think he's moved out.'

'Perhaps I've got the wrong house.' Caroline stood back on the path and assessed the doors again. No, this was definitely Tom's house.

'Well, I say moved out but I don't know. He's the one with the goat, yes?'

'Yes,' she confirmed with disappointment.

'Don't know where he is, I'm afraid. I saw him packing stuff up a few weeks ago. Took the animals so I don't suppose it's just a short trip.'

'But –' Caroline bit her lip.

'Sorry about that. Does he owe you money or something?'

'Money?' She sighed. 'No, he doesn't owe me money. In fact, he doesn't owe me anything at all. He's just a friend and I wasn't expecting him to leave, that's all.'

458

'Well,' the other woman had smiled apologetically as the baby had started to cry.

'Sorry to have disturbed you.'

All night Caroline had rolled over and over under her *Star Trek* duvet, tangling her sweaty skin up in the cotton, fretting about Tom's disappearance. Soon Phil would be coming out of hospital and it was most likely that he would come back to stay with her. She didn't want to be a mass of confused hormones when he arrived. He needed peace, calm, happiness and stability while he got over the shock of his injuries. Besides, she had spent her entire adult life managing to avoid being a mass of confused hormones.

But why had Tom vanished? The question would not go away. It woke her up again the moment she'd drifted off. It dried out her throat and sent her down the stairs four times in the night to fetch more water. It made her sweat so much that at five in the morning she was standing under a lukewarm shower. At least when Phil was released from hospital they'd have something in common. They'd both know how it felt to be inside the emotional wind tunnel Phil had talked about before. Ultimately the mystery of Tom's disappearance left her feeling so exhausted from a sleepless night that she'd let the register slip out of her hand in the corridor, had dropped it, then Antonia had stopped as she passed by and suggested that they talk over a glass of wine.

She must have gone a long time without answering, because Antonia then said, 'It's all right, it was just an idea.'

Caroline quickly put out a hand and touched her arm. 'No, please. I'd love that. Are you free tonight?'

Antonia had looked a little surprised. Perhaps she'd

seen the urgency in Caroline's eyes. Antonia had been asking after Phil on a regular basis, but they hadn't talked about anything much more personal since their brush with familiarity in the hospital. Caroline also knew that Antonia received updates on Phil's progress from Daniel, who was a surprisingly regular visitor. She hadn't felt a need to double up on every minute detail when Antonia was already aware of it. So every time they'd passed comments so far, they'd been friendly but casual. No doubt Antonia was slightly surprised by Caroline's dilated pupils.

'How about a meal?' Antonia said warmly. 'You know Zizzis?'

'Yes.'

'Well that's about halfway between us, and if you fancy a glass of wine or two, not far for either of us to get a taxi.'

Antonia had already been at the table when Caroline arrived.

'I didn't want us to sit at one of those tables for two where you're cheek by jowl with another couple, so I picked this one in the corner. Is it okay for you?'

'Oh yes, lovely.' Caroline sat down, her coat having been taken by the waitress at the door, and settled herself. The restaurant had a wide, airy seating area with a shiny, wood-panelled floor and a high, spotlit ceiling. Their table was near a window where the softer lights of the gabled shops floated through the night towards them, providing a cosy atmosphere. 'Yes, this is great.'

'Red or white?' Antonia asked, surveying the wine list.

'Er, white I think.'

Antonia nudged the card across the table. 'I was thinking Pinot Grigio. What do you reckon?'

Caroline glanced at the wine list but didn't pay it a great deal of attention. 'Sounds great.'

'I'll get a bottle then.'

'Lovely.' Caroline nodded and took the menu that the waitress offered her. She gazed at it for some time, then Antonia cleared her throat.

'I'm glad to meet up with you like this. The last time you and I went for a drink together, Gerry started sermonising and I rudely shot off.'

Caroline had been drifting away on her thoughts but was brought back abruptly. 'Oh God, that evening? Yes, I remember. Gerry's fault, not yours. He's a bit old-fashioned and annoying but I'm sure he's not that bad at heart. Let's not dwell on it.'

'The delectable Gerry Bream. You're very gracious not to want to dwell on him.' Antonia quirked an eyebrow. 'He's not quite so gracious about you.'

'What do you mean?'

'Well, let's just say that he's got his eye on being Hilary's replacement.'

'Oh yes, well he would have now that Greg's made it public that he's leaving.' Caroline let out a sigh. 'Yes, Greg. What a bloody shame. I'll miss him.'

'We all will. But you know why Gerry's been particularly prickly with you ever since it became clear that the Head of Science post was coming up, don't you? I mean, long before Greg told everyone that he was going off to a new job?'

Caroline shook her head. Antonia waited as the wine arrived and was poured for both of them. She asked for

461

more time to decide on their food and leaned forward with a sparkle in her blue eyes.

'What is it, Antonia?'

'He knows you're going to get it, and he can't stand it.'

Caroline shook her head slowly. 'Me? Don't be silly. I've only been at the school for five minutes. These sort of senior jobs go to those who've put in hours of service. Even Greg had been there eight years. With no Greg, Gerry will walk it.'

'Try the wine,' Antonia said, a smile playing about her lips. 'Go on, have a few good slurps. Did you drive up here tonight? No? Fantastic. It's Thursday night, we've only got to stagger through tomorrow, so I say we let our hair down a bit. Now do as you're told and have a drink.'

Caroline blinked and obeyed. 'All right, I've had plenty of wine. What are you talking about? I'm no competition for Gerry. I've been in my job much less time and –'

'And the girls love you. Have you looked at the stats? Do you know how many girls are turning scientific in their exam choices because they want to be in your classes?' Caroline shook her head again and Antonia tutted at her. 'You should have your ear closer to the ground. They adore you. Heather Martin knows this.'

'Okay, steady on.' Caroline put out her hands as the name of the headmistress was brought up. 'Heather is somebody who values merit above anything else. Gerry will be the obvious candidate. He has years of experience at the school and he's well thought of.'

'By whom?' Antonia queried, sipping her wine. Caroline noted again the impish look about her. What was it with her in the last few weeks? She seemed to be the same Antonia and yet on extra batteries.

'Well . . .' Caroline tried to turn her attention back to the menu.

'Caroline,' Antonia said in a very low voice, leaning across the table. 'Do you want the truth or do you want to nurture your fantasies? Greg was never in the running for that post. We all like him, but he was always too restless. Gerry doesn't stand a chance. He's a dinosaur and the girls need him as a role model like they need Peter Stringfellow to take them on their first date. Heather can't wait for an opportunity to push him out to graze. The fact is, you're the outstanding candidate and it's very likely Heather will back you. Provided you impress the governors, of course, which you have anyway.'

It was hard to know what to say to Antonia. She seemed so sure of herself. Caroline shook her head doubtfully. 'This isn't because of his wife leaving, is it? I know he's been acting pretty strangely recently, but we know there's a reason for that now.'

'He's been lecturing me for years about the solidity of his marriage. I think he's got everything he deserved.'

'Even so. If he wants this head of department post so desperately, perhaps he should have it.'

Antonia tutted again. They were distracted by the return of the waitress, and gave their orders. As she glided away, Antonia leaned forward.

'I know what you should do,' she said mischievously, tipping more wine into both glasses. 'Pay a visit to this guy that I know. He's a . . .' A pretty frown furrowed her brow. 'Actually I don't know what he is, but he's amazing. He's a sort of fortune-teller and psychic, or something along those lines. I met him quite by accident. My daughter wanted a theme birthday party, so we dragged him along as the star turn. But then I had a consultation on my own with him and he completely changed the way I saw myself and my, well, my problems. His attitude is so contagious, it really turned me around. It was like being showered with positive energy. In fact, I haven't seen him for about a month, I must ring him and talk to him again.' She lowered her voice. 'The truth is, I wasn't very well. But with all the energy I've had since I saw him, I've really started to believe that I've beaten it off. I'm having some minor treatment next week, so we'll see. But I've never felt better. Anyway, I know you're a scientist and don't believe in anything that doesn't have an atomic number, but it's just a thought.' She added with a twisted smile, 'And he's bloody gorgeous too. And single, from what I can work out. Can't do any harm to introduce yourself, can it? He lives in your neck of the woods.'

Caroline listened, growing paler. 'You know Tom?'

'You know him?' Antonia was amazed. She elegantly draped an arm over the back of her chair and sipped at her wine. 'You are a dark horse.'

'I knew him.' Caroline let out a long sigh. 'He seems to have moved.'

'Moved?' Antonia put her elbows on the table and concentrated hard on Caroline. 'How can he have moved? He hasn't had time to move since I last saw him.'

'Apparently he has.'

Antonia looked thoughtful. 'How bizarre. Then again, I wouldn't really be that surprised at anything he might do. He's that kind of guy. I'm sure he's got Romany blood. In some people it's a necessity, you know.'

'What is?'

'Being on the move.'

Caroline fiddled with her knife and fork to avoid Antonia's eye. A strong desire to cry had crept into her throat and lodged itself there. Her fingers were jittery, and her spoon flew off the table onto the floor. She bent to pick it up. 'Sorry.'

Antonia's hand stretched across the table and touched hers. 'No, I'm sorry. I've been a clot. Jumping around in my hobnailed boots and completely missing the point. I can see there's something between you two. Am I right?'

'Yes.' Caroline's voice was small.

'Well I'll be damned.' Antonia shook her head. 'Of all the unlikely couples. But the more I think about it, the more perfect you are. Remarkable.'

'I think you should talk about it in the past tense.'

'He really does mean a lot to you.' Antonia's tone had softened. There was understanding and warmth in her eyes.

'He's . . .' Caroline shut her mouth again. She was getting ridiculously emotional. 'I just wish I understood why he's gone like this.'

They sat in silence for a while. 'Did he say anything the last time you saw him that suggested he might just take off?'

'No.'

'Mind you,' Antonia muttered to herself, 'most men's idea of letting a woman down gently is to promise to call her the next day. But I'd never have put Tom in that category.'

Caroline lowered her voice. 'The last time I saw him

465

we'd just spent the night together so I think you could safely say we were both pretty distracted.' Antonia raised her eyebrows in response. 'But he did seem very torn up about my brother's accident. No doubt he was picking up on my state of mind. It was all still a shock. Tom kept saying how sorry he was.'

'That would be normal. I'm sorry about Phil too.'

'No, I mean as if he was sorry for something he'd done.'

'Or something he hadn't done.' Antonia was quiet again. She turned the cold wine bottle around on the table. The condensation left a smear on the polished wooden surface. 'Had he ever met your brother?'

'No.'

'But he met Daniel, and when he did there was something . . . I can't tell you what. It was as if Tom picked up a bad vibe. Perhaps it was to do with the accident.'

'Perhaps it's just to do with me,' Caroline said under her breath, her stomach buckling at the thought. 'Perhaps he just didn't feel the same way about me.'

'I think he did,' Antonia said firmly.

They waited while their food was served. Antonia had chosen a warm salad that looked delicious. Caroline's was a pizza the size of a tractor wheel. She tried to hang onto her rapidly receding appetite. Talking about Tom was tying her intestines up in knots.

'Well, anyway.' Caroline forced a smile. 'At least Phil's in good spirits. He knows how lucky he is. He says he's going to make a brand new start to his life when he gets out. It's given him time to think about his priorities. He tells me he wants to live every moment as if it's his last now.'

'I know just how he feels.'

466

'Were you – I mean, are you better now? You said you hadn't been well.'

'I'm fine.' Antonia smiled confidently.

They ate for a while, comfortable in each other's presence. The restaurant had a regular flow of custom, but wasn't busy enough to interfere with their respective musings. Caroline, at Antonia's prompting, was now running through the comments Tom had made on their last night together. The echoes of his voice brought back delicious memories of his touch, his kisses, his love-making. She put down her knife and fork, the pizza defeating her.

'That was lovely, but I can't manage any more.'

Antonia seemed lost in thought. 'You say you last saw him on the night of Phil's accident. Did you make any attempt to contact him after that?'

'I've either been at the hospital, or at the school, or at my parents' or with my cousin. I've hardly been at home. I thought – I suppose I thought he'd contact me.'

'I mean, did he think you stayed the night with him because you particularly wanted to be with *him* or because you didn't want to be on your own?'

'I'm not sure.'

'What I mean is, does he know how you feel about him?'

Caroline thought for a moment, but images of Tom were making her feel dizzy. This was not how she normally lived her life. Up until recently she had been even-tempered, controlled, organised. Now she understood how irrational the world became when you were in love. How Phil would laugh about this if she ever shared it with him. He wouldn't be able to call her

Spock any more. Her appetite extinguished, Caroline concentrated on drinking her wine instead.

'Well, if he doesn't know how I feel about him, it's too late to tell him now.'

'Don't underestimate him.' Antonia put out a hand. 'He's not like other people. He's one in a million. That means, unfortunately for you, that you can't even attempt to predict what he'll do.'

'It sounds like my grandfather,' Caroline said in a choked voice.

'Either way, he needs his guardian angel just as much as anybody.' Antonia chewed heartily on a mouthful of salad. 'Can I have a slice of that pizza if you've finished with it?'

Lizzy was seated on the low stool in front of her chest of drawers, in her underwear, putting her make-up on, when David walked in. She continued to stroke colour onto her cheeks with her blusher brush, then dabbed some coral gloss onto her lips. David lay down on the bed fully clothed, and picked up a book from his bedside table. She sprayed perfume onto her neck and wrists, then she crossed to her wardrobe and tried to decide what to wear.

David flopped face down on the bed and abandoned the book.

'You know you look like Melanie Griffiths in your underwear, don't you?'

Lizzy absorbed the compliment, but couldn't quite produce the coquettish grin, or the bottom wiggle, or the chest pout, or the flirty quip that she normally would. She nodded without looking at David and cast her hands through her coat hangers, wiping her clothes from side to side on the rail as her edginess increased. She was picking her mother up tonight, then taking her for a drink. Lizzy had suggested, unusually, that they dress up a little and go somewhere nice. Doe knew things were wrong, but she had no idea what. Lizzy wasn't certain that she was going to give her the whole story yet. She'd see how she felt. First, she'd have to be sure that she could trust her mother with absolute discretion. Then she had to be sure that she wanted somebody else to know. She wasn't certain about that at all. The more people who knew, the more difficult the decision could be.

'You are bloody gorgeous.' David rolled over on the bed, his eyes indicating to her that he was turned on. 'Come here.'

'I can't come there, David. I'm about to meet my mum and I don't want to be late.'

'What's the point in the boys growing up if we don't get a bit more time to ourselves?' David grinned and rolled over again, playing the fool and sticking his arms into the air.

'Where are the boys?'

'In their bedroom, perfectly safe.'

'I thought you were meant to be looking out for them while I got ready.'

'I am,' David defended. 'Their door's wide open and so is ours. It's not as if the house is that big. I can hear them both babbling. Listen for a sec. Can't you hear them?'

Both the boys' voices came gambolling through the silence. What David didn't realise, Lizzy thought with a burst of smugness, was that a mother could hear her child's voice from several thousand miles away, let alone a yard or two. Of course she'd been able to hear the boys playing in their adjacent bedroom. She hadn't really been asking him where they were. She'd been asking him to go away.

'So is it really Doe you're meeting?' David rambled on. 'You seem to be making a big effort to look nice.'

'No, I'm meeting the Harlequins. Fifteen of them, one me. Can't wait.'

'Okay.' David pulled a rueful face. 'I don't mean that, I just mean I haven't seen you look so smart in a long time. What are you rehearsing for?'

Lizzy was going to argue, but realised that she was rehearsing. She was trying to make more of her business associations with Criss-Cross and had been thinking a lot about the extra money her activities could bring in, if only she could channel them properly. She and David had both wanted extra income, to live a life that wasn't bound by the children's need for new shoes. Well, what could she do about it? More than she was doing at the moment, she'd realised. But these were tentative steps.

'Looking smart is important to me now.' Lizzy put on a pair of black brushed cotton trousers and found a smooth shirt to go with them. 'I have to look business-like and professional. Cassie wants to introduce me to some friends of hers who run a craft exhibition. It could mean bigger contacts. Through that I could get to meet people who are connected with greetings-card companies. That's what happened to Cassie. Her designs were bought, for a lot of money, because she was spotted by a greetings-card company.'

'A whattie?' David laughed. 'Hang on, Cassie's the woman in Tunbridge Wells?'

'Cassie is the manager of the shop that is buying my

work,' Lizzy said, straight-faced. 'I thought I'd explained that to you.'

'Yes, I'm sorry.' David sat up. 'Really, I'm sorry. You did tell me about it, and I know that you bringing in a bit of extra money for us is important.'

Lizzy buttoned her shirt, her skin tightening across her cheeks. It would help if David didn't seem so amused by the steps she was taking. And all the time, scraping at her from the inside like a beetle in a jar, was the burning need to tell him that she was pregnant. And yet, because of his shock and his injuries in the car accident and their mutual distrust and distance ever since, she couldn't find the right words. It was a strange situation to be in, one that she could not have anticipated in her wildest dreams. But how did you tell a man who had suddenly developed a need to distance himself from family life, that his family was about to grow bigger and more demanding?

'Do you want to go back to work full-time? I'd suggest it myself,' David went on, 'but I can't imagine we'd earn enough to pay for the child-care. I mean, what kind of a nonsense is this? You get back to work, you spend all of your money on paying some strange woman to bring up our children, we're no better off, the children are brought up by a stranger. What's the logic in that?'

Lizzy offered nothing other than an arch look over her shoulder as she fixed a gold necklet in place.

'Oh come on,' David said defensively, reading her look as a line of argument. 'Is that what you want? We both agreed that we wanted to have some say in the boys' upbringing. Otherwise we might as well have all the money in the world and send them off at seven years old to be brought up by sadists. We don't meet them

471

again until they're eighteen, at which point we give them their inheritance and they go and spend it all on therapy.'

'What the bloody hell are you on about?'

'Well that's what the upper classes do, isn't it?'

'I can't talk to you tonight,' Lizzy said calmly, brushing her hair and clouding it with hairspray. 'You're very hyper.'

'Well perhaps one of us should be hyper.' David's voice was tight. 'Since this business with Phil you've been as cold as an ice cube towards me. I don't know why but I do know that it's not healthy.'

'Healthy?' Lizzy put her hands on her hips and stared at him. 'Do you want to lecture me about what's healthy? Or are you complaining because we haven't had sex since the night you were in the car accident and I discovered that you had lied to me about every single thing that was important?'

'None of it was important.' David gaped back at Lizzy as she marched around the room rearranging her clothes. 'It was silly stuff. We tried to sneak a trip on a helicopter. It was just *Boys' Own* fantasy.'

'How about if I live out a *Girls' Own* fantasy and go and live in France with David Ginola? Will that be unimportant too?'

'This was something Brendan and I had dreamed about for years but knew we couldn't do because we couldn't afford it. Or maybe we just hadn't done it because we hadn't had the balls to book it. So we did. It was impulsive and naughty, I know, and we were found out. And I'm sorry about it, but it was a stupid, frivolous act. And hiding Phil being here from you, that was only at his request. He wanted to keep his split from Luzie secret from the family for as long as possible. He knew Stephanie and Howard would put pressure on him to make it up. He knew he couldn't make it up with her, so he needed our understanding. That's why I couldn't tell you.'

'And you don't think any of that was important?' Lizzy savagely stuffed a lipstick into the pocket compartment of her handbag.

'No,' David said elaborately. 'My stunt with the guys was a private, stupid thing, but it wasn't important to our marriage. You'd have found out about Phil in time, but that was his decision. It was horrible that things happened the way that they did.'

'Oh for God's sake.' Lizzy went back to the wardrobe to find a jacket.

'For God's sake?'

'Yes, for God's sake. Can you not see that your need to secretly spend shitloads of money on yourself, rather than on our family, was important to us?'

'Hang on, it's not just about me spending money, is it? It's about the fact that I didn't tell you. Is it the secrecy element that is really driving you mad here?' David asked.

'It's both. But of course you being secretive is a problem.' Lizzy rifled through the make-up on the top of her dressing table. It rattled under her fingers. 'When did we ever have elements of secrecy in our marriage before?'

'Well, let me see.' David sat on the edge of the bed, his face flushed. 'Everything you've ever discussed with Caroline is secret. There are things you don't tell me about her, or your mother, or your other girlfriends. In fact, it's completely normal for you to keep a load of secrets from me, and I never complain about it.'

'That's completely different. Those are other people's private affairs. Things that don't affect you.'

'Well.' He raised his eyebrows ironically. 'I think that you going into business is our private affair rather than other people's. But you didn't tell me about that until we were at the hospital. You'd already sold three lots of cards to Cassie and yet you hadn't said a word to me. And strange as it may seem to you, I was pretty amazed that you had that ability to hold information back. I always thought you were a heart-on-sleeve sort of woman. I was wrong. You were keeping that to yourself and waiting for a moment that suited you to tell me. Isn't that secretive?'

'I was trying to make a positive difference to us,' Lizzy growled, tears of frustration rising in her throat, which she bit back. She squirted more perfume on her neck and inhaled it to give her spirits a lift. 'It's not the same as spending money on yourself just so that you can – what did you call it? – live a little.'

'But Lizzy.' David stood up. 'If we don't live our lives, what sort of parents can we be?'

She flinched away from him, pulling out a jacket with a fake fur collar that was ten years old and that would normally have cheered her up, and pushing her arms into it. 'If we don't put our children first, what sort of parents are we?'

'I do put my children first.' David took Lizzy by the upper arms to hold her still. 'Listen to me. I love my boys. I'd give them anything, and you know it. And now that we've got a full family, two lovely boys and us, we can build on what we've got. Michael's four now, and already he's doing pre-school activities. Just think what it'll be like in a couple of years. They'll both be in primary

474

school full-time. We'll have so much more freedom. And when they're both in the same routine, maybe we can get a childminder for an hour or two either side of their school day. And then, just think what we can do again. All the fun we used to have. The holidays. The adventures. You and I used to take off and do the wildest things. Don't you remember?' He laughed. 'I remember when we went snowboarding. We had such a great time flying down the slopes. You were so bloody hopeless, crashing into trees, piles of snow, everyone else. That was just before we knew you were . . .'

David tailed away. Lizzy allowed time to pass. She had no urge to prompt him, to remind him of anything so important. And unusually for her, she had no desire at all to make him feel better about the terrible *faux pas* that he'd just inflicted upon them both. She watched his expression change from animation into sorrow.

'God Lizzy, I'm so sorry.'

'You're sorry? Why should you be apologising to me? It was *our* daughter that we lost, not mine.'

'I'm sorry, I didn't want to bring that up.' David made a move to leave the room.

'So now you walk away,' Lizzy observed so sharply that David turned around with his hand on the door. 'Do you remember how you felt when we lost our daughter?'

David was silent for a moment. 'Oh for Christ's sake, don't take me back to that.'

'Why not?'

'Have you been drinking?'

'Have you?'

'Your reactions seem a bit odd tonight. I think I'd better get back to the boys and let you get ready to meet Doe.'

475

'On the contrary, David, I think your reactions are a little odd. Why don't we ever talk about it?'

David splayed a hand by means of explanation. 'Because we can't *do* anything about it, that's why.'

Lizzy stood still, her breath whistling in and out of her nostrils. What was it with men? Why were they incapable of talking about anything unless they could actually do something about it? Was that why they blocked any discussion of anything emotional, no matter how damaging it was? Anything that could not practically be acted on didn't exist for them? It was like slamming a lid on a jam jar and blocking out the oxygen. If only Caroline could witness this situation she would understand why Lizzy had been compelled to go and sit in a church to allow herself the freedom to think. Lizzy had known that at least her grief would be respected there.

'You think you're the only one with secrets,' Lizzy said, tears biting the back of her throat. 'But you're wrong.'

'Oh terrific.' David followed her to the top of the stairs as she flounced away. 'That's really good parenting. Eye for an eye, tooth for a tooth.'

'You have no fucking idea,' Lizzy said, flashing an angry look to where David stood with his hands gripping the banisters at the top of the stairs, before she found her car keys in the pot and yanked at the front door.

'Give Doe my love,' David said sardonically.

'Make sure my children are still alive when I get home,' Lizzy called back.

Daniel was up when Antonia got home. He was in the living room. The television was on, but he wasn't

476

watching it. His head was in his hands and the haunted look that had dogged him for the last few weeks was stronger than ever.

'Hey, how's things?' Antonia took a mug of tea in with her and sat on the sofa. It was too late to do any more work, and she was nicely tipsy. Some tea and a late programme before she went upstairs would relax her thoroughly. She would sleep well. Now that Audrey had returned to her house and Antonia's double bed was her own again, she had been catching up on all her lost sleep. So far, Emile hadn't stayed over, apart from the night of the car accident when he had finally retired to the sofa. That was only after they had shared an exquisite experience of love-making. They had seen each other since then, for dinner, for walks, and once Antonia had taken Sonia up to London for the evening, and Emile and Natalie had joined them. They'd had a steak dinner and seen *Chicago*. They'd had a riot, but Antonia had insisted on getting the last train back to Kent. For Sonia's sake, she wanted to tread very carefully, even if her heart told her that she'd come home.

Just a week ago, Antonia had driven her mother to the hospital to have her plaster cast removed from her wrist. Audrey had been in boisterously high spirits, and had cried with relief to have the cumbersome plaster removed, then cried with horror at the sight of the white, wrinkled skin beneath. The physiotherapist had assured them both that the skin would return to normal very soon. Finding that she was able to move her hand freely, Audrey had brightened on the drive back. Then she'd insisted on returning to her own home.

'I'd stay here for you, love, but you don't need me now. You need space to find out what's what.'

477

'You can stay as long as you like.' Antonia had hugged her mother tightly. 'I love having you here. I'm so glad we've got to know each other better.'

'I'll be around for your op,' Audrey had stated. 'I'm coming with you, no matter what you say. But now that we've had those biopsies back, I'm a lot happier. After your op I'll stay here if you want me to, for as long as you like. You might want a hand fixing supper or making cups of tea for a day or two. But for now you need a bit of privacy.'

Antonia, too, had been relieved beyond measure to find the biopsy results showed that the cells that had presented a problem had not got any worse, and in fact seemed to be shrinking back. Treatment was still necessary, but it seemed very likely that only one session would be needed. Having looked her illness in the face, she knew it was no longer an ogre to be hidden from. She could see it now as something localised, minor, and routine. It was like having a bad tooth out. It was a bugger that it had to be done at all, but her spirits were so high she was quite sure that this would be the end of it. One lot of treatment, problem solved. Ever since she had seen Tom in his kitchen, and he had held her hand and shown her a glimpse of pure, positive energy, she hadn't looked back.

And so Audrey had left. They spoke daily on the phone, and most evenings either Antonia or Sonia dropped in on her to help her with any jobs that needed doing, to drink tea, or to eat with her, or just to chat. The house had now returned to a semblance of normality. Sonia was either shrieking with laughter down the phone to one of her friends, lying on her bed listening to music, trying out a new hair product or nail varnish, or shooting sarcastic remarks at the room. Soon, Antonia would find a gentle way to warn her that she was going to have a little time off work for some medical treatment. She wasn't afraid of Sonia's reaction. She just had to find the right way to phrase it for her.

So now Antonia crossed one leg over the other. It had been an interesting evening with Caroline. She was finding that she liked her much more than she'd thought possible. Despite their different approaches to life – Caroline with her scientific rigidity, Antonia with her eager pursuit of the vague and obscure – it seemed they had a lot in common. Perhaps it was because they were both in love? It was just a shame that Tom had disappeared. Where would he have vanished to?

Antonia pondered the question, sipped her tea and regarded Daniel again. Ever since the accident he had been morose, but on occasions he seemed to be utterly surrounded by black cloud, so opaque that nobody could see in and he couldn't see out.

'Daniel?'

Daniel rubbed at one of his eyes, tracing a finger down his cheek. 'This is where Phil's going to have an almighty scar.'

'You saw him again this evening?'

Daniel nodded. 'I took him in some flowers.'

Antonia picked her words carefully. 'Nobody's to blame for the accident, Daniel. You do know that, don't you?'

Daniel let out a heavy sigh. 'We're all responsible. We were all mad that day.'

'What do you mean?' she asked tentatively.

'Have you ever felt the need to pretend that you've got no responsibilities, no ties, no commitments? To

479

throw off the shackles of everyday humdrum existence, to escape from the sheer, flat ache of the boredom and the predictability of it all? Do you know how it feels to reach a point where you're so close to screaming that it just doesn't matter what you do any more, and it matters even less what anyone thinks? Have you got to that point where you want to break all the rules, for no other reason than because they're *there*?'

Antonia swallowed. 'I think so.'

'Well, we did. We went up there in really high spirits. We had music on full blast, and David was telling stupid air-force jokes. Brendan kept doing an impersonation of Skippy that had us all doubled up. We were all crazy that weekend. It was such a release, such an opportunity to be young and stupid together. Then the helicopter trip was cancelled and we all felt flat. I can't say how it happened. We went straight from the Biggin Hill airbase to a pub on a back road, no more than half a mile away. I don't know why suddenly anything seemed possible, but everybody drank. I wasn't over the legal limit, but I was as high as a kite on atmosphere. When the tree came down, we were all yelling and singing on our way back from the pub. None of us saw it. Not a thing. Can you imagine that? Not a moment of warning. We were too busy acting like maniacs who'd escaped from the asylum.'

Antonia tried to visualise what this orgy of a weekend must have been like, how it must have felt. No wonder Lizzy, David's wife, had been so furious. It was just what her husband had been running away from. Answerability. And Daniel too, running away from the stresses of his job perhaps, of expectations, of being nice and polite all the time. Perhaps escaping from the strains that had been created inside her household: her mother, her daughter, herself. Yes, she could see just why they'd all gone off and had a blast. A rebellion against the cry of 'You shouldn't!' A manic attempt to leap away from a preplanned route. A futile yelp in protest against predestination. Through her illness, she had rediscovered the wildness of wanting to live each moment to excess. Daniel and his friends had found it in a state of health. Everybody's idea of constraint was different. The consequences had been shocking, but she envied them their wild collusion.

'I understand better than you think,' she said at last. 'You mustn't blame yourself.'

'Look, Antonia,' Daniel sighed. 'I know you mean well but now that you and Emile are an item, the chances are that we're going to be around each other for a very long time. Sonia and I are resigned to it, so don't look so surprised. But that means you have to know when to let me torture myself in peace.' He got to his feet and pushed his way out of the door. 'Night.' He let the door swing shut behind him, leaving Antonia to stare after him.

Chapter Twenty-Three

'At last,' Stephanie said. She took Phil in her arms and held him tightly. Caroline hovered on the doormat holding a bottle of wine, peering over her mother's shoulder at her father, who gave her a wave. 'Let me look at you. My God, it's good to have you home.'

'Well, I have been out for nearly two weeks now.' Phil kissed her cheek.

'No, I mean *home*. Our home, our family home. Here.' Stephanie sparkled.

'I think Phil was timing it for your anniversary,' Caroline commented, stepping past them into the hall and handing her father the wine. 'You both look splendid. Is that a new dress, Mum?'

'Of course.' Stephanie did a twirl. 'I wasn't going to turn up in any old rag for my anniversary, was I?'

'You just need to zip it up at the back.'

'Lovely, can you help me then, dear?'

'Come through, Phil,' Howard said. 'The others are all here and we're dying to get stuck into the wine. You can help me pour. Or maybe not, with that dodgy arm of yours. Will it be out of the sling soon?'

'Another week, they reckon.'

'Good, good. Well follow me then.' Howard lowered his voice to a hoarse whisper. 'There's a bit of an atmosphere through here. The kids have been yelled at by Lizzy, and I think David's got a hangover. They're going to put the boys to bed up in the spare room at any moment. It is late for them and they're getting a bit overexcited. Still, let's go and liven things up even more.'

'Okay.'

They all tried not to watch as Phil limped through the hall, his hands on the wall to steady himself. Howard put out a hand but Phil shook his head. He'd abandoned the crutch he was generally using. He'd told Caroline it made him feel shackled, so he'd promised instead not to stay on his feet for too long. Father and son disappeared through the hall in the direction of the back of the house.

'His face is looking much better,' Stephanie said to Caroline with relief.

'Yes. Better week by week.' Once Caroline had caught Phil looking at himself in the bathroom mirror, pushing back his hair and grimacing. She'd reminded him that he could have lost an eye, and he'd nodded. It would take him time to adjust, but perhaps it might lead him to be a little less vain. She hoped he'd find a way to live with it. He'd always been a chameleon before this, capable of adapting to almost anything.

'And how is my beautiful daughter?' Stephanie held Caroline's hands and surveyed her. 'You do look so well. What a good colour you've got. And you've filled out. Are you on the pill?'

'Mum!' Caroline tutted. 'No I'm not on the pill.'

'Maybe it's that black jumper then. It does fit you very well. You seem, well, more buxom.'

Caroline gazed down at herself. 'No, I don't think so. It's probably hormonal.'

'Speaking of hormones, I heard that you'd been seeing

a chap.' Stephanie wiggled her eyebrows, and as if on cue a strand of hair loosened itself from its pleat and fell in front of her eyes.

'You don't mean Brendan, do you, because there's nothing to say. Has someone been wittering to you about that?'

'Brendan? No, I know all about the Paris mission and the aborted luxury hotel trip. No, I didn't mean Brendan.'

'You knew about all of that?'

'Yes.' Stephanie cleared her throat. 'Well, it's all in the family.'

'Yes, how cosy that is,' she said drily.

'No, I meant this other . . . Well, I'd heard you'd seen someone else on a date.'

'I did see someone once or twice but . . .' Caroline hesitated. She was still in love with Tom, but she had no idea what he thought about her. It wouldn't exactly be true to say that it hadn't worked out. It had never really even started before he'd disappeared. 'Well, he had to leave town.'

'People have all sorts of long-distance relationships these days,' Stephanie insisted. 'What with the phone and the Internet. No reason not to stay in touch.'

'Well, in this case it's a bit more tricky.' Caroline gave a smile that indicated finality.

'If you don't want to talk about it, it's your business, my love. Just remember that I'm here. Such a shame, though. Doe said Lizzy said you'd said you're quite smitten.'

'I *was* quite smitten.'

'So a possibility bites the dust, then?'

Caroline hesitated for a second before answering.

'Well, that's quite a negative way of looking at it. On the bright side, I've got a thousand things to do now the spring's here. Clear skies are on their way.'

Stephanie's eyes lit up. 'You know your grandpa always said you were the one who should be going up there, not sitting down here doing all the theory.'

'I think it's a bit late for that now, Mum.'

'You could always go back into research, you know. You're still young. I always thought you'd be a pure scientist, like Howard and your granddad before you. If anyone had it in them to do something really important, it was you.'

'I thought I was doing something important.'

'Oh you are. It was just that I thought you'd make something special of your life.'

'What?'

'You know what I mean,' Stephanie blustered. 'I thought you'd be the one to discover something.'

'I did. I discovered that I love teaching.' Caroline was surprised at how narked she was by her mother's casual comments. Didn't anybody value a good science teacher? She'd always known that it was one of the most important things she could do.

'Oh, I know, love. I'm sorry, I didn't mean to offend you. I'm worried about Phil really. He's been drifting for all these years and now here he is again, at another full stop, about to drift into something equally as vague no doubt.'

They stopped in front of the dining-room door. Inside, everyone was talking loudly and Caroline could hear her father offering the wine round. She frowned at her mother critically. She was still annoyed with her for the remark about making something special of her life.

485

Was that what they'd all secretly thought while she'd been busy inspiring girls and young women to have the vision and confidence to take up careers in science? It made her more defensive of her brother.

'Phil will make something of his life, Mum. He just needs time.'

'Yes well, trust him to be fashionably late. I still can't believe he's walked out on Luzie, and I'm shocked that he wouldn't even let her visit him in hospital.'

'She didn't want to come. Believe me, I spoke to her on the phone myself.' She squeezed her mother's hand gently. 'His marriage is over, Mum. It was never meant to be. Try to accept that if you can.'

Stephanie shook her head briskly as if it would help to blow away the image of her separated son. 'Not a divorce. Not in our family. And Phil's so young too.'

'Thank heavens he is so young. He'll have time to start afresh.'

'And I suppose you've been talking to him about all this at home, since he got out of hospital? He's bent your ear, I can see that. He was always able to charm the living daylights out of everybody.'

'He hasn't charmed me. He's just helped me to understand that it's the right decision for him.'

'He'll come round to Luzie. Once he realises that this is one responsibility he can't run away from,' Stephanie said firmly, and opened the dining-room door.

'I'll get it. I'm closest to the door.' Caroline stood up at the sound of the bell.

'Who can that be then?' Stephanie's cheeks were flushed. She'd been enjoying the wine they'd had with the meal.

'It'll be Brendan.' Lizzy glanced at Caroline conspiratorially. 'Or at least, it'd better be. He's bloody late.'

'Oh Brendan, that darling boy,' Doe opined, refilling her own glass as Ron seemed too engrossed in his trifle to notice that she needed a top-up. 'Get him in here so I can have another look at that lovely bum.'

'Mum!' Lizzy hissed.

'Oh cheer up for heaven's sake.' Doe pulled a face at her daughter. 'Why aren't you drinking? Have a glass of wine, it'll melt the ice.'

'Thanks but I'm driving.'

'One glass won't hurt.'

'Don't,' David said, instantly putting a hand out and trapping Lizzy's fingers. 'Don't have even one glass.'

'I wasn't going to,' Lizzy snapped back.

'I'll just let him in then.' Caroline left the room as her father was announcing that he thought he'd heard the doorbell and if it was the Hope-Potters he'd find something imaginative to do with the telescope.

It was Brendan.

'If I say you look sheepish, will you think I'm stereotyping you?' She stood back to let him in.

'You're in better spirits.' His dark eyebrows rose. 'Has Phil been cheering you up?'

'I've been enjoying having him living with me, yes. We've been getting on very well.'

Brendan nodded, then smiled slowly. 'And if I say that you look gorgeous will you think I'm being a stereotype?'

'No, I'll think you're being honest,' she quipped. 'Phil had said you were back in shape and he's right. You look great. It was good of you to take him to his physio appointment the other day too. I just couldn't

487

get the time off. I'm really pleased you both made such a day of it. He needed that. He's been getting so claustrophobic.'

'Of course he has. Locked up in hospital for weeks, and now he's still got a dodgy leg and can't get about independently as he'd like to. It'll heal fast, though. He reckons he'll be off the crutch in another week. He's fighting like fury.'

'He's off it today. It's a big improvement. And your day together really gave him a boost. He's been in such good spirits ever since.'

Brendan nodded and looked thoughtful. 'So you really are well. I mean, you look fantastic. Better than I've ever seen you. But you're happy, are you? That's what I mean.'

Caroline was surprised. She was expecting just to cavort back into the dining room with Brendan in tow in time for the toasts and presents, but he'd put a hand on her arm.

'Of course. I'm fine.'

He searched her expression. 'You're not sorry. About . . . anything.'

'Like what?'

'About us.' Brendan cleared his throat awkwardly. 'I've wondered whether you ever had second thoughts.'

Caroline relaxed and touched his face. She put a soft kiss there, amazed that she didn't feel inhibited or embarrassed in doing so. 'The honest truth? Yes, sometimes I've wished we'd made it off to our luxury hotel that night. I was curious about it. And you are a nice-looking bloke, and I'm very fond of you.'

'You mean,' Brendan pulled a heroic, jutting-jawed face, 'you wish you'd had my body.'

She laughed. 'Okay, sometimes I've wished I'd had your body. It's an all-right body. Happy?'

'Very. I think the bed would have caught fire.'

'Maybe.' She gave him a warning look. Perhaps it was best not to dwell on what the bed might have done had they both managed to be in it, and awake, at the same time. 'But I'm fine with it as it is. You're a member of the family, and that's even better.'

'Thank you, princess.' He held her for a moment and she inhaled his scent. It was a clean, lime-edged smell. Attractive, but it didn't speak to her. He kissed her lips softly. 'I'll never forget you. Ever. Wherever I am.'

'I'd hope not.' Then she studied him more seriously. 'You're not going anywhere, are you?'

'I'd better deliver my present,' Brendan said, nodding at the dining room, which was erupting with cheers and laughs. 'Hope I'm still in time.'

'Yes, just. You've missed dinner, but if you're hungry there'll be tons left. With any luck you're bang in time for . . .' Caroline pushed open the door just as a champagne cork flew through the air. 'The toasts and speeches. Lucky you.'

Brendan was greeted with the usual oohs and aahs, especially from Stephanie and Doe. Somehow Howard and Ron had always liked him just as much as their wives did, probably because he was a man's man at heart. Caroline took her place at the table again, shuffling up as Howard added another chair. Stephanie took some pictures and they all grinned. Caroline noticed that even Lizzy forced a smile, though she knew she must have been finding it hard. Then Howard and Stephanie stood up and went to the dresser where the presents were amassed. Howard insisted on reading every card out loud and putting it carefully to the side as a memento. Stephanie was already on to the presents and managed to spill red wine on Howard's pile of cards, earning herself a kind reprimand and a chair to sit down on to prevent further damage.

They were thrilled with the presents. An engraved silver dish; an antique vase; an intricately carved hand-made picture made entirely out of wood and painted in tiny detail, which Lizzy had apparently been working on for weeks; tickets to see *The Graduate* from Brendan; a jeroboam of champagne from all of them; air tickets for a weekend in Venice together with a night in a five-star hotel, which caused a great stir. This was Doe's gift to her sister and brother-in-law, and she promptly produced a brochure with a photograph of a sumptuous hotel foyer in marble, cream and tangerine, which made everybody's mouth water. Then Stephanie opened Caroline's present, and her eyes lit up.

'Ooh Howard, look,' she squealed excitedly. 'Ballooning. We've never done that.'

Ron handed out more champagne as there were general guffaws. Howard took the information and retrieved the strap-on head set with the magnifying glasses in it so that he could study it closely. 'Well, good grief,' he said, his cheeks tinged pink with pleasure. 'A day's instruction in hot-air ballooning at a date to suit us. In the West Country? What's all this then, Caro?' He looked up, his eyes huge.

'Gloucestershire. And you've got a night's stay in a country hotel, though it probably won't compare with your Venice pad.'

'How wonderful.' Stephanie grouped all the presents together on the dresser, her eyes moist. 'How very kind you all are. What luck we have, such a complete family. So much love between us.'

'You sound like you're making your speech already,' Howard twinkled at her.

'Is that it then? Great, nice and short,' Phil teased.

'Now you.' Stephanie wagged a finger. 'You all know how I like to give my little speeches.'

Caroline smiled to herself. Christmas, birthdays, anniversaries. It was always her mother who summed things up for them all. It was something her grandfather used to do. He'd tap a spoon against the side of his glass and it would ring across the table. A hush would descend, and he would stand up, a small, thin figure with large, expressive eyes and long fingers. Then he would say something profound, with a joke and a smile attached, and they'd all listen with great intensity. Caroline remembered those speeches well from her childhood. Then when he'd died, her mother had, hesitantly at first, assumed the mantle of speech-maker at big family events. Caroline had listened to her grandfather's speeches in total awe, silent and spellbound. Perhaps the adults had teased him as he spoke, but she couldn't remember that aspect of it. Stephanie on the other hand always expected a good barracking, and she generally got it.

'Shall I do it now, then?' she asked.

'Well, we're all sitting comfortably,' Doe said, waving a glass. They were all still gathered around the table. 'As good a time as any to listen to a speech. Although we could do with a refill. We don't want to have empty glasses when it comes to the toast.'

And as Stephanie was gathering herself ready to speak, Caroline tried to remember the last time they'd all been together. They often visited each other for Sunday lunch, sometimes here at her parents' house, sometimes at Ron and Doe's, less often at Lizzy's unless it was only a small gathering, once at Caroline's but her microwaved potatoes had exploded, so they hadn't repeated that experiment. But often at least one element of the family would be missing. Even at the last big gathering Caroline could remember, in early January, when the frost was encasing the earth and she was getting depressed with the endless dull days and cloud-filled nights, Phil had been in Germany. In fact, the last big dinner she could remember where they'd all been gathered as a family was Christmas, two years ago. And then Luzie had been with them, and they'd been toasting Phil and Luzie's recent marriage. The thought made her feel a little sad. Now her mother had started to speak, and everyone was listening.

Smiling at the way Stephanie came alive in front of an audience, Caroline wondered if she'd inherited just a little of that. People always spoke of how like her grand-father Caroline was, with her passion for astronomy, her talking hands when she explained something, her fiery interest in scientific discovery. But her grandfather had been more enigmatic, more of an inventor than a teacher. He'd been fascinating, unfathomable and unique, and others had been obliged to probe him for explanations. Except for Caroline. She would follow him around, and he would tell her what he was doing as he was doing it. But Stephanie was a communicator and loved to explain things. Perhaps some of that energy had come through to Caroline. She watched her mother hold court with a thread of pride. It didn't matter that the zip on Stephanie's dress had come undone again at the back and a flash of bra strap revealed itself whenever she swung round, or that her hair was falling out of the pleat she'd attempted to put it in, or that whenever she moved her hands she knocked something over. They were all used to that.

She had made generous remarks about the presents and about the occasion, and had kissed Howard and talked of their happy years together. Caroline tried to put her grandfather from her mind and tune in again.

'Because it's our anniversary and we've had years of happiness together, I want to talk about marriage.' Stephanie took a sip of her champagne and eyed them all seriously as Howard spotted the undone zip and did it up again for her. 'Thank you, Howard. We all know what a terrible time we've had over the last two months. My son was in the country but didn't tell me. He was staying with my daughter, who also didn't tell me that he was in the country. I have to tell you all what a blow that was to me.'

Caroline stiffened in her chair. She glanced at Phil. He was staring straight ahead. She looked over at Lizzy instead and they exchanged expressions of surprise. The family speeches weren't normally used as opportunity to dress people down. At least, if so, only with much teasing. She picked up her glass and fiddled with it.

'I love my children. Everybody knows that. But I have to say that they've let me down this year. It seems that the first time it was deemed appropriate for me to know that my only son was ten miles down the road from me was when he needed my blood.'

Caroline met Doe's eye. Doe was grimacing. Perhaps she would come up with one of her timely heckles soon. It was getting a little uncomfortable.

'What you did was wonderful, Mum.' Phil looked down at the carpet.

'Yes, it was wonderful!' Doe chimed in. 'Well done, Stephanie. Even if it was your fault for handing on such a rare blood group to your poor son. All those who are O positive, raise your hands! We may be common as muck but we're a lot better off in a crisis.'

A couple of them privately smothered smiles, but the atmosphere was still tense.

'Yes, of course we're all relieved beyond measure that Phil is so much better and here with us today for our anniversary. And let's be grateful that Phil came out of his accident so well, given how much worse it could have been.'

'Amen,' Doe said robustly, winking at Caroline. 'Let's have a glug to that. C'mon Phil, give us a rattle of all those metal pins in your knee.'

'Doe!' Phil laughed under his breath.

'But I want to say more. And I want us all to consider the family photographs here on the dresser.'

'We can't see them,' David protested. 'All the presents are in the way.'

'Oh yes. Well, let's move the presents then. Come on Howard, help me. Steady with that vase.'

'Wouldn't it be quicker to move the photographs?'

'And less expensive?' Doe grimaced, watching the vase slip in Howard's hands before he caught it again. She whispered across the table to Caroline, 'That cost us ten quid. I don't want to see it in pieces on the carpet.'

'It's very pretty,' Caroline hissed back. 'You'd never know it was only ten quid.'

'I think the ladies in Help the Aged were a bit confused. It cost less than a photo frame with a denim jacket on. I think it might be quite valuable. But we'll never know if they drop it, will we?'

Once the presents had all been moved to a coffer near the window, the selection of photographs on the dresser were clear to be seen again. They were familiar to everyone. Marriages, christenings, birthdays. About fifteen photographs that they'd all seen a thousand times.

'I want us to look at these,' Stephanie said, slightly out of breath. 'And particularly the sense of continuity. Of purposeful activity.'

'Lovely.' Doe clapped heartily, and nobody joined in. She shrugged and refilled her glass.

Caroline hadn't clapped because Stephanie had edged to the front of the photographs a large, colour picture of Phil and Luzie. They'd got married in a registry office. Afterwards they'd all gone to a country hotel and had a sumptuous dinner with dancing. There hadn't been that many people there, but it had been an event with a lot of good feeling behind it. The respective parents had met, everyone had stayed overnight at the hotel, and a couple of days later Phil and Luzie had sped off to Germany to start a new life. At the time, it had felt as if everything was rubber-stamped.

'Today's a time to think about the meaning of marriage. It's about compromise and reason. It's about being kind to each other. It's about treasuring a commitment and turning it into a family. I mean, look at us all here. You and me, Doe, you children, Lizzy, Caroline and Phil, and the boys. We're all here, forming this loving unit of a family because we understand that relationships are what build families. It starts with a spark, then romance, then marriage and children. Then we have an occasion like this.' Stephanie was pleading softly. She couldn't remain censorious for long, if she ever was. It was hope that motivated her.

Caroline understood that, but she was still worried about the effect of this plea on Phil. And, as Stephanie slid an old photograph of Caroline as a baby to the front of the display, she started to feel uncomfortable on her own account too.

'Oh Mum, I think we can leave that one at the back,' she protested.

'No, because I want to look at my two children. Phil and Caroline. Well, let's see. Caroline is unlikely to marry, at least, she probably won't bring grandchildren to us. She's her own person. So we accept that, and let's move on to Phil.'

Caroline narrowed her eyes. It wasn't easy to be brought up and dismissed so efficiently. It was very unlike her mother to be so clumsy, but it seemed that since Phil's arrival and especially since news of his separation, Stephanie had become far more blunt. It was as if she couldn't quite help herself. Caroline nearly said something but caught Lizzy's eye. There was so much support there that she sat back again.

Stephanie prodded the photograph of Phil's wedding. 'I just want you to think about this. It was never easy at first for Howard and me, however much you might think so now.' She laughed and her hair flew away from her head, reminding them all that they loved her, even if she was being dogmatic. 'It was hard for Doe and Ron too. Yes, let me say this, Doe, you had your troubles when you first set out. I remember.'

'So do I,' said Ron.

'And so do I,' said Howard.

'Well I bloody don't,' Doe drawled, smirking at Lizzy and Caroline. 'Pass me the fizzy.'

'And that's my point,' Stephanie emphasised. 'A marriage doesn't happen by accident. You can't live in a marriage as if you're two single people occupying the same space and expect it to work. It changes everything, but you see, we do know how hard it is to adjust because we had to adjust too, and that involved rows and hurting each other and all sorts of mean behaviour in those first few years that you wouldn't be able to imagine. I want you to know that although you think of us as the crusty generation, we went through exactly the same thing when we were at your stage too.'

'I think Phil's probably got your point,' Doe said. Caroline bit her tongue. Resistance was mounting within her but she fought it back. Phil sat silently.

'Oh, I don't want to get onto you all. I mean, I can't think of a couple less in need of a lecture on how to have a happy marriage than David and Lizzy.'

'Well that's lovely,' Phil said edgily. 'I'm delighted.'

'It's all right Phil, don't worry,' David said in a very low voice.

'This is a wonderful time to use us as role models,' Lizzy muttered to nobody in particular.

'It's just that time is moving on. I want to impress on you all how important marriage is to providing a secure grounding for your life. And I want to tell you just how happy marriage and children can make you, even if you don't realise it. I mean, here's Doe with her one daughter and two grandchildren. And here Howard and I are, after all these years, with our two children and not a hope of a grandchild in sight. I just hope that—'

'That's enough.' Caroline got to her feet. She'd stood

497

up before she'd realised that she was going to do it. The words that were coming next, she knew in a flash, were going to be based on her gut reaction. She hoped fervently that they wouldn't be too damaging. To her relief, her voice was low and calm when she spoke. 'We're all united in wishing you and Dad a happy anniversary, and we're all thrilled that you've been this lucky with your marriage. But you've said some things which I've found hurtful and I think I've got a right to defend myself.'

'Caroline?' Howard seemed amazed.

She put a hand up to silence him. 'No, Dad. I've tried to be a good daughter to you. I've been close by, I've helped you when I can, and we've all been company and a comfort to each other. But I'm Caroline, the single physics teacher, and this evening it's been suggested that both what I do and what I am are a disappointment to you. You've actually said that your children have let you down by keeping secrets from you. Well, I can only say this, Mum. The reason we had to keep certain things from you was because we knew that you'd make the situation ten times worse by piling on the pressure to do things your way. We just want you to be proud of what we are, not what you think we might have been. We're not living your life. We're living our own.'

Stephanie's eyebrows had mounted her forehead, but she was listening and Caroline was grateful for that. But then Ron piped up.

'Now look here, Caro. I'm sure you've got a good point and we're all sure you should say what you think but is now really the right time? I just mean, anniversary, fizzy, you know, all the—'

'Shut up, Ron,' Doe said, sounding totally sober for an

instant. 'Caroline is an adult woman and totally capable of deciding when to address issues with her family. Just as Stephanie has decided to. So be quiet. We're all family, so just listen. And if you're not drinking that, give it to me.'

'I'm not going to force a relationship with somebody just so that I can have a respectable family before the cut-off point.' Caroline knew that everybody was looking at her now, but she didn't care. 'I may be single for ever, but the only reason I'd ever be unhappy about it is if you make me feel unhappy about it. And as for grand-children . . .' She took several long breaths, but emotion, unwelcome and choking, crawled up into her throat. She put a hand on the table.

Lizzy stood up and blurted out, 'And as for grand-children, what Caro's trying to say but is struggling with because she's too decent to blow the whistle on me, is that we're all expecting another grandchild.'

'Thank you, Lizzy,' Caroline whispered, sitting down again with relief.

'So,' Lizzy said, 'there's no reason for anyone to worry about a lack of small children, is there? You can all share visiting and babysitting rights, so I don't see the need to hassle Phil and Caro about this any more.' She remained standing, her chin defiantly held up.

'What do you mean?' David shot at Lizzy.

'I mean, David, that I'm expecting another baby.'

'Oh you beauty.' Brendan reacted first.

'Lizzy?' David stared at Lizzy, his mouth open. 'What are you saying?'

'Well, when I said that I was expecting another baby, what I was really trying to say was that I was expecting another baby. Sorry to be so cryptic.'

David stood up, his face crumpling. He was silent for a moment, then the tears began to flow. 'Oh my God, that's so fantastic. I'm so happy.' His voice broke inelegantly into a croak. 'Come here my gorgeous creature. Come here, let me hold you.'

Doe stared in amazement. 'You're pregnant, and you didn't tell me?' Then her mouth opened into a circle of delight. 'Ron, do you hear that? We've got another one on the way. Where's that jeroboam? Can we open it now?'

'My goodness,' Stephanie said, her hands fluttering. 'Lizzy, how delightful. How exciting. I'm so pleased. Oh dear, yes, let's open the big bottle. Howard, you do it.'

'You don't seem surprised.' Brendan leaned towards Caroline with an arched eyebrow.

'There are a lot of things Lizzy and I know about each other.' She gave him a blank look in return.

More champagne was tipped into glasses. People hugged each other. Lizzy looked relieved. David looked delighted. Caroline was happy to see them holding hands tightly. And Doe seemed utterly content, what with a pregnant daughter to one side and a full glass to the other.

Then Brendan tapped on a glass with a spoon and everybody quietened down. He stood in front of the dresser. They'd all moved about since Stephanie's speech had been interrupted, so they sat on the nearest chair. Looking at Brendan, Caroline couldn't help regretting the fact that it could never have been a greater thing between them. Why couldn't she have fallen in love with him? But she couldn't, and she was in love with somebody else. There was nothing she could do about it.

'I hate to distract from such a great reason for celebration,' he began. 'And I mean, of course, Steph and Howard's wonderful anniversary achievement. Fantastic. Then Lizzy tells us she's expecting. It's tremendous. I can't imagine how to top that, but I'm not even going to try. My great mate David already knows what I'm about to tell you, but I feel I should share it with the rest of you formally like this because you are my English family and I think you should know now.' He paused, and pushed his hand over his hair, smoothing down his ponytail. 'The fact is . . .' Caroline was alarmed because she knew exactly what was coming next. She sat perfectly still and waited while Brendan put it into words. 'The fact is that I'm going back to Australia.'

'Oh Brendan, don't do that,' came Stephanie's voice. And Lizzy, who seemed amazed, said, 'You can't! You've got to be a godfather again!' And Doe cried, 'Not on my bloody nelly. You're the best bum for fifty miles.'

'You must be missing your home,' Caroline said. 'You've been away for a long time.'

Brendan clicked his tongue and winked at Caroline. 'Thatta girl.'

They smiled at each other. That look was the beginning of a newly defined friendship between them that would last a lifetime.

'But there's something else,' Brendan said seriously. 'Phil's coming with me.'

'You what?' David said.

'Phil's coming with me, to Australia. He wants to see how it is out there, and initially at least I can put him up while he works it out.'

'Oh God,' Stephanie said. 'How is Luzie going to find him in Australia?'

'She's not going to find me there,' Phil said grittily. 'I'm going out there to try a new life.'

'Like all your previous new lives?' Stephanie was getting upset. 'And at what point will you settle down, and create a happy home and atmosphere and fill it with people who care about you? When will you see sense and be happy with what you've got?'

'I'll create a happy home when I am happy. I can't do it before then.' Phil's voice was clear and loud. Even Doe stopped in her wine-pouring and Ron stopped in his efforts to generate diplomacy. 'I can't be like you and Dad. I wish I could, but I can't.'

'We're used to you travelling the world. It'd be strange if you suddenly stopped doing it,' Caroline said calmly. 'I wouldn't expect anything less of you. You've never been to Australia and I bet the curiosity's been driving you mad for years.'

Phil's lips curled into a smile. 'Well, yes. And when I talked to Brendan it made sense.'

'All right, stop this right now.' Stephanie took an empty bottle of champagne and thumped it on the dresser. 'I won't have my children becoming drifters. They were brought up to read, to think, to analyse things, to experiment. We were imaginative parents, I like to think so. I'm delighted that we gave you both that confidence to try new things out. But if it's not too taxing on the memory, I'd like to take us back three years to a wedding we all attended. I mean, look at these photographs. Were we all in fancy dress? Did it actually mean anything to the people concerned? I feel hoodwinked. I can't help it if I do.'

'Perhaps we're all feeling a bit stirred up by the plonk,' Lizzy suggested quietly to Caroline. 'I think your mum's moving on to the tired and emotional phase.'

Caroline went up to her mother and gently took away the empty bottle that she was holding.

'Caroline?'

'Mum. It's time to stop lecturing us all about marriage. We love you and Dad, so let's have a happy anniversary evening.'

'But Phil's going to Australia. He's going to end up living abroad. I'll never see him.'

'But you thought he was going to live his life in Germany. It was just the same.'

'No, it's closer. The time difference is less. We could phone more.'

'In reality you'll talk to him as much in Australia as you would in Germany.' Caroline touched her mother's shoulder. 'He'll go anyway. You can make it hard for him, but nothing's going to change.'

Stephanie stamped a foot, an action that had everybody in the room looking up in surprise. 'I thought we had set you a good example. What else could we have done? I did *not* strive my entire life for a happy marriage so that you could be failures!'

The room was silent. Stephanie's words seemed to echo around the walls. Caroline felt the colour ebbing away from her cheeks. She withdrew her hand from her mother's shoulder.

'That's an awful thing to say, Mum. You'd better take it back.'

Stephanie's jaw dropped in dismay. 'Caroline! Darling! I didn't mean you, I was talking to Phil.'

Phil stood up and stalked across the room. 'Well you can stop lecturing me about marriage, Mum, because I'm gay.'

503

Stephanie gasped. 'No you're not!' she said on reflex.

'Yes I am.' Phil's face was burning. 'So I'm truly sorry if it messes up your vision of grandchildren and the continuation of the family name. What with me and Caroline, it looks like you'll never get your grandchildren.'

'Oh I wouldn't be so sure about that,' Caroline uttered under her breath. But the conversation was gaining momentum.

'But why Australia?' Howard said with an agonised expression. 'Of all the countries that are intolerant of homosexuals, Australia's got to be right up there.'

'Howard!' Stephanie interrupted. 'Can you not say "right up there" in reference to this topic. This isn't about Australia, it's about Phil. We have to reason with him. He's confused.'

'I think you should apologise to Phil for assuming he doesn't know his own mind,' Caroline said, unnerved.

'You knew about this?' Stephanie gasped to Caroline, who was silent in response. 'Then you should apologise to me!'

'Stuff that. I think we should apologise to Brendan for making such rude comments about Australia,' Doe said, swaying on her chair. Caroline wondered if she really had a grasp of what was happening, or whether it was the moment that proved that her aunt Doe was genuinely as cool as she'd always suspected.

'I'm sorry Brendan, no offence,' Howard said gruffly, 'but our impression of Australia is of burly, masculine types who give short shrift to those who embrace alternative lifestyles. I'm afraid the spectre of the homophobe follows closely up the rear.'

'Oh Howard,' Stephanie protested, sitting back on her chair and fanning her face with an anniversary card.

'What?'

'It's all right,' Brendan soothed. 'I know what you're getting at, but I have to tell you the bigger cities are just as cosmopolitan as a lot of other big cities. You get your bigots, sure, but you get your gay clubs and communities too. You shouldn't believe everything you see on a lager ad.'

'Oh I see. You know about this.' Ron nodded at Brendan with such an expression of elaborate understanding that silence descended like a fog. Puzzlement was on every face. One by one, eyes turned to Brendan, who didn't react at first then stared back belligerently.

'Fuck, you mean me? I'm not a woofter,' he defended.

Further silence followed. Howard fingered his spectacles with such agitation that they broke into two even pieces. Stephanie's mouth remained open. Lizzy looked as if she'd been caught in a snapshot taken on a funfair ride, going over an unexpected hoop. David was expressionless. Doe drank her wine, grabbed Caroline's glass and drank that too. Ron glanced gingerly around the room. Caroline was frozen to the spot, waiting for something to happen. It seemed that they had all finally managed to stun each other into silence, an event so rare in that household that she knew she would never forget it.

The silence was broken by the sudden trill of Caroline's mobile phone. Everybody jumped. She scrambled for it, panting.

'I can't talk now,' she barked into it. 'Who is it anyway?'

'Caroline? It's Nina. I am sorry to disturb you. I got

505

your number from Carl. I phoned him and he said I should phone you on your mobile.'

'Nina?' Caroline breathed, then she placed her. The blonde woman with the inquisitive eyes and elfin face. She was a regular attender of meetings now, but the two of them had never had a chance to chat. The last thing on her mind right at that second was the astronomy club. It could honestly be said that it was one of the few moments in her life when all aspects of astronomical activity were absent from her thoughts.

'I'm so sorry, I've disturbed you.'

'No, no. I'm sorry for sounding sharp.' She frowned at the room full of people who were listening to her phone call and turned her back on them to face the wall. 'I'm at my parents' anniversary dinner just now.'

'How nice. Is it going well?'

'Yes, it's going brilliantly,' she lied, crossing her fingers.

'I wouldn't have dreamed of troubling you, and especially on a weekend too. But I had some rather bad news and I thought you'd want to know, and Carl said I should tell you straight away.'

'Bad news?' Caroline frowned.

'Yes. I'm afraid that Roderick's dead.'

Chapter Twenty-Four

They were a sad huddle on a sharply chill but sunny morning, dressed in their dull hues. Starlings chattered in an adjacent copse, the sparrows hopped between the dry twigs of the forsythia, probably noting the tiny bulges of green as the first, shy buds began to emerge. Caroline drew in a deep lungful of breath. There was a sweet smell in the air. Perhaps the copse hid a cluster of bluebells. They all listened respectfully as Dylan's speech drew to an end.

'Roderick was very well thought of as an amateur astronomer and dear friend. He inspired me with his ceaseless energy and dedication.'

'Inspired us all,' Carl muttered in a thick voice. He wiped a leather-gloved hand across his face and blinked at the gaping hole in the earth along with the rest of them. Lesley, standing next to him, gazed morosely down into the earth.

'The club exists because of his drive to start it all those years ago,' Dylan went on sombrely. 'He never missed a meeting. Not a single one. He was ferociously independent and set an example of both passion and individualism to us all. We amateur astronomers know just how important those two qualities are to somebody in our field. Speaking on behalf of the astronomy club, I know that I can say that we will forever be in his debt.' The small gathering nodded as they shuffled in the dewy grass. A duet of crows cawed as they dived between the cypresses.

Caroline glanced at Nina again. She was the only relative present. She looked pale and delicately beautiful in a dark suit, her curly fair hair touching her shoulders. She seemed very badly shaken by Roderick's death and had been extremely quiet all day. Caroline had touched her hand as they'd left the church but hadn't known quite what to say. They all knew that Nina had only got to know Roderick recently and it was a little embarrassing to suspect that they'd known her great-uncle better than she did herself. It was doubly awkward as the astronomy club members had somehow assumed that some relatives would appear out of the woodwork to take control of the proceedings at the church. Perhaps Nina, who was now clearly the only member of the family to care enough to attend, had assumed that other people would say something if they wanted to, or perhaps she'd been too surprised by Roderick's sudden death to authorise anything other than a standardised farewell. The unfortunate result had been that the vicar had galloped through an impersonal service which had left everybody feeling as if justice hadn't been done. As the club members had transported themselves from the church to the graveyard, they'd all expressed their need to do more before Roderick was finally earthed over. Caroline had brought along a tribute herself which she was hoping to be able to give at some point. It was something that she'd consulted Antonia about.

So Nina stood by looking strained and fragile as the club members excelled themselves in their attempts to say goodbye. Caroline could hear Roderick's voice now, proudly declaring that he was on his own, always had been, always would be. She knew he'd never married. She didn't know why. She wasn't even sure if he'd ever had girlfriends, or even boyfriends. She'd known nothing of his private life.

What was more clear to her today than ever before, though, was that he had lived alone and died alone. Even Nina's recent arrival into his life hadn't altered the fate that he had predicted for himself. Caroline had found out from Dylan that it had been a wine merchant who had discovered that something was wrong. Apparently Roderick had maintained an account with a distinguished vintners, and when his supplier had called with an order, he was disturbed by the fact that Roderick didn't answer the door. They always pre-arranged delivery times and Roderick was always there to receive his goods. Further investigation had revealed milk bottles on the doorstep and junk mail wedged in the letter box. Roderick was found in an armchair with his cat on his lap. A plate of beans on toast had hit the floor, judging by the chewed-up remains left by the cat. But the beans had sustained the animal, who was disgruntled but otherwise well. Hearing this, Caroline had thought it was a shame that it was such an inauspicious end to an auspicious life. Died, eating beans. It would have been so much more poetic if he'd been out star-gazing, or crouched over a wealth of astronomical data, or even if he'd tripped over his famously long scarf in his eagerness to get to another club meeting.

Then it had made her wonder how long it would take people to find her if she suddenly died at home. She sometimes screened calls. She didn't have a vintner who'd pop in and realise something was amiss. What if it was during a school holiday? At what point would her friends or somebody from her family raise the alarm? It was an uncomfortable thought. But on the other hand, Roderick had gloried in his independence. He'd never appeared sad or regretful about his lifelong bachelor status, neither had there been even an inkling of bitterness. He loved his life, exactly as it was, and he hadn't seemed to miss marriage and children, or even the permanent companionship of a partner. From what she'd observed, he hadn't even been particularly joyous in his reception of Nina in these last cold months. He'd seemed to grow philosophical about her presence at the club meetings, yes. Perhaps they got together once in a while for cups of tea, even. But he was a loner to the core. He'd celebrated every day in his own way, fuelled by a craving for intellectual gratification, so overwhelmed by the realisation of how much was yet to be discovered that the quest for cramming as much information as possible into his brain had become a joyful obsession that had filled his days. In short, Caroline had realised that in many ways she was just like Roderick. And at that thought, she swallowed.

'So now I'll pass over to Caroline, our club secretary, who I know would like to say her own personal farewell to our old friend.'

Caroline nodded, and as Dylan stepped away from the head of the grave, took his place. She opened the small book that Antonia had lent her at the point that she'd marked. Before she began she gazed over the faces of her friends. She had been planning a short speech of her own. She was going to talk about her impressions of Roderick when she first joined the club. Of how challenging he had been of her knowledge, of how she'd

510

come to understand that this was his way with all new members, and then of how kind he had been in accepting her wholeheartedly onto the committee. But as she tried to formulate the words that she wanted to express in tribute to the old man she had respected so much, she found they were too mundane. They weren't fitting to be the final beacon lit above his shiny oak coffin. She struggled to voice her thoughts, then launched straight in.

'It's taken me a little while to realise that some things can't be expressed in the language of science.' She read the poem that Antonia had found for her:

> ' "I am gone into the fields
> To take what this sweet hour yields;
> Reflection, you may come tomorrow,
> Sit by the fireside with Sorrow.
> You with the unpaid bill, Despair,
> You tiresome verse-reciter, Care,
> I will pay you in the grave,
> Death will listen to your stave." '

Caroline closed the book again, tears edging their way down her face. There followed a pensive silence as they all stood together.

'Well, if we're ready now,' Dylan said gently.

'I would, please, like to say something.'

'Of course, my dear. You must speak.'

They all looked up as Nina's quiet voice commanded their attention. Her eyes seemed enormous within her white face. She stepped forward to the edge of the grave and gazed down at the coffin, then looked around the group.

511

'Roderick Vinnicombe was my grandmother's brother. I came to find him because I don't have anybody else. I – I just want to say that I was thrilled to meet him and his friends. You've all opened my eyes to a new way of thinking. I only knew him briefly but he gave me a great gift, which was to see the world in a different way. He made me realise how little I was experiencing life. I was seeing it from the ground, but he showed me shooting stars.' She paused, looking down. 'I'm so sad that he's gone just as I was getting to know him. I wish he hadn't done that. But I have Perseus now and he's living with me very happily.'

She stopped as suddenly as she'd started.

Caroline wiped away a tear and considered Nina carefully. She had nobody else? Nobody other than her great-uncle Roderick, a complete stranger to her? No wonder she was so intense today. While she carried herself well and maintained her dignity, it was clear to anybody that her spirit was utterly crushed. Roderick's affectionate Siamese cat Perseus, sweet as he was, could be little compensation for a family. She found herself thinking of her own robust, boisterous, unpredictable, chaotic, irrational family. Of expectations and disappointments, halcyon days and nightmare evenings. And Brendan was going away, and would without any doubt leave a chasm in his wake.

As a family, they were rather adept at adopting waifs and strays, after all.

'I wonder where Roderick is now.' Dylan offered his arm to Caroline as the gathering of friends walked away from the grave. They stopped, as one, and tilted back their heads to stare up into the forget-me-not blue of the spring sky. A ghostly white moon glimmered like a Chinese lantern above the town rooftops. Beyond, the fields seemed as soft and mossy as velvet.

'He's free,' Caroline said. Together the astronomy club members stared up and pondered this.

'Atoms, man,' Carl said. 'Brilliant.'

'I'm afraid I think that's it for him,' William said, decked out in a fine black suit. Like many of them, he'd taken time off work to be there. 'I know it's hard for us all, but I think death is a full stop. You're conscious one minute, then you're not.'

Carl shook his head. 'It's too finite. I can't believe it.'

'But no reason to pity Roderick,' Patrick added, catching up with them and smoothing back his few strands of hair. 'He doesn't know a thing about it.'

'I don't agree,' Carl reasoned, his crash helmet swinging from the crook of his arm. Nobody had fluttered so much as an eyelash when he'd arrived at the church in full biking leathers. Anyway, his leathers were black. 'I don't think that Roderick's spirit's just been snuffed out. I mean, that was everything that was Roderick. The weird sense of humour, the attention to detail, those sudden convictions he got sometimes. And just when you thought he wasn't listening, bang! He'd hit you with the most unanswerable logic you'd ever heard. That's not a heap of bones. That's a ball of energy.'

'Ah. Energy,' William said. 'So you're talking about the conversion of energy?'

'Well,' Dylan observed as they tromped on through the wet grass. 'Perhaps Roderick has been converted into a different kind of energy.'

'But what would that be?' William pondered. 'What

513

was he before and what has he become? Kinetic energy? Light energy? Heat energy?'

They all looked at Caroline. 'I don't really want to discuss Roderick in terms of a GCSE assignment.'

'It can't be potential energy. I don't think there's much potential about being dead.'

'Oh please!' Caroline protested as they reached the road. 'There are some things we can't explain. I mean, what if you were a fish in a pond?'

'A what?' William adjusted his tie and Patrick wiped his bald pate. They seemed to like being told off. Caroline had noticed it before but tried to concentrate on her point.

'A fish. If you were a fish and I told you that – I don't know, that there was a whole world of black suits and oak coffins and,' she put a hand out to the air, 'the smell of bluebells and a spring sun, and a beautiful green view from this spot. My God, it's lovely. Would you believe me?'

'Yes, of course,' William nodded. 'It's picturesque.'

'No, if you were a fish,' Lesley explained, rolling her eyes.

'Oh, I see.' There was a puzzled silence.

'Yeah, that's it,' Carl said emphatically. 'We can't possibly understand things that we can't . . . understand.'

They watched from a distance as the vicar shook Nina's hand. He turned to smile appreciatively at everybody else and headed off with his cassock flapping. She was left standing on her own. They hadn't realised that they'd taken off in a group like that. Caroline instantly felt awkward. She waved a hand at Nina, who walked over to them. They stood in silence, watching her approach.

'Nobody mentions Roderick in terms of molecules in Nina's presence. Understood?' Caroline instructed them all.

'How are you doing?' Carl asked with concern as she reached them.

'For heaven's sake,' Nina said. 'Let's go and have a wake somewhere.'

It was many hours later when Dylan thumped on the glossily polished pub table, now smeared with the treacly evidence of several rounds of beer and wine, and tried to gain their attention.

It was a robust wake. Caroline was full of ideas which she thought were being appreciated. Patrick, in particular, seemed to be all agog. Dylan, clearly, was relishing a day off work as much as he was hating the reason for it. Perhaps they all were. They'd all deposited their various means of transportation elsewhere until the following day and had reconvened at a pub that Carl had recommended which was hidden from the town, on a quiet, winding back road studded with small houses. There was hardly anybody else there, and the landlord was wonderfully tolerant, probably due to keeping up with their rounds, albeit from behind the bar and in a solitary fashion.

'Now listen up all,' Dylan proclaimed. Two scowling old men looked around from their bar stools and Dylan genially waved their attention away. 'No, not all. Just all of us. Sorry. Do carry on with your evening. Fellow club members, I have something to say.'

'Okay,' Carl said, his hand reaching for Nina's, Caroline couldn't fail to notice. 'Fire away.'

'I think there is a final duty to be done this evening, so

I'm going to do it. Roderick was a hard taskmaster, as we know. It took him a while to get used to people, because he only decided whether to like somebody or not after he was in possession of all the facts.'

Nina laughed, warming them all. It was such a relief after the agony they'd been able to see in her eyes all day to witness her laughing. 'It wasn't just me, then.'

'Most certainly not just you,' Caroline said. 'It took him months and months to like me too.'

'Now, Roderick was the president of our club. But now he's gone, we don't have a president.'

'We didn't really need one in the first place,' William said. He'd given up straightening his tie a couple of hours ago and put it into his pocket instead. 'It was a sort of honerr, honyerrery title.'

'I bet you couldn't say *orrery* if you tried,' Lesley teased him.

'No, I couldn't.'

'Don't agree about a president not being wanted, man,' Carl said, flicking back his hair. 'I think it was great to have a president. I really enjoyed it. It's a real mark of status and, well, it was fun. Why shouldn't we have one? We can have anything we want. We can have a fairy godmother if we want. It's our club.'

'I think so too,' Lesley said positively.

'And me,' Patrick voiced.

'I think a president sounds stately,' Nina contributed.

'Well I don't mind then.' William coloured. 'It was only a thought, but I'm fine with a president. Why not?'

'Well then, Dylan,' Caroline raised a glass to him as she sank back into the bench seat. 'You are our president and we salute you. Respect!'

'No, no.' Dylan shook his head. 'It so happens that I

516

have already rung around the members who couldn't make it here today. As we know they've all sent their regrets, messages, flowers, etc. That's understood. But what I asked them was, who do you think is best fitted to take over the role of president of the club after Roderick?' They all looked at Dylan. 'So, I'm going to ask you that same question now.'

'Secret ballot?' Patrick was confused. 'Shall we write it down?'

'What about hustings?' William scratched his neck.

'No, no.' Dylan waved a hand carelessly and broke into a laugh. 'It won't be that difficult. I'll ask you each, one by one, and you have to be honest. That's it.' He'd pointed a finger at Patrick before they'd all had a chance to think about it. 'Who's our next president?' he shot at him.

'Caroline,' Patrick said, then blustered. 'I'm sorry, Dylan, you took me by surprise. You do a fabulous job, it's just that Caroline's put so much in.'

Dylan nodded and turned to William. 'I'd have to say Caroline. Sorry Dylan. You're great, but she's shit-hot.'

'William!' Lesley pulled a mock-shocked face at him and they laughed.

'Carl,' Dylan said, pointing his finger. 'President please.'

'Caroline,' Carl nodded, smiling. 'She's fabulous. I love you too, Dylan man, but if anyone should be running things most of the time, it's her. And I mean that with the greatest respect.'

'Lesley?'

'I'd say Caroline too. She's had a lot of ideas and she does seem to have the explanations to almost every-thing. And she does stay in touch about observing evenings and star parties and things. I think you and Caroline are a fantastic team and I'm grateful for everything you organise for us, so I'd like you to carry on working together, but I think Caroline should be president. I like her.' Lesley buried her nose in her glass of wine.

'And the all-important endorsement . . . Nina, please give us your view.'

'Yes, Nina, what do you think?' Caroline asked.

'I know that Roderick respected Caroline more than anybody else, so I'll vote on his behalf,' Nina said, smiling shyly at her. 'Caroline should take over. I know it's what he'd want because he talked about her so much to me.'

'Caroline?'

She gaped at them all. She couldn't believe what she was hearing. 'I vote for Dylan. He's fantastic.'

'Yeah well,' Carl snorted, 'it's exactly because you would vote for Dylan that we all love your pants off.'

'But listen.' Caroline struggled to make sense of it all. 'I'm the secretary and that's the only reason why you think I do so much. It's my job to do that.'

'Your job, like you get paid,' Carl grinned.

'Somebody has to be the secretary.'

'Are you saying that if you were the club president you would only take a notional role?' Dylan smiled at her. 'It's fair to say that we all think that you'll continue to contribute a huge amount as president.'

'But who'd be the secretary?'

There was a long pause while they all thought about it.

'The fact is, I wouldn't mind being secretary,' Carl said. 'I'm always at the meetings and I'm pretty reliable.

518

Been doing this a few years now, so I've got lots of contacts.'

'Perfect. I'm very glad you volunteered, Carl, because when I rang around the absentees and asked them also who they'd most like to replace Caroline as secretary, they all voted for you.' Dylan eyed the others. 'Any comments?'

'Brilliant idea,' Lesley said.

'Yes, got my vote,' William said.

'And mine,' from Patrick.

'Caroline?'

'Well yes. Of course, Carl would make a superb secretary. I've always thought so.'

Dylan picked up his glass and they all did likewise. 'I would like to propose a toast to our new club secretary, Carl.'

They all clinked glasses.

'And now, ladies and gentlemen of our club, on behalf of our esteemed outgoing president Roderick, I would like you all to be upstanding for a toast. By unanimous verdict, her own vote not counting of course, our new club president, Caroline Blake.'

Before they all left the pub, Caroline at last managed to do something that she'd been meaning to do for weeks. She talked to Nina on her own, away from the others.

'I was wondering,' Caroline said. 'Would you like to come over and have Sunday lunch with me and my family?'

It was something of a shock to Nina when she received a phone call on her mobile some days later from a solicitor, claiming to represent the estate of Roderick

Vinnicombe. She was summoned to an office and asked to bring identification, which she did.

Afterwards, she met Carl, Lesley and some friends of theirs for a drink in a wine bar in the Pantiles of Tunbridge Wells.

'You all right?' Carl quizzed her as they stood at the bar together getting in a round for the group. 'You're bright pink.'

'Something has happened,' Nina said. It was all she could bring herself to say about it.

'There's something up,' Carl laughed at her. 'Don't tell me by all means, but it's like you've got a firework inside you this evening. It makes you look incredibly pretty, I have to tell you. Although you're always pretty. I think so, anyway.'

'Carl.' Nina took his large, clumsy hand and held it. 'You've become a wonderful friend to me. You've taught me a lot already, and there's so much I still want to know.'

'Glad to hear it,' he grinned.

'But I need to find out who I am, and that may take me a very long time. I'd love you to be my friend, but in any other sense I need to be on my own. Do you see?'

Carl nodded and a gentle smile crossed his lips. 'Yep, I can see that. Now let's get these drinks to that thirsty lot over there.'

Later in the evening, Nina met Caroline as they'd arranged, in an attractive and relaxed restaurant near the auction house. It was a table that Nina had booked earlier in the day. She had now been to Caroline's family for Sunday lunch. She'd never felt so warmly welcomed by anybody as by Caroline's mother and father. She'd also met Caroline's cousin, Lizzy. She'd spent so much time playing with Lizzy's children after lunch that Lizzy had hinted that if she ever wanted to babysit she'd be more than welcome and also get paid. They'd exchanged phone numbers.

'Wow, this is posh,' Caroline exclaimed as she'd stripped off her jacket and sat down. 'What are we celebrating?'

'Well, a couple of things,' Nina said, indicating to the waiter that he should now bring over glasses of chilled champagne for them.

'Good God, what's this?' Caroline's black eyes were alive with curiosity. 'Have you had a promotion?'

'No, it's something far more bizarre than that.'

'The lottery?'

'No, no.' Nina shook her head.

'But we should drink to something.'

'Then we should drink to Roderick.'

Caroline gasped and touched Nina's arm. 'No! He didn't leave you some money, did he? I can't think of anyone who'd deserve it more than you.'

Nina smiled. She'd told Caroline just a little of her circumstances whilst at lunch with her family. They'd taken a walk around the back garden together and Caroline had fired questions at her. It had been quite painful to reveal facts about herself to Caroline, but on the other hand she trusted her. And so had Roderick.

'I don't want to dwell on the past, Caroline,' Nina said, unable to keep the delight from her voice. 'Because thanks to Roderick, it's time to think about the future.'

Caroline slapped the table. 'He left you money. Well, good on him. I'd hoped he wasn't so selfish that he'd take it all with him, and I mean that in the nicest possible

521

way. I'm thrilled to hear it. Good old Roderick. There was a heart under all that dust after all.'

'No, Caroline, you're not listening. He's left you his observatory.'

'What?'

'His observatory in the garden, and everything in it. And everything that he owned to do with astronomy, a couple of older telescopes and lots of books on the subject. That kind of thing. He's left it all to you.'

Caroline put her hand over her mouth. 'To *me*?'

'Yes. I spoke to the solicitor today and asked them if I could tell you first. I thought it was more personal coming from me, distant relative as I am.'

'Well I'll be goddamned.' Caroline shook her head, dazed. 'But that's just amazing. I can't believe it. Oh my God. And what about you?'

'Oh, he hardly got to know me, as you know. But he left me the house and the rest of his stuff. It's all pretty old.'

There was a pause while this sank in. Nina and Caroline stared at each other with mutually bemused expressions.

'His house on the hill? In that exclusive road? He's left you that? You do realise that place is worth thousands, don't you?'

Nina nodded. 'The solicitor explained it. I can't believe it. You're the only person I've told. I trust you, and I don't know what to do. It's so different from anything I expected to happen to me that I'm shocked. I'm scared, actually. That sounds silly, doesn't it?'

Then they both burst out laughing.

'Oh heck, you need very good legal and financial advice from this point on,' Caroline said, concentrating.

'The house is worth a bomb in itself. Heaven knows what the estate's worth.'

'The thing is,' Nina said, leaning forward earnestly. 'It's got me thinking about all sorts of possibilities. Like, how about if it was possible to open up his garden to kids from London or something who never see a view over the fields like that, or have never thought about what's up there in the sky. Or maybe the house could be a language school. Or what about something – I don't know – something creative. Or charitable. Or something that could educate people. I know why Roderick's done this. It's not because I'm a relative, I'm sure it's not, because there must be relatives who are more obvious links on the family tree. It's because he knew it meant something to me to meet him. He knew it altered my horizon. He knew that in the brief time since I met him, he changed the way I saw the world.' Caroline watched Nina as she spoke. Nina finished with, 'I just knew you'd be able to help me sort it out. And apart from anything else, the observatory's yours so we need to get together on it anyway.'

'Well I'll be blown away.' Caroline smiled across the table. 'Have you ever thought of going into teaching, Nina?'

'When I was a little girl.'

'You should look at it seriously. I bet you're a natural.' Caroline reached into a bag she'd brought with her. 'And I got you this. When we talked in my parents' garden you told me about something that had meant a lot to you, something that had helped you to feel alive.' She handed Nina the video of *Dances with Wolves* with a smile. 'Although I have a feeling that from now on you're going to feel alive every minute of the day.'

'He left without saying goodbye.' Stephanie shielded her eyes as she looked out to the horizon.

They both gazed down the green at the smooth lawn fringed with black, sienna and yellow branches. Ahead a chalk-white bunker glinted back at them in the sun. From the terrace of the golf club they had a first-rate view over the players leaving and returning. In the rough, primroses were sprouting like light yellow measles, peppering every dark rust thicket with life. The wild cherries were covered with a thin, shivery pale green. Beside her mother, drinking tea and chewing on a chicken salad on the lichen-spattered wooden slats of the picnic table positioned there, Caroline was appreciating a deliciously warm spring afternoon. Golf clubs were not at all her parents' thing, but Ron and Doe enjoyed them. Today, Howard was doing a round with Doe, having been challenged to the point of exhaustion. Caroline watched her father's shot in answer to Doe's before she turned her attention back to her mother.

'I'm not really surprised.'

'Aren't you?' Stephanie turned on her a profoundly hurt expression. 'Really? Was the anniversary do that bad?'

'From Phil's point of view, it was pretty bad.' Caroline set aside her empty plate and turned back to her tea. The small figures of Doe and her father evaporated from view as they walked in an arc that took them round a corner towards another hole behind the trees. 'But he'll be in touch, don't worry about it.'

'Did you see him off at the airport?'

Caroline paused before answering. 'Yes. Him and Brendan. They travelled together.'

Stephanie absorbed this. It had been a very emotional event, not many days ago, and personally Caroline was glad that her parents hadn't been a part of it. It was a dramatic enough farewell as it was, and she had cried for hours when she'd got home. But Phil had rung her immediately on arriving in Australia, then Brendan had rung her two days later to chat. Somehow Caroline couldn't imagine the line going cold for very long.

'Well,' Stephanie said. 'He didn't leave me a number or an address. I assume he's staying with Brendan for now. I'm supposing he gave you details of everything.'

'Yes,' she said gently.

'I thought mothers were the pivot.' Stephanie proudly put her head back. She had a sheepskin jacket around her, but her flimsy cotton skirt flapped around her shins in the breeze, making her seem more vulnerable. 'I used to be the control centre of information. You have to understand, it's a bit of a shock to me to find out that I'm no longer needed in that role.'

Caroline shook her head slowly. 'I don't think anybody is. I don't think there's any such thing any more.' They both looked out into the beauty of the scene in front of them.

'You will give me Phil's number, won't you?'

'Of course I will. He'd expect me to pass it on to you, Brendan too.'

'Is he really gay?' Stephanie turned blue eyes on her.

Some time had passed since Phil's stunning revelation. Stephanie now seemed curious rather than anything. It was a good development, Caroline thought, but given her mother's analytical brain, it was one she'd been expecting. She had to bury a smile when Stephanie asked her the question. With Phil you never quite knew if something was intended to create an impression, or was a stony reality. The truth was that Phil had played with Caroline before the anniversary party. On the one hand, he'd insisted that if their parents pushed him, he'd just announce he was gay to get them off his back. On the other hand, Caroline didn't know for sure whether it was true or not. Speaking for herself, she didn't care. She hadn't asked Phil much more about it, and he hadn't volunteered anything. They'd talked about everything else, but they seemed to have reached a point of mutual discretion in terms of their personal lives. Or perhaps it was less about discretion and more about respect.

'To tell you the truth, Mum, I really don't know. Maybe.'

'It doesn't bother you at all?' Stephanie asked, but at least it was a question and not a statement.

'Why would it?'

'No nieces or nephews?'

Caroline laughed under her breath. She took the bread roll that Stephanie had left, broke it in two and chewed on it. 'Well, who knows?'

'You're different, Caro. I can't pin down when you became different, but it's recently. Maybe it was Phil coming back to stay with you that did it.'

'I feel different, but I'm not sure if it's due to Phil.'

'You and Phil became much closer after his accident, didn't you?'

'We bonded, that's true, although we had a grotty teething process before we got there.'

'There's something else, though. It's as if somebody's turned a light on inside you. Like one of those night lights with a candle inside them.'

Caroline shrugged. 'Probably work inspiration.'

'Oh yes!' Stephanie turned around properly, pointed her knees at Caroline and covered her face with enthusiasm. 'I'm so sorry darling, you said you had something to tell me about work. I want to hear about it. But let's order another cup of tea first.' Stephanie gestured to the waiting staff.

'And some dessert,' Caroline said. 'No good thinking on an empty stomach. I'll have apple pie.'

After they'd ordered, they both looked out at the green again. The breeze sprang up and the heads of the trees nodded whimsically in reply.

'There's something you have to know, Caro,' Stephanie said. 'We're both proud of you, whatever you do. I've thought hard about why I managed to offend you on our anniversary night. I talked it through with Howard as well. I realised that I'd said a lot of things without thinking. About your job, suggesting to you that we don't rate what you do, about you not getting married or having children. I mean, those comments weren't meant to hurt you and we're both so sorry you felt attacked. We love you for who you are, and we wouldn't have you any other way.'

'Oh, well,' Caroline blustered.

'No, it's important. We think what you do is amazing. I sat there with Howard and asked him if he could remember any of his old teachers. He came out with such a eulogy for a Mrs Bradbourne that I started to feel jealous. And it turns out that she was maths.' Stephanie's face dimpled into a smile. 'She fired him up to do engineering. And of course I had your grandfather behind me all the time, but there was another teacher. A young man with chestnut hair called Mr Ridley. He was fabulous and I've never forgotten him to this day. We always knew that you loved what you did, but it wasn't until we saw how outraged you were with us that we stopped taking it for granted. That night I realised that the path you've chosen is where your true gift lies. It's very rare to have such a talent. We think it's wonderful.'

'Well that's great, Mum. Thanks.'

'So.' Stephanie put her hands together cheerfully after the tea and dessert had arrived. 'The important thing is you. What's your news?'

'The thing is,' Caroline found herself smiling, 'I've been offered the post of Head of Science at the school.'

Stephanie leapt up and engulfed her daughter in a hug. 'You clever girl! How exciting!'

'When Heather Martin offered the post to me I felt a tingle all over. I had a vision of all the things I could do. The clubs, the activities, the ways I could inspire the other staff to join me in big projects, exhibitions, theme days, to turn the whole science department around. Bring it to life. I was surprised at how great it felt. It may sound odd, but as she and I talked, I actually felt bigger. As if my image of myself was bigger, I don't know if you know what I mean.'

'So what did you tell her?'

Caroline's smile spread. 'I told her I'd take it, of course.'

'I am so delighted.' Stephanie beamed at Caroline. 'Just wait until I tell your father. We'll have to have a special celebration for this. And perhaps you could invite Nina back again. I did like her.'

They talked for a while about the new job and what it would entail, then Stephanie patted Caroline's hand as a nippy breeze sent them both shivering. 'I know it's a wonderfully clear sky, but it's blimmin' cold out here. Shall we go inside now?'

'There's just one thing before we go back in.' Caroline held onto her mother's hand in a sudden but important need to feel her skin against hers.

'What is it, dear?'

She was now the sole object of her mother's concerned attention. Caroline marvelled at it. Whatever it was that had passed across her eyes, or was in her body language or her tone of voice, Stephanie had picked up on it. Perhaps that was what happened to a mother when her daughter spoke to her in a way that she'd never done before. Perhaps Stephanie realised that she had to concentrate because what was about to be said was going to change everything.

'I know that in your heart you've wished for marriage and children for me.'

Stephanie nodded, her eyes wide.

'Well,' Caroline took a deep breath. 'I haven't exactly done things in the right order, but one out of two can't be bad.'

Lizzy watched David's fingers as they traced a pattern over the sensitive skin of her stomach. Already she could feel the tightening and swelling there as her waistline thickened. Slowly, he slid down the bed and followed the trail of his fingertips with soft kisses. His cheeks were flushed, his eyes closed, a smile playing across his mouth. He looked as rapturous as she'd seen him.

'David?'

'Hmmn.'

'You are really happy about the baby, aren't you?'

He rested his head on her stomach and looked at her. She could see the truth in his eyes as they shone.

'I can't tell you how happy. And how proud I am of you.'

'I just – I was worried about telling you. You know that.'

'Shh.' He pulled himself up and kissed her. Then he placed a finger on her lips. 'Let's not go over it again. I was an idiot. I felt under pressure because of money, and like some sort of naughty kid I just rebelled against it. I'm not proud of myself, love. But it did make me grow up. I've always wanted a big family. It's all I ever dreamed of. I think we're the luckiest two people alive.'

'And the cards will bring in more money now.'

'Yes, you clever woman.' He stroked her hair. 'And who knows where it might take you. If that bloke from the Paper Rose company who spent so much time with you at the craft fair gets back to us . . .' He raised an eyebrow at her in excitement, and her smile spread.

'Imagine that. One of my designs in card shops all over the country.'

David drew her into his arms, a warm hand protectively covering her stomach.

'Believe me, Lizzy. I've got everything a man could want, right here, right now.'

She closed her eyes and before long she had fallen into a peaceful sleep again.

The wind had dropped completely, and the sun was offering a lazy, golden preview to the spring as Caroline left her car and ambled down the path towards her house.

Poor Stephanie, she thought with a smile. The perfect

mother in so many respects, and this was how her children repaid her. And yet her mother was resilient, and there was already a glimmer of humour lurking in the depths of her blue eyes. It wouldn't be long before she would be taking it all in her stride.

Somebody was using a sandblaster and it droned through the cool air, mingling with the occasional whine of a car heading down the hill. How beautiful the view over to the horizon was, the domes of the fields fringed with black bushes peppered with lime-green buds. A bonfire trailed woodsmoke across the furrows of a ploughed field way off into the distance. In a front garden, daffodils swayed on springy stems. A dog barked hoarsely. The smell of freshly mown grass floated in the air. A wonderful suggestion of summer filled Caroline's senses.

The future held so many possibilities, and each of them was exciting. The joy of being alive filled her chest and burst from her lungs in an exhalation of air. She quickened her step, jogging gently towards her house. She let herself in and strode straight through to the back door, opening it wide to allow the early spring scent to flood in. Soon it would be evening. The white horizon was already tinged with pink and the evening stars were coming into view.

An hour later, it had deepened into violet. Next would come the mouth-watering ultramarine that made her heart beat fast. She scrambled into a thick sweater, put on her windcheater and grabbed her woollen hat and gloves. Tonight she wanted to be at one with the sky, with her sky.

When she heard the scuffling coming from the bottom of her garden, she didn't register it at first. After all, it was a sound she had become used to over the last year. She had first thought of it as a neighbour's dog, and then realised it was a goat.

'Daisy,' she murmured down the garden as she undid her shed door. Then she paused with her hand on the latch. 'Daisy?'

In response the rustling became louder. Caroline headed down the path, squinting in the half-light. Then she stopped and gaped at the small, white, hairy form. It was Daisy, and she had managed to create a cavernous hole at the bottom of the flimsy wooden fence. Following that, she had come through it, and was now proudly standing in Caroline's garden, chewing everything that she could see.

'Oh my God, Daisy! It's you. You made it through the fence!' Emotionally Caroline dropped to her knees and put her arms around the animal's neck. She forgot to be nervous, even when Daisy clipped her skin with determined teeth. She laughed, rubbing the stiff hair with delight. 'It's so good to see you! Even if you have got a hairy chin that tickles.'

'Thanks.'

Caroline jumped to her feet at the sound of Tom's voice. Her heart thundered, her breath catching in her throat. She watched him climb over her fence as if it were a little wooden stile. He dropped down to the ground and walked towards her. Her eyes filled with tears. She tried to swallow them away but they shot in hot streams down her face. She gasped, struggling to recover her voice.

'You went away,' she managed to say.

'Yes.'

'Why?'

'It all got out of control.'

'Are you back now?' she whispered.

'Yes.'

'Why?'

'Because I love you.'

It was simple. After everything she'd imagined, every thought she'd nurtured, every fretful moment she'd spent without him, she found that she was utterly fulfilled by that explanation. He didn't have to say any more. She understood him. She stood still, her knees trembling, as he walked towards her. He took her in his arms and encircled her possessively. Then he lifted her up and carried her towards the house.

'There's something I have to tell you, Tom.'

'What's that?'

She gazed into the limpid green eyes she adored, at the soul of the man who had stolen her heart. So much to tell him. So much they shared. A precious life created in a moment of magic. She had plenty of time to tell him, and they had all the time in the world to experience it.

'I love you too.'

'I know,' he said, smiling.